THE SEDUCTION OF AN EARL

LINDA RAE SANDE

Twisted Teacup
PUBLISHING

The Seduction of an Earl

ISBN: 978-0-9893973-7-7

Library of Congress Control Number: 2013912069

Linda Rae Sande, Cody, WY

PRINTED IN THE UNITED STATES OF AMERICA

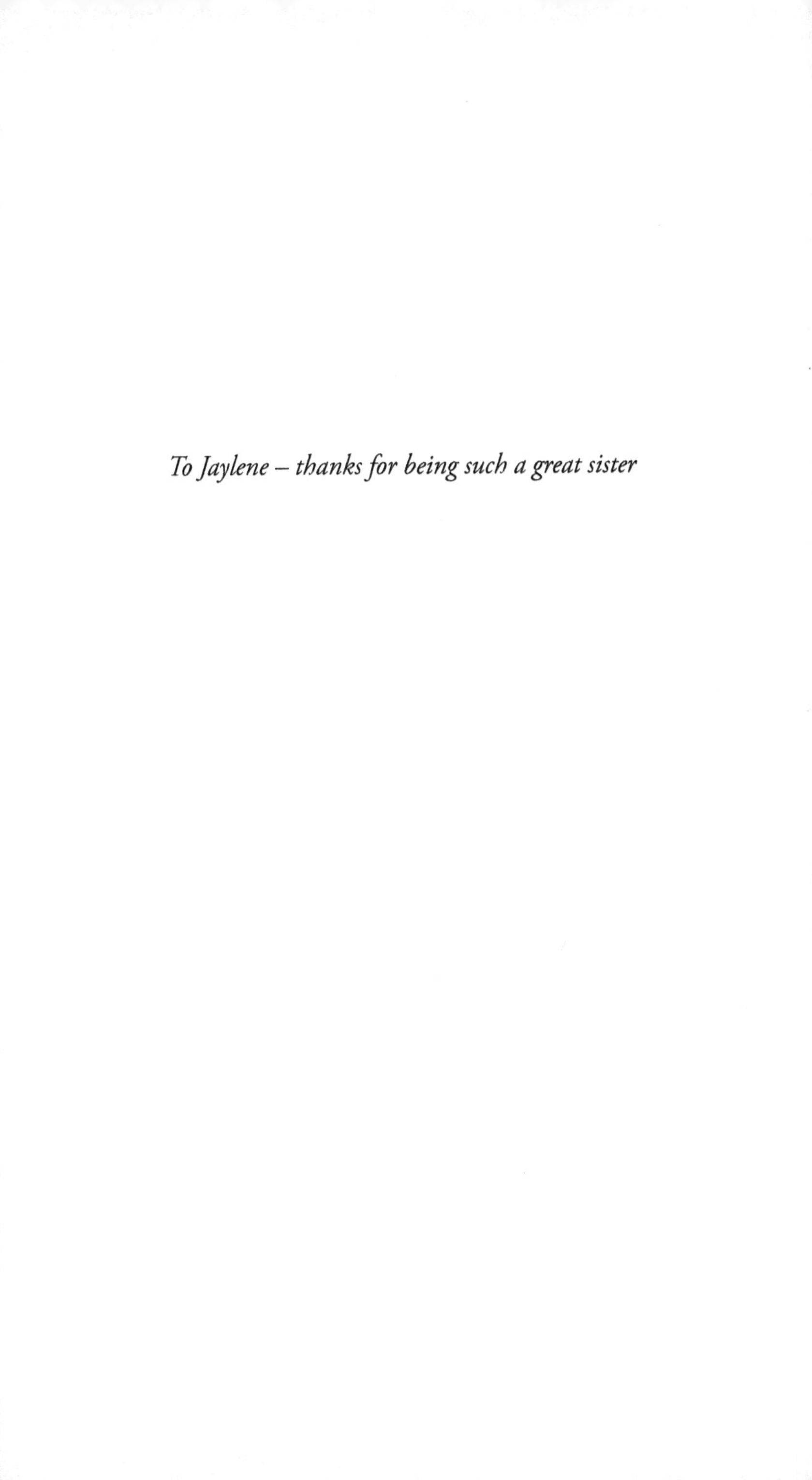

To Jaylene – thanks for being such a great sister

ALSO BY LINDA RAE SANDE

The Daughters of the Aristocracy

The Kiss of a Viscount

The Grace of a Duke

The Seduction of an Earl

The Sons of the Aristocracy

Tuesday Nights

The Widowed Countess

My Fair Groom

The Sisters of the Aristocracy

The Story of a Baron

The Passion of a Marquess

The Desire of a Lady

The Brothers of the Aristocracy

The Love of a Rake

The Caress of a Commander

The Epiphany of an Explorer

The Widows of the Aristocracy

The Gossip of an Earl

The Enigma of a Widow

The Secrets of a Viscount

The Widowers of the Aristocracy

The Dream of a Duchess

The Vision of a Viscountess

The Conundrum of a Clerk

The Charity of a Viscount

The Cousins of the Aristocracy

The Promise of a Gentleman

The Pride of a Gentleman

The Holidays of the Aristocracy

The Christmas of a Countess

The Knot of a Knight

The Heirs of the Aristocracy

The Angel of an Astronomer

The Puzzle of a Bastard

The Choice of a Cavalier

The Bargain of a Baroness

The Jewel of an Earl's Heir

The Vixen of a Viscount

The Honor of an Heir

Beyond the Aristocracy

The Pleasure of a Pirate

The Making of a Mistress

Stella of Akrotiri

Origins

Deminon

Diana

CHAPTER 1
THERE BE PIRATES

arch 1815, near Bampton, Oxfordshire
Nathaniel Forster regarded his best friend, Andrew Barnaby, with a quirked eyebrow. The expression was familiar to anyone who knew Nathan's father, Henry Forster. The man's eyebrow made a similar arch whenever he was puzzled by something, such as a problem that needed solving. At the moment, Nathan was considering Andrew's assertion that they needed something to use as booty if their foray into playing pirates was to be the least bit believable.

"A treasure?" he asked his best friend. "You mean, like *gold?*"

Andrew nodded enthusiastically, causing his crudely made eye patch to slide down his face. He quickly pushed it back over his right eye. "Aye. Or jewels. Or *coins,*" he added, this time holding the eye patch in place while he nodded.

Nathan considered what he might find in Gisborn Hall that could be used for booty. "And what would we *do* with the treasure?" he asked, not being particularly familiar with pirate stories. His mother, Sarah Inglenook, didn't have any pirate stories in the library at the dowager house where they had taken up residence earlier that year. Since he had never been in the library at Gisborn Hall, Nathan didn't know if there were any pirate books on the shelves there, either. He would have to ask his father the next time the earl paid his mother and him a visit.

"Bury it!" Andrew answered, as if everyone knew that's what pirates did with their treasure. "To hide it from other pirates. And anyone else who might want the treasure." This last was said as Andrew crossed his arms, challenging his friend to counter his claim.

"Oh, I understand," Nathan replied, nodding as he considered where they could find gold or jewels or coins. He had a few sovereigns his father had given him on the occasions of his birthday. And he knew there were some jewels in a box in his father's bedchamber. He had seen a ring his father was trying on one day, a gold ring in which a ruby was mounted. A signet ring, he remembered his mother explaining to him later that night when he asked her about the ring.

"He's an earl, now, Nathan," she had said. "The ring is something passed down from one earl to the next. It will go to his heir when he dies." And then she had suddenly looked away, her hand going to her mouth as if she had to stop her words, her usually happy demeanor replaced with sadness.

Seeing his mother's reaction whenever she spoke of his father, especially since Henry had become an earl, made Nathan realize he had to change the subject or risk seeing his mother sad again. For, despite the fact that Nathan was the earl's son, he was not the heir to the Gisborn estate. And his mother, Sarah, was not the countess.

"I have some money we could use," Nathan offered finally, deciding they could use his coins as the treasure, "And I think I can find a ring."

Andrew's eyes widened in delight. "That's perfect! Now we just need a box we can use as a treasure chest, and we'll put the money and ring in it and bury it!"

Grinning broadly, the boys hurried off toward Gisborn Hall to gather their treasures and plan their next adventure.

The two lived about a mile south of Bampton in Oxfordshire and had been standing in the middle of Henry Forster's farmland as they plotted their pirate story.

Actually, the farmlands belonged to the Gisborn earldom. At the age of nine-and-twenty, Henry had just inherited the title of Earl of Gisborn from his late uncle. Within a month, Sarah Inglenook and her son, Nathaniel Forster, were moved from their small cottage near Bampton to the dowager house on the Gisborn lands. Henry, who had lived with them in the cottage, moved into Gisborn Hall and took up his duties as earl. Given the Gisborn earldom was primarily made up of farmland just north of the River Isis, Henry's duties revolved around maintaining the farm, planning crop rotations, solving irrigation problems and overseeing the tenants who farmed the lands.

Since he had been farming for his uncle almost his entire life, Henry found he couldn't leave the life of a farmer to take up the life of a member of the *ton*, a life for some gentlemen that included too much leisure, too much gambling, too much drinking and too many women. Henry opted to remain on his estate, working to modernize the farm and restore Gisborn Hall to its former glory.

"What are you two up to today?" Parkerhouse asked as he answered the knock at the front door of Gisborn Hall. The ancient butler stared down at Nathan and Andrew, suppressing a grin at the sight of the two dressed as pirates.

"We're going to bury our treasure!" Nathan announced, passing Parkerhouse on his way to the stairs leading to the second floor where his room was located. Although he didn't live in Gisborn Hall, he occasionally spent the night at his father's request. "I have to get a box."

Parkerhouse sighed and watched the boys disappear into Nathan's bedchamber. Deciding they couldn't get into too much trouble, he continued with his duties on the main floor. He was unaware of their entry into his master's bedchamber, of them retrieving the gold signet ring from Henry Forster's jewelry box, of Nathan emptying his coin collection into a pasteboard cheroot box. He was only aware of their retreating steps when he spotted Nathan outside with the box under one arm and a shovel from the stables hoisted over Andrew's shoulder. He watched with a small smile as the two boys made their way toward the farmlands to the south.

The following day, after Nathan had finished his studies with a tutor, and Andrew had finished his chores, the two met at Gisborn Hall. There they planned their expedition to retrieve the buried treasure from the place in the field where they had buried it the day before. Decked out in pirate regalia, or in borrowed clothes that at least made them look somewhat like pirates, and each sporting black felt patches over their eyes, they stood at the edge of the field in which they'd buried the pasteboard box.

They stood, and they stared.

For at some point in the twenty-four hours since they had buried the treasure, the field had been plowed. Furrows running parallel to one another had replaced the flat land that extended as far as the river. Tenant farmers were following the furrows and using seed drills to plant wheat. The rock the two boys had put into place to mark the location of the box was gone. And, despite their best efforts to locate the treasure, it was nearly dark when the two, disheartened and disappointed, made their way to their respective homes.

It was two days before Nathan admitted to his mother that his birthday money was somewhere in his father's wheat field. Stunned that her son would do such a thing, Sarah sent him to bed without supper, weeping as she did so. Although she had threatened to tell his father, Nathan begged her not to, claiming he would one day find the money.

It was another month before Nathan found the courage to tell his father that the Gisborn signet ring was somewhere in the middle of his field. He only did so because his father's valet had reported the ring missing when he was searching for a pair of cuff links, and when a maid was accused of the crime of thievery, Nathan knew he had to admit his involvement in the ring's disappearance.

Henry's first reaction had to be kept hidden from the boy. Given the small size of its ruby, Henry was rather amused that his son would consider his signet ring suitable as part of a pirate's treasure.

Henry's second reaction was far more severe, however. His son had taken something without asking, and because he had not admitted his involvement from the start, a maid had quit his household in shame. Upset at his son and saddened at the same time, Henry did what his own father had done to him under similar circumstances, back when his father had still been alive to discipline him. The whip, made from a willow branch, left its mark across the boy's bottom and the back of his legs. Having never suffered such discipline, Nathan cried in fear and pain at the lashing. But it was Henry who wept later that night, wondering if he had done the right thing. He was sure he could find the missing treasure—he knew from the boy's description its approximate location out in his wheat field.

But by the time he learned of the missing ring, the field of wheat had grown too tall to allow a search to take place. When the harvest took down the wheat, there was still no sign of the pasteboard box and its treasure.

Deciding it was a lost cause, Henry decided he would simply arrange for a jeweler to make another signet ring on his next trip to London.

And Nathan's coins had been his to lose.

CHAPTER 2
LADY BOSTWICK CALLS ON
LADY HANNAH

March, 1816, Mayfair

At precisely nine o' clock in the morning, Elizabeth Ben-nett-Jones, Viscountess Bostwick, stepped as lightly as she could from the pristine black carriage bearing her husband's family crest onto the semi-circular drive of Devonville House.

Stepping lightly wasn't something Elizabeth could do well these days. She was six months into her first pregnancy, and given the size of her expanding belly, her largest carriage gown just barely covered the evidence. At some point, probably within a fortnight, she and her husband George would retire to their country estate in Sussex, and she would go into confinement. If her husband didn't dote on her as he did, rubbing her ankles every night after dinner, bestowing various gifts on her for no particular reason, and making love to her every night and sometimes in the morning, she might have been one of those women of the *ton* who complained about breeding. But George Bennett-Jones did all those things. And he did them well.

"Good morning, Lady Bostwick," the butler greeted her as he opened the double doors and let the young matron sweep into the vestibule. Except for Sundays, Elizabeth's visits to Devonville House occurred every other day of the week.

On the opposite days, Lady Hannah Slater, daughter of William Slater, Marquess of Devonville, paid a call upon Lady Bostwick at Bostwick Place, just a few streets down in Park Lane. "Lady Hannah is expecting you in the parlor," the balding man said as he took Elizabeth's pelisse from her shoulders. He led the way.

"Of course she is, Hatfield," Elizabeth replied with a roll of her eyes. "If she were not, I would have to hire a Bow Street Runner to locate her," she deadpanned, for if Hannah Slater was not where she was supposed to be, Something was Wrong.

The butler barely turned to give her a nod, not quite certain of the viscountess' sarcasm.

"Elizabeth!" Hannah gushed as she hurried to greet her best friend, her hands held out in front of her. A very large dog, brown and white in coloring, with a square head and floppy ears, raised itself from the hearth to regard the visitor.

"How do, Harold," Elizabeth said by way of greeting the Alpenmastiff. "No kisses, please," she added with a wave. The dog settled his massive body back down onto the tiled hearth, as if understanding her ladyship's refusal of one of his primary functions in life.

Smiling, Hannah kissed Elizabeth's cheek and stood back to have a look at her attire. "You look splendid in that shade of green," she said as she fingered the superfine. "Whenever did you have time to have a fitting?" she asked, realizing the carriage gown had to be new.

"I left the office early last week to see Madame Bouvier. The worker bees had everything under control, so I gave myself the afternoon off." Elizabeth's charity, Lady E and Associates—Finding Work for the Wounded, had its recently enlarged office in Oxford Street and boasted a staff of four full-time office workers and several part-timers. They also had contracts with several tailors, hat makers, and boot makers in London for the purpose of outfitting war veterans for employment. The burgeoning charity, which Elizabeth had begun just before her introduction to the viscount nearly seven months prior, was a huge success. The men she had hired were from among those who responded to her ads offering help in locating employment. The ex-soldiers were responsible for finding positions in which wounded soldiers could work, despite those men having only partial sight or hearing, missing limbs, or some other malady resulting from their time spent in the war against France.

Sometimes those employers were only willing to hire a wounded man if a bribe was involved. In those cases, Elizabeth sent out one of her employees to negotiate the employment contract. At one time, she had been the one to see to that part of the business. With her growing belly, her husband had suggested, very carefully and with a good deal of tact, and perhaps using a bribe of his own, that Elizabeth allow her minions to do the jobs for which they were paid out of the charity's coffers and allow her to do the part of the charity she did so well—matching men to jobs.

"Spoken like a true queen bee," Hannah teased as she motioned for Elizabeth to take her favorite chair. She waved to the butler for tea to be brought and settled in the chair opposite her friend. "And when did you start using Madame Bouvier?" she asked, never before having heard Elizabeth mention that particular modiste.

"Oh, there's a first time for everything," her visitor sighed. "Lady Pettigrew suggested her because she specializes in maternity gowns, and ever since I saw her niece Lucy wearing that peach confection at Lady Worthington's musicale last month, I thought to try her."

Hannah leaned back in her chair, admiring her auburn-haired friend. Beautiful, with aquamarine eyes, full lips, and a peaches and cream complexion, Elizabeth was not much older than Hannah's twenty-one years. Her condition made her look as if she was lit from within by a dozen candles. "And?"

Elizabeth regarded Hannah for a moment. "She's brilliant. And she eschews corsets! Which means George approves." This last was said with an elegantly arched eyebrow, which was Elizabeth's way of pointing out anything that might be considered naughty by gentlewoman standards.

"And how is George?" Hannah asked, noticing the maid rolling the tea cart over the threshold. "Thank you, Rose, I can serve this morning," she said as an aside. Normally, she would allow the maid to do the honors, but she knew her friend would not speak freely with a servant in the room.

Angling her head to one side, Elizabeth grinned but didn't say anything. Hannah's eyes grew wide. "Oh! What have you two done *now?*" she asked as she leaned forward to pour the tea. There was something positively salacious about having a friend who shared tales of her sexual exploits. Despite the embarrassment she felt at hearing them described in such detail, Hannah found herself looking forward to Elizabeth's tales.

"Characters from storybooks," Elizabeth offered, not immediately elaborating on just what she meant.

Hannah handed over a cup and saucer and poured one for herself, adding milk and sugar. "Like Cinderella and her Prince Charming?" she guessed.

A very unladylike snort erupted from Elizabeth. She lifted one foot from the floor and pulled up her gown to reveal her unfashionably large feet. "I think not," she replied with a shake of her head. "And I'm not about to be an ugly stepsister. No, my dear, more like..." And here, she paused, for there were times her friend could be a bit of a prude, and she dared not shock the poor girl too much. Given Hannah's appearance—*she* was the one who looked like a fairy princess with her cornflower blue eyes, berry colored lips, pale complexion and pale blonde hair pinned up in a mass of curls atop her head and wispy ringlets scattered about her temples—*she* would have been the perfect person to play the damsel-in-distress captured by a fire-breathing dragon. George, with his finely honed skill at fencing, slew the dragon, used the tip of his sword to deftly remove every last button from Elizabeth's new French chiffon gown, and then, despite her swollen belly, had his way with her.

Her maid was, at this very moment, sewing all the buttons back onto the gown.

"Oh!" was all Hannah could say when Elizabeth described the scene.

"Really, Hannah," Elizabeth admonished her with a shake of her head. "When it comes to a husband, you must keep him guessing. Keep him interested. Keep him entertained," she said with a naughty eyebrow. "You just have to use your imagination."

"I will remember," Hannah replied with a grin, her face having turned a bright shade of pink. How could she forget such a tale?

And how would she ever be able to look at George again without blushing?

CHAPTER 3
AN EARL SPIES A LADY

At precisely ten o'clock on the very same morning, Henry Forster, Earl of Gisborn, peered out the carriage window at the grand Palladian mansion of the Marquess of Devonville. An odd excitement was building in his gut, one that made him wonder if he might be sick or if he was merely nervous. He had done this same reconnaissance mission the evening before, after making the journey from Kirdford in West Sussex to London in what might have been record time.

His sole purpose for the trip was to secure a bride. Which, considering how much he really didn't want to get married, seemed suddenly ludicrous. But inheriting an earldom from a deceased uncle more than a year ago, and being nearly thirty years of age, apparently required one to have a wife and a nursery with an heir and a spare. Henry could only hope this could be done as quickly as possible (the marriage, of course—the heir and the spare would just have to come on their own time).

He intended to call on the marquess, and then, once he had secured permission to court Lord Devonville's daughter, he planned to request an audience with Lady Hannah Slater. But propriety had prevented him from approaching the front door of Devonville House last evening. It was after seven o'clock, far too late in the day to be paying a call on a member of the *ton*.

Last evening's trip proved somewhat successful, though, for when the coach pulled up to the carriageway in front of the stately home, Henry spied a rather large brown and white dog bounding about in the gardens next to the house.

At least, he was fairly certain it was a dog.

His initial guess had him thinking it was a short, over-weight horse. Then he heard the unmistakable sound of a bark and remembered Lady Charlotte's description of the hairy beast. *Harold MacDuff,* she had called him. Lady Hannah's pet and constant companion. Lady Charlotte had assured Henry that if he was able to befriend the Alpenmas-tiff, he was sure to be more readily accepted by the dog's mistress, Lady Hannah.

At second glance, Henry thought perhaps the dog was no larger than a collie or sheepdog. But when a vision in pale lavender appeared from behind the house and ran up to wrap her arms around the dog's neck, the earl stared in disbelief. The beast had to be at least twelve stones! And then the girl began to laugh, the musical sound barely reaching his ears, as she angled her head to one side while the dog licked her neck.

He was sure she was a fairy.

Her pale blonde hair was braided and wrapped atop her head like a coronet, while ringlets danced around her deli-cate, rosy cheeks. Her eyes, closed as if she meant to protect them from her pet's long tongue, were slightly upturned and surrounded by dark lashes. With her berry-colored lips shaped into a gleeful smile, her teeth shown white despite the deepening twilight. And then she was up and running away from the dog, giggling in delight as her long limbs were silhouetted in the fabric of her gown. She disappeared from view as quickly as she had appeared.

The beast finally lifted his massive body from the grassy lawn and lumbered after her, barking and jumping about, his tail wagging about behind him. A stick flew through the air and landed very near to where the two had just been sitting in the grass, the dog barking and bounding back to where it landed. Rather than retrieve the stick and take it to his mistress, however, the dog settled his heavy body back onto the lawn and began chewing on the large twig. "Harold," he heard then, the word called out in a voice that had Henry wishing his own name was Harold. "Time for your dinner, you hairy beast," the girl called from somewhere out of sight. And then she reappeared, all proper and ladylike as she strolled toward the dog. She slapped her hand against the front of her gown and then turned back toward the house, disappearing once again.

Her brief appearance just then afforded Henry the best view of her. Almond-shaped eyes, rosebud lips, a pert nose.

Good God, the girl wasn't a girl at all, but a gorgeous young woman!

Not gorgeous like the elegant painted courtesans who frequented the theatre in Drury Lane, or the beautiful debutantes Henry noticed during the few soirées and musicales he had attended two Seasons before. No, this woman truly looked like he imagined a fairy tale princess to look. Was *she* Lady Hannah? *Could I see myself married to her?* That was the only reason he was here, after all. He needed a wife. She wasn't betrothed. And Lady Charlotte had assured him that Lady Hannah would be the perfect match for him and his situation.

His situation.

His mind wandered once more to the predicament he found himself in. Just a week ago, a mail coach had arrived at Gisborn Hall in Oxfordshire with a summons from Harold Bingham, the Earl of Ellsworth. Could Henry make the trip to Mayfair on an urgent matter regarding Ellsworth Park? The land, which included a beautiful but slightly shabby country mansion, bordered his own land in Oxfordshire, and it was Henry's intention to purchase the property at a fair price and annex it to his own. He thought Lord Ellsworth's summons meant the man was finally willing to sell him the property.

Unbeknownst to Henry at the time, it seemed Ellsworth was quite insistent his daughter, Lady Charlotte, be married to someone other than the second son who had recently inherited the Chichester dukedom. With most of the Wainswright family having perished in a fire last August, Joshua Wainwright was now the duke, and since Charlotte had been betrothed to the heir apparent and now deceased John Wainwright II, she was quite sure her betrothal now applied to Joshua.

Her father, however, was not about to have his only daughter married to a man who had been badly disfigured in the fire. *His Grace with half a face*, some in the *ton* called him. With her twenty-first birthday just a couple of weeks away, Ellsworth was determined to see his daughter settled.

To Henry Forster, Earl of Gisborn.

Henry thought Ellsworth's summons rather timely. There being no evidence the Earl of Ellsworth planned to occupy the estate house at Ellsworth Park nor employ more than a few tenants to work the lands that extended south to the River Isis, Gisborn hoped to simply purchase the property. He had plans for the Gisborn lands—plans to employ more productive farm implements and to create a gated irrigation system using the nearby river as a water source. So he made the trip to London expecting to pay a fair amount for Ellsworth Park.

He was not expecting Lord Ellsworth to offer Ellsworth Park as a *dowry*.

But in Ellsworth's apparent haste to marry off his daughter, he had already made arrangements with his solicitor to sign over the title of the unentailed property to Henry. Had the man no knowledge of Henry's own betrothal to Joshua Wainwright's sister? Jennifer Wainwright had died in the same fire that took the lives of John and the duke and duchess. Although Henry had met the girl, it had been years ago, when she was still in leading strings and he was barely twelve. He hadn't seen her since and found it difficult to mourn a girl he couldn't remember. At the same time, he found the circumstances uncomfortable at best.

According to Ellsworth, if Henry could wait a couple of weeks, Lady Charlotte would reach her majority and could marry without her parents' permission. Or Lord Ellsworth assured Henry he could marry her by special license the very next day.

Henry left the Ellsworth townhouse with the title and the intention of calling on Lady Charlotte later that week. Given his infrequent visits to London, he had errands to run, such as ordering a signet ring from a goldsmith in Bond Street (to replace the one his son had lost while using it as pirate treasure), choosing a wedding ring from a jeweler in Ludgate Hill, obtaining a special license from the bishop in Doctor's Commons, meeting his boot maker and tailor, and, perhaps the most important of all, taking possession of newly built coach at Tillbury's.

And then, the unthinkable had happened. That very night, Lord Ellsworth had taken a nasty fall in his study, hitting his head on a massive mahogany desk as he did so. Since he had dismissed the servants for the evening, his poor wife and their daughter, Lady Charlotte, apparently found the man unconscious on their return from an evening out.

A Bow Street Runner had investigated the scene. Finding no evidence of foul play, the Runner ruled the fall an accident.

Only Lady Bingham and her daughter knew what had truly happened that night. At least, they were the only ones who knew until Lady Charlotte explained it to him the day before, whilst Henry was at Wainwright's home near Kirdford. Henry winced as he recalled the sight of the scar on Charlotte's back, a long, ugly wound put there by the hand of her angered father. She had boldly refused his order to marry the Earl of Gisborn and been horse whipped for it. But her mother, appalled at her husband's drunken behavior, had pushed him as he was about to raise the whip to strike his daughter a second time. In his unsteady state, the earl fell, his head hitting the desk and rendering him unconscious.

Harold Bingham now lay in St. Bartholomew's Hospital, Lady Ellsworth at his side. The heir to the Earl of Ellsworth's estate, Nicholas Bingham, was said to be anxious to inherit the earldom if for no other reason than to secure more funds for his gambling habit. And there was the issue of his having drained Lady Charlotte's ten-thousand pound dowry account. It seemed Nicholas intended for the empty escrow account to go unnoticed and unnecessary by arranging for her to be killed in an explosion.

Henry shuddered to think what would have happened if the Duke of Chichester's home had been set afire again—it was still under reconstruction due to the fire that had disfigured the new duke and killed his family. Nicholas' hired henchman had attempted to pull off that very scenario when he set gunpowder to explode in a nearby tree. The oak tree, located just outside the bedchamber in which Lady Charlotte was staying, blew apart in the subsequent explosion. Charlotte could have been killed. And, upon the death of her father due to the head injury, her cousin would inherit the earldom and all of its assets, just as he planned.

The henchman had failed in his assassination attempt, though. And even though Henry held the title to Ellsworth Park, Lady Charlotte still intended to marry the Duke of Chichester.

Which left Henry without a bride.

If only Sarah would agree to marry him!

He sighed as he considered the only woman he had ever loved. The mother of his son. His bastard son. Although the ten-year-old was the light of life, his mother, Sarah, refused all his requests that she marry him. Over the years, she was quite insistent that Henry would one day need to marry a woman suited to the *ton*. A woman who would be accepted by the peerage because she was already a part of it. The daughter of an earl or a viscount or even a baron would suit just fine, Sarah thought.

The daughter of a marquess would be even better.

After a rather restless night spent at his rarely used town-house in Bruton Street, Henry had decided that he rather liked the idea of being married to a beautiful fairy princess.

Which was why Henry sat in a town coach in Park Lane at ten o'clock in the morning, the driver waiting for space to clear in the drive in front of the house. He would have stepped out of his coach and made his way up the steps, but another town coach, a very new one with a glossy black finish, sat in the semi-circular drive.

He watched as a beautiful, somewhat overweight woman descended the stairs and, with the hand of a groom supporting her, stepped into the marked coach. From her auburn hair and rounded front, Henry knew it wasn't the woman he had watched in the park the night before. Which meant Lady Hannah was probably still in the house.

Once the town coach departed from Devonville House with its passenger, the driver of his coach set the horses in motion. Another minute, and the coach had come to a halt.

Yes, Henry decided, *I could see myself married to Lady Hannah.*

Now he just had to convince her to marry him.

Henry pulled his thoughts back to the present. The driver was dismounting and about to open the door. The last thing Henry wanted was to be caught daydreaming about the woman he had seen the night before. If she truly was Lady Hannah Slater, then Lady Charlotte had been almost remiss in not describing her with the more generous attributes the woman deserved. "This is the Marquess of Devonville's resi-dence, my lord," the driver said, motioning to the grand house with the wide expanse of parkland to one side. Henry noted that the driver had pulled into the semi-circular carriageway. The equipage was parked at the base of the five stone steps leading up to the massive double doors framed by a portico and Grecian columns.

Nodding to the driver as he stepped down, Henry gave the man a coin and asked if he could wait. He silently chided himself for not yet having visited Tillbury's to claim his newly built coach for the trip from his townhouse. Besides the added comfort of his new coach, the marked equipage would signal to the household staff that he was a member of the peerage. He had considered riding in his late uncle's ancient coach— the one he had used to get to London from Oxfordshire—but the springs were long gone, and the condition of the exterior made for a poor first impression. The only other equipage the earldom owned was a curricle, but he had left it behind on the off chance Sarah might require it for a trip to Bampton. She might not be his wife, but everyone in his earldom knew she was under his protection.

In lieu of a marked carriage, he made sure he had a calling card to hand to the butler.

Taking the risers with quick and efficient steps, Henry found one of the front doors opening even before he could pull the brass lion head knocker. "Is Lord Devonville in residence?" he asked, handing the pasteboard to the butler.

The stout servant took only a quick glance at the card before nodding to Henry. "Indeed, my lord. If you'll follow me, please, I'll see you to the drawing room." He took Henry's hat and placed it rather fastidiously on a polished shelf before leading the earl down the ornately decorated hallway.

Henry had to resist the urge to answer; the butler's welcome was spoken with more words than he heard from his own butler in a entire day.

If there was any question as to the financial status of the marquess, a quick look at the artifacts displayed on caryatids throughout the alcoves they passed would hint that he was quite flush. The thought of the dowry associated with Lady Hannah hadn't even crossed his mind; he already held the title to Ellsworth Park free and clear, despite not having convinced Lady Charlotte to marry him.

The time he had spent on the ride from Kirdford to London gave him time to reflect on the situation, though. Lady Charlotte and Joshua Wainwright, the new Duke of

Chichester, were a perfect match for one another. He could only wish them well in life. Joshua had been most accommodating despite Henry's poor treatment of the disfigured man when he had first arrived at the recently rebuilt estate home. Any evidence of the fire that had left the new duke with burn scars had long been washed from the exterior stones of the west wing. From the whiffs of new cut lumber that made their way to the east wing of the house, it was evident the west wing interior was well on its way to being restored to its former glory.

The butler waved Henry into the drawing room and asked if he wished for refreshment. Henry considered the offer for only a moment; with any luck, William Slater would offer an alcoholic beverage. He politely declined and made his way around the room, studying the paintings, listening to the faint strains of music coming from another part of the house, admiring the tasteful decor and the fashionably current furniture, including a Grecian couch set in front of a window overlooking the side yard where he had witnessed Lady Hannah and Harold MacDuff playing the night before.

The vision of Hannah's head, thrown back in delight as the dog licked her neck, came unbidden to his mind. He found himself wondering if she would look like that when she was in ecstasy, her long, dark lashes resting on the tops of those beautiful cheekbones, her rosebud shaped lips parted slightly, her nipples ruched and ready for his mouth to plunder. His loins stirred at the thought.

Stunned at his body's reaction to the thought of Lady Hannah in ecstasy, Henry had to resist the urge to look down at his breeches. Sarah was his first and only love. He couldn't remember having such a reaction to any other woman, at least not since his days as a randy student at Oxford. Nor could he remember having daydreams about how a woman might look like in ecstasy!

He shook himself from his reverie. In order to get himself under control, Henry had to concentrate on the painting of some stern looking naval officer staring down at him from above a velvet settee.

"My father probably never looked quite that serious."

The comment was made in a deep Scottish burr that spoke volumes of its owner. "Ya can't when you have eyes that give away your penchant for mischief."

Henry turned to find a distinguished looking man regarding him from the doorway. When he was younger, the marquess had no doubt been quite popular among the ladies of the *ton*; even now, he carried himself as one who was aware of the effect his very presence had on a room. His salt-and-pepper hair was long but pulled back into a queue and secured with a black ribbon. His dark blue suit coat and dark breeches set off the snowy white linen of his cravat and the red waistcoat he wore beneath. Crinkles at the sides of his eyes suggested he was in his late forties or early fifties, but his darkened skin was a surprise for one from the northern counties. The man obviously enjoyed riding or other outdoor pursuits.

"But I am sure his officers were quick to obey him," Henry countered, hurrying to stand before the marquess. He bowed formally before the marquess, hoping the man would offer his hand. He was not disappointed.

"Probably," the man replied. "William Slater, Marquess of Devonville," he stated with a nod. "I have to admit surprise in seeing you here in London, Gisborn. I was under the impression you were quite busy installing upgrades on your estate in Oxfordshire. Not one for owning sheep, I take it?"

Henry could barely hide his surprise that the marquess would even know who he was, let alone be familiar with what he was trying to accomplish on his lands. "Until I received a summons from Lord Ellsworth a week ago, I actually was," he replied with a shrug. "And I am of the opinion that there are already far too many sheep in the Cotswolds."

Lord Devonville considered the earl's words for a moment. "Oh, yes. That matter of his daughter," he said with a hint of disappointment. "Can't say I blame him for his concern, but..." He allowed the sentence to trail off, his eyes squinting in Henry's direction. "Tell me, Gisborn. What exactly *are* you planning on that estate of yours?" he asked, his hands sliding into the pockets of his breeches as he wandered farther into the room. He made his way to a sideboard, where a crystal decanter and several glasses were placed on a silver salver. Pouring a finger's worth of liquor into one glass, he turned to regard Henry as he held out the glass.

"Thank you," Henry said as he took the heavy tumbler, knowing almost immediately the liquor within was scotch. Malt scotch. Probably from Scotland and no doubt aged at least twelve years. "I have designed a series of irrigation ditches for the farmland on my property as well as the neighboring estate. It's my intention to be able to drain the lands during heavy rains as well as to provide water for the crops during drier times." He didn't add that he had purchased new seed drills for the planting and cradles for the harvest, nor that he was working on a design for a more efficient plow.

The marquess regarded him for a moment and then poured a glass for himself. "So, you're aware of what Aldenwood has prognosticated for this summer, eh?" he asked as he held his own glass out toward Henry.

Not recognizing the name in association with predictions for the future, Henry regarded the marquess for a moment. "Aldenwood? I'm afraid I'm not familiar with him, my lord," he replied as he noticed the marquess holding his glass out in his direction.

"James Aldenwood. The world explorer," Devonville stated, as if that was information enough.

A surprised Henry clinked his own glass against Devonville's before taking a sip of the amber liquid. The scotch burned his throat as it made its way down, but the effect was as comforting as it was restorative. "Oh, that's very good, my lord," he said with an appreciative nod.

"Isn't it? My brother makes the stuff up in the Highlands," the marquess responded proudly. "Good thing he was born second. He's not good for anything else," he added with a mischievous grin.

Henry smiled in response, realizing the younger brother of a marquess was merely the spare heir in a *ton* family. "I am, of course, familiar with Mr. Aldenwood's writings about his various travels," he admitted then, wanting to be sure the marquess knew he had at least *heard* of the man, "But I was not aware he was a prognosticator," Henry added as he wondered how his intent for his lands and Aldenwood were related.

The marquess moved to the fireplace. "Aldenwood and I are old friends. I used to travel with him on occasion. He has seen things—amazing things. His writings do not begin to cover all that he has witnessed in his lifetime. Last year, he was in Australia when a volcano erupted in the Dutch East Indies. The thing apparently put so much debris into the air, the sky was completely black down there for several days. The sun was so dim, you could look at it with the naked eye for many weeks afterward. And the debris hasn't come down. All that stuff in the air—he says it's why we have these gorgeous sunrises and sunsets, you see," he explained, finally taking a sip of his scotch. He seemed to hold it on his tongue for a moment before swallowing it with a great deal of relish.

Henry stared at the marquess for a moment before taking another sip of his scotch. "And is all this... debris... the reason we've had a colder winter? More rain?" he asked, a sense of dread settling into his stomach. Would the bad weather continue into the summer? Shorten the growing season? The spring was already proving to be cooler and rainier than usual. Although the Gisborn earldom was fairly flush economically, he could not afford to have a bad growing season. There were tenants who depended on the crops, several nearby villages that existed because of the farming done on Gisborn lands.

Devonville pointed a finger at him. "You catch on quick, my son," he said in a manner that suggested he was pleased with Henry's deduction. "Aldenwood is convinced that Northern Europe and all of Great Britain will have a terrible growing season. So, anything you can do now to ensure a better yield on your crops will be beneficial. May keep your tenants from starving this winter." The marquess drained his remaining scotch in a single gulp.

Following suit with his own scotch, Henry stared into his empty glass before regarding the marquess. "I appreciate your telling me this. I may have the right idea about draining the fields of excess water. But now I may have to rethink what crops to plant."

What choice did he really have? Wheat, barley and beans were the only crops grown in his part of Oxfordshire. Although his words were meant to appease the marquess, on further reflection, an uneasy feeling was building in his gut; how much credence should he give the information? Devonville seemed pretty convinced of Aldenwood's conclusions, though. Even if Aldenwood's prediction didn't come true, it wouldn't hurt to be prepared in any case.

"And while you're doing that, tell me, Gisborn. About your meeting with Ellsworth, I mean," Devonville said as he moved to the sideboard and refilled his glass. He motioned for Henry to bring his glass so he could pour more scotch into it.

Henry held out his glass. "I was there to speak with him about property. Ellsworth Park is adjacent to the Gisborn lands." He didn't mention the discussion concerning his marrying Lady Charlotte as part of the deal.

"Are you planning to marry the girl?" Devonville asked then, his gaze so direct that Henry was forced to look away.

He sighed quietly. The marquess certainly didn't mince words. "Joshua Wainwright, the new Duke of Chichester, will have that honor, my lord. Probably in a day or two, in fact," Henry added, trying not to allow his disappointment to show. Charlotte had seemed the perfect woman to be his countess. She would make Wainwright the perfect duchess.

Devonville let out a grunt. "Can't say I blame Lady Charlotte. I think she is quite in love with the younger Wainwright. The older brother ..," he paused for a moment and shook his head quickly. "Not so much. Most wouldn't say so out loud, but I think the world is better off without his despicable character staining the reputation of the Wainwrights."

Henry forced his face to remain impassive. *So the marquess was not a fan of the Earl of Grinstead—the man who would have been the Duke of Chichester—had he not died in the fire.* "Indeed," Henry answered with a nod. "Lord Ellsworth was quite insistent that I marry Lady Charlotte, even gave me a generous dowry before the fact. And I would have honored his arrangement had she *wanted* to marry me," he said carefully. *Good God, I am here to inquire about Lady Hannah's availability for marriage. I shouldn't be commenting on my first choice in a wife!*

"A marriage of convenience is not always the best approach, lad," the marquess said in a soft voice, his eyes somber. "I miss my wife. Terribly. Didn't realize what a catch she was until after she had borne me a fine heir, and a beautiful daughter, and put up with my philandering ways for a good decade. I must have had five mistresses before I came to my senses and realized I was in love with my own wife!"

Henry stared at the older man, stunned that he would admit such personal details to someone he had only just met. "She must certainly have returned the favor," he commented, cocking his head to one side.

At this, the light in Lord Devonville's eyes dimmed. His head lowered a notch. "She used to. She died a couple of years ago."

Stunned at the comment, Henry struggled for the correct words to say. *Why hadn't Charlotte warned him that Lady Devonville had died?* "I am so sorry for your loss, my lord," he said in a solemn voice. "It must have been very hard for you. And for your children."

At the mention of children, the marquess lifted his head again. "William is the oldest. He has his own naval command, but Hannah... she isn't yet settled. She's had a harder time of it. Spent a year of what would have been her first Season in mourning for her mother and the second Season in mourning when my when one of my sisters died. My other sister, Adele, has just become betrothed to the Earl of Torrington," he explained with a shrug, waving a hand to indicate Henry should take a seat. Henry did so when the marquess settled himself into an overstuffed chair near the fireplace.

Henry realized then that the woman he had seen with the dog the night before *had* to be Lady Hannah. "She had six suitors this past Season," Devonville continued, a hint of pride in his voice. He took another sip of his scotch. "And not a one of them were worthy of my only daughter," he added before regarding Henry with a critical eye.

Although not surprised that Lady Hannah would attract so many suitors her first Season out, the earl had to struggle to hide his initial shock. *So, I'm not the only one to find her beautiful,* he thought, a sense of sadness settling over him. "It is Lady Charlotte's opinion that your daughter would be a suitable match for me," he said as a way to introduce his reason for calling on the marquess. "I know we have only just met, but do you suppose you might find me worthy enough for your daughter?" Henry asked, holding his head up and meeting the marquess' direct gaze without flinching. Better to discover how he fared with the father before even trying to convince the daughter of his suitability as a husband.

William Slater regarded him for several seconds before turning his attention to the fireplace. He drained his glass, setting the empty tumbler on the table next to this chair. "Did you ever meet your first betrothed?" he asked in a quiet voice.

Henry had to stifle a gasp. How did the marquess know about that? "I met Lady Jennifer when she was quite young. I... We did not renew our acquaintance prior to her death," he stammered. "She was quite young," he repeated, not sure what else to say about his first betrothal.

"Is it true you have a bastard son?" Devonville asked then, his visage so stern, Henry thought perhaps the marquess had already decided he wasn't good enough for his only daughter.

"I do, my lord," Henry answered with a nod, not allowing his surprise to show. *How does the marquess know of my son?*

"I have raised him as such since his birth."

Nodding, Devonville leaned forward. "And what of his education?"

Henry wondered at the man's curiosity. "He had a governess until early last year, he has had a tutor ever since. He will go to Abingdon this fall and Eton when he is thirteen. I hope he will wish to attend a university after that, but it will be up to him to decide which one and for what discipline."

Devonville's bushy eyebrows hiked up on the man's forehead, as if he was surprised by Gisborn's answer. "And what of the mother?"

Bristling at the question but deciding it was better to offer the truth, Henry sighed. "I have wanted to marry his mother since we were quite young, but she has refused all my offers."

Devonville seemed taken aback by his response. "Whatever reason could a woman devise to turn down an earl's offer of marriage?" he asked, his bushy eyebrows now furrowed in disbelief. "Is she frequently beset by the vapours?"

At that moment, Henry wanted nothing more than to disappear into the expensive Turkish carpeting that covered the floor of the drawing room. The marquess had voiced the very question Henry had asked of Sarah the last time he proposed marriage to her. "She was not born to our class. She has known I would inherit the Gisborn earldom since we were in our teen years," he explained quickly, wanting the marquess to know he had tried to legitimize the son. "She feels it is my duty to seek a wife at least equal to my station, so she has rebuffed all my offers to make her my wife."

Although he had given a very similar answer to Lady Charlotte just the afternoon before, somehow it seemed a rather lame excuse when he was saying it to a marquess.

There were several instances of viscounts and earls who had married women from outside the aristocracy. Some of their wives had done just fine in assimilating themselves into the life of the *ton* in London. Some others, however, were never accepted by the fickle aristocracy. They spent their lives on their husband's country estates, never to be seen in London.

The marquess seemed impressed by his answer—or impressed by the mother of his son—Henry could not be sure which. "So, she is your mistress, then?" Devonville half-asked.

Again, Henry remembered his conversation with Lady Charlotte from the day before. He had never considered Sarah his mistress, and yet, that's exactly the role she had played over the years. He intended to continue their relationship even after he wed. He loved her. "I... Yes," he finally agreed, embarrassed at having to admit to keeping a mistress when he was there to ask for the man's permission to court his daughter. "If we suit and if you allow me to wed your daughter, my lord, I promise I will provide protection and the very best of everything for her and our... children," Henry stammered again, cursing at himself for losing his confidence in the middle of the exchange with the marquess. "Lady Charlotte implied..." He stopped then, wondering if he should tell the marquess what Lady Hannah's friend had told him about the younger woman's opinion of husbands.

"Lady Hannah has rather peculiar ideas when it comes to men," the marquess interrupted, realizing Lady Charlotte had probably shared Hannah's odd opinion of men with the earl. When he noted Henry's arched eyebrow, though, he wondered if she had explained it in terms the earl could understand. "It is my daughter's opinion that men only really love their mistresses and merely need their wives to bear them children," Devonville admitted with an exaggerated sigh. He recognized the earl's discomfiture for what it was. "Although I kept all those mistresses for several years, I know now I was a fool to do so. I loved my wife. And I have tried in vain to convince my daughter of that fact for the past couple of years," he insisted then, his ire increasing with every word.

"I do not require she love me," Henry stated then, his head shaking. "And, as long as she loves the children she bears, I should consider myself a very lucky man, my lord."

The Marquess of Devonville stared at the Earl of Gisborn for several moments, his features set in an unreadable expression. And then a hint of mischief appeared in his eyes. "Then I suggest you get on with the business of courting her," Devonville stated before rising to his feet. "To the extent she can be courted," he added with a grin that seemed to indicate more mischief. "The third time is the charm, they say," he murmured, referring to his daughter being Gisborn's third wife apparent. "I wish you luck, Gisborn," he added as he extended his hand to the earl.

Henry stared in disbelief at the marquess. What was the man not telling him? He finally took and shook the proffered hand. *The third time.* "Thank you, my lord. I..." He stopped as he considered why the marquess would even give him permission to court Lady Hannah. "May I ask why it is you're allowing me to court your daughter?"

The gleam of mischief still in his eyes, the Marquess of Devonville regarded Henry with a slight grin. "You're an earl, and yet you work your land. Most of the idiots in the *ton* would find that offensive, but I do not. You've done right by your son. I expect you'll do right by my daughter. And whatever grandchildren you manage to produce." He straightened. "By the way, you'll find Lady Hannah in the parlor."

Henry nodded, surprised at the man's candor. "May I call on her now?"

"Of course. Her earlier caller, Lady Bostwick, left a bit ago. She's Hannah's other best friend, by the way," he said in an off-hand manner, but Henry got the distinct impression the information was provided to help him in his quest. "Oh, and Harold is with her. Let me tell you a bit about my daughter's pet. Just so you're prepared."

And for the next few minutes, the Marquess of Devonville described the abilities and antics of the Alpenmastiff that had been with the family for ten years.

Allowing a smile at Devonville's descriptions, Henry realized the dog had become equivalent to another child in the Slater household. And he was obviously near and dear to Lady Hannah.

"Now, off with you," Devonville said with a wave as he indicated the drawing room door.

Henry grinned. "I will not disappoint you."

The marquess regarded him, his eyes narrowing. "See that you don't."

CHAPTER 4
LADY HANNAH MEETS LORD GISBORN

Standing to the side of the front window of the Devonville House parlor, Lady Hannah Slater watched as the unmarked coach pulled up into the semi-circular drive and deposited its rather handsome occupant onto the crushed granite. A coin was tossed to the driver, who nodded and set his crop aside once he'd climbed back onto the box. So... the coach was no doubt hired and expected to stay put for the duration of the gentleman's visit.

But who was the fare?

She watched as the tall man approached the front doors, his gaze directed straight ahead. His top hat was well suited to his height, his dark topcoat and buckskin breeches tailored to fit him precisely. There was a shine on his boots that suggested his valet had seen to them that very morning.

Hannah wondered why he didn't seem to direct his gaze to the rest of the house as most did when they approached the Palladian mansion in Park Lane. Perhaps he had already caught sight of her staring out the window and did not wish to embarrass her by looking in her direction.

She stepped back and to the side a bit more, to keep his figure in view until he passed one of the Grecian columns that flanked the entry. Dark hair, long sideburns, a square jaw—he looked familiar, but Hannah could not be certain she'd met him.

Oh, if only Lady Charlotte were still in town. She would know the man who was now being let into the vestibule by Hatfield. Charlotte knew all the gentlemen of the *ton* and several cits, besides. Having been betrothed nearly her entire life, Charlotte had no need of considering every man she met as a potential suitor. As such, she made friends with men for the sole purpose of having dance partners at balls. For Hannah, though, two Seasons lost to mourning meant she was still becoming acquainted with the available bachelors of the *ton*. Although she'd had six suitors her first year out, none were particularly interesting, and all but one were clearly angling for her dowry more than for her hand in marriage. The other was barely eighteen and apparently wanted to get married so he could escape his domineering mother.

Almost one-and-twenty, and with one best friend married and, in Charlotte's case, another almost so, Hannah had decided she would have to be settled before summer or die of boredom. She could only hope this Season would present some better prospects.

Moving to the parlor door but making sure she stayed within its walls, Hannah listened intently. The man had apparently asked to see her father. A sense of disappointment settled over her, and she wondered at her reaction. The Season had only just begun. There had only been two balls and a *musicale*. Why would she expect a gentleman caller already?

Perhaps it was Elizabeth's visit, she decided. Lady Bostwick was so *happy* in her marriage to George Bennett-Jones. She'd spent most of her visit espousing the virtues of having an attentive husband—a man she had thought was a cit until Elizabeth's father, the Marquess of Morganfield, set her straight and informed her he was a *viscount*. That was the day back in October when Elizabeth became engaged to George. They were married so quickly, the *ton* had gossiped for nearly a week. And Elizabeth was already with child. In another three months, she would give birth!

A stab of jealousy caught Hannah by surprise. *Oh, to be with child!* She thought it rather unfair that one had to have a husband before you could have a baby. At least, in the legitimate sense. She couldn't imagine being a poor, unmarried woman with a child.

Sighing, Hannah moved back to a chair near the fireplace. Her abandoned needlework lay on the chair cushion, and her dog, Harold MacDuff, lay napping on the floor directly in front of the chair. Rather than insist he lift his huge body and move it so that she could retake her seat, Hannah directed her attention to the piano-forté. Music would do her spirits some good, she decided. Rifling through the sheets of music she'd picked out at Birchall's the week before, she pulled out a few and began to play.

So engrossed was she in studying the music she played, Hannah was unaware of the visitor who stood on the threshold of the parlor. It wasn't until she completed a selection by Bach and was moving a new sheet of music into place that she noticed her father's caller. "Oh!" she managed as a hand went to the top of her bosom.

"Brava, my lady." Henry Forster bowed deeply, not wanting to take his eyes off the beauty at the piano-forté. He did so to complete the courtesy. Then he had to force himself to breathe. Lady Hannah was far more beautiful up close than she had appeared in the garden the night before. The pink muslin gown she wore complemented her skin as well as her figure, the bodice fitted enough to display the fullness of her breasts. With her slender arms and long fingers uncovered, it was apparent to Henry she had long since left the schoolroom. *Twenty, perhaps*, he thought as he allowed his gaze to rest on her face. Had Devonville mentioned her age? If so, he couldn't remember. His brain was suddenly a bit addled.

Hannah stood up from the piano bench and curtsied.

Where is Harold? And why hadn't he warned her there was a man awaiting her attention? She dared a quick glance in the direction of the fireplace and saw that the hairy beast still napped in front of her chair. *Some guard dog you are,* she thought with annoyance. As if reading her thoughts, Harold opened one eye for a moment before yawning and closing it again. "Thank you, my lord. I'm afraid it's the first time I've played that piece—"

"And yet you played it perfectly. Bach himself would have to agree, I'm sure," Henry stated with a nod as he moved toward her. He stopped directly in front of her and reached for her hand. Lifting it, he brushed his lips over the back of the knuckles. *Even her hands are beautiful,* he thought as he held the one longer than propriety would allow. "Henry Forster, Earl of Gisborn," he said by way of introduction. "At your service."

Hannah blushed, the pink spreading over her cheeks in an instant. "You are too kind," she answered, daring to return the man's gaze. *Gisborn?* That made no sense. The Earl of Gisborn was an old fart of an earl. A wrinkled, disagreeable, mean old man. So old he was... *dead,* she just then realized.

And this man was his heir.

Henry Forster. She recognized the name, but the man who stood before her was not someone to whom she had been introduced at a ball or *musicale.* Lady Charlotte had spoken of him. She knew him from her youth. Nearby estates, or some such. "And I am Lady Hannah Slater," she stated, shaking herself from her brief reverie. "I am pleased to make your acquaintance." Her mind raced. Had he only come to the parlor because of the music? He had called on her father. Their business must be complete. "Would you care to join me for tea?" she asked, surprised she would invite him, but if she did not, she was afraid he would take his leave of Devonville House, and she'd never see him again.

Stunned at the invitation—he was alone with her in the parlor, with not a footman nor a maid in sight to act as chaperone—Henry angled his head to one side. He wasn't about to question his good luck. "I would be honored," he replied with a nod.

Hannah dipped her head in return and moved to the bell pull. "I thought perhaps I would have had another caller by now, so it shan't be long."

Henry remembered what the marquess had said about her earlier caller being her 'other best friend.'

"Won't you take a seat?" she offered, waving to the only chair her father would sit in when he was in the parlor.

Hannah made sure to sit in an adjacent chair with a low table in front. She watched as Henry took the proffered chair. He seemed nervous, as if it was the first time he was alone in a room with a lady. "Did you have business with my father?" she asked, not sure how else to start the conversation.

Henry considered the question. "Something like that. I find him quite... agreeable," he offered, daring to look at her as he made the assessment.

About to respond, Hannah waved toward the parlor door. A maid rolled the tea cart into the room, her eyes widening at the sight of her mistress with a man and apparently no other servant in the room. She placed the silver tray with the pot and cups on the low table in front of Hannah along with a plate of lemon biscuits. "Did you by chance bring a biscuit for the dog?" Hannah asked, hoping the mention of the hairy beast would put to rest any qualms the maid might have about leaving Hannah alone with the visitor.

"Aye, milady," the maid replied, her voice sounding ever so relieved at the mention of the dog. She placed a plate with an odd looking brown shape onto the table next to the biscuits.

"Thank you. I'll see to pouring the tea," Hannah said by way of dismissal. Turning to the earl, she asked, "How do you take your tea, my lord?" as she lifted a cup and saucer.

"Gisborn," Henry stated emphatically. At Hannah's

widened eyes, he wondered if he had erred in insisting she use his name so soon after their introduction. "No sugar, a bit of milk," he added. He dared a glance in the dog's direction. "Will Harold be joining us, milady?"

Hannah was pouring the milk and didn't see the glint in Henry's eye as he asked about the dog. She wondered how he knew her pet's name. *Did Father talk about Harold with him?* She lifted her gaze to his as she handed him the tea. "I am sure he would love to. That is, if you were not asking in jest."

Henry smiled. "I was not," he answered with a shake of his head. "Unless I have taken his chair, in which case I should like the opportunity to move to another before we invite him."

Smiling at his joke, Hannah turned her attention on her pet. "Would you like a biscuit, Harold?"

The Alpenmastiff raised his head in surprise. A very small but deep 'woof ' erupted before the beast raised his entire body off the floor, a move that seemed to take a great deal of effort and at least two or three whines before he lumbered over to Hannah's side. He appeared to notice Henry for the first time, but, not sensing any danger to his mistress, he pulled his haunches under him and sat up as straight as his bulk would allow.

"May I?" Henry asked as he pointed toward the dog's treat.

Hannah regarded her guest with uncertainty. "I... I suppose."

Lifting the biscuit from the plate, Henry rose from the chair and walked over to the dog. Standing directly in front of Harold, he allowed his eyes to make contact with the dog's. They were large, brown eyes, rather expressive despite the overall look of boredom the rest of his expression seemed to convey. His huge black nose was surrounded by a white snout that featured a collection of black freckles. Beyond that, his body was covered in brown fur which extended to a white band of fur around his entire neck. The rest of his body seemed covered in the brown fur, except his front legs, which were quite white, as if the dog had been recently bathed. Henry wondered if there was a copper tub anywhere in London large enough to accommodate such a huge beast.

Henry lowered the biscuit until it rested on top of the dog's rather wide snout. Harold stared at him with lazy eyes, as if he had done the trick a thousand times and was bored by it. Henry returned to his chair and sat down. "Now, Harold!"

he commanded. Harold dutifully tossed the biscuit into the air with an upward shake of his nose and caught the treat in his mouth as it came down. For a few seconds, a crunching sound emanated from the animal.

Hannah's mouth dropped open before one of her hands could cover it. "How did you... how did *he* know how to do *that*?" she asked in surprise. "I... I didn't know he knew that trick!" She stared at Henry for several seconds. "I haven't taught him how to do it!"

Fighting the urge to laugh at her expense, Henry shook his head. "I think your father might be the guilty one, my lady," he said in an apologetic tone.

The pink flush that colored Hannah's face nearly matched her gown. "I cannot believe he would keep that from me," she murmured, feeling a bit indignant. She glanced up to find the earl watching her, his head angled to one side. He was a very handsome man, she decided. Broad of shoulder, tall, with a full head of dark hair that could almost be black, and eyes that were so blue, she almost dared not look at him directly.

"It is just a parlor trick. Your Harold," he nodded his head toward the dog and was not surprised to find the beast watching him intently, "Is quite a majestic dog. Perhaps he could join us on a ride in the park. 'Tis a beautiful day for it." In truth, it was a bit chilly, but the sun was finally burning off the early morning fog, and the sky would be clear soon.

A frisson passed through Hannah—just the thought of

riding in the park with this very handsome man made her belly flip and her heart begin to race. "I... I would have to ask my father, of course, but... I would be delighted." Even if the earl wasn't handsome, she would have welcomed the opportunity to get out of the house. A ride in the park seemed just the thing.

"Have I heard my name, perhaps?" the Marquess of Devonville asked from the threshold. He seemed rather pleased by what he saw, but Henry placed his cup on the table and stood up at the man's comment, hoping the marquess didn't find the tableau he was witnessing too inappropriate. Here he was, sitting very close to the man's daughter, and next to her was the family dog with his tongue hanging to one side and a bit of slobber about to drip off it. Henry bowed to the marquess.

"Sit, sit," Devonville insisted as he moved into the room.

"Good morning, Father," Hannah said by way of greeting, tilting one cheek up so her father could kiss it. The marquess gave Harold a pat on the head and moved to sit in a chair opposite Henry. Hannah was already pouring tea and milk for him.

"If you'd like to take my daughter for a ride in Hyde Park, you're welcome to take my phaeton, Gisborn," he offered as he took the teacup from Hannah. "I've got a groom seeing to it now. Of course, there really isn't room for Harold, but I trust you'll get her home in one piece."

Working hard to hide his astonishment, Henry nodded. "That is very gracious of you. I was just asking her ladyship if she would join me for a ride."

Hannah was sure her face was bright red. Her father had never offered such liberties to her other suitors. Nor had he ever offered his high perch phaeton!

"Henry here is the new Earl of Gisborn," the marquess said, directing his comment to Hannah. "And the new owner of Ellsworth Park," he added, a bushy eyebrow arched in a manner that suggested his daughter should be impressed.

"Seems Lady Charlotte will be marrying her duke any day now."

Her mouth opening in astonishment, Hannah quickly changed her expression to one of delight. "I am so happy for her," she said, the sound of relief in her voice. "She has wanted no other than Joshua Wainwright since she was sixteen!"

Fighting back the urge to wince at her comment, Henry merely nodded. "I just came from Wisborough Oaks late yesterday," he said as lightly as he could manage. "Lady Charlotte is already settled, and has taken on the responsibility of overseeing the decoration of the rebuilt portion of the estate," he added in a tone of voice that was all business. "I believe she has become Wainwright's chatelaine." His words were obviously important to Lady Hannah, though, as her face brightened and she gave him a smile that was so glorious, he wanted nothing more than to repeat whatever word it was that made her so happy.

"Did you have occasion to speak with Lady Charlotte?" Hannah asked, leaning forward as she made the query.

Henry nodded, keeping his eyes on hers in order to avoid the urge to stare at her suddenly more apparent décolletage. He hadn't noticed *that* last night as she cavorted with Harold in the park. "Yes, I…" He paused, realizing he couldn't tell her he'd been there to claim Lady Charlotte as his wife. "I had business there with the duke," he amended quickly. "But I made Lady Charlotte's acquaintance many years ago. The estate I just *acquired* belonged to her father. It sits directly to the west of the Gisborn earldom," he explained, hoping he wasn't boring the poor girl.

"If you have acquired the estate, Gisborn, you must have plans for the land," she supposed, hoping her barely hidden query wasn't too personal. She only meant to keep up her end of the conversation.

Hearing his name spoken in her voice made something shiver deep inside Henry. *Gisborn.* She had said it as if she was put on the earth for the sole purpose of speaking that word. Henry gazed at her, remembering too late that she had hinted he had plans for Ellsworth Park. "I... I mean to add it to my existing farmlands and modernize the entire tract," he finally got out, hoping he didn't sound like a dullard.

"And what will modernizing entail?" she countered, the tilt of her head suggesting she was truly interested in the topic. She refilled his teacup and followed it with a dollop of milk.

Henry watched her hands as she saw to his tea. She had elegant hands—smooth, pale hands with long, perfectly shaped fingers. He could imagine those fingers traveling over his body, gripping his shoulders as he kissed her senseless, teasing his manhood into hardened steel, digging into his back as he rode her during intercourse, the fingernails leaving little half-moon brands in his skin as he brought her to ecstasy.

What the hell? Mentally pinching his swelling manhood, Henry swallowed. Hard.

He dared a glance in Devonville's direction. The marquess seemed quite interested in farm modernization, as well. "My lands border the River Isis. It's my intention to have irrigation ditches dug on both ends of the land as well as down the middle, at right angles to the river, to allow the fields to be watered during dry times and drained in times of too much rain." Pausing a moment to be sure his audience was still interested, he saw Lady Hannah's brow furrow.

"How, then, will you keep the river from flooding your fields when there is too much rain?" she asked, her body barely perched on the edge of her chair. She was leaning forward again, apparently very interested in irrigation.

The thought of river water spilling into the ditches he planned to have dug in the next few weeks was quickly replaced with the thought of Hannah's breasts spilling forth from her bodice and into his eager hands. He was sure one of them would fill a hand completely, perhaps even overflow the edges of his fingers and flood onto his...

Gates! he admonished himself. He had to think of gates. *The gates of hell.* And higher necklines.

"At the points where the irrigation ditches and the river meet, there will be a sort of gate—a large, flat piece of iron with a rope attached that can be strung over a pulley. Then the gate can be raised and lowered between two guide tracks," he explained, his hands motioning in the air as he described the devices, making sure to include the marquess in his explanation. "A sort of dam that can be put into place when no water is needed, and then lifted up when the ditch needs to be filled."

Hannah's mouth opened as she listened to his explanation, understanding immediately how the system would work. "That's brilliant! Did you come up with the idea yourself?"

Henry couldn't help but allow a grin at Hannah's enthusiasm. "Thank you," he murmured, nodding as he said so and feeling as if her assessment was the last bit of encouragement he needed to actually put the irrigation system into place.

I could name the system the Gates of Hannah.

"Some of it, yes. I like to design things to... to solve problems," he admitted.

The Gates of Hannah. He found himself imagining Hannah, naked and atop his bed, her milky white thighs spreading apart, gates to the heaven that could be his as his manhood thrust into her warm, wet cocoon, flooding her with his seed... *Christ! We're talking about farm modernization here,* he chastised himself, shifting his position in the chair and lowering his teacup and saucer to better cover the evidence of his erection.

Devonville was watching him with a good deal of interest. "You'll have to excuse Lady Hannah's ignorance of modern farm techniques. Her other best friend recently married Viscount Bostwick. His farmlands in Sussex are undergoing the same modernization." He turned his attention to his daughter. "I don't suppose Lady Bostwick talks of such things when she visits, though," he added, a hint of derision in his voice.

Her face displaying a sudden wash of pink, Hannah regarded her father with a mix of surprise and embarrassment. "Certainly not today," she agreed with a shake of her head, not adding that Elizabeth Bennett-Jones wouldn't be the least bit interested in anything having to do with farming techniques. Her primary interests of late seemed to revolve around activities that could be performed in a bedchamber. Or in other rooms of a house when servants were not present.

Alarmed at the marquess' comment, Henry felt a twinge of embarrassment on behalf of Lady Hannah. Did the man realize how critical he sounded of her wish to understand the topic at hand? Henry remembered Hannah's response to her father's query about Lady Bostwick. So, she *was* the woman who had left just before his arrival.

Hannah sighed and gave a wan smile. She set her teacup on the table. *How could Father say such a thing in front of a guest?* she wondered, her joy at having so easily followed the earl's explanation gone. Her father had never done such a thing to her during dinner parties.

Was he chastising her because of her conversations with Elizabeth? Did he even know the topics of Elizabeth's every-other-daily visits? Had he overheard the viscountess telling Hannah of her bedroom antics? Of how much she loved being married to George Bennett-Jones—because he was so attentive and because there was such joy in their marriage bed?

Or had he simply decided his daughter shouldn't know such things as how irrigation gates worked? It seemed to her he should be more concerned about Elizabeth's titillating conversation.

"Perhaps we can go for that ride now?" Henry spoke, his tone suggesting he was trying to lighten the mood in the room. He also needed something to concentrate on besides Hannah. Never in his life had the presence of a woman had him so addled. And never had he experienced such vivid thoughts of what he might do with one should he get her in his bed.

The marquess brightened. "The phaeton should be in the drive by now," he said as he stood up. Both Henry and Hannah stood as well. Harold, sensing the change in the dynamics in the room, was already standing. His brown eyes seemed to focus on each of the room's occupants for only a moment before moving to the next, as if he was trying to size up the situation. Then he concentrated his attention on his mistress, as if he took cues from only her.

"My bonnet is in the vestibule," Hannah said with a nod, "But I must go to my room for some gloves and a shawl. Please excuse me. I'll be but a moment," she added as she moved to the parlor door. Both gentlemen bowed as she and the dog took their leave of the parlor.

As Hannah climbed the stairs to her room, she wondered at her last comment. Perhaps she shouldn't have seemed so eager. Perhaps she should make the Earl of Gisborn wait a few minutes. *Did I sound desperate when I said I would be but a moment? That I so wanted the earl to like me that I would hurry so as not to keep him waiting?* And if he did find her biddable, did he plan to court her? A frisson shot through Hannah's body at that thought, nearly causing her to gasp as she stepped over the threshold and into her bedchamber. Despite not being invited to do so, Harold followed on her footsteps.

Hannah's father regarded Henry for a moment. "You probably think she's a feather-headed twit, don't you?" the Marquess of Devonville stated, his apparent disappointment displayed quite clearly on his face and in how his shoulders slumped.

Henry had to suppress the first thing that came to mind by way of a response. "Actually, I found her interest in the topic quite unique for her sex, and she seemed intelligent enough to follow my explanation. *I* see no reason to be critical of her," he countered, hoping his annoyance at the marquess wasn't too apparent in his response.

"Indeed?" Devonville replied with a tilt of his head. He made a sort of humming sound in his throat as he considered Henry's comment. "Then, if you should wish to, you may continue the topic on your ride in the park," he said with a shrug. "But I must remind you, Gisborn. She is just a chit. Although she had a governess and attended a finishing school, don't expect the topics of her conversation to be too challenging."

Henry bristled at hearing the marquess' words as the two of them made their way to the vestibule. "I assure you, my lord. I don't really have any expectations at this point."

"Expectations of what?" Hannah asked as she finished pulling on a glove. A deep pink shawl was carelessly draped across her shoulders. From where she stood on the last step of the stairs leading to the second floor, she had been able to watch her father and Henry as they continued their conversation outside the parlor.

Admiring her figure from where he stood, Henry considered how to respond. Should he make light of his last comment to the marquess? Or lay it all on the line and explain exactly why he was there? To do so would risk her possible derision at his intentions. It might also result in her admiration of his forthright manner. At the moment, Henry decided he didn't have the time for a drawn-out courtship. If Hannah Slater wasn't interested in becoming the Countess of Gisborn, he may as well find out right now.

Henry walked to the base of the stairs, his line of sight nearly equal with hers. Regarding Hannah for a moment, he took a deep breath and reached for her hand. "Expectation that you would allow me to court you, in the hope that we could marry next week, so that I might return to Gisborn Hall with you as my countess, and see to it an heir is on the way, and those irrigation ditches are dug, and the gates are built and working before seeds are planted in the fields next month," he managed to get out quite calmly. "Are you ready?" This last was delivered in a completely different voice, as if his other words were merely spoken in rote, rehearsed over a dozen times to sound nonchalant and wooden.

Lady Hannah blinked once and considered every word he had just spoken. She blinked again, realizing Henry Forster was quite serious. A slow smile spread over her face. "I am ready," she answered as she took his proffered hand and made her way to his side.

CHAPTER 5
A RIDE IN THE PARK

"Tell me truly. Are you the least bit interested in irrigation ditches and water gates?" Henry asked. He had just offered his hand as Lady Hannah made to climb up to the bench seat of the bright red phaeton. She paused in taking the first step up and raised her eyes to meet the earl's.

"I must admit, I was not at first. Until you explained them in terms that I could understand. Now I find myself rather curious as to how they will look when they are operating." She resumed her climb onto the seat, thankful the earl had provided a strong arm for her to grasp for balance as she ascended the equipage.

Henry caught sight of an ankle above her silk slipper as she lifted her skirts to clear the side rail. The shiver passed through him again, forcing him to close his eyes and take a deep breath to steady himself.

What is happening to me? He had seen Sarah's ankles plenty of times, even massaged them while she was in the later months of her confinement. But there was something about Hannah's ankle that made him want to stroke it, kiss it, hold it between his hands and write poetry... *What the hell?*

Henry Forster had never written an ode to anything in his life!

Noticing Henry's reaction, Hannah felt a sense of disappointment settling over her. Had she been too bold in admitting her lack of interest in irrigation ditches? Should she have lied and claimed she was eminently interested and could think of nothing else more important to the future of agriculture in Great Britain? In the few instances where it was easy to speak the truth, she had just done so and now found herself regretting it.

Before climbing up to the seat and taking the ribbons from the groom, Henry nodded his thanks to the young man and asked if he would see to the coach and driver still waiting for him in the carriageway. Handing him a coin, he told the groom to request the coach return to Devonville House in two hours.

Once up and onto the phaeton, Henry found the seat didn't provide much room. He was careful to leave space between the edge of Hannah's skirts and his thigh. He turned and regarded Hannah with a grin that grew into a brilliant smile. "Someday soon, I hope you will be there to witness the first time I raise the gates on my irrigation system," he said before turning his attention to the grey horse. *As to those other gates...*

Staring back in surprise, Hannah gave him a tentative smile in return. "I rather hope so, too."

He allowed the impatient beast a loose rein and steered the phaeton up Park Lane toward Oxford Street. "I have other plans for the farm, of course. I'm afraid my late uncle —the ninth Earl of Gisborn—was not interested in modernizing, so there is much to do," he remarked, avoiding a vegetable cart that had suddenly been pushed into the street. Although Hyde Park would not be crowded this time of the morning, the streets leading to it were teaming with carriages and carts and all manner of equipage and horses.

"What else has to be done?" Hannah asked, her face turning up to regard the earl's profile. He was a truly handsome man, she thought. And not at all like the gentlemen she had met at last Season's balls. Gisborn was bronzed from the sun, his torso and shoulders shaped as if he performed manual labor. She wondered what he looked like without a shirt, wondered what it would be like to stroke skin that stretched over hardened muscle, to see him over the top of her as he moved to claim her virtue, to feel him enter her, thrust into her, bring her to ecstasy like Elizabeth described in such vivid detail.

Henry shrugged and gave her a quick glance. "It is more a case of what doesn't need to be done," he answered finally. "I have some new cast iron plows on order. But I am thinking there must be a way to make one that will do the work of three or more, if I can just figure a way to mount the plows and have them pulled behind several draft horses. Then it would be possible for one man to plow ten or more acres a day."

She was thinking that being plowed once a day would suit her just fine if it was everything Elizabeth described. Angling her head to one side, Hannah tried to imagine what Henry was describing. "Wouldn't you have to be seated above the plows then? So you could drive the horses?"

A costermonger selling oranges darted onto Oxford Street, forcing Henry to rein in the horse. The sudden jerk in the phaeton caused Hannah to shift dangerously on the bench. There was a moment when she seemed suspended in mid-air and might have been forced completely off the high perch. But Henry had his arm around her back in an instant, his hand pressed against the side of her waist and pulling her towards him. She let out a squeak of surprise and grabbed onto his thigh. And then blushed a bright pink as she quickly pulled her hand away to instead take purchase on the bench front.

"I've got you," Henry said calmly, although it took everything in his power to keep the horse reined in and her body on the bench seat. "Are you injured?" he asked then, fighting the urge to yell at the costermonger for his negligence.

Hannah held her breath, the sensation of his arm and hand sending a startling jolt of *something* through her body just then. "I am fine. Truly. I... I apologize. I should have been holding on," she murmured.

"No apology is necessary, my lady," Henry countered, not removing his arm. "Especially since you have given me a rather brilliant idea." This last was said in a quiet voice, as if he were deep in thought.

Wondering what she had said or done to give him a brilliant idea, Hannah glanced in his direction and rather hoped the brilliant idea was something that could be done in a bed. She supposed she should ask him to remove his arm, but she found she rather liked it right where it was. When he turned to look at her, Hannah felt her face heating up again.

"I believe I can make a plow that will do three furrows at a time," Henry said, as if he was still deep in thought and having an epiphany at the same time. "Two shire horses and a seat on top of the yoke that houses the plows. And there would be the yoke for the horses." His eyebrows arched as a grin settled on his face. Then he seemed to realize his arm was still around Hannah. "Oh, pardon me," he said as he quickly removed it. He changed hands on the reins and then moved to take Hannah's gloved hand and place it on the arm that had been around her back. "Just in case," he said as he noticed Hannah's questioning look.

Hannah grinned, trying hard to put out of her mind the feel of his thigh beneath her hand as she moved to steady herself a moment ago. It was solid muscle. He obviously rode a horse or exercised regularly. And now his arm, under the same gloved hand, felt just as solid.

"By the way, Lady Charlotte sends her regards," Henry said as he negotiated the phaeton between two ancient barouches just inside the entrance to Hyde Park. Their occupants, looking at least as old as the equipage in which they rode, were waving to one another just as he made the turn.

Surprised at the mention of Charlotte Bingham again, Hannah angled her head up to stare at Henry. She also wanted to avoid being recognized by Lady Fennington. Should the dowager viscountess notice she rode unchaperoned, she was quite sure she would be the topic of drawing room conversations for a week. At least the earl blocked her from being seen by Lady Fletcher, although the baroness wasn't much of a gossip. She was George Bennett-Jones' aunt, in fact, and would probably encourage Hannah to take a turn with an eligible bachelor, chaperoned or not, and would probably offer to provide the equipage, too. "May I ask when you spoke with her?" Hannah asked, hoping to keep the surprise out of her voice. She and Elizabeth Bennett-Jones had said their good-byes to Charlotte not even a fortnight ago. The daughter of an earl and betrothed to a duke, Charlotte had departed for Sussex with the intention of marrying when she turned one-and-twenty. Hannah remembered that day would be Saturday.

"Yesterday, in fact," Henry answered, expecting to feel a sense of disappointment at having to say the words aloud. Charlotte should have been his wife. Instead, she would be marrying the Duke of Chichester. He realized he had accepted Charlotte's devotion to her duke, though. She would be a duchess, a role she had planned to play for her entire life. But, once again, Henry was left looking for a countess.

Or, perhaps not, if Lady Hannah was of a mind to marry him.

He could imagine taking her as his wife. He had already imagined what he might do to her in his bed, already imagined her as his countess. He had already voiced his intention to take her as his wife, although he wasn't sure Hannah had given his earlier litany any serious thought.

When he glanced over to find Hannah regarding him, a look of anticipation animating her fairy tale princess features, a sense of calm settled over him. His eyes darted to the horse, just a quick look to be sure it was following the road, before he gave her his full attention.

She was a lovely woman. Not a classical beauty, nor as beautiful as Charlotte, but very pretty. Very soft and fair and princess-like. And she smelled like honeysuckle. He had to resist the urge to plant his nose into the space along the column of her neck just so he could inhale the scent of her. And those lips. Perfect rosebud lips just begging to be kissed. He could imagine kissing those lips. Every night and every morning and perhaps several times throughout the day. He wondered if she would allow such a thing. Sarah certainly wouldn't.

The thought of Sarah brought him back to reality.

Hannah was still regarding him, her lips parted slightly. "Is she... well?" she asked finally, deciding the earl wasn't going to offer any more information about her friend. He seemed to be staring at her, in a way that suggested he was remembering something. She hadn't wanted to interrupt his thoughts, especially when she thought he looked like he was about to kiss her. Her belly did a little flip at that thought, sending a sensation of soft pleasure coursing through her. She had to resist the urge to look down at her bodice to be sure her breasts were still hidden beneath the pelisse she wore. They felt too heavy. She was sure her nipples were puckered. Heat pooled between her thighs. A slight flush rushed up her body, turning her face that pale pink. Again.

And if Henry didn't maintain a tighter rein on the horse, they were going to end up on the grassy lawn to the side of the carriageway. She reached out with a gloved hand to grasp his larger hand.

"Oh, pardon me," Henry said, his hands tightening on the ribbons. The horse tossed his head in response but straightened his progress on the path.

"A penny for your thoughts." The words were out of her mouth before Hannah realized she had said them.

Trying hard to suppress a grin of embarrassment, Henry shook his head. "I was woolgathering. Which is a horrible thing for someone such as me to admit to when I find sheep so..." He paused, not sure if he should tell her of his disdain for the livestock that were so important to the region where his lands were located. Oxfordshire could boast of the Cotswolds, and while the region was synonymous with sheep, his lands were devoted to farming. And farming was what he did. It was how he had made his living before he inherited the earldom. And he continued to do it, although he did so because he could not imagine not doing it. One of the few members of the aristocracy who worked for a living, Henry could actually afford not to, should he choose. But he was used to laboring in the fields surrounding Gisborn Hall. Just because he had inherited an earldom and enough money so he could spend his days in leisure didn't mean he intended to live like his peers.

"Offensive?" Hannah offered, not quite sure if it was the correct adjective.

Henry glanced over at his passenger, finding the word perfect. "Yes. I'm a farmer. I don't own sheep. Nor will I ever. Nor are there any on my lands." His words were delivered with a firmness that suggested he despised the sources of wool that were so important to the economy of Great Britain.

"Should there be?" Hannah countered, her expression one of puzzlement.

Henry laughed. "Not if you ask me." He reached over to where her hand was resting on his arm, his gloved hand patting hers. "But they are a fixture of the Cotswolds," he added with a shrug. "And, in answer to your earlier question, when I left the Wainwright estate yesterday, Lady Charlotte was busy with her decorating project for the duke's house. I expect Wainwright has asked for her hand by now. He planned to do so after I left them to return to London."

Hannah sighed, her face brightening at the news of her best friend. "I am very relieved to hear it," she said with a grin. "There was gossip suggesting her cousin tried to have her killed, and other gossip that had her father on his deathbed at St. Bart's."

Henry angled his head. "And he is not?" he asked, his brows furrowing. He had heard the very same gossip shortly after he had met with the Earl of Ellsworth. Although he never went to White's, he did visit Boodles during his occasional visits to London.

Dipping her head, Hannah shook it before returning her gaze to meet his. "He has a bump on his head, but apparently wanted everyone to *believe* he was going to die. He wanted to learn if his nephew was truly as awful as he feared."

Henry gave her a sideways glance. "And?" he urged her to continue.

"He is. He's been arrested for theft and attempted murder," she answered, her voice kept low, as if she were afraid of being overheard. "I tell you only because..."

She paused, not wanting to admit she knew of his betrothal to Charlotte.

"Because it is important to me," Henry stated, glancing again in her direction. He wondered if what Hannah knew of Bingham's condition was really the case. Was the man truly recovered? Or was he on his deathbed? And would the authorities truly arrest a man who was due to inherit the Ellsworth earldom? It seemed rather unlikely to him. Members of the *ton* seemed impervious to matters of the law. "But Lady Charlotte is under Wainwright's protection now, so I can rest easy knowing she is safe from her own cousin."

Hannah nodded, feeling a sense of relief at learning of her friend's current situation. Charlotte would be married soon. With Elizabeth already married and with child, and Charlotte about to be wed, it just left Hannah without a betrothal in place. "So, what brings you to London, my lord?"

Henry had to resist the urge to say, "You do."

And then he couldn't help himself.

"You do, my lady," he said aloud, holding his breath as he tried to guess how she would react. "And you're supposed to call me 'Gisborn'," he added.

He was not surprised by the sight of her slightly parted lips, of her face as her expression changed from delight to puzzlement. He directed the horse to pull into a parkway along the side of the path where a tree provided shade. After he jumped down from the phaeton, he tied the reins around the trunk of the tree and stepped to the side of the phaeton where Hannah sat. Holding his hands up as if he intended to bodily capture Hannah, he noticed her widened eyes at how far down she would have to step to make it to the ground. "Place your hands on my shoulders, and I'll do the rest."

Hannah did as she was told, and next she was floating to the ground, Henry's hands planted firmly on either side of her waist. Once her feet were under her, she expected he would let go. But he stood before her, his heavy lidded eyes letting her know he wasn't about to let go. Instead, his lips came down onto hers in a very light, feathery kiss that tickled as well as tantalized. It was over too soon, she thought, and she was disappointed when he straightened slightly.

"I meant what I said earlier," he said in a quiet voice. "Lady Charlotte recommended I call on you. She thought... that is, she..." he closed his eyes for a moment, as if seeing her before him was too much of a distraction. "I believe she was right in thinking we might suit one another for marriage. So, I would ask if I might be allowed to court you," he got out finally. "Your father has already given his permission," he added, not sure if that bit of information would help his case or not.

Hannah stared up at Henry, her lips still parted slightly as she considered his words. He was talking seriously of courting and marriage. Not like he had back at the house, where she had been left to think his comments were made in jest. And Lady Charlotte had recommended he call on her. Surely Charlotte had been his first choice for a wife, though.

Had he wanted Charlotte because he felt affection for her? Or was it because of a dowry? No, he was an earl with somewhat of a fortune, so a dowry couldn't explain why Charlotte was his first choice. But why had Charlotte recommended her? "Tell me, Gisborn. Do you have just one mistress? Or several?" Hannah asked then, her manner quite matter-of-fact. The question had worked in Elizabeth's favor at one point.

Henry stared at her for several seconds, stunned by the question. Gently bred ladies didn't speak of mistresses. Or ask gentlemen about their arrangements with their mistresses. "I don't employ a mistress," he finally answered. Then he remembered he needed to tell her about his son. And about Sarah. "I have a son with a woman I have known since we were children."

When Hannah did not seem to take offense at the comment, he continued, "Although I love her and have asked her to be my wife on several occasions, she has steadfastly refused. She is not of the *ton* and thought I required a wife who was." When Hannah continued to regard him, her expression not changing in the least, Henry swallowed. "As an illegitimate child, my son cannot inherit, so I seek a wife with whom to have legitimate children. Heirs," he stated with a shrug, thinking that at any moment, Hannah would ask him to drive her home, and tell him she never wanted to see him again.

So he was rather surprised when Hannah placed her hand on his arm and turned, as if she intended them to walk on the crushed granite path leading away from the carriageway. They began to stroll, neither saying anything right away.

Hannah remembered Elizabeth's description of her first foray into Hyde Park with George. They, too, had stopped and walked along such a path, although it wasn't to discuss such serious subjects as bastard children and mistresses.

Hannah was quite sure it was so they could engage in stolen kisses behind a hedgerow.

"What is your son's name?" Hannah asked, her face not indicating how she felt about hearing of Henry's son and the woman he claimed to love.

Henry could not have been more surprised at Hannah's simple question. "Nathaniel. Nathan," he amended quickly, keeping his attention on where they were going as much as on her.

When he didn't offer more information, Hannah asked, "And how old is Nathan?"

Henry increased the speed of their walk, still surprised at how calm Hannah seemed. Wouldn't any other woman of the *ton* give him the cut direct for having mentioned something as crass as a bastard child? But then, Hannah had mentioned mistresses. "He is ten. A tutor is seeing to his education this year, but he will go off to Abingdon School in the fall," he said, wondering if that information might help his cause.

After all, what potential wife would want an illegitimate child underfoot whilst trying to raise legitimate heirs? The thought made him bristle, but at the same time, he could understand why a wife would not wish there to be daily reminders of a man's past indiscretions.

Nathan is not an indiscretion. I loved Sarah. Love Sarah, he amended to himself.

"So soon?" Hannah countered, her brows furrowed as if she were truly concerned about a boy being sent off to boarding school.

Henry lifted one shoulder. "I was eleven when I went off to Abingdon," he countered. "And thirteen when I went to Eton, and seventeen when I went to Oxford."

Hannah regarded him with surprise. From his earlier comments about being a farmer, she wouldn't have expected him to attend the same schools where so many of the gentlemen of the *ton* had been educated. "So, you *knew* you would be an earl someday?"

A chuckle erupted from Henry, a rather pleasant sound given the man had seemed so serious only a moment ago. "Someone did, I suppose." He considered asking her why she didn't request he take her home immediately. He still half-expected her to do so. And she still hadn't answered his question about whether he could court her, although she hadn't dodged the question, either.

"I only ever had a governess until I went to finishing

school in town," Hannah said wistfully. "I was rather jealous of my brother. He had a tutor, of course."

Henry grinned. "Ah, yes. The older brother," he said as he remembered the marquess mentioning an heir. "Is he in Town now?"

Shaking her head, Hannah sighed. "He's a naval officer. I've no idea where he is, nor have I seen him since..." Her voice trailed off as she considered just when it was she last saw her older brother. "Our mother's funeral," she finally realized. "Goodness, it's been over two years since he was in Town!"

Secretly glad she hadn't turned into a watering pot at the mention of her mother's funeral, Henry found her revelation about her brother's absence amusing. "Do you miss him now that he's in the Navy?" he asked, realizing conversation came easy with the chit. He could imagine speaking with her like this on a regular basis; over breakfast, should she rise early enough to join him, of course, or at luncheon, although he wasn't always good about coming in from the fields to eat (however, knowing she would be there might be the impetus he needed to do so), and during dinner, for propriety's sake they would dine together every night. He was about to imagine them conversing in bed, perhaps after having made love, when sleep was just about to claim them as they held one another. But he found she was gazing up at him rather expectantly, and he had to put the thought from his head. "I apologize."

"You were woolgathering again, weren't you?" Hannah accused with a teasing grin.

Damn! So the chit had a sense of humor, too. "Guilty as charged, my lady. So..." And then he realized he had forgotten the question he had just asked her only a moment ago.

"I do miss my brother, although not because Will was particularly loving or a joy to be around," she answered in a tone that suggested she had just said the very same words only a moment ago. But she was smiling as she said them, making Henry realize she had forgiven him.

He frowned, wondering what kind of brother William Slater was to his sister. "It sounds as if there's a story or two there," he hinted. The path on which they walked split into two; Henry led them along the path to the right, thinking perhaps it circled around and would bring them back to the same place.

Hannah dipped her head, the pink flush appearing where her bonnet didn't hide her neck from view. "I will have to know you much better before I tell those tales," she countered lightly. She raised her head back up to find him looking down at her with a much more serious expression than she was expecting to see. "What is it?" she asked, wondering if she had spoken out of turn.

"I was serious. About what I said back at the phaeton. About courting you," he stammered, chastising himself for making such a cake of his declaration.

"I know," Hannah said with a nod, her slight smile not indicating how she felt about the topic.

"So, may I?" he countered, taking the hand that rested on his arm and bringing it to his mouth. He placed a kiss on the back of her gloved hand, tempted to peel back the fabric until he could expose her knuckles and kiss them directly.

"I thought you already were," Hannah whispered, an eyebrow arching suggestively.

Henry's face split into a huge grin. "You minx!" Glancing about to be sure no one could see them, he cupped her face with one hand while he placed his other at the small of her back at the same time his lips met hers.

Henry nearly chastised himself. He hadn't intended to kiss the chit. At least, not like this. Their earlier peck next to the phaeton could hardly be considered a kiss. But she had looked at him as if she expected him to kiss her, a gaze that clearly invited him to at least press his lips to hers. So he had done it, and, out of a sense of propriety, ended it as quickly as he could. They were in the park, for God's sake. Anyone might have spotted them.

But now they were hidden behind a series of hedgerows and trees that already displayed their early spring greenery. He had asked if he could court her, for what? *The third time?* And she stood there with an expression that gave away nothing, and then informed him that she thought he had already begun. *The minx, indeed.* Of course, he had to kiss her at that point. What else could he do? And should her lips remain parted, as they clearly were as his lips settled onto them, well, it was her own damn fault that his tongue was going to want to participate.

He hadn't expected hers to get involved, too!

For a girl who had only been out for one Season, Henry was astonished at her behavior. How many men had she kissed like this? And did she leave them all feeling as if their kiss was the most important act of courting in the world of courtship?

Perhaps a kiss was, he considered. This one certainly ranked at the top of his list as the most satisfying, most all-consuming, intimate, powerful kiss he had ever bestowed on a woman. Which probably wasn't saying much since he had only ever kissed Sarah. And she didn't *like* to be kissed.

At some point, he would have to end it. At some point, his cock was going to make itself readily apparent behind the fall of his doeskin breeches. And given her close proximity to that particular location—she was practically plastered against the front of his body—she was about to find out just how aroused this kiss was making him. In her defense, though, he had been the one to pull her that close, his one arm lashed about her waist while the other had moved from her jaw to her neck to the back of her head, just under the damned bonnet that he wished he could remove so he could undo the pins in her hair and run his fingers through the silken strands.

He had to end this. Now.

Hannah gently pulled her lips away from Henry's, her

eyes still unfocused and her lips feeling every bit as swollen as her breasts and that space between her thighs. Even knowing he would kiss her, properly this time, she was sure, Hannah was still unprepared for the sensations his lips and tongue created as their mouths met. This was the kind of kiss Elizabeth had spoken of, the kind of kiss where lips were parted and tongues tasted and explored and debutantes were ruined. *What have I done?* she wondered as she tasted him on her tongue, the sensation of his teeth and tongue still lingering there. She had allowed him to pull her against his body, so there was very little, if any, space between them. His lips on hers had been perfect. A perfect fit. And he was gazing down at her with just a hint of surprise on his face, as if he, too, couldn't believe what they had done.

She placed a hand along the side of his jaw and lifted her lips back to his, giving him a quick kiss before removing her hand to rest on his shoulder and settling her feet back onto solid ground. No wonder she had been pressed against the front of his body—she had been standing on tip-toes and would have fallen over otherwise! Well, except that his hand was still firmly at her back.

Henry blinked. And then, because he didn't know what else to do, he lowered his lips onto hers in a quick counter-kiss to hers. As he raised his face from hers, he watched as her lips curled up into a mysterious little smile. "You've done this before," he accused, his voice kept light despite the fact that he was feeling possessive? *Jealous?*

Hannah's eyes widened. "I assure you, Gisborn, I have never been kissed like that. Nor have I ever..." She allowed the sentence to trail off as she shook her head, as much in denial as in wonderment.

Henry's eyebrow arched so that it nearly touched the errant curl that rested on his forehead. "Never?" he countered. There wasn't any malice in his question, but Hannah clearly heard the disbelief in his voice.

Hannah dipped her head. "When I was twelve, my brother dared my elder cousin to kiss me, but, I assure you, it was more like the peck you gave me back at the phaeton," she explained with another shake of her head. She didn't notice Henry's sudden look of offense; he had replaced it with an impassive expression before Hannah lifted her head so that she could regard him directly. "And I do not believe Harold's kisses count, but if you insist on including them, well, I assure you, I have never kissed *him* back," she stated rather firmly, feeling a great deal of shame at her wanton behavior. Her face had to be bright pink. She had never done anything so impulsive in her life! She had behaved like Elizabeth! But at least Elizabeth had been kissing a man who had already declared his affection for her, if not his intention to marry her.

Henry had only asked if he could court her.

The sound of Henry's chuckle brought her eyes back up to his. He was shaking his own head back and forth as he noticed the soft pink blush that colored her face. She was rather fetching when she was embarrassed. "Well, should you ever wish to bestow such kisses on me again, I think I shall not mind," he murmured, his face a study in controlled mirth. And then, as quickly as his humor had shown itself, it disappeared. "If your father hasn't already sent out a rescue squad for you, he will do so momentarily. I should get you back home."

Surprised at his remark—did he really mean she was invited to kiss him should she wish to again?—Hannah took a deep breath and nodded. Given how eager her father had been to have her join Gisborn on the ride in the park, she rather doubted he would send a search party so quickly.

Perhaps only after a fortnight or so.

After all, wasn't that how long it took to get to Gretna Green and back if a couple decided to elope?

"Will you be at the Attenborough's ball this evening?" Hannah asked, thinking she would save him two dances if he so wished. She placed her hand in his and climbed up and onto the phaeton, forgetting about keeping her ankles covered as she did so. The earl's attention had moved from seeing her safely onto the conveyance to the briefly exposed ankle when she pulled her skirts onto the bench seat.

Henry lifted his head and considered the question. "I do not know if I have been invited," he replied with a shrug. "There is a stack of correspondence at my house in Bruton Street, but I fear I've not yet had a chance to read it." He undid the horse's reins from around the tree where he had parked the phaeton and easily climbed up into the seat. He didn't add that he rather doubted there would be an invitation to a ball given by someone he had never met.

"Lady Attenborough is quite vexed that there won't be enough gentlemen at her ball," Hannah stated, placing her hand on his arm when he had the horse and phaeton back onto the carriage way. "If I could secure an invitation on your behalf, would you consider attending?" Even as the words left her lips, she realized how *fast* she sounded. She was practically inviting him to be her escort!

"Will you allow me to escort you?" he asked, negotiating the phaeton past a curricle that had stopped so its occupant could converse with a man on horseback. Hannah recognized the man in the curricle as one of her suitors from last Season, but his attention was squarely on Lady Penelope, a veteran of two Seasons who had yet to make an advantageous match despite her considerable dowry.

Hannah grinned at his query. "If my father allows it, then, yes," she hedged, her facing pinking up again.

Henry grinned, thinking how easy it was to court a lady. "I must warn you. I have not yet taken ownership of my new town coach, and the one I have with me on this trip is positively ancient," he started to explain.

Her grin broadening, Hannah leaned in so her shoulder grazed his. "The Attenboroughs live across the street from Devonville House."

"I'll call on you at nine," he countered as the phaeton passed through the park gates. "You must promise me three dances."

Hannah's gasp could probably have been heard by the

coach that followed them. "Gisborn!" she started to admonish him. A debutante never danced more than twice with any gentleman. But he was already holding up a finger, as if to make an additional request.

"Including the supper dance. And I plan to take you for a turn on their terrace, or in their gardens, or wherever it's dark or dimly lit."

Hannah's mouth was now open in a most unbecoming expression of shock. "Gisborn!" she said again.

"Well, I shouldn't want us to be where just anyone could see us should you wish to bestow another kiss on me," he explained, his barely contained mirth finally turning into a teasing smile.

"Gisborn!" was all Hannah could say in reply, not yet realizing his comments were made to shock her for the sole purpose of hearing his name said in her lyrical voice.

And, despite the impropriety of his requests, Hannah was quite sure she would grant him every one.

Dearest Charlotte,

I hope this letter finds you happy and in good health. I write quickly and with a happy heart as Henry Forster, the Earl of Gisborn, has brought word of your impending nuptials to your beloved duke. You may even be married as I write! (I am led to believe Wainwright would obtain a special license.) I also write with a happy heart to Thank You for your recommendation of me to Lord Gisborn. He called on Father this morning to ask permission to court me! Which, of course, Father was happy to provide. He seems most impatient to see me settled. Gisborn then took me on a ride in the Park, where conversation came easily between us. He asked if he could court me; I don't mind telling you I waited until his third query on the matter before giving him my blessing and kissing him (Elizabeth has been most firm with me as to kissing, assuring me it is Necessary to kiss a man to whom you expect to wed). As Gisborn is in a hurry to return to his farms in Oxfordshire, and to his son and the boy's mother, I am led to believe that, should he ask for my hand, he, too, will obtain a special license and see to it we are wed within a week! Can you imagine? This evening, we are to attend a ball at Lord Attenborough's house. As Lady A. is always concerned about a lack of gentlemen this early in the Season, I was able to secure an invitation for Gisborn. He will join Father and me for the walk across the street. Although it is only fashionable to arrive at a ton ball by carriage, I can think of nothing more ridiculous when a ball is merely across the street. I shall feel quite special being escorted by not just one, but two gentlemen. I must end this in order that Lily can dress me for tonight. I wish you happy, Charlotte! Or, should I say, Your Grace? Sincerely, Hannah.

CHAPTER 6
A BALL AND A WEDDING

*L*ily completed ironing the last of a series of ringlets into Hannah's hair and stepped back, admiring the series of tiny braids that wrapped around a tumble of curls atop her mistress' head. Hannah had been quite clear with her instructions for her hair and seemed more concerned than usual about which ball gown to wear. A white chiffon Grecian column gown with braided chiffon ties crossing beneath her breasts won out over the white satin de Naples gown for the simple reason it made her look like a titled woman. *A countess?* she hoped as she reviewed her profile in the looking glass.

"Is there something special about the Attenborough's ball, milady?" the lady's maid asked, placing a series of pearl-tipped pins into the elaborate coiffure.

Hannah opened a pot of lip color, a cosmetic she rarely used. She had not yet told her maid about the earl who had asked to court her just that morning. Gisborn had returned her to Devonville House, along with the phaeton, and given his thanks to her father for the use of it. With one last kiss on the back of her hand, the earl took his leave, saying that should she be able to secure an invitation to the ball for him, he would return at precisely nine o'clock. Hannah glanced at the mantel clock, a surge of nervousness welling inside her. It was nearly that now.

"An earl has asked to court me," she admitted, a lifted shoulder suggesting earls asked for permission to court her every day.

"Oh!" Lily replied as a smile spread on her face. "The gentleman who called on your father earlier today, perhaps?" she asked, attaching pearl ear bobs to Hannah's earlobes. She had attempted to catch a glimpse of the man from her vantage point at the top of the stairs, but he had already passed by the time she dared take a peek.

Even before Hannah could dip her pinky into the color pot, the sound of horses pulling a carriage came from the street below. *Of course, there should be the sound of horses and carriages*, she scolded herself. A ball was about to start across the street. But just as she finished applying the barest hint of lip color, she heard the front door closing. "I think he's here," she whispered, the nervousness in her belly growing. Just the thought of Henry Forster set flutterbies to tumbling in her stomach. She remembered the feel of hardened muscles beneath her hands when she'd had to hold onto him as he helped her down from the phaeton—twice! And the feel of his hands as they gripped the sides of her waist—she was sure she could feel their warmth even through his driving gloves and her gown and corset. Hannah pulled on her long white gloves and watched as Lily placed a string of pearls around her neck.

"There," Lily said with a great deal of satisfaction. "Now you truly look like a fairy princess." She continued to admire Hannah's reflection. "And who will be your prince?" she asked, curious as to the identity of the man.

Hannah grinned, a dimple appearing in one cheek. "The Earl of Gisborn."

Lily's face fell in an instant. "I beg pardon, milady?" she whispered, one hand going to her chest as if she had been physically struck.

Noting her maid's look of shock, Hannah turned to face

her directly. "What is it, Lily?" Becoming alarmed, she reached for the servant's hand. "You look as if..." She paused. "Do you *know* the earl?" she asked, remembering the girl had come to London from Oxfordshire.

"Randolph Forster?" Lily whispered, her eyes too wide. "He's awfully... *old*," she managed to get out.

Relaxing back into her dressing table chair, Hannah dipped her head. "So old, in fact, that he has passed on," she whispered back. "Henry Forster, his nephew, inherited the earldom."

The news seemed to take a great deal of time for Lily to process. "*Henry? The farmer?*" she asked, her attention no longer on her mistress. Her eyes came back to regard Hannah. "He is..." Her face reddened and she stepped back.

"In love with another," Hannah finished for her. "Yes, I know. He told me about the mother of his son," she explained, wondering how much more Lily knew of the family.

Taking a deep breath, Lily's nodded. "Mr. Forster is a very handsome man," she offered finally. "I saw him a time or two when my mother and I would go to Bampton to shop."

One of Hannah's eyebrows popped up. "Indeed? Did you actually live near the Gisborn estate?" she asked, her hands folding in her lap. Should Gisborn offer for her hand, perhaps the maid had information she could use to help her decide if she should accept the man's suit.

Lily shook her head. "I am from a farm near Witney. We only heard stories about the old earl. He didn't pay his tenant farmers very well, and he seemed angry all the time."

Considering her maid's words for a moment, Hannah felt as if a stone had dropped into her stomach. "And what do you know of his nephew? Besides him being handsome?" she added, giving her maid a teasing grin in an attempt to hide her sudden unease.

But Lily merely shrugged. "Not much, I am afraid. He was away at school and then he was with his woman and their son..." Her voice trailed off. "Do you expect he will ask for your hand?" she asked then, her eyes lit with excitement. "If you should accept, I would be very happy to be your maid at Gisborn Hall!"

Hannah smiled, deciding that she would indeed want Lily to join her. Lily would be closer to her home, closer to relatives. "I am glad to hear it," she offered. She turned back toward the mirror. "So, what do you suppose the earl will think of me like this?" she asked, angling her head to be sure her hair held its elaborate coiffure.

"He'll think you're a fairy princess," Lily answered with a firm nod. "He'll wish to kiss you before the evening has even begun."

About to roll her eyes, Hannah caught her reflection in the glass and stared at herself. Pearls instead of her mother's diamonds had been the better choice, she realized. She looked sophisticated, and yet, she also looked like she had stepped out of the pages of Sleeping Beauty, after the prince had kissed her awake and sworn his undying love.

Well, Gisborn wouldn't be doing *that*. He loved another.

There was a knock at the door and her father's voice sounded from the other side. She hurried to open it, allowing Lily to follow with a satin shawl. The maid draped it over her elbows just as she opened the door.

The marquess stepped back upon seeing Hannah emerge from her room, a look of shock on his face. "Did you see my daughter in there, by chance?" he asked, his Scottish burr more pronounced than usual and a hint of amusement in his eyes. "Good God, Hannah! You look as if..." He clasped his hands in front of his body as if to still them. "Well, you look... lovely," he stammered, the humor turning to admiration. *She looks like her mother did when I married her!*

"Thank you, Father," Hannah said, dimpling. Her father had never reacted like *that* before! "Has the earl arrived?" She immediately regretted asking; she knew she shouldn't seem so eager, so nervous.

"Just got here. He may not live in town very often, but he's obviously got a chronometer and a decent valet." He held out his arm and Hannah took it. "Makes a rather dashing figure, he does. Asked me if he might be allowed to dance with you more than twice this evening."

"Oh?" Hannah answered, trying to sound shocked. "And, of course, you would not grant him permission to do such a thing," she suggested with a hint of humor, trying to quell the flutterbies that were at it again in her stomach.

"Oh, I told him he could have as many dances as he wished," the marquess answered, his face contorted into a smirk.

"Father!" she admonished him. "If you truly did that, then you had best inform Lady Jersey, or I will never be allowed in Almack's again!"

William Slater shook his head, his eyes truly full of humor. "I rather doubt you'll ever have to go to that despicable place again," he countered with a shudder.

Hannah was about to ask why he would say such a thing, but they had reached the bottom of the stairs, and she was breathless. The Earl of Gisborn stood before her in black satin evening clothes, his snow-white cravat perfectly tied. A ruby pin gleamed from within the folds. Bowing deeply, he moved toward her as she completed her curtsy to take her gloved hand and kiss the back of it.

"My lady, you look like perfection embodied," he murmured, holding his arm out for her.

Hannah blinked. She could think of no one who would dare say such a thing to a lady, unless it was said in private, perhaps. Or by George Bennett-Jones. *He* would say something like that to Elizabeth. Probably had done so a dozen times or more, now that she thought about it. "Thank you, my lord," she murmured, her face taking on the familiar pink blush. Goodness, she hardly knew what to say! He was so regal, so handsome. She couldn't believe it was the same man who had paid her a call that very morning and taken her on a ride in Hyde Park! *The farmer?* Lily had said. The Henry Forster who stood before her certainly didn't look like any farmer Hannah had ever seen, nor could she imagine him working in the fields.

Hannah placed her hand on his arm and realized she would, indeed, be escorted by two gentlemen this evening. They all paused as Hatfield opened both front doors before they proceeded down the steps and across the street to the Attenborough's.

Henry held himself as erect as possible, aware of Hannah's occasional glances in his direction, as if she couldn't believe her eyes. He could hardly believe his. How had this woman managed to make it through an entire Season without being claimed by the first available duke or marquess? How could she possibly *still* be on the Marriage Mart? She was perfection, he repeated to himself. Lovely. Gracious. A good conversationalist. With a good disposition. Despite her huge dog that would more appropriately be called livestock than a pet, she was the perfect woman to be his countess.

He thought of the ruby signet ring tucked into his waistcoat pocket. If he was brave enough to ask for her hand during a walk in the gardens, he would have something to put on her finger tonight. A jeweler in Ludgate Hill was making the ruby and diamond ring he planned to give her on their wedding day. He had Lady Charlotte in mind when he had ordered it, but somehow he thought it would look better on one of Lady Hannah's long fingers. With luck, the goldsmith could have it finished on the morrow. The special license he had procured from the bishop in Doctor's Commons was back at his house in Bruton Street. If she accepted his suit, they could be married in a few days, and be on their way to Oxfordshire the day after that. After all, every day he was gone from home was another day lost in starting the irrigation ditches and in preparing the fields for planting.

"Did you attend any balls last Season, my lord?" Hannah asked, allowing Gisborn to step them around a carriage parked in front of the Attenborough home.

Henry turned his head slightly. In the dim light of a

nearby gas lamp, he tried to see her face and found it mostly in shadow. What was visible seemed almost angelic. "I did not. I was only in town in February, so I was able to attend Mrs. Worthington's musicale and a few lectures at the Royal Academy," he replied. He noted that the marquess was quiet.

In fact, the man didn't seem to have his attention on either of them but rather on the crowd of ball guests as they made their way up the flagstone path to the front doors. "Will there be a card room, my lord?" he asked, curious as to Devonville's silence.

The marquess seemed reluctant to tear his gaze away from the crowd in front of them. "Lord Attenborough always has a lively card room, Gisborn," he responded. "And the supper is quite good if you're of a mind to eat at midnight," he added, his tone suggesting he was not.

Henry turned his attention back to Hannah. "Are you of a mind to eat at midnight?" he asked in a subdued voice.

Shivering at the sound of his question, Hannah had to swallow before she could respond. "Lady Attenborough's lobster patties are the best in all of London," she hinted.

"My favorite!" Henry replied, giving her his best smile. "Will you stay and have one or two with a glass of champagne?" he asked, his voice lowering.

"It depends on the company," Hannah replied, feeling like a coquette, her lashes hiding her eyes as she made the remark. Her lip curled, though, and gave away her answer.

"And will there be company you wish to keep?" he countered, enjoying the opportunity to flirt.

Hannah angled her head to one side, realizing she didn't know whom to expect at the ball. Elizabeth and George would be there. This would be their last ball before they headed off to Sussex. "I expect Lord and Lady Bostwick will be in attendance," she replied. "I would like to introduce you if you'll allow it," she offered, wondering if he might already know them from prior Seasons.

"I would like that," he replied, lifting the hand that rested on his arm so he could bring it to his lips and kiss the back of it. "And I would like to dance every waltz with you, if you'll allow it." Henry heard the slight inhalation of breath Hannah made on hearing his words, wondering if he had shocked her with the request. He thought her father's permission to dance as many as he wanted had been said in jest; now, he wasn't so certain.

Given there would probably be only two waltzes played during the entire ball, Hannah lifted her head and said, "I will allow it, of course," the flutterbies tumbling in her middle.

Once they were in the crowded vestibule, Hannah gave up her shawl to a footman as her father and the earl waited. It was then she realized she hadn't brought a reticule or a fan. How could Lily allow her to get out of the house without at least a *fan?* She could only hope the early Season ball would not become a crush. But if it did, she hoped Gisborn would escort her on the back terrace so she might get some air.

As she rejoined them for the receiving line, she glanced about to look for anyone she knew. She looked for Elizabeth and George but saw neither. She did notice Lady Fletcher—George's aunt—with Lady Pettigrew as they joined the line. The two older women had their heads together, apparently continuing whatever conversation they were having in the park earlier that morning.

Lady Attenborough raised her eyes to meet Lord Gisborn's. Hannah watched the older woman's reaction, pleased to see the delight in the viscountess' face. "Why, Lord Gisborn, you're not at all who I expected!" she said as she allowed Gisborn to raise her gloved hand so he could brush his lips over her knuckles. Lady Attenborough was positively blushing!

Henry realized their hostess probably expected his late uncle and wondered at how they would know the man. He rarely visited London in his later years.

Hannah, having completed her greeting to Lord Attenborough, turned and noticed the raised eyebrows of those behind them in the receiving line, realizing they had overheard Lady Attenborough's curious remark. Afraid they would think Gisborn was a gate crasher, she was about to say something like, "Lord Gisborn inherited the title from his late uncle last year," when Henry gave Lady Attenborough a winning smile. "I do hope your invitation is not withdrawn, my lady. I had so looked forward to a dance with you."

Beaming, Lady Attenborough turned to her husband. "Attenborough! Look who 'tis. Randolph's nephew, Henry!" She turned back to the surprised earl. "We spent a very lovely week at Gisborn Hall many years ago," she explained. "You were still in short pants and…"

Lord Attenborough nudged his wife. "Livvie, darling, let the poor boy be," he admonished her. He held out his hand to Henry and the earl stepped over so he stood in front of the familiar man.

"Lord Attenborough, so good to see you again," Henry stated with a slight bow.

"And you. How are the Gisborn farms?" he asked, his head tilted up as he was a good deal shorter than Henry. "Still growing wheat, beans and barley?"

"Indeed, and on a bit more land now," Henry replied with a grin. And then he was at the end of the line and holding his arm out for Hannah. Her father had her other arm. A footman announced them to a ballroom not yet crowded. The orchestra was playing somewhere off to one side and footman scurried about with champagne on trays as the three of them descended the seven steps to the ballroom floor.

The Attenboroughs had spared no expense on candles. The three massive chandeliers hung above the room had hundreds of them, giving the room a bright, golden glow. The French doors to the flagstone terrace and gardens were already opened. Outside, paper lanterns bobbed in the gentle breeze, giving off light that seemed to dance. The ball had barely begun and yet everything seemed magical.

"If you two will excuse me, I need to make someone's acquaintance," the marquess murmured, giving Gisborn and

Hannah a nod before he walked off toward one of the corners.

Surprised at his sudden departure, Hannah followed his apparent path to where Lady Winslow stood next to a potted palm. The widow's face split into a smile when she spotted the Marquess of Devonville approaching her. "Oh, my," Hannah breathed, not intending Gisborn to overhear her.

"Something amiss?" Henry asked, following her line of sight. He watched as the marquess lifted both of the woman's hands to his lips. And then the woman had her arm on his as he escorted her toward the French doors.

"Not really, I suppose," Hannah murmured, finally turning her attention to the earl. When she realized he had been watching her father and the widow, she added, "I had no idea he had a *tendre* for Lady Winslow."

Henry regarded Hannah for a quick moment. "Does it bother you if he does?" he asked carefully. He took two glasses of champagne from a passing footman's tray and offered her one.

Hannah grinned as she wrapped her fingers about the stem. "No," she replied with a quick shake of head. "I am rather happy for him, in fact," she said, realizing she meant it. Her father had missed her mother, his bouts of melancholy less often these days but still evident when he spent too much time alone.

Touching his champagne glass against the rim of Hannah's, Henry cocked an eyebrow. "To your father's happiness then?" he offered, wondering how Hannah would react.

She responded with a brilliant smile. "Yes!" she said before taking a sip. The bubbles danced on her tongue and continued dancing down her throat, leaving her feeling a bit giddy.

Smiling broadly, Henry took a sip of his and let the liquid stay on his tongue as long as he could. Champagne was not something kept in the cellars at Gisborn Hall. There hadn't been much to celebrate at the estate in many years, but perhaps with Hannah as his countess, there would be a reason to stock it. "Tell me, Lady Hannah. As the lady of Devonville House, have you had to host an entertainment such as this?" he asked, the hand holding his champagne waving in a small arc to indicate the ball.

Hannah shook her head. "I assisted my mother with her last ball, of course, so I know the requirements of hosting such a production, but my responsibilities to my father have been to play hostess for his dinner parties."

Henry seemed to think about that for a moment, his brow furrowing. "Does he host them often?"

Smiling so her dimple appeared in her right cheek, Hannah nodded. "Every week," she replied. She took another sip of her champagne, wondering why Gisborn would ask such a question. Was he interviewing her to determine if she had the necessary skills to be a countess? "How many do you host as an earl?" she asked before finishing off the champagne and allowing a footman to take the glass from her.

The question caught Henry off guard. He glanced to the side quickly, his attention briefly captured by a familiar woman who had just kissed the cheek of the man who was escorting her. She hadn't even tried to hide the kiss! And now she was angling her head against his shoulder as they made their way toward a couple near the center of the ballroom floor. "I admit, I have not had the opportunity to do so," he answered with a shrug.

Hannah turned to glance where the earl's attention had been diverted a moment ago. She smiled when she recognized Elizabeth and George. "Did Lady Bostwick do something scandalous?" she asked with a teasing grin, her voice seductively quiet.

Surprised by the question, Henry blinked. "I have not been introduced to a woman of that name," he countered, his eyes moving back to the center of the room. Hannah's question had him wondering if he was too staid for the ball. Was it common practice for ladies to kiss their escorts out in the open? If so, when had the rules of society changed to allow such a display of affection?

"She is the former Lady Elizabeth Carlington. Of the charity, Lady E and Associates' Finding Work for the Wounded. What did she do?" Hannah asked as she placed her hand on his arm and turned toward the couple, making it clear the two of them would be heading in the couple's direction.

Henry started walking, slowly at first. "She kissed him. She didn't even try to hide it," he whispered, trying not to act too scandalized.

Hannah leaned toward him, her mouth inches from his ear. "Lady Bostwick and her husband are quite in love with one another. Prior to their union, she was a prim and proper young lady, with nary a hint of scandal associated with her. Then, she and George married," she said with a sigh, one that did not sound as if she found fault with the union. "Ever since, Elizabeth has been quite obvious about her feelings toward her husband. It does not excuse her action, but she has a hard time keeping her kisses to the privacy of their home," she managed to get out before they were standing before the happy couple.

"Hannah!" Elizabeth brightened, her arms coming out so her hands could grasp her friend's shoulders. Hannah did likewise as the two women hugged. "You look exquisite, as usual, and..." Her attention turned to Gisborn. "I see you have arrived on the arm of a Greek god this evening. Do tell me which deity he is. I'm terrible at mythology." This last was delivered with a good deal of mischief and to the astonished earl himself. Hannah had to fight down the urge to gasp in shock.

Henry did his very best to keep his face as impassive as possible, but he found himself allowing a small smile. The woman was most outrageous! And he recognized her as the woman who had come out of Devonville House that very morning before he had called on the marquess. He immediately realized that his earlier assumption of her being overweight was incorrect—she was quite round with child. And she was one of the most beautiful women he had ever seen.

Her husband had turned to join them at that moment, his eyes rolling and his head shaking at his wife's comment. "Please allow me to beg your pardon for milady's mistaken assumption," Lord Bostwick intoned, a hint of a smile giving away his humor. "Elizabeth, he is most assuredly a *Roman* god," he corrected her. "I'm thinking... Apollo?" he guessed, a dark eyebrow cocking. The man's stern features didn't allow him to be particularly handsome, but with his devilish grin making his eyes light up, he appeared friendly and very approachable.

Quite certain his face was taking on the reddish cast of embarrassment, Henry bowed, realizing their comments were all in good fun. "Neither, I'm afraid. Henry Forster, Earl of Gisborn, at your service," he answered, not waiting for Hannah's introduction.

"Elizabeth and George Bennett-Jones," George replied in kind, bowing as Elizabeth curtsied. She held out her hand and the earl kissed the back of her knuckles.

"Viscount Bostwick," Hannah added, since George never seemed to mention his title when introducing himself.

The viscount reached over to lift Hannah's gloved hand to his lips. "And you are looking as if you stepped out of the pages of 'Sleeping Beauty', perhaps?" he guessed, giving Hannah a mischievous grin.

Hannah's inhalation of breath was soft enough that only Henry was aware of it. He wondered what it was about the reference to Sleeping Beauty that would make her react so. Had he been given time to consider what fairy tale princess she looked like this evening, he would have to agree Sleeping Beauty was a good guess. A thought of kissing her awake crossed his mind, but he had to erase it as quickly as it appeared—his satin breeches did not allow room for the erection that was forming.

"George!" Hannah admonished him, not wanting to admit it was her thought while in front of the dressing table mirror. Turning to Henry, she said, "George is a fencer."

A look of recognition passed over Henry's face. "Bennett-

Jones, of course," he spoke. "You are Angelo's champion, are you not?"

George dipped his head. "Guilty as charged, my lord," he responded. "But I'll probably lose the title during the next few months. I'm about to whisk my wife away to Sussex for her confinement. And I have estate business to attend to," he explained quickly, his gaze on Henry's one of calculation. "May I assume you are the Forster who is a friend of Lady Charlotte's?" he asked then.

Stunned that a man he hadn't met would know of his connection to the Binghams, Henry nodded. "Indeed, I know Lady Charlotte—her entire family, of course—since one of their estates is adjacent to the Gisborn lands in Oxfordshire," he explained quickly, hoping there was no hint of scandal associated with him or Lady Charlotte. "Have you heard if her father is recovering?" he asked, not having ascertained the truth as to the health of the Earl of Ellsworth since returning to London.

Moving to stand by the earl's side, George nodded to his wife. "I know you two are dying to gossip," he whispered, giving her a peck on the temple as permission for her to take her leave of him. When the women were out of earshot, having moved off to join a group of other young matrons forming in one corner, George returned his attention to Henry. "Truth be told, the Earl of Ellsworth is in quite good health, although he does have a bump on his noggin," George said *sotto voce*.

Henry's eyes widened, wondering at George's need to keep the news quiet. "That is certainly good news," he replied, although there was a part of him that thought the man deserved to die for what he had done to Charlotte. *How could a father horsewhip his daughter, even if he was in his cups when he did so?*

"News that must be kept under wraps for at least a few more days," George intoned, his voice still low. "According to my sources, Lady Charlotte's cousin is to be charged with attempted murder and embezzlement, but until he has been dealt his sentence, he must believe the earl is on his deathbed."

Noting the man's seriousness, Henry nodded. "I understand. I... I just came from Sussex yesterday," he said, deciding to share his knowledge of the situation with George. "Lady Charlotte was in good health and," he paused, wishing Charlotte was truly in good health—the stitches along her whip scar were still in place just yesterday—"If the Duke of Chichester did not lose his nerve, the two of them will be saying their wedding vows in a couple of days." The words tripped off his tongue, sounding somehow *right* despite how he had felt about the situation just a day ago. *My, how things have changed in only a day*, he considered.

A slow smile spread over George's face. "Your news is the best I've heard in days," the viscount claimed. He glanced to where his wife stood with the cluster of friends, a look of obvious adoration on his face. Turning his attention back to the earl, he said, "If I may say so, it seems to me our uncles were men of a similar mind."

Henry wasn't familiar with George's predecessor, so he gave George a cocked eyebrow. "How so?" he asked, noting George's sudden interest in him instead of the wife that was still gossiping with her friends.

"My uncle was a miser," he whispered, leaning in toward Henry so he could be heard over the growing din of the ballroom. He thought of adding, "and a molly," but decided he didn't know enough about Randolph Forster to make the comment inclusive.

His head angling, Henry finally nodded, deciding it wasn't treasonous to admit his uncle had been tight-fisted. "Mine, as well," he murmured. "These past two years have been a struggle just to return the Gisborn lands and buildings to some semblance of normalcy." He frowned. "When did you inherit?" he asked, wondering if George's viscountcy had suffered the same lack of oversight and care.

"Just over a year ago," George answered. "I, too, have been spending a good deal of blunt trying to right the wrongs of so many years of deferred maintenance." This last was delivered with a definite hint of disgust.

"Oh, I like that terminology," Henry said in admiration, taking a drink of his champagne. "May I inquire as to how you have handled your tenants' cottages?"

George nodded to the earl's compliment and helped himself to a glass of champagne from a footman's tray. "Since I don't have much in the way of farmland, I don't have many tenants, but all ten families have new cottages as of last month," he said, not intending for the pride he felt to come through in his statement.

Good grief!

"You must have an estate manager very different from mine," Henry spoke quietly, not wanting to be overheard. The Gisborn earldom could claim at least twenty cottages in all—at one time, there might have been nearly thirty. But, as far as Henry was concerned, every one of them required major work or complete replacement. He had directed his estate manager to see to the rebuilding of one when he first inherited. The man had argued that the tenant had allowed the cottage to deteriorate through lack of regular maintenance, but time and weather had been the true culprits in its disintegration. It was only after Henry had threatened to replace the manager when the matter was finally resolved. *Nineteen to go*, he thought, *and another ten to build from scratch*, wondering if he would still have to replace Edward Grainger. The man was downright stubborn when it came to expenditures of the maintenance sort, as if he thought his compensation was tied to how much of the earldom's coffers he saved.

"If you are suggesting that your man of business is as miserly as our uncles were in life, then I must admit, mine was as well," George retorted, taking a drink and holding the bubbly liquid on his tongue as if he was truly appreciating the sensation.

Surprised by the comment, Henry regarded the viscount

with a cocked eyebrow. "What did you say to change his mind?" he asked, his curiosity piqued.

Laughter bubbled up from George, the sound making his wife turn from where she stood to give him a wink. "There was nothing I could say, so I didn't. I fired him and hired one who was a bit more accommodating," he admitted with a good deal of amusement, his gaze returning to meet his wife's for a moment. "I found the danger from poorly maintained coal mines a far greater problem than cottages that were on the verge of collapse," he added, his countenance turning serious.

Still fighting to hold down a blush at the couple's outrageous behavior, Henry considered George's words. The man owned coal mines in addition to farmland! But the idea of replacing his estate manager was suddenly at the top of his mind. The man rarely spent time out of doors and could barely ride a horse, a necessity given where his lands were in Oxfordshire. *It wasn't as if you could drive a curricle over the farmland.* And lately, Henry had been the one overseeing any work being done in the fields, riding out at first light to check on his foremen and laborers and sometimes staying out until almost dark. Why pay a man who couldn't do the job to his satisfaction?

Henry remembered the Marquess of Devonville's comment about Aldenwood's prediction for a colder summer and wondered what George might think. "Tell me, Bostwick, are you familiar with an adventurer named Aldenwood?" he asked then, hoping George wouldn't be too surprised by the change of topic.

"Of course." He turned from having winked at his wife to regard Henry, his brows furrowing. "Why do you ask?" he asked, his curiosity piqued.

"The Marquess of Devonville claims Aldenwood is predicting a colder than usual growing season—"

"Because?" George drained his champagne, his manner even more serious.

Embarrassed at having brought up the topic, Henry was

about to ask the viscount to forget he query when he realized George really *wanted* to know.

"He paid witness to a volcano erupting somewhere near Australia. Apparently, the volcanic ash and... the debris, dust, whatnot... from that explosion and some others that happened before that one... it's all still in the air, blocking some of the sun's heat from reaching land. Aldenwood has said the summer won't be warm enough for crops to grow and there will likely be a famine as a result."

"Jesus," George breathed, his eyes focused internally. He shook his head. "You would think, that as an owner of three coal mines, I might welcome the opportunity to sell more coal in the summer," he commented with a hint of wonder in his voice. "But if there is a famine as a result of crop failures, no one will be able to *afford* coal, much less any food that is available. The prices will be too high." He rolled his eyes before turning them onto Henry. He studied the earl's face. "Do you *believe* the prediction?" he asked, his brows furrowing.

Henry shrugged, not wanting to seem gullible. What if Aldenwood was wrong and the growing season was like any other? He would look like a fool if he spent too much preparing for a possible shortage of food for his tenants.

But what if Aldenwood *wasn't* wrong?

"I think I must," Henry said with a sigh. "At least, I must prepare as if the growing season will be poor. To do otherwise condemns my tenants to possible hardship in the fall and winter."

Nodding, George seemed to agree. "What will you do?"

Pressing his lips into a thin line, Henry took a deep breath. "I have already planned irrigation ditches to drain excess water from the fields and provide a means to irrigate when it is dry. I have two large fields scheduled to be fallow. If I build greenhouses on them, at least there will be a way to ensure some food."

Biting his lower lip, George raised his gaze to one of the chandeliers overhead. "A capital idea," he said with a hint of awe. "I believe I shall do the same. If it comes to pass that the weather is fine, then I shall always have a greenhouse in which to grow flowers for my wife," he reasoned, his attention once again on the auburn-haired beauty who stood with Lady Hannah.

Henry's eyes followed George's, but his gaze rested on Hannah. "You have a very beautiful wife," Henry remarked as they helped themselves to more drinks from a passing footman.

"Thank you," George replied, his attention finally returning to Henry when he had caught Lady Bostwick's eye and winked in her direction. "I fell in love with her six months, two weeks and four days ago," he spoke in reverent tones. "And I thank my lucky star every day. She almost ended up married to a pompous ass of an earl hell-bent on ruining her father," he said in a manner suggesting he was not the woman's first choice for a husband.

Surprised by George's comment, Henry wondered how the man had managed to usurp an earl in Lady Elizabeth's estimation. He was a viscount, after all, and Henry rather doubted he was due to inherit an earldom. "If I may say so, she seems to show a great deal of affection toward you," Henry commented, his own gaze turning to Hannah's figure. When she bent over to hear something another young lady was saying, the shape of her bottom was suddenly silhouetted in the fabric of her gown. Henry had to suppress a groan and bite the inside of his cheek to tamp down what was about to come up.

"You may say so," George replied happily. "There is much to be said for marrying for love. We of the *ton* seem to have it all wrong, sometimes. Unions of convenience must be *unsatisfying* in so many ways. And the children born from them cannot be happy knowing their parents are spending their lives bed hopping. No, I am quite happy with my wife."

The lifted eyebrow as he mentioned this last bit made it quite clear to Henry that Lady Bostwick's beauty was not the only reason George was happy.

He thought of Sarah and how strained their relationship had become over the past few months. "May I ask as to how it is you *stay* happy with one another?" he ventured, casting another quick glance in the direction of Lady Hannah, as if to make sure he was keeping track of her whereabouts. The orchestra had started to play another tune, but it was a prelude to the dancing music, so no couples yet formed on the dance floor.

George smiled. He had seen Henry look after Hannah several times during their conversation. "We share a bed. Every night," he replied quietly. "We make love as often as possible and wherever we wish. I bring her a gift every fortnight or so, although she does not ask for baubles or gold. We take a drive in a park once a day, even if it's raining. And I allow her to run her charity, although I have seen to it she has trustworthy men on her staff and protection on the days when she is in the office and I cannot not be with her." After a moment, he added, "Oh, and we tell one another of our love and adoration at least once a day."

The viscount's prescription for a happy marriage was both a surprise and a source of embarrassment for Henry. The earl struggled to prevent the color he knew was suffusing his face. "So obvious and yet..." He tried to find a suitable word to use to indicate the rarity of what George described. He felt emboldened by the information, knowing he could probably renew his relationship with Sarah if he were to employ the same approach with her.

"Unfamiliar to so many," the viscount finished for him. He nodded toward where the women were still conversing with friends. "When will you be marrying Lady Hannah?"

Henry blinked at the bold question, surprised enough that he thought to admonish George. He was embarrassed by his thoughts of Sarah when the young woman he intended to ask to be his wife stood so near. But the man had been blunt enough with him that he should not have been surprised by the question. "I only asked permission to court her this morning," Henry answered with a shrug. At George's impish grin, he added, "I was considering as soon as this evening," he admitted then, wondering if it was entirely too early. "Is that entirely too early?" he asked in a teasing voice.

Smiling, George shook his head. "Her father wants to see her settled so he can see to his own life," he said as he motioned for them to retrieve the women. "He has been calling on a widow for a fortnight," he added, a glint of humor reaching his eyes, as if the idea of the marquess calling on a widow was somehow scandalous.

"Lady Winslow?" Henry guessed, remembering how the marquess had hurried to the woman's side when they first arrived.

George was smiling. "Yes." He sidled up to his wife and placed a kiss on her ear. "My love, it is time to dance," he said in a voice loud enough for the young matrons in the group to hear. A round of embarrassed titters erupted from the women. Henry took the opportunity to offer his arm to Hannah. After a startled pause, she put her own on it, said her pardons to those whose eyes had lit up with curiosity, and left the group with her escort.

"Take a turn with me?" Henry suggested, deciding he would ask for Hannah's hand once they were beyond the ballroom.

"Of course," Hannah said with a smile, her dimple appearing briefly. They walked in silence for several moments as the orchestra completed its prelude and began tuning for the dance music. "It appeared as if you had an opportunity to speak with Lord Bostwick," she half-questioned, noting the crowd had increased to nearly fill the ballroom. Lady Attenborough had every right to be proud of hosting a crush this early in the Season.

"I did. He is a very interesting man," Henry commented. The viscount had given him much to consider. Despite not having asked for advice, Henry was secretly thankful George Bennett-Jones had been so forthcoming with his opinions. As a result, Henry was quite sure of what he had to do when he returned to Oxfordshire.

Henry motioned toward a set of open French doors. "Would you like to take a turn in the gardens?"

Hannah regarded him with a lifted eyebrow. *Did he intend to kiss her so early in the evening?* The ball had barely begun! "Certainly," she agreed, allowing him to lead her onto the flagstone terrace. The pace he had set in the ballroom remained the same once they were out of doors. Despite the days being chillier than usual, the night air felt comfortable enough for a walk.

"Are you warm enough?" Henry asked, glad there were paper lanterns to light the path from the terrace into the gardens below and off to the side of the estate.

"Yes, thank you," Hannah replied, her nostrils filling with the scent of newly turned earth and the few flowers that had managed to bloom in the cooler weather.

Henry glanced about, certain no one else had taken their leave of the house. "I wish to thank you for securing an invitation for me to attend this evening," he managed to get out, his nervousness increasing with each step they took.

"It was no trouble," Hannah replied, sensing his growing unease. "I was surprised the Attenboroughs knew you. Why didn't you mention it earlier?" she asked, curious as to why he would keep his history with the elderly couple a secret.

"I didn't know. I... I didn't recognize the name when you mentioned it, and it wasn't until Lady Attenborough looked at me with such delight that I figured out she must have known me when I was a child." The path continued around some dormant rose bushes and under an arched trellis. Within moments, they were out of sight of the ballroom. "George was quite right when he mentioned you looked like Sleeping Beauty this evening." He felt more than heard Hannah's gasp of surprise. "From the moment I first saw you, I thought you looked like a fairy princess."

Hannah gave him a tentative smile, her gaze on his profile quickly turning away when he glanced over at her. "Just so you are aware, I am not endowed with any magical powers," she said, hoping to deflect whatever platitudes he was about to say regarding her appearance.

"Oh, I disagree."

Hannah paused in mid-step, forcing Henry to turn and stand in front of her. "Indeed?" she replied uncertainly. She couldn't decide whether to offer him a smile at his tease or keep her face impassive. Whatever had he meant by such a comment? The flutterbies returned to her belly. She could feel her breasts swelling against her corset, her nipples responding as if his fingers had delved past the edge of her bodice and touched them.

"You have bewitched me since our time in the parlor this morning," he countered quietly, not wanting to admit she had done so the night before while playing with her giant dog. "I... I know I only just asked you if I might court you, but now I wish to ask you for your hand in marriage. Lady Hannah, will you do me the honor of being my wife?" He lowered himself to one knee during his question while he removed his new ruby signet ring from a waistcoat pocket. Holding up the ring, he was disappointed it wasn't visible in the dim light of the lanterns.

Hannah stood very still, her heart beating so fast she was sure he could hear it. "Oh, Gisborn," she breathed. *This is so unexpected!* She thought he had brought her out to the garden to kiss her—not to *propose!* But how to answer? Certainly she always intended to say 'yes' to a proposal as romantic as this one. "I... I..." Placing an open hand against her bosom, she lowered her face to his. "Yes," she said with a nod. And then her lips were on his, inviting him to kiss her as he rose from his knees and wrapped his arms around her shoulders. His lips never left hers, their hold gentle but possessive, his tongue tasting the champagne and a hint of strawberries that lingered in her mouth. A moment more and Hannah's fingers were at the nape of his neck. As Henry's hands slid from her shoulders to her waist, his thumbs brushed along the sides of her breasts, sending shivers of pleasure though her very core, their intensity so surprising and so delightful her mouth broke with his for a moment so she could breathe. And then they were kissing once again.

"If there was a vicar in attendance, I would insist he marry us this instant," Henry spoke against her lips, thinking he could remove her gown and bed her within the hour. For a moment, he was stunned to hear the words, stunned he had been the one to say them. But lust was a powerful feeling. *That's all it is*, he told himself. He loved someone else, although damn him to hell, he couldn't think of her name.

Gratified he would say such a thing, Hannah feigned surprise, her mouth molding to his until she had to break from him. "Must we wait three weeks?" she countered, surprised she would sound so impatient, so wanton. Banns needed to be read, after all. A wedding had to be planned. But she was wishing he would move his hands back to the sides of her breasts. *What had happened a moment ago?* The sensation had been so delicious, so amazing. But his hands had moved to below her waist, sliding over the curve of her bottom and the back of her thigh. *How scandalous this is!* If she didn't stop it, he might have her gown pushed up her legs, his hands directly on her heated skin, sliding up her thigh, up to that place where she was turning into molten lava.

Henry's quick shake of his head could be felt through his kiss. A guttural sound erupted from him. "No. I obtained a special license today," he spoke, again with his lips still against hers.

The information seemed to bring Hannah back to reality. "Today?" she murmured, her lips rejoining his in a mutual feast.

"Hmm," he replied, finally trailing his kisses down her throat and to her collarbone. "I had to," he murmured. "Bewitched, I tell you," he spoke into the hollow of her throat.

Hannah giggled at the tickling sensation his lips created against the spot where her pulse raged, her head thrown back as she cradled his head in her hands. She could never have imagined such pleasures from kissing.

And if this was how Henry kissed, how would he behave in their marriage bed? Something skittered beneath her skin, sending a wave of pleasure through her. Awareness of everything around her was suddenly sharp, her senses awakened with his every kiss, his every caress. "Gisborn!" she whispered, suddenly aware they were no longer alone. When he didn't stop his gentle nips and kisses, she moved one hand to the side of his face and chin and lifted his head away from her.

He groaned his disappointment and then was suddenly standing straight, a look of guilt etched on his features as he pulled his hands from around Hannah's body and took one of her hands in his.

George and Elizabeth stood only a few feet away, their bodies pressed against one another as they, too, kissed behind the hedgerow. Although they seemed involved enough in one another not to take notice of Hannah and Henry, George pulled his head away from his wife's kiss, turned, and nodded in their direction. "If best wishes are in order, then please accept them," he whispered hoarsely, before returning his amorous attentions to his wife.

Glad for the darkness hiding her reddening face, Hannah suppressed the urge to giggle. She instead lay her head against Henry's chest and wrapped her arms around his waist. "Thank you, George," she murmured.

Stunned at being caught, and even more surprised by the viscount's reaction, Henry lowered his lips to kiss the top of Hannah's curls. "My lady, I do believe you owe me this dance," he said.

*T*he Marquess of Devonville awoke to an unfamiliar sensation. And a familiar scent. *Lilac.* Cherice Dubois, Lady Winslow, was using her tongue to amazing affect on one of his nipples. Could the woman be ready for him again already? *I'm too old for this*, he thought as he felt the fingers of one of her hands splay over his chest and travel ever so lightly down his torso, their nails occasionally scraping his skin and sending shock waves of pleasure coursing through him. He was surprised when her fingers curled around his hardening shaft. *Or, perhaps not*, he amended his thought, realizing he was already recovered enough to bury his manhood in her warm, welcoming sheath at least one more time. Just the thought of spending every night with Cherice was enough to make him ready for her.

The younger widow was obviously not shy in the bedroom, a trait he wondered about when he first called on her. She had only been out of widow's weeds for a fortnight. He had kept track of when Winslow had died, timing his visit to ensure he would be the first, and with luck, the only gentleman caller she would entertain. She offered tea and he accepted. He offered a ride in the park and she accepted. She wondered if he would be at the ball. He said he would be; he lived across the street and could hardly decline the invitation. She said she would save him a dance. He asked for all of them. She smiled at him, her gaze quite telling through her long, dark lashes. "All of them?" she had repeated, her large, green eyes suggesting a demure demeanor.

And then the minx had agreed! *So much for her being demure.*

Had anyone taken notice of them, at least when they weren't hiding behind a potted palm or a hedgerow in the garden, they would have been quite convinced Lady Winslow would soon be the Marchioness of Devonville. Much like the two in question were convinced Lady Hannah was about to become the Countess of Gisborn when they were on their way to hide behind a hedgerow and noticed the Earl of Gisborn kneeling before Devonville's daughter.

Devonville hadn't watched beyond the moment he saw Hannah give her obvious answer of 'yes,' but Lady Winslow had sighed with such heartfelt joy, Devonville wondered if it had been a mistake not to ask for her hand at that very moment. But the marquess wanted his daughter settled before he remarried, and Cherice seemed more interested in a tête-à-tête that involved more kissing than conversation. He had to accommodate her, of course, even if Lord and Lady Bostwick had decided to carry on their mutual affection only a few feet away.

Who knew the Attenborough's garden could be such a popular and delightful destination for amorous encounters?

Devonville had no intention of bedding Cherice before asking for her hand; she had been the one to suggest they share a night of carnal pleasure so they could determine 'if they suited one another.' Well, he wasn't absolutely sure how she felt about their suitability, but he had decided quite early on—an hour after leaving the Attenborough's ball, in fact— that they suited one another just fine. Cherice Dubois would be his next wife. And should another expect to court her, well, there was a reason he was an excellent shot.

A special license, granted by the Archbishop of Canterbury, was a rather powerful piece of paper, Hannah was learning as she and Elizabeth made arrangements for her wedding. Although Henry could have left for Oxfordshire and returned to marry her at some point a few months in the future, he seemed quite eager to marry her as soon as possible.

He suggested the following day.

At Hannah's widened eyes and sudden look of distress, he amended his suggestion to the day after that. Given her father's surprising news over breakfast of his own upcoming nuptials with Lady Winslow, Hannah realized it made sense to simply agree to an early wedding and leave for Oxfordshire with Henry.

Elizabeth, hell bent on seeing her best friend wed before she and George left for Sussex, assured Henry a wedding would take place before noon Saturday as long as a vicar could be located. Then, just as soon as the breakfast was complete, the Bennett-Joneses could be on their way to

Sussex. And the Forsters could leave for Oxfordshire the following day.

Hannah didn't seem to have a say in the matter. She clung to Harold as Elizabeth took charge, sending footmen this way and that to acquire flowers and ribbons, ordering her kitchen staff to move into Devonville House to help in the creation of a cake and the breakfast foods, and summoning a modiste and her crew of seamstresses to construct a wedding gown overnight. Henry was dispatched to find a vicar or a bishop, a task he seemed most willing to do. Hannah wondered if his enthusiasm was due to a desire to take his leave of the chaos or to avoid Lady Bostwick. Either way, he took off on horseback directly after tea was served, assuring Hannah he would see her at dinner that night, if not before. And when he asked if she knew what was being served for dinner, she listed ham and a variety of side dishes among the five courses.

"My favorite!" he replied, his face lighting up as if she had made his day with the recitation of the dinner menu.

Even the marquess seemed eager to share in the festivities as he took off for White's to make the announcements to those who hadn't been at the Attenborough's ball the night before.

Shortly after luncheon, which featured another round of discussions about who else should be sent an invitation, how Hannah's hair would be dressed for the ceremony, and what to pack for the trip ("Everything I own," Hannah answered, reminding Elizabeth she was moving to her husband's house), Hannah found herself amazed at her best friend. When had Elizabeth acquired these kinds of skills? She hadn't planned her own wedding; had it been up to Elizabeth, she and George would have been married by a vicar the very day she proposed to him. Instead, the Marchioness of Morganfield had arranged a church wedding that took place five days later. So, when had Elizabeth become so organized? So efficient? *Is this how she runs her charity?* Hannah wondered.

How could a woman, already round with child, have so much energy?

Because it didn't last, of course.

About two o'clock in the afternoon, George arrived at Devonville House to remind his wife it was time for her nap. Hannah thought perhaps George intended something else once he got Elizabeth back to Bostwick Place, just a few streets down Park Lane, but Elizabeth really was quite tired. Hannah insisted they take one of the guest bedchambers at Devonville House. George agreed, saying he could rub his wife's feet there just as well as he could at home.

"Rub her feet?" Hannah repeated in a whisper, stunned that the viscount would do such a thing, let alone speak of it. The thought of having her own feet rubbed brought a mixture of disgust and the sensation of flutterbies in her stomach. *Would Gisborn do such a thing?* she wondered. The flutterbies seemed to cause her entire body to spasm in delight at the thought.

"Of course," George said without the least hint of embarrassment. "The poor thing can barely walk when her ankles are so swollen," he said as much to Hannah as to Elizabeth, who was leaning against him for support. With a quick glance to ensure no servants were about, George lifted Elizabeth's skirts a few inches to show what he meant. Hannah gave Elizabeth a questioning glance before she dipped her head to confirm that, yes, Lady Bostwick's ankles were indeed swollen. Her slippers seemed too small for her feet.

"Up the stairs, second door on the right," Hannah ordered, pointing a finger in the general direction of the staircase. It was her first and only order of the day.

Once the viscount and his viscountess were locked away in the guest suite, Hannah was about to settle herself into a chair in the parlor when the modiste and a team of seamstresses invaded Devonville House with yards of sarcenet, a light blue satin gown, strings of tiny seed pearls, and rolls of silver satin ribbon. Whisked into her bedchamber, the girls soon had the plain gown fitted and the hem pinned up. As the modiste, who spoke with a faux French accent, flitted about the room giving her seamstresses various orders, she occasionally stopped to inspect the work being done, her delicate eyebrows rising and lowering as she studied the results. Soon, the sarcenet was fluttering over the top of the blue satin, ruched by loops of the seed pearls that were then anchored into the gown with tiny stitches. The ribbon was then strung through the loops and fashioned to follow the lines of the ruched sarcenet as it crisscrossed into diamonds down the length of the skirt. The bodice was then trimmed with the ruched sarcenet, pearls and ribbon.

Hannah watched in her cheval mirror as the simple dress was transformed into a wedding gown worthy of a princess. By four o'clock, the seamstresses had all they needed to complete the gown without requiring Hannah to be in it, but she made sure Elizabeth approved before she dared step out of it. Lady Bostwick had emerged from the guest bedchamber looking quite refreshed and very happy, leading Hannah to believe George had done far more than rub her feet.

The thought of Gisborn doing those things to her set the flutterbies to tumbling in her belly. She had to suppress a gasp at the surprising sensation she felt, realizing with a bit of shock that she was looking *forward* to her wedding night! Could any other woman of the *ton* claim to have felt this way *before* their wedding? From the talk she had heard in various parlors in Mayfair, she rather doubted it.

As the seamstresses took their leave, the modiste promised the gown would be delivered in the morning. With Elizabeth once again locked away in the guest bedchamber with her husband, Hannah descended the stairs to reflect on the day's preparations. Devonville House had only seen this kind of activity during her mother's last ball.

It was during the lull in the late afternoon, after Hannah had settled into a comfortable chair in the parlor and Harold was napping peacefully at her feet, when the butler delivered a white parchment. She examined the stamp in the red wax seal on the back of the missive, not recognizing the ducal insignia. Breaking it, she opened the fine, white paper and smiled.

> *Dear Hannah,*
>
> *I received your news of Henry's arrival and his request to court you. I do hope you find him a suitable match! I should be so happy that one of my friends from childhood would marry my best friend. I write with happy news of my own impending nuptials. Joshua has (finally) asked for my hand! We are to be married Saturday at eleven o'clock in a chapel a few miles from here. I apologize for the late notice; it seems my Joshua is more romantic than I first thought. He obtained a marriage license, and his household staff is seeing to the wedding and breakfast. I do hope you can join us, although I have reason to believe Henry might have other plans for you. Would it be possible you are to be married at the same time as me? I do hope yours is the fairy tale wedding we always thought you would have. Best wishes! Please give my love to your father and to Elizabeth and George.*
>
> *Yours very truly, Charlotte.*

Hannah sighed, tears forming in the corners of her eyes as she reread the letter.

"Is something wrong, my lady?"

Startled by the sound of the masculine voice, Hannah gasped and stood up, her feet still under Harold. The dog, startled by her sudden movement, made to remove himself from in front of her, causing her to lose her balance. "Oh!" she cried out, hoping she could grab onto the dog before falling completely to the floor. Strong hands caught her before she could pitch forward onto Harold, though. Her own hands were suddenly holding onto broad shoulders, their muscles bunching beneath her grip. When she glazed up, she was surprised to find Lord Gisborn regarding her with a look of concern.

"Are you well, my lady?" he asked, his face an unreadable mask.

Hannah stared up at him, her lips parting before she gave him a huge smile. A tear streamed down one cheek. Although she had her feet safely under her, she rather liked the way Gisborn's hands had grasped her on either side of her waist, at the sensation she felt of being nearly weightless as her feet barely touched the ground, of the flutterbies that were sending shivers of pleasure through her entire body. "Oh, yes, Gisborn," she murmured. And then, in a move that was bold beyond measure, she reached up and kissed him.

Henry had only a moment to react. He had returned to Devonville House with the news that a bishop would be there on the morrow to marry them. Hatfield met him at the door, but Henry assured the butler he could find his own way to the parlor. He intended to make his presence known at the threshold, intended to bow and give his future bride a kiss on the back of her hand. But he had found her reading a letter, a letter that obviously contained bad news, for he was aware of tears brightening her eyes. Not wanting to interrupt her, he had made his way into the room a quietly as possible, hoping to offer his condolences and perhaps a shoulder on which she could cry.

Instead, Lady Hannah had been so startled by his query, she nearly tripped over her damned dog. Seeing the tears stream down her cheek had made his heart clench. He had wanted nothing more than to hold her just then, to comfort her and assure her all would be well. That's what he did when Sarah cried, after all.

So, the last thing he expected was for Hannah to bestow him with a smile and a kiss. In that moment of surprise, and the sudden change from feeling sorrow on her behalf to feeling the joy in her kiss, Henry allowed Hannah to have her way with him. When had a woman ever initiated a kiss with him? He couldn't recall this ever happening, not even a bar maid in a tavern had done such a thing!

When he was aware she was ending the kiss, he allowed

his grip on her waist to lessen so her feet could take purchase on the carpet below. Then he raised his face from hers and saw the pink blush color her cheeks.

"I have never been welcomed like *that* before," Henry spoke after he had blinked once, his tone of voice not giving away how he felt about such a greeting.

"Oh!" The sound was as much an exhalation of air as it was surprise at what she had done. *I kissed my betrothed! He'll think me fast. He'll think me a hoyden!* "I... I apologize, my lord." Hannah stammered, realizing too late what she had done.

"Do not," Henry commanded, one of his hands lifting to her cheek to brush away one of the tears still left there. "I believe I rather like being greeted by my fiancée in such a manner. It assures me she has not changed her mind about marrying me," he added with a hint of humor. He pulled a handkerchief from his waistcoat pocket and wiped another stray tear from her face. "Now, pray tell, what was it that made you cry?"

A brilliant smile lit up Hannah's face. "Charlotte and her duke are marrying tomorrow morning!"

A hint of panic gripped Henry. The news wasn't unexpected, but did Hannah expect to attend Charlotte's wedding instead of her own?

"At exactly the same time we're getting married!" Hannah added, her delight so infectious, Henry was forced to smile, although his was due more to relief than news of Charlotte's wedding. "That is, if you were able to schedule a vicar?" she half-questioned, her brows furrowing so a tiny line developed between her eyebrows.

Henry lifted a finger to the spot and pressed lightly. "The bishop will be here at ten-thirty," he assured her as he continued to hold her lightly.

Her eyes still bright, Hannah gave him an embarrassed grin. "Truly, I did not doubt you," she claimed, wondering how it could be she felt comfortable standing so close to a man, closer than she would if they were waltzing.

Giving her half a shrug, he cocked an eyebrow. "And how did my lady fair in her plans?" he asked, the amusement back in his voice.

Hannah took a deep breath. "I do not know how Lady Bostwick can accomplish so much in such a short amount of time, but there will be flowers and a gown and a cake and a breakfast feast..." She allowed the sentence to trail off, her face turning more serious. "I don't know that we'll have any *guests* at the wedding."

Henry shook his head. "Not to worry. I have spoken with some friends who are not making the trip to Sussex for the duke's wedding. I expect they will make an appearance." At her raised eyebrow, he gave a shrug. "A few invitations were delivered by courier to some members of the *ton*. It is a ducal wedding, after all," he explained, hoping she wasn't disappointed that their hastily planned affair would take second to that of her friend's wedding. He was surprised when she seemed relieved by the news.

"I feared there would be no one at Lady Charlotte's wedding," she said by way of explanation. Both of her hands still rested on his shoulders from when she kissed him. She lowered one so it rested on his chest, the feel of his heartbeat beneath her fingers.

Sometime tomorrow, she imagined her hand would be at the same spot, but there would be no topcoat, no waistcoat, no linen shirt separating her fingers from his bare skin. A shiver of anticipation shot through her. What had Elizabeth done in telling her all about the joys of the marriage bed? Her friend had described intercourse in so many varied versions, she found she could not imagine half of them and otherwise blushed at the ones she could. But instead of dreading her wedding night, Hannah found herself looking forward to the time she could share her bed with Gisborn. With luck, he would get her with child shortly after the wedding, and she would have a baby to love and care for while Gisborn and his mistress continued their lives.

Hannah had to rein in her thoughts of the future. First,

they would spend the night at Devonville House and then leave for Oxfordshire the following day. If the weather held, they would make the entire trip in one day. "Lord and Lady Bostwick have agreed to stay in London for one more day so that Elizabeth can stand with me. Have you someone who will stand with you?" she asked, not sure how many members of the *ton* he knew. He hadn't yet taken his seat in Parliament; instead, he had stayed in Oxfordshire, seeing to his estate and the farms surrounding it.

"My man, Murphy, will stand with me," he said with a nod, marveling at how calm she seemed, as if she arranged her own wedding every day. Nervousness gripped him. A quick glance around the parlor made it apparent a special event was planned somewhere in Devonville House. Vases of flowers were already scenting the air around them. Footmen were hauling items in from a dray parked in the front drive. An impeccably dressed woman with an Italian accent was giving instructions to a team of maids as to where dozens of large bows were to be hung. Henry was quite sure he had seen her at a *ton* event, but knew he had never been introduced.

This wedding was going to happen. *Tomorrow morning.* It was too late to back out, too late to apologize and beg forgiveness.

A sense of calm settled over him as he regarded the bride standing before him. She seemed happy to have him, satisfied with the arrangement they would have. *The third time's the charm*, he thought as he considered any debutante in the Marriage Mart would do at this point.

Well, perhaps not *any*. But Lady Hannah Slater certainly would.

CHAPTER 7
WEDDING NIGHT JITTERS

Hannah stood before him in a pristine white night rail, its neckline edged in delicate lace while a ribbon bow held the top edges of the bodice together. From the way her lower lip trembled slightly, Henry realized she was nervous, frightened even.

Probably even more than he was at the moment.

What was wrong with him? He had bedded Sarah for over ten years! He knew how to do this—how to caress and stroke and kiss until Sarah's quiet cries told him she was ready for his manhood.

But the woman that stood before him wasn't Sarah.

She was Lady Hannah Slater. She was a fairy princess. She was a virgin. *My countess.* And she looked scared to death.

"Perhaps, for this first night, I should..." Henry shook his head, astounded that he could feel so uncertain about how to proceed with his new wife. This was their wedding night. He should simply carry her to the bed, pull the gown from her body and mount her, take her virtue just as he had imagined doing down in the parlor. He was her husband, after all. But there was that trembling lip, the fright in her eyes.

Hannah reached out and clasped her hand around his wrist, her long fingers warm as they pulled him forward.

"You should come all the way into the room, my lord," she said in a voice that sounded far steadier than she felt at the moment. Her entire insides were in a jumble. Anticipation, fear, the need to feel as if she had made the right decision, and the awareness of the very male gentleman who stood before her made for a heady mix of emotions. Reaching around him, she gave the door a gentle push and waited until the latch clicked into place before returning her attention to his face.

"Henry," he stated. When Hannah only arched an eyebrow at the sound of his name, he added, "When we are alone like this, you shall call me 'Henry'," he explained, hoping his words didn't sound as impatient to her as they did to him. Her fingers had loosened their grip on his wrist but were still touching him lightly.

Henry glanced around the room, desperately trying to keep his nervousness from showing. Decorated in feminine peach and green, there was no doubt the room belonged to a young lady. *She is my wife*, he kept thinking, the scent of honeysuckle wafting up to fill his nostrils and make his brain even more addled, if that were even possible. "My lady, I..." His gaze fell on her bed, the coverlet and blankets folded down to expose the wide expanse of white linens. Good grief! Her bed was larger than his own! He could take her right then and there, truly make her his wife. God knew his cock wanted to—his manhood had hardened the moment she opened the door and gave him a tentative smile. And then, when her hand touched his arm to pull him into the room, the heat he felt inflamed him even more.

"We are alone," she said simply, wanting to assure him her lady's maid, Lily, wasn't still somewhere in the suite.

I could kiss her at least, Henry thought, wondering if he would be able to leave before they made it anywhere near the bed. This was the bedchamber she had slept in since she was in the nursery. He dared not deflower her here. He really should wait. Take her back to Oxfordshire, to Gisborn Hall and one of the bedchambers there. The one that was adjacent to his, with the connecting dressing room and a bath. Yes, that's where he would do it.

"Henry?" Hannah whispered, her eyes round. Her body seemed to be shaking.

She's frightened, of course, he thought. Her mother had probably died before telling her what to expect on her wedding night. Christ, he didn't know exactly what *he* was supposed to expect on his wedding night! It had been so long since that first time with Sarah, when he had been too anxious and too impatient and too aroused to understand how to make love to a woman. Sarah had cried afterwards, huge tears accompanied by sobs that wracked her body. She told him to leave her alone. And he had. For two days, in fact, until she found him working in the fields near the river and slammed her fist into his face. He had dropped like a rock, the pain under his eye so acute he thought he would be sick. But Sarah was suddenly there, begging for forgiveness and gently kissing his blackening cheek.

Had he fallen in love with her then?

He must have, for he had promised he wouldn't pursue any of the other girls in the village (not that there were many of them). He bedded her again the next evening, and again after the village dance. When her condition was noticeable a few months later, his uncle boxed his ears and shipped Sarah off to his aunt's house near Oxford. Henry visited her frequently, using each trip as another opportunity to ask for her hand in marriage.

But she was a stubborn girl, refusing him every time, even when the babe was about to be born. At that point, his aunt had even tried to convince Sarah to marry him, telling the poor girl Henry would eventually be the tenth Earl of Gisborn and Sarah, who was no better than a low-born commoner, could be his countess.

Sarah never relented.

A few weeks after his son was born, the three of them made their way back to the village nearest Gisborn Hall. Despite his uncle's directive that he denounce the child as his own, Henry set up a household for Sarah and made sure everyone knew the babe was his son. The earl could denounce *him*, he had decided. Used to laboring in the fields, he could make his own way in the world.

And then something amazing had happened.

When Nathan was but six weeks old, the Earl of Gisborn paid them a visit at the unfashionable hour of eight o'clock in the evening. Upon seeing his grand-nephew, Randolph Forster announced he was again making Henry his heir. His large hand had settled on Henry's shoulder and given it a shake. "You did right by your son. Even if she," he had pointed at Sarah and lowered his voice so only Henry could hear, "Is too proud or stupid to realize it."

Had the entire situation been a test? Henry always wondered at the earl's pronouncement that evening. And he hadn't counted on the earl actually bequeathing the *entire* Gisborn estate nor the earldom to him (although Henry found out later he would have been granted the earldom no matter what—he was the late earl's closest living male relative).

So, now he stood before his very lovely, very nervous bride and allowed the smell of honeysuckle to addle his brain some more. *I should kiss her. Say a few sweet nothings. Say good night and take my leave.* Lowering his lips to hers, he kissed her ever so lightly. When she raised her hands to his shoulders and then wrapped them around his neck, he deepened the kiss.

Her body was warm and soft beneath his hands, the entire front of her body pressed against his in open invitation. One of his hands drew up the side of her body, its thumb caressing the side of her breast before he gently drew it over the taut nipple, the fabric of her night rail thin enough so that he could almost believe he was touching her heated skin directly. He took satisfaction in feeling Hannah's reaction against his mouth as her lips were forced to break from his in order for her to inhale sharply.

Perhaps one more kiss and then he would leave her. The

hand that caressed her nipple opened over her breast, gently lifting the mound that was, indeed, a bit larger than his palm. He captured Hannah lips to stifle her cry and then slowly slid the hand down to her hip. Gathering the fabric of her night rail beneath his palm, pulling up the gown as he did so, soon Henry had the flat of his hand smoothing over the side of her thigh, the globe of her bottom and to the front where he barely touched her belly. Hannah's body spasmed in response, a moan rising from her throat as his kiss continued to consume her cries. When he slid his palm through the crisp curls and into the space between her thighs, he gripped her bottom with his other hand and held her hard against his body, knowing in a moment her legs would turn to gelatin and she would require his support to remain upright.

"Henry," she managed to whisper against his lips.

Pulling his mouth away from hers, he kissed her hair and the column of her neck as his fingers searched for her womanhood. He was about to force her legs apart with a knee, but she slid one foot sideways, and then his fingers were sliding along her wet, swollen folds of flesh. The scent of feminine musk reached his nostrils as his fingers found their prey. He felt Hannah's grip on him tighten, felt her tremulous breaths, as if she dared not breathe until whatever was about to happen, and then she arced her body. With her hip solid against his erection and her head thrown back in ecstasy, Henry waited until he heard her quiet keening before stilling his fingers.

He was suddenly aware of his own body, of his own arousal, of her hip pressed against him. The sight of her head thrown back set off something in him he found he could not stop. His climax, so sudden and so unexpected, gripped his entire body. Pulling Hannah hard against the front of his body, he planted his mouth on her shoulder to stifle the growl, struggled hard to keep his legs beneath him, and wondered at how his body seemed to be trembling so hard. Stunned that the sight of his wife in ecstasy could have such an effect on him, Henry finally inhaled and gentled his hold on her.

Shaking like a leaf, Hannah struggled to regain her sense of self, tried to pull herself back into a single body, sure she was lost in some oblivion where her physical being didn't exist.

Slowly, she became aware of Henry's quiet whispers in her ear, of his hands stroking her back, stroking her shoulders, of her body being lifted and moved into a cloud of white and covered in warmth, of Henry's lips on hers, of his lips on her neck. And then, as if it was all just a dream, she found herself dreaming.

Still breathing heavily, Henry gave Hannah one last kiss before taking his leave of her. It was a very long walk to his room at the other end of the house.

CHAPTER 8
THE NEWLYWEDS ON A
LONG RIDE

*H*enry glanced at Hannah. She sat on the other side in the coach, facing the direction of their travel while he sat opposite. Her gaze was directed at something beyond the window. They had barely looked at one another the entire morning, each of them stealing glances at one another and then quickly averting their eyes should one be caught staring by the other. Their conversation had been stilted, so uncomfortable at one point that Henry thought Hannah might cry. So he had dropped the subject of her possible need for warmer gowns and a mantle in favor of silence.

Well, it would have been silent in the coach had Harold MacDuff not been sprawled on the floor between them. The dog's snoring was sometimes so loud Henry was sure he once saw Hannah grin before covering her mouth with a gloved hand. She was beautiful when she grinned like that, as if she harbored some secret to which only she was privy.

Actually, she was beautiful with any expression on her face, Henry decided.

Every time he thought to stretch out his long limbs, his boots ended up nudging the hairy beast so that it would lift its head and snuffle and snort in surprise. Earlier that morning, Henry had thought to simply leash the dog to the back of the coach, but realized very quickly the dog wouldn't have been able to keep up with the coach-and-four as it made its way out the Great West Road for the seventy-five mile trek to Gisborn Hall. And then he wondered if the dog could sit up on the box with the driver, but one glance at the size of the box, and another at the size of Harold, and Henry realized there would be no room for the driver. Perhaps Harold could be relegated to the older carriage that would follow with the rest of Lady Hannah's trunks and her maid the following day, but with the volume of stuff still being packed and loaded onto that conveyance, Henry wondered if there would even be room for Lily.

He had spied the maid when she was hurrying about with an armful of gowns, sure he had seen her somewhere before. But his attention had been diverted and the chance to ask about her passed.

In one of her few comments that morning, Hannah suggested the dog ride inside the coach for the sole purpose of keeping her slippered feet warm. "A hot brick won't be necessary, my lord," she had assured him when he was about to order a servant to have one brought out from the kitchens. "Harold serves the purpose quite effectively."

Henry found he had to agree. Good God, the dog was huge, covering nearly the entire floor of the coach. Having realized his own feet would be far warmer if he sat with Hannah and placed his feet next to hers under the back of the dog, he was about to ask if he could do so when he realized Hannah was turning in his direction. Not wanting to be caught staring, he quickly turned his head to look out the window.

Hannah stole a glance in the direction of the earl, sure his gaze had been directed at her, and then, suddenly, it wasn't. He was looking out the window to his right, she realized as she dared a longer look. His profile was quite striking, she thought, with its strong nose, square jaw and wide chin. His neatly trimmed almost-black hair included one forelock that seemed determined to curl above one eyebrow, and despite his having shaved that morning, there was already a hint of dark shadow along his jawline. A quick glance might have the viewer thinking him a rogue or even a highwayman.

My husband, she thought for at least the tenth time that morning. So handsome, so tall, so uncomfortable. Despite the roomy interior of the new coach in which they rode, Henry Forster seemed somehow scrunched into the squabs, his limbs too long for the leather seat and his torso too tall for the seat's back. And then Hannah noticed how his knees had to bend so that his feet could take purchase on the floor next to Harold's sprawled mass. "Oh, goodness, my lord. Wouldn't you be more comfortable sitting on this side?"

The words were out of her mouth before she realized she had said them, and she wondered if she had made a mistake in suggesting he share the seat with her. Would he think her fast in suggesting such an arrangement? She had to suppress a giggle. *I am his wife, not some chit fresh out of the schoolroom*, she chided herself. She struggled to think of what to add when she saw his startled expression, as if he were surprised she had the ability to speak. "Then you could put your feet under Harold. Keep them warm," she added, resisting the urge to roll her eyes when the reasoning sounded lame to her own ears. Harold raised his head at the sound of his name but allowed it to plop back down onto his front paws when he realized he wasn't being addressed directly.

Hiding his astonishment at his wife's insight, especially at the very moment he was thinking the very same thing, Henry nodded. "If you would not mind, my lady," he answered quickly, moving carefully to step over the dog and reposition himself on the bench seat next to Hannah. To be facing the direction of travel was a relief; he despised not being able to see ahead as they made their way west toward Oxfordshire.

"Not at all, my lord. I should wish for your comfort, of course," Hannah replied shyly, one gloved hand gathering her skirts so they were no longer spread out across the seat. She left the hand resting on a thigh, not wanting to appear as if she couldn't sit still.

Henry settled himself into the squabs and let out a sigh of relief as his limbs stretched. Warmth crept into his feet where his boots were tucked under the dog. "Thank you, my lady. This was an excellent idea," he said, placing a black-gloved hand over hers where it rested on her thigh. *So tiny*, he thought as his fingers curled slightly. If Hannah was surprised or made uncomfortable by his touch, he couldn't sense it in her hand.

Hannah had to suppress the start she felt at his hand closing over the back of hers. The heat from his palm actually permeated their gloves, leaving her hand bathed in comforting warmth. She wondered if she would feel that same warmth when their bodies were pressed together in their marriage bed. A frisson passed through her body at the thought.

She should already *know* how it felt to have him next to her in bed. He should have been *in* it last night! Why hadn't he simply bedded her when he had the chance? She had been quite ready for him, her white-blond hair loose and brushed to a gleaming shine, her new night rail clinging to her slight curves, her feet encased in daring half-slippers that displayed her toes. She had made sure the maid was gone and the bed linens were turned down. Having been told what to expect by her friends who were young matrons, especially by Elizabeth, she was quite prepared to be ravished.

Then Henry had come to her door, and instead of coming all the way in, he had stood there on the threshold acting like some shy boy barely out of Eton attending his first ball and telling her he was very glad to meet her, but could he reserve a dance for the next ball instead?

She had almost said, "Of course not. You're here. Dance with me now!" Or something to that effect. *How dare he?* It was their wedding night. He should have claimed what was rightfully his right then and there.

At least he'd had the decency to kiss her, although the

slight pressing of lips could hardly be called a kiss. But then he had kissed her more deeply, and used his hands to great effect on her body. And then he had pleasured her quite thoroughly— her body seemed to quake even now as she remembered the sharp sensations he had created with his caresses. Who knew a man's hands could deliver so much pleasure?

Elizabeth knew, of course. Hannah couldn't keep herself from blushing at the thought of some of the things George had done to Elizabeth. The woman had described them in detail, all the while seeming to re-experience the sensations she had felt when her husband had created them in the first place. George had probably pleasured her to within an inch of her life before they had even wed!

Blast and damnation! Hannah had been *ready* for Gisborn last night. After traveling seventy-five miles in a coach over roads that were proving a bit rough, she rather doubted she would want him in her bed tonight! And then she wondered if she would even have her own bed, or if they would always share a marriage bed. Nothing had been said as to the sleeping arrangements at Gisborn Hall.

Chancing another glance in his wife's direction, Henry couldn't help but notice Hannah's delicate features, her skin so smooth and pale and fine, it was almost translucent, eye lashes so long they seemed to collide with the tops of her cheekbones with every blink, lips that were full but not too large—kissable lips, he thought. He had wanted desperately to spend the entire night kissing those lips, kiss them with far more passion than the simple kisses he had placed on them when he came to bid Hannah good night.

She had looked ravishing in her night clothes, the thin fabric of her nightgown barely hiding her *charms*. And her hair. He'd had no idea she had such long, lustrous hair. He wanted nothing more than to step into her bedchamber and strip her bare and slide his hands over her breasts and bottom and spread her legs and take her virtue as was his right as her husband. But the idea of taking her maidenhood in her own bed, the bed she had probably slept in every night of her life since being out of the cradle—it seemed *wrong,* somehow. Had he taken her virtue, she might be left feeling sore. Given their long coach ride to Oxfordshire, he considered she would be uncomfortable the entire trip. There was no use putting her through that. It might be a week or more before she would allow him to bed her again. And, truth be told, he wasn't sure he would have been able to muster the courage. The effects of the champagne served just after the vicar declared the couple legally wed had long since worn off.

So, instead, he had allowed his hands to wander and his lips to take hers more so he could keep her cries quiet than to impart any meaning to it.

But something had happened. *Lust,* he told himself. His body—the traitor—had made it clear he should be with his wife. Even now, he wondered at the sudden and glorious sensation he had felt as Hannah's pleasure crested, as if she were determined to take him along on the wave. But the thought of bedding his new wife made him feel as if he were betraying Sarah.

He had only ever been with Sarah. His modest income prior to his inheritance hadn't afforded him the life of most gentlemen. He didn't have the funds to gamble or spend his nights in brothels, and there certainly wasn't enough to hire a mistress, not that he ever wanted to. He had Sarah. She was the mother of his child. She was everything he had ever wanted in a wife. Damn her for thinking she wasn't good enough to marry him!

"Why didn't you take my virtue last night?"

The question, tinged with what might have been anger and probably some hurt, rang out in the cramped coach, a shock to the three sets of ears that heard it. Harold lifted his head and angled it to one side, regarding his mistress and her look of utter astonishment for a full five seconds before realizing he, for once, wasn't the one being accused of some wrongdoing. Henry, who had sat very still for that full five seconds and displayed the look of the one being accused, slowly turned to find his wife's hand, the one he wasn't now holding in a death grip, covering her plump lips. Her pale peaches and cream complexion had turned a bright pink. And, despite how tightly her eyes were closed at that very moment, a tear was forcing itself out of the corner of the eye nearest Henry.

Oh, God, she's going to cry.

Henry ceased to breathe as he wondered what to say. What to do. And then instinct took over. He let go of her hand and wrapped his arms around her shoulders, pulling her hard against his chest. Her bonnet collided with his shoulder, but he had it stripped from her head in an instant, the quick flick of his wrist sending the offending velvet hat sailing onto the seat across from them. Although he wanted to kiss her just then, cover her lips and take possession of her with a punishing kiss that proved just how badly he wanted her the night before, how badly he wanted her right now, Henry simply held her body against his and kissed her forehead. If there had been any fight in her, he did not sense it. Nor did she feel stiff or unyielding in his arms. It was as if she melted against him, molding herself to fit into the empty spaces along the front of his body. "I wanted nothing more than to bed you last night, my lady," he whispered hoarsely. "But it would have been..." *Wrong? Awkward?* "Inappropriate," he finally got out, rather proud that he was able to make such a sensible sounding excuse for himself.

Hannah apparently didn't agree, however. He felt her body become rigid, felt her head tilt until he could see her eyes. Angry eyes. *Oh, God.*

"*Inappropriate?*" she repeated in a voice tinged with outrage. "I am expected to bear you an heir and a *spare*. How can I do that if you don't *bed* me?" This last was delivered with the hint of a sob, as if she might really be on the verge of tears.

Swallowing hard, Henry gave some thought to countering her annoyance with his own sudden ire. How could she talk to him like that? He thought he had spared her a night of embarrassment at having to host her husband in the room in which she had spent her childhood nights. He thought he spared her the discomfort of having to ride in a coach while tender *down there*. He thought he had done right by her by not insisting on sexual intercourse in her father's home. *We'll have intercourse when I am damn good and ready!*

And then he noticed Harold staring at him.

The dog's head seemed to shake ever so slightly from side to side, as if warning Henry that he was about to make a huge mistake. Or, perhaps he was warning him that it didn't matter what he said or did. He had already made a huge mistake and there was no getting out of it.

Henry used one hand to cup his wife's cheek as he stared down into her bright cornflower blue eyes, made more so by the unshed tears. Even limned with tears, they were gorgeous. He settled his lips over hers, barely pressing against her plump lips until he had completely captured them. And then he kissed her, deepening the kiss until she let out a slight moan that either signaled she was appeased or that she needed to breathe. Either way, Henry slowly let go and pulled away, his eyes watching her lids as they fluttered open. He saw defiance there, he thought, and realized he still needed to explain himself. "I did not wish to take your virtue in the bed in which you've spent your maidenhood," he stated quietly. "I intend to do so in our *marriage* bed. I think perhaps my bed will be most suitable." Although, now that he thought about it, that was where he and Sarah sometimes made love. "Or we can use the bed in the mistress suite. Your suite," he amended quickly, realizing she knew nothing of Gisborn Hall. "I have every intention of bedding you." *Frequently? Often? A couple of times a week?* He was suddenly at a loss.

How often did husbands bed their wives?

"Every night," Hannah stated quietly, her head nodding. "At least, until I am with child, and then as often as you wish," she added, her face turning that shade of pink he was finding quite fetching. *He wanted to spare me the embarrass-*

ment of losing my virginity in my own bed? Perhaps he is as considerate as his words make him out to be.

Henry stared down at her. *Every night?* He and Sarah... well, things hadn't been very comfortable between them these last few months. She had come to the house the day before he made his trip to London, agreeing to spend the night in Gisborn Hall while Nathan and his friend Andrew stayed in the nursery upstairs. And she had been willing, although he sensed something was wrong when he had been unable to pleasure her quite like he was used to doing. His simple strokes and touching were no longer effective in bringing her to ecstasy. It was as if her body demanded a harder, more forceful union—a faster, more urgent coupling. Although it had left her satiated, he felt as if he had violated her in some way.

Then, in the morning, when he was quite prepared to make love to her in the light from a golden red dawn, he turned over to find her already gone from his bed. She was dressed and pulling on stockings in front of the fireplace, her attention on the dying embers. He wondered how long she had sat there, staring. He had kissed her on the cheek, hugged Nathan as hard as he dared, and bid them both good-bye as he stepped into the ancient Gisborn coach.

He hadn't intended to get married while on this trip; he went thinking only to obtain the title to Ellsworth Park. So why had Sarah seemed so distant? So distracted? Now that he was going home with far more than he bargained for—a willing wife who would apparently tolerate his continued relationship with Sarah—*Men only love their mistresses*, she had said—he wondered if Sarah would be more like she had been for all the years before this one. Or would she become even more distant? *Damn it, what was going on with the woman?*

"I shall come to your bedchamber every night then," Henry finally agreed, nodding his head. "And should there be a night you do not want my company, you only need say so, and I shall take my leave of you." *There. That should be a suit-*

able arrangement, he thought, rather glad they had the discussion done before arriving at Gisborn Hall.

"Agreed," Hannah replied with a nod of her own. Having carefully watched him as he made his proclamation, she wondered if he might kiss her on those occasions. Or were kisses reserved only for Sarah? For the kiss he had bestowed on her only moments ago was quite pleasant, really. Very satisfactory. Thrilling, even, when she thought for a moment she was about to be dumped on the floor of the coach—or rather onto poor Harold—had Henry let go his hold on her.

Henry continued to stare down at Hannah, thinking of the kiss they had just shared. She had allowed it quite readily, returned it even. Had he wanted to continue the kiss, he realized she would not have objected. *She's gazing at me. As if she expects something.* "What... what is it?" he asked, his face lowering to just inches above hers.

"I would not object to being kissed, of course... whenever you should think it... appropriate," she stammered.

Appropriate? How could her command of the English language leave her with such a poor choice of words? She could have said *whenever you desire* or *whenever you wish* or *anytime of the day or night.*

Good God, can she read my mind? "I... Thank you. I will remember that," Henry answered, watching her face as it pinked up again. Before he was quite aware of what he was doing, his lips were back on hers, completing the kiss he had started only moments ago, his attention so thoroughly on the kiss and the feel of her lips and the texture of her teeth against his tongue and the taste of her mouth and the scent of honeysuckle that wafted from her hair, that he didn't realize the coach had taken a turn into the yard of a posting inn until the driver jumped down from the box and opened the door to the coach. Ending the kiss as quickly as he could, and then chiding himself for feeling embarrassed at being caught kissing his own wife, Henry straightened Hannah on his lap and nodded at the driver as the man put down the steps.

While the horses were being changed out for a fresh team, they would have time to get tea and sustenance in the posting inn. For Henry, the time would give him a chance to learn more about his new wife. For Hannah, the time would give her a chance to realize her new husband was far more than she expected.

As for Harold, it was a chance to relieve himself and to take a nap in blessed silence.

CHAPTER 9
WELCOME TO GISBORN HALL

After nearly nine hours of traveling in the well-sprung coach, Henry was relieved when they made the turn toward Tadpole Bridge and his lands just north of the River Isis. Hannah had fallen asleep shortly after their luncheon a few hours before, and only stirred when the coach took a nasty bump or swayed more than usual. Her head lay in the small of his shoulder, his arm wrapped protectively across the back of her shoulders. His thoughts went to later, when he would join her in the mistress suite at Gisborn Hall and make her his wife. He wondered if she would allow him to share her bed for the entire night, or if she would insist he return to his bedchamber.

"Is that Gisborn Hall?" he heard in an awed whisper. Henry smiled, feeling a sense of pride. "Indeed," he answered, giving Hannah a kiss on the forehead before allowing her to raise herself to a sitting position. Harold noticed the slowing coach and raised his head, his ears perking up.

The imposing gray stone structure appeared to have been dropped from high up, it was so embedded into the earth, its foundations quite solid and at an angle to the road leading up to the circular drive. Rectangular except for where the front doors were encased in a portico, the house was symmetrical down to the two topiary trees that flanked the entry. Dozens of windows stretched along the second story, each placed in perfect symmetry. The windows on either side of the front door were in triplets and pairs, suggesting the rooms there were larger, perhaps the library and parlor. From a distance, it looked simply grand.

Hannah felt a stirring and grinned; she would be mistress of this house. Once they had pulled up into the drive and the horses were slowing in front of the double doors, she noted how the façade was weathered, one window was cracked and the plantings along the front of the house appeared in need of a gardener's touch. A bit of work and it would be a proper looking house for an earl, she thought.

The coach door opened. Harold lifted himself and stepped out, apparently aware that neither human would be able to do so until he was out of the way. Gisborn squeezed Hannah's hand and stepped out, turning to hand her down. Once Hannah was sure her feet were under her and her skirts were shaken out, she glanced around. A man not much younger than her was hurrying up to see to the horses, and a footman was undoing the straps that held their valises to the back of the coach. She allowed Henry to escort her up the five steps and to the front doors. She couldn't help but notice Henry inhale before he pulled the brass knocker. Harold sat next to her as they all waited.

No one answered. At least, not immediately.

Hannah glanced at Henry, wondering if they had arrived on the butler's day off. Hadn't Henry sent word ahead that they would be arriving today? She was about to ask when the door opened to reveal an elderly man, so stooped he had to lean back in order to determine it was his master who stood at the door. "Ah, Gisborn," the butler said as he stepped back to allow them entrance, a gnarled hand waving them in.

"Parkerhouse. I'd like to introduce my wife, Hannah Forster, Lady Gisborn," Henry said. "Oh, and this is Harold MacDuff," he added as he indicated the dog.

The butler, who was dressed quite formally and looked as

if he had been on staff at the house for at least fifty years, bowed in her direction. "Countess," he said by way of acknowledgment, not showing the least bit of surprise. "Harold," he said, affording the dog a nod. "May I take your cloak?"

Henry aimed a cocked brow in Hannah's direction, an expression which seemed to say that Parkerhouse was always unflappable. Hannah undid the buttons on her pelisse and allowed the ancient butler to help her out of the coat while Henry gave instructions. "Could you let Mrs. Batey know we've arrived? And Mrs. Chambers, too? I believe we'll have dinner in the smaller dining room. And have the mistress suite readied for my wife."

Parkerhouse nodded and shuffled off. Hannah watched him go. "How long has he been in service?" she asked, taking Henry's proffered arm. He led her down the long hall to the right, and Harold followed, as if he wasn't quite sure what to do.

"He was my uncle's butler and my grandfather's butler before that," Henry said with a shrug. Stopping at the first open door on the right, he waved her in. "The parlor, my lady," he said with a nod. "If you'll pull the bell, we may get some tea."

Hannah glanced around, noting the rich fabrics, the elegant furnishings. Despite the exterior looking as if it needed some attention, this room did not. Surfaces gleamed, and the Aubusson carpet was recently cleaned. "Take me on a tour of the whole house," she suggested, moving to stand before him.

Henry looked down on her, surprised by her request. "As you wish," he agreed. Taking her hand, they left the parlor and wandered the halls of Gisborn's estate home, Henry reciting interesting facts along the way, pointing at various artifacts and explaining their significance. Hannah hung on his every word, determined to learn everything she could about the house. She also noticed very few servants about; a footman or two bowed as they passed, but she saw no maids.

When they reached his study, the room to the left of the front doors and the last stop on their tour of the main floor, he hurried to leaf through the notes that lay on a silver salver, shaking his head as he did so. "Looks like I chose a good time to be gone," he murmured. He watched as Hannah slid her fingers over the backs of the chairs, gazed at the shelves of books and studied the framed drawings hung on the walls. Harold seemed to understand the significance of the room. He settled himself in front of the hearth.

"You are an inventor, aren't you?" Hannah asked rhetorically, studying one of the drawings that lay unfolded on a library table. It was a detail of the irrigation ditch where the gate would be installed, along with drawings of the gate and tracks in which it would ride when it was installed. It was exactly as he had described it in the Devonville House parlor just a few days ago.

Moving to stand behind her, wrapping his arms around her arms and holding her hands with his, Henry kissed her temple. "I am a farmer, my lady, but I admit to indulging my whims when I think it best for the estate," he acknowledged, his lips barely touching her ear as he said the words.

Hannah grinned, turning her head so she could regard him. "Indulging your whims?" she repeated, thinking he meant spending money on luxuries. Although the rooms they had toured were elegant and well-appointed, nothing was done to excess, nor were there expensive objets d'art on display nor were there paintings by masters decorating the walls. Henry dressed well and wore boots that suggested they were custom made, but other than a ruby cravat pin, he didn't wear jewelry. Hannah glanced at her wedding ring, obviously the signet ring for the earldom. The ring was so large, she had to wear it on her middle finger, and even then, the band was wrapped with yarn to ensure it stayed put on her finger. "When have you ever done such a thing as indulge your whims?" she asked with a teasing grin.

"When I bought this for you," he said, pulling a diamond and ruby ring from his pocket and settling it onto her left ring finger, next to where his signet ring already rested. "And when I married you," he kissed her when she turned around in his arms, obviously surprised by the ring.

"Henry," she breathed, holding her hand up before her face as he held her around her waist. "It's... it's beautiful," she said, her tone reverent. She placed her other hand against his face and stood on tiptoes so she could kiss him. Henry pulled her against him, returning the kiss in equal measure.

At the sound of a throat clearing, the two quickly ended the kiss and turned to the doorway.

"Dinner is served, my lady, my lord," Parkerhouse stated.

Stealing guilty glances at one another, the two made their way to the small dining room and had their first dinner together as Lord and Lady Gisborn.

Henry found Hannah sleeping in the copper tub, her knees slightly bent and her breasts barely covered by water that had probably been topped with bubbles when she first climbed in. *She looks like a mermaid,* Henry thought, not quite sure what a mermaid should look like but deciding she was what he would imagine one to be if someone ever brought up the topic.

He dipped a finger in the water. *Still warm.* And the tub, a rather large one as it was designed for a man of his size, had plenty of room for him even given the mermaid who occupied it.

Slowly, Henry stepped into the scented water, making sure one foot was secure on the bottom of the tub before bringing his other foot up and into the tub. Hannah's body moved forward, her head leaning to one side as she dozed. Henry lowered himself behind her, his arms sliding along her back and gently pushing her so her knees bent a bit more. His own legs folded on either side of her body as he lowered himself to sit behind her. Wrapping one hand around her waist, he pulled her body back against his and watched with barely contained lust as Hannah's head lolled onto his chest. The scent of honeysuckle caught in his nostrils. He breathed deeply, the inhalation interrupted when he noticed her bare breasts. Their curves were just above the surface of the bubble-topped water, her rosy nipples beautifully on display. No longer in the warm water, they tightened into ruched buds. Kissable buds.

At that moment, Henry wanted nothing more than to reach down with his lips and kiss one of those nipples. Or both, really. And ever so slowly pull them into his mouth and suckle each until she was crying with pleasure and wet and ready for him. His cock hardening at the thought, he had to readjust Hannah's body as it rested against him. She stirred and her head rolled to the other side of his chest, leaving the side of her neck fully exposed. Lowering his lips to the space under her ear, he ever so carefully kissed her. His tongue reached out and captured her earlobe, his lips closing over it to suckle it as lightly as he could manage given his odd position. Hannah's slight moan spurred him to move his mouth down her neck, his kisses continuing as he sipped and suckled the skin there. In order to kiss the tops of her breasts, though, he would be forced to move her body slightly to one side. One arm cradled her side as he used the other to pull her closer.

Perhaps his lips came down too hard on the mounded curve of her breast, or perhaps the chill of her breasts being entirely out of the water roused her. Whatever it was, Hannah was suddenly wide awake.

And had there been anyone else with a bedchamber on the second floor, they would have been as well.

Henry was reminded of the first time his father took him fishing. There was the sensation of rolling waves lifting and lowering the boat. There was the feel of the fish as it caught his line, the smooth way in which it swam up as he pulled back his rod, the weight of it barely noticeable until the fish broke the surface of the water. Then its tail lashed about, sending a cascade of water over the top of him while the rest of its body undulated uncontrollably, making the fish so heavy he couldn't hang on and finally had to let go or be drowned in the effort to take it aboard.

When the water in the tub evened out, a thoroughly drenched Henry was staring at his very startled wife. She had somehow managed to turn herself completely over so that she was now on her hands and knees in the tub, her shoulders, back and rather beautiful, white bottom clearly out of the water. Henry knew at once where her hands were—one was planted firmly on one of his thighs while the other was proving to be rather bothersome in its current location. "My lady, if you do not move this hand," he wrapped one of his own around her wrist and pulled up to release the pressure on his groin, "I won't be able to father the children you so desperately want, and I apparently need as heirs," he managed to get out between gritted teeth.

Gasping, Hannah lifted her hand, but in doing so, lost her balance and pitched forward, one cheek and her breasts colliding with his rather solid chest, the dusting of crisp hair that covered it now soaked and plastered to his skin. She let out a rather audible "Oof ". The resulting wave of water from the sudden movement rebounded from the end of the tub and then lifted and landed her torso farther up onto his body. Capturing her around the waist with one arm, Henry held onto her until the waves subsided. She was about to attempt to push away from his body—he could tell from her startled expression and the way one palm of a hand was pressing against his chest— when he secured her completely by wrapping his other arm beneath her bottom. His still engorged cock, now made even harder as he realized the position into which she had managed to place herself with the help of the water, was pressed firmly against her soft belly.

"Oh!" she got out, her eyes round as they regarded his face. She then lowered them to take in the sight of his bare chest and his equally bare arms. She dared not lift herself and look between the breasts that were pressed quite firmly into his chest. She might have been a virgin, but Elizabeth had described a man's member in extreme detail, so even Hannah knew what caused the throbbing sensation she felt pounding against her belly. There was a matching one deep inside her, its throbbing rhythm the same as the one against her belly. The tension in her body left as she sighed and allowed her body to be buoyed by the water and held in place by his arms.

"I think I might have enjoyed fishing a great deal more had I known I could catch a mermaid as beautiful as you," Henry murmured, his voice so husky he barely recognized it.

If the words suggested he was humored by what had occurred, Hannah could not detect it in his eyes nor in the tone of his voice. Whatever ire she had felt at discovering Henry in her bathtub—well, *his* bathtub, actually, but her bath water—was quickly replaced with her need to be held by him. "And what does a man do when he catches a mermaid?" she countered in a whisper, her gaze traveling from the line of slight stubble along his jaw to his lips. Her own lips parted in anticipation.

"He kisses her senseless, of course," Henry replied, again with no hint of humor. "And then he dries her off and takes her to a very soft bed and makes love to her until she is completely and thoroughly pleasured."

Hannah held her breath. "Oh," she whispered. "I think I would like to be that mermaid. May I be... May I be that mermaid?" she asked in a voice so alluring, she barely recognized it as her own.

Henry lips were on hers in an instant, his arms pulling her body farther up his while he allowed his own to slide down the back of the tub. *Good God, she is wanton when given the chance*, he thought as he slipped his tongue between her lips and teeth. She tasted of mint and smelled of honeysuckle and whatever citrus scent the disappearing bubbles gave off.

As his hand caressed one of the globes of her bottom, hers were sliding up his chest and out to his shoulders. His other hand moved up the side of her body, his thumb seeking the side of her mounded breast where it pressed against his chest. Barely touching the wet skin there, he was thrilled when he felt her body shudder, her lips pulling away from his for only an instant so that she could gasp. When he had recaptured her lips, he used his other thumb to caress the side of her other breast. He smiled at her similar reaction.

Everything Henry did felt so wicked, so decadent, so wrong to Hannah, and yet she had to remind herself he was her husband. Did he do this to Sarah? Was she as receptive to his touch, to his kisses? Did she feel these pleasures? Was she wanton or demure or …?

Henry moved a hand back to her bottom and attempted to slide a finger between her thighs. Opening her legs— she could if she bent her knees slightly around the tops of his thighs—Hannah cried out as the finger made contact with that rather sensitive spot he had touched the night before. Arching her back in response to the sharp and sudden stab of pleasure, her breasts came off his chest.

Henry watched, fascinated, as Hannah's head fell back, her lips parted as the wave of ecstasy gripped her. He was reminded of the first time he had seen her, playing with Harold in the yard, her head thrown back in delight as the dog licked her neck. Except now, her expression was far more mature, wanton. And her swollen breasts, with their ruched buds, were suddenly at a rather advantageous position with respect to his mouth.

Circling his finger around the swollen nub of her womanhood one more time, he placed his lips over one of her breasts and began to suckle and kiss it. A shudder passed under his lips. Sensing how close she must be to her release, he drew the side of his tongue across the nipple while his finger stroked her womanhood one last time before he slid it into the warm, wet sheath. *God, she is tight.* He wanted desperately to be inside her, his own cock so engorged he was sure it was leaving a mark on her belly where it pressed into her. But he concentrated on her pleasure, on the cresting wave that was about to break.

He felt a great deal of satisfaction as she suddenly tensed and then cried out his name. In another instant, her body went limp and fell down onto his. Even as he held her, as he stroked her back and her arms and gentled her to relax against him, he could feel the trembling of her entire body.

A moment more and he would need to get them out of the water. Already the ends of his fingers were showing signs of wrinkling, and despite the heated condition of his own body, the water was cooling quickly.

Not able to push herself up and not necessarily wanting to, Hannah lay with her head resting in the small of Henry's shoulder. Never could she have imagined the pleasure of a marriage bed, or a bath, rather. No one had described being pleasured in a copper tub, not even Elizabeth. The thing wasn't truly large enough to accomplish what she was sure Gisborn wanted just then, judging from the throbbing mass squashed into her belly, but surely he would help her out of the tub and onto the bed. She rather doubted she had the strength to do so on her own.

As if he could read her thoughts, Henry slowly straightened in the tub, repositioning Hannah so he could get his legs beneath him and stand up. Once he was out of tub and had a linen wrapped around his middle, he reached down to capture Hannah beneath her arms and pull her up and out of the tub. He grinned as he saw her skin turn to gooseflesh, her nipples tighten into tiny buds. Winding a linen around her shoulders and another around her bottom, he reached down and captured her knees in one arm while his other supported her shoulders. Grinning again when he heard her gasp of surprise, he easily carried her to her bed. The downturned linens left a large, white expanse on which to place her still wet body. The soft mattress gave way as they settled onto it.

Henry leaned down and touched his lips to hers. Hannah responded by opening her mouth and meeting the pressure of his lips against hers. She felt his arms press into the mattress on either side of her torso, enclosing her body as the kiss continued. She inhaled the scent of him, a subtle musk that emanated from his entire body, and she breathed in the scent of the citrus soap from their bath.

And the kiss! His lips were firm, but he was careful in

how he held them against hers, at once tasting hers and pulling away slightly before pushing them against hers again and again.

When his mouth finally moved away from hers, it was to gently kiss her cheek and neck. "I have wanted to kiss you like this all night long, Hannah," he whispered just before his lips took her earlobe into his mouth.

Hannah gasped at the sensation as his tongue caressed her ear. She was aware of how her body was responding to his kisses and his touch, sure her breasts had escaped from beneath the bath linen, and if they hadn't, she wanted them out and in his warm hands.

A shiver passed through her body as his lips moved to her neck and throat. Arching back, she took a deep breath as his tongue made its way down to the space below her collarbone, as his lips moved to hover over the swell of her breasts. Her thighs quivered, the heat between them making her very aware of the male that hovered over her. She could think of nothing but giving herself to this man. "Take me, Henry," she whispered as she gasped for air.

CHAPTER 10

GISBORN AND HANNAH IN
THE MIDDLE OF THE NIGHT

*D*espite Lady Bostwick's insistence she would enjoy it, Hannah was still anxious about what was to come. Perhaps these waves of pleasure Henry was inducing were part of what Lady Bostwick had alluded to the week before. *Do not be afraid to take whatever pleasure your husband wants to provide you. You will return it ten-fold without doing much more than opening your body to him and giving him an heir.*

Henry lifted his lips from her collarbone and stared at her for only a moment. He placed a hand against her cheek and brushed his thumb over her lower lip, caressing the fullness of it as she wrapped a hand around his wrist and rested another on his shoulder.

Henry's bare chest was of more importance to Hannah. She had seen it when it was soaking wet in the tub, but now it glowed in the candlelight, the light dusting of black hair tickling her nose and the pads of her fingers as she kissed the area around his nipples. At his sudden gasp, she moved her lips to his upper arms and moved her trembling fingers to play over his back.

Henry shuddered at the sensations that coursed through his body. *She is truly giving herself to me*, he realized, his gaze traveling the length of her body before he placed his mouth against one of the round breasts. He suckled the nipple.

Hannah inhaled sharply in surprise at the feeling of his wet lips and the tip of his tongue against her. A shiver of pleasure passed through her and settled just above her thighs. A whimper escaped her lips as the throbbing sensation deepened within her and demanded attention.

Moving his hand to the front of her body, Henry slowly skimmed his fingers over her belly and breasts, his thumb extended so as to brush the tip of her engorged nipples as he continued his caresses. Despite the growing heat of her body, her skin shivered under his touch, and he heard her sudden but quiet gasps.

Pulling away to look at Hannah, Henry's gaze took in her entire body before returning to her face. "You are so beautiful," he whispered urgently. Naked, now that the linens were unwrapped from around her shoulders and waist, she was the most erotic sight he had ever beheld. This was not the body of a fairy tale princess, but that of an enchantress, ripe and ready to cast her spell over him. She had already done that, he realized, when she had played mermaid in the tub. His arousal was proof of it, his cock becoming uncomfortable in its unrequited state.

Bending down, he kissed her other nipple while Hannah slid her trembling hands down the side of his body. Her touch was tentative, unsure. *Where am I allowed to touch?*

"Anywhere you wish," Henry managed to get out between kissing her breasts and the inside of her elbows.

She gasped, her fingers stilling on the front of his hips. Had he read her mind? Or had she spoken aloud just then?

Emboldened, she traced a fingertip toward his manhood, explored his erection with her fingers. The silken skin, tight and already wet at the tip, throbbed against her hand. She marveled at the feel of it, surprised that it did not frighten her as she expected and relieved it was not quite as large as she had feared. Sliding her forefinger down along a pulsing vein, she gingerly touched his balls and then cupped them with several fingertips.

Releasing his grip on her nipple to catch his breath, Henry closed his eyes and placed his face next to her shoulder, his hand moving down the front of her, across her hips, and down as far as he could reach along one leg and then slowly up to the dark space between her thighs. Hannah could feel her entire body trembling in anticipation, and then she inhaled sharply as he slid first one finger and then another through her dark curlies and between her thighs. The warm moistness spread over his fingers as he felt for the nub that, if rubbed just so, would send her into ecstasy once again.

Startled by his intimate touch, Hannah inhaled and clung to him, her hands moving to his arms, her fingernails digging into his flesh, branding him with a series of half moons in his skin.

At Hannah's instinct to clench shut the opening to the space between her thighs, Henry coaxed her legs apart as he continued to massage the engorged nub just inside the honeyed folds.

Hannah's breaths came faster as a sharp but exquisite sensation gripped her. She cried out, her back arcing so that her breasts were within reach of his mouth. He licked one hardened pebble with the side of his tongue before pulling it into his mouth. She cried out his name as her body convulsed against him. Even before she had recovered from the sensation, a pleasure so intense and sharp, it was almost painful, she felt his slick fingers stroke the tender folds of skin.

There was a pause in their exploration as Henry lifted himself and moved his kisses from one peaked nipple to another, his tongue playfully licking the other hardened pebble. When he slid a finger inside her, Hannah jerked, clenching instinctively around the intruder. Henry held his breath as he watched her eyes widen, her bee stung lips parting slightly. When he felt her relax from around his finger, he pushed it in a bit further and used the pad of his thumb to circle her swollen sex.

Whimpering, Hannah lifted her hips slightly, forcing his finger to bury itself deeper inside her. Her breath catching, she slid a hand down the side of his body, pausing when she realized his manhood rested against her thigh. She gingerly touched the taut silken skin, feeling a great deal of satisfaction when her ministrations elicited the same reaction from Henry that she had expressed only seconds before.

Henry closed his eyes, fighting the urge to simply allow himself the release his body was demanding. Realizing Hannah was as ready as he could make her, and hoping he wouldn't hurt her too terribly, he slowly removed his finger from inside her. He lifted his hips over hers and placed the tip of his throbbing manhood where his finger had just been. "Wrap your legs around my back," he whispered, nudging himself into her just an inch or so. As she watched him through lowered lashes, the euphoria from her climax still on her face, Henry entered her slowly. He felt her entire body trembling—in anticipation or fear, he did not know—he merely knew he had to have her.

"This may hurt a bit," he whispered, his lips brushing against hers. He was aware of her nod of acknowledgment, and when he lifted his head so that he could see her face, he saw desire in her eyes. Lowering his lips onto hers, he kissed her gently and then slowly pushed into her, his manhood demanding he thrust while what was left of rational thought told him he had to take it slow. This was her first time; there might be pain. When his manhood stretched her maidenhood, Henry paused, pulled himself out, and then thrust his cock deep into her.

Hannah winced at the pinch, but stifled any sound as the warm sensation of fullness filled her lower body. Her husband's motions were careful and deliberate—Henry pushed into her quickly and then slowly pulled out, repeating his movements rhythmically as if he wanted to make it last as long as possible.

With the combination of her body clenching on his manhood with each thrust, and her lips taking purchase on one of his nipples to gently suckle it, and her fingers lightly stroking down the sides of his torso and around his hips to hold onto his buttocks, Henry could no longer hold back. With Sarah, this would be the time he would pull out of her body, spill his seed on her belly or on the bed linens. But this was Hannah. This was his *wife*. He could take his pleasure while deep inside, her wet warmth gripping him, inviting him to spill his seed within her. As he pushed into her as hard and as fast as he could, the release he felt was intense, consuming his entire body in a spasm of pure pleasure.

He nearly yelled out as Hannah arched her back in response to his body's wave of pleasure, her thighs gripping him tightly. He forced his mouth onto one of her shoulders to stifle the growl emanating from his throat. He felt Hannah's body shudder under him and he slowly relaxed, all his energy expended and the last vestiges of his climax waning.

Lowering himself onto her and collapsing in exhaustion, Henry allowed his head to rest on Hannah's shoulder as he felt her fingers wind themselves into his hair on the back of his head and lightly stroke his back. He felt her kiss the top of his head as he continued to lie on top of her. When he finally stirred, it was to kiss her and slowly roll off of her body. He repositioned them both so their heads were on the pillows, tossing the damp bath linens from the bed as he did so. A blood stain on one was proof of her virtue, he realized, his comprehension slowed from the lovemaking. With his last ounce of strength, he covered them both with the bed linens before pulling Hannah closer to his body. He felt her head come to rest on his shoulder. He kissed her hair. "Now, you're my wife," he murmured sleepily.

Hannah purred in response, not quite sure what to say. She didn't even know what to think of her first time. She had felt the warm wetness spread deep inside when he had spilt his seed. That was the moment his body had suddenly stilled, his eyes closing while his face contorted and his muscles tensed. She hadn't realized a man could appear to be in such agony when he was apparently experiencing his ultimate pleasure.

"Are you well?" she asked in a ragged whisper. Her body still trembled, her skin still sensitive to touch, and a new warmth radiated from it.

She felt rather than heard his chuckle. "God, yes," came his equally ragged reply. Overcome with fatigue, Henry fell asleep with his nose in her hair and a grin on his face.

Hannah sighed as she realized it was better that they had waited to consummate their marriage. She could not imagine doing what they had just done in her bedchamber back at Devonville House. Her cries of pleasure would have been heard by the entire household staff. She would have been the source of below-stairs titters for weeks to come. Here, the room seemed to swallow up the sounds they had made. Even the solid bed never protested under their weight or Henry's violent movements.

The cool mattress was soothing beneath her heated skin. The soreness between her thighs seemed almost a pleasant sensation. And her husband, rather than removing himself to his own bedchamber, had drifted off to sleep. Hannah smiled at the thought of their shared nakedness. This part she knew she could get used to. Welcome, even. "Good night, husband," she whispered.

CHAPTER 11
LIFE AT GISBORN HALL

*T*he coach loaded with Hannah's three trunks, her maid, and Murphy arrived at Gisborn Hall at four o'clock in the afternoon the following day. Murphy was all business as he unfolded himself and stepped from the coach, waiting a moment to hand down Lily.

The maid stepped from the coach and inhaled the scent of early spring grass and horse manure. As much as she looked forward to getting back to Oxfordshire and to her true love, there were some things she decided she hadn't missed when she was employed at Devonville House. She wrinkled her nose but quickly recovered her impassive facial expression. She was a lady's maid to a countess! Or, at least, she would be for a day or so. She had other plans for her future.

From his place at the front of the horses, Billy O'Conlin watched as a young lady emerged from the coach. She was wearing a cloak and bonnet that concealed her honey brown hair, but he didn't need to see it to recognize Lily Parker. His heart stutter-stepped as he tried to keep his gaze from being noticed by the maid. She was here. She was back. She was *gorgeous*, he thought, deciding his sleepless nights thinking of her had somehow caught up with him and he was seeing an apparition of Lily instead of whomever had really stepped down from the ancient coach.

Returning his attention to the horse that was growing impatient, he concentrated on the task at hand before stealing another glance in the young woman's direction. It was Lily. There was no doubt. And from the greeting she was receiving from the earl's new wife, Billy realized almost at once that she was Lady Gisborn's maid!

A mix of dread and excitement gripped him. Lily Parker would be a member of the servant staff at Gisborn Hall. Her room would be mere steps from his, although those steps would require one to descend a ladder, walk the length of the stables, cross the backyard to the kitchen door and shuffle down a thin hallway to the servants' quarters. But it was the idea that Lily, who used to live in Witney before her family went into service for the Coley's household, was back in the Gisborn earldom. Back to a place that was close to home. Back to where he could bask in the glow from her smile and imagine a life with her.

Out of the corner of her eye, Lily watched as a stable hand approached the coach-and-four. A shiver passed through her when she realized she recognized the boy. *Billy O'Conlin?* she wondered, sneaking another look in his direction as she made her way to the front steps of the decrepit mansion that was Gisborn Hall. She wasn't positive, but she might have actually said something by way of a greeting to the poor boy.

She had to suppress a shudder at the sight of the late Elizabethan monstrosity planted onto flat land and surrounded on two sides by farmland and the barest hint of parkland on the other two. Whose idea had it been to plow a mile or more of beautiful lawn that ended at the River Isis to plant wheat, beans and barley? Ugh! *The late earl's, of course.* The miser had turned every bit of available Gisborn land into farmland. *Anything to make money*, she thought, remembering her father's comments on the topic. Well, this might be her home for a day or two, but if her plans worked out, she would soon be gone and married to her true love.

Did Lily just wave at me? Billy wondered. *Did she call me by name?* Billy looked up from where he was undoing tack and gave her a nod. *A nod?* He could have said something. Could have said, "Welcome back, Miss Parker. We missed you," or something to at least let her know her absence has been noticed. But the opportunity was lost as she ascended the steps to Gisborn Hall.

Sighing, Billy went back to work. There would be other opportunities to gain her attention, to draw her into conversation, to propose marriage. *What the hell?*

Lily hurried to where Hannah appeared at the double-doors of the front entrance, a matching smile on her face as she hugged her mistress.

Hannah let out a sigh of relief upon seeing Lily again. Other than Harold, Lily was her only other acquaintance from London. To have her in the household might help to make Gisborn Hall feel comfortable, to feel like home. Even though Hannah didn't intend to share anything about her first night with her husband, she was still eager to tell the maid about her new life at Gisborn Hall.

Although Hannah expected she would feel homesick—it was the first time she had been away from Devonville House since visiting friends in the Lake District before her mother's death—she found the wonder of a new home and surroundings enough to keep her mind off of London. And after her late night with the earl, she had slept quite late, waking to a brightly lit room. The new sensation of soreness at the top of her thighs was not unpleasant, especially considering the pleasure that had radiated from that spot only hours ago, but she wondered if it would fade with time.

By ten in the morning on any other day, she would have had tea with Lady Bostwick. Even if she was still in London, though, Lady Bostwick would not have called on her today. Elizabeth and George were on their way to their estate in West Sussex.

"Welcome, Lily, Murphy," Hannah offered as her maid curtsied and Henry's valet bowed. "I hope you had a pleasant trip."

"Thank you, milady. I did. Your husband's coach was most comfortable," Lily lied as she made her way through the vestibule, noticing Hannah's simple coiffure. Braids of her pale blonde hair were wrapped atop her head, and where the leftover wisps weren't captured into the braids, they simply floated around her face. *Wasn't there a maid in the household who could have seen to Lady Hannah's hair?*

Murphy took his leave of them, hurrying off to his master's suite. Mrs. Batey introduced herself and took Lily in hand, telling Hannah she would see to giving the servant a tour and show her to her quarters. Footmen brought in a trunk, setting it aside as they returned to the coach to unload another. Lily pulled a folded parchment from her reticule. "Would it be possible to have this posted? I wish to let my family know I am no longer working in London," she explained when she noticed the housekeeper's raised eyebrow. Another trunk appeared in the vestibule, forcing the women to step into the hall to make room.

"We'll see to it, of course," Hannah said as she took the parchment and placed it with her own letters. In all the excitement of the quick wedding and making the trip to Oxfordshire, she had been unable to send announcements of her marriage from London. She had spent her morning writing correspondence to several friends. In addition, letters to Elizabeth and Charlotte as well as her father were piled on a salver.

Hannah added Lily's missive, noting the address on the outside. *Thomas Babcock, Witney.* Glancing over at her maid's back, Hannah thought of the girl's name. *Lily Parker. Odd,* Hannah thought, wondering if Lily's mother had remarried.

"Lady Gisborn," Parkerhouse spoke from the parlor door. "Tea is served."

Hannah turned her attention to the butler. "Thank you, Parkerhouse," she replied, wondering if tea time was at four o'clock every day or if the servants simply started the practice with her arrival. She made her way to the parlor and took a seat, realizing it was her first opportunity to sit since she'd had luncheon with Henry at one.

Her husband—the thought made her smile to herself—had come in from what she had thought was a ride for pleasure. But he had been out in the fields, overseeing a crew of laborers digging the trench for an irrigation ditch and then down to the village to see his son's tutor, and by default, his son, and out to the stables to see the new colt that had been born while he was in London. Upon his arrival at the house, he had given his hat and greatcoat to Parkerhouse and joined her in the small dining room.

Their first moment alone had been a bit awkward. Should she curtsy and hold out her hand, or lift her cheek in anticipation of a peck, or tilt up her head and, if there weren't any servants about, kiss him? She had seen married couples together at dinner parties, but they arrived on each other's arms at the same time. Whatever did they do when one arrived while the other was already present?

Apparently, Henry wasn't familiar with the protocol, either. He entered the room, the scent of sandalwood and *man* emanating from him as he made his way to the table. And then, upon seeing her, he paused. "Good afternoon, milady," he said as he gave her a formal bow.

Hannah stood up and curtsied, saying her own, "Good afternoon, Gisborn." Moving to meet him where he stood, Hannah paused mid-step; Henry had already begun walking toward her. The hand she was going to extend for him to kiss seemed to take on a life of its own as it lifted to his cheek. She angled her head up intending to kiss him—there were no servants in the room—but he misinterpreted her move and simply lay his own hand over hers.

"Has it already begun to bruise?" he asked in a quiet voice, a hissing sound coming from between his teeth.

Bruise? His cheek? Hannah's eyes widened in alarm. "What happened?"

Henry pulled her hand away from his face and kissed the back of it, his lips sending a shiver through her bare fingers.

She could hardly believe a kiss could incite such sensations in her skin!

His cheek was red, although no bruising was evident. "It's nothing, milady. A bit of horseplay with my son is all," he added when her look of alarm remained on her face.

"I do hope the horse survived," she replied with a hint of humor. "Perhaps a cold compress?" she suggested, about to ring the bell next to her place setting.

Henry's hand settled over hers before she could lift the bell. "Perhaps the kiss of a fairy tale princess instead?" he suggested, a teasing light in his eyes.

Hannah grinned, her dimple appearing as she lifted her lips to his cheek and, ever so gently, kissed him. Moving his head, Henry was able to capture her lips and finish the kiss against his mouth. With the sound of footsteps just outside the servant's door, the two were suddenly a foot apart, Hannah's face pinking up and Henry staring at her with a look of amusement. Sheepishly, the two took their seats at either end of the table.

When the footman had departed, having filled their wine glasses and left plates of bread and cheese and bowls of savory stew, Henry waved at her from his end of the table. "I do believe we need a shorter table, milady," he pretended to shout.

Giggling at his antics, Hannah lifted her wine glass. "And if I'm to call you Gisborn, you should call me Hannah," she countered.

Henry sobered. "Hannah," he repeated, as if saying the name for the first time in his life. "I shall call you Hannah, but only when we are alone," he stated finally. He took a drink and set his glass down. "May I ask, did our servants arrive from London yet?"

Shaking her head, Hannah said, "Not yet. But my lady's maid, Lily, is very glad to be coming back to Oxfordshire."

His brow arching at the comment, Henry stared at his

wife. "Lily? Lily Parker?" he asked. He remembered thinking the lady's maid he had seen at Devonville House looked familiar.

"She's your abigail?"

Hannah smiled. "Yes. You must have known of her before she went to London?" she asked, hoping Lily had left with a good character. She actually hadn't hired the girl; Lily was sent from an agency shortly after Hannah's mother died.

"Just knew of her, I suppose," Henry replied carefully. "Her parents are in service to my new estate manager, Frank Coley," he explained. Hiring the man to replace Grainger had been his second order of business following his return to the earldom; the first had been to order the building of two greenhouses. His construction foreman was seeing to their plans and building details and promised one finished structure, ready for covering in glass or oilcloth, in two weeks.

"What became of your old manager?" Hannah asked, deciding she rather liked the stew Mrs. Chambers had made.

Henry seemed reluctant to tell her anything about Edward Grainger, but he finally angled his head to one side. "I fired him." At Hannah's look of surprise, he added, "He could not ride a horse, and he did not share my desire to keep the tenant cottages in good repair."

Hannah's look of surprise had him wondering what he had said to evoke such a reaction. "How could a man claim to be an estate manager and not know how to ride a horse?" she asked rhetorically, obviously sharing his opinion on the matter.

"Exactly!" he agreed, holding up his wine glass in a salute. "By the way, what we might be having for dinner this evening?"

Surprised by the question, Hannah had to think a moment to recall the list of courses that would be featured at that evening's dinner. She had gone to the kitchens, Harold following on her heels, intending to ask about creating menus for the next week's meals. As the new countess, she knew she would be expected to complete certain duties, the menus for dinners being one of them. Mrs. Batey was not in the kitchens, but the cook, Mrs. Chambers was. Hannah nodded her head and introduced herself, but the cook took no notice of Hannah.

Her attention was on Harold, whose nose was sniffing everything he could get near, including the cook.

The woman let out a yell worthy of a Welsh milkmaid, the sound so startling to Harold, he froze in place and barked once. "Out! Out with ya', ya' big beastie!" Mrs. Chambers shouted, her meat cleaver pointing to the nearest exit. Harold backed up and then high-tailed it to the doorway that led to back door of the house, sounding one lone 'woof ' as his body plowed through it and toward the stables.

Hannah stood rooted to the floor, one hand at her chest as she regarded the large, rosy-cheeked woman who still wielded the meat cleaver as if Hannah might be her next target. "Pardon me," Hannah managed to get out as she backed up against the wall. "Could you tell me where I might find Mrs. Batey?"

The cook turned her attention on Hannah, her eyes widening in surprise. The woman blinked, as if she thought Hannah was merely an apparition. Then she turned back to her stove and slowly looked over her shoulder. "Oh, my," she murmured. "You are real, aren't ya'?"

Her eyes darting to the right and left, wondering at first if the cook was referring to her, Hannah took a deep breath and nodded. "I am Lady Gisborn," she introduced herself. "And you are ..?"

The cook's mouth dropped open, a look of profound astonishment on her face. "So fired," she whispered, her entire body seeming to sag with her words. "Oh, milady, please forgive my impertinence." Her eyes drifted to the door. "That was *your* dog, wasn't it?" she asked rhetorically. A whimpering sound, quite at odds with her size, emanated from her.

"Yes," Hannah nodded hesitantly, trying to decide if she should put on airs at the treatment of her dog, or give the cook her due. But the kitchen *was* the cook's domain. "His name is Harold. Harold MacDuff," Hannah stated softly, deciding it was better to be nice. The woman would be cooking her meals, after all. "He is a very good kitchen dog. He'll eat anything. And he's a good mouser," she claimed, realizing too late she needn't make excuses for her dog.

The cook looked at the door again before dipping her head. "I never saw a dog that large, milady. Well, exceptin' for Mr. Cavenaugh's Maggie, but even *she's* not as big as that... that..." She pointed toward the door.

"Alpenmastiff," Hannah finished for her. "A very noble dog." She took a deep breath. "I came... what may I call you?" she asked, realizing just then the cook hadn't yet said her name.

Sighing loudly, the woman hung her head. "Mrs. Chambers," she said quietly, apparently still thinking she was about to be sacked.

"I came, Mrs. Chambers, because I believe I need to do menus for this week's dinners."

The large woman seemed surprised by the comment. "But Mrs. Batey does the menus, milady," she said as she set the meat cleaver on the large wood block in the center of the kitchen. She backed away as if trying to distance herself from a loaded gun.

Hannah wondered if the woman was challenging her. Without a lady of the house, the housekeeper would be responsible for creating menus. "Very good, then," she said. "Might I ask what we're having for dinner this evening? I should like to know as I expect the earl will ask me."

Holding up her hand as if she understood, the cook stood very still and listed that night's dinner. "Onion soup, lobster patties, aspic, pot roast, potatoes, carrots, turnips, rolls, apple tarts and walnuts with coffee."

Hannah blinked, thinking the combination seemed a bit off, but she didn't offer her opinion. Perhaps the meal was her husband's favorite. Perhaps the lobster patties would be better than those served at *ton* balls. "Thank you, Mrs. Chambers," she said with a nod. "Carry on."

The cook's eyes widened. "You mean," she paused, her eyes darting to the left and right. "I'm not to pack up and leave?"

Glancing back at Mrs. Chambers, Hannah shook her head. "No, of course not, Mrs. Chambers. Good day," she said as she stepped out the same door Harold had disappeared through moments before.

So, when Henry asked Hannah if she knew what they were having for dinner that night, Hannah sat up and proudly recited that night's menu. "Onion soup, lobster patties, aspic, pot roast, potatoes, carrots, turnips, dinner rolls, apple tarts and walnuts with coffee."

Henry's eyes widened at her list. From her recitation, she had obviously memorized it, but he knew she wouldn't have been the one to combine such disparate dishes together in a single meal. "Oh! My favorite," he said, a look of appreciation appearing on his face.

Hannah couldn't hide the surprise she felt at hearing his words. "My lord?" she countered, stunned he would think the meal worthy of being his favorite.

But a footman came from the kitchen and placed a note next to Henry's plate. She watched as Henry lifted and read the missive, his face taking on a look of worry.

"Is anything wrong?" Hannah asked, seeing his brows furrow.

Henry glanced up. "One of the men digging the east trench has been injured. The foremen has taken a horse to fetch the physician from Bampton. I should get back there," he said as he stood up. "Please forgive me, my lady. I will see you..." He paused to consider just when he would next see his wife. "At dinner," he decided as he gave her a bow and left through the door to the kitchen.

Hannah watched as her husband departed, feeling as if the air had left with him. It was at that moment that Hannah realized Henry Forster was truly a unique member of the *ton*.

The man would probably never claim his seat in Parliament — he would always be too busy working his estate. And men who were busy with their lands had less time for leisure pursuits, like drinking and gambling and whor...

The last word of that thought was quickly squelched before she could think it. The only woman her husband would bed besides her was Sarah.

A small smile of appreciation lit Hannah's face. *I'm married to a working gentleman!*

CHAPTER 12

HANNAH MEETS SARAH
AND NATHAN

Hannah walked with purpose but was still uncertain about her intent. She only wanted to meet Sarah. She wanted to put a face with a name, and, should the mistress seem the least bit, well, likable, she thought to appear as approachable as possible and offer her friendship. Although she was a countess and Sarah was apparently a low born commoner, Hannah wished desperately for them to be friends. Sarah was the mother of Henry's son Nathan, and they had Henry in common, after all.

She slowed her step to regard the dowager house on the edge of the Gisborn property. If she continued past the flagstone path that led to the front door, she would be on the main road to the earldom's village, its collection of cottages and businesses clustered almost another half-mile down the lane.

The stone house, which featured well-maintained shutters on all its windows and a newly painted front door, was smaller than Hannah would have imagined given Henry's mistress and son lived there. She regarded the cut stones that made up the exterior walls. They had no doubt been dug up from the nearby fields when they had been converted to farms. There was a stately elegance to their arrangement, although their shades of gray made for a somber backdrop.

The darker gray shutters did little to liven the look, but the front door's cheerful yellow paint and a cluster of brightly colored flowers near the single front step proved welcoming. For a cottage that was to have housed the earl's mother, it was passable. At some point in the future, that earl's mother would be her, Hannah realized with some surprise.

Walking up the flagstone path to the door, Hannah took a deep breath and knocked three times. She carried two baskets of fresh-baked scones and loaves of bread from Gisborn Hall's kitchen, the cook having been goaded into the show of hospitality by Mrs. Batey the day before. Apparently, the cook had little regard for Sarah, although she seemed to accept Nathan without question. Hannah wondered at the disparity. Sarah had borne Henry a son nearly ten years before; why would Mrs. Chambers begrudge the woman some baked goods? She set one of the baskets down on the stoop, intending the contents to go to some elderly ladies she would visit in the village after she concluded her call on Sarah.

The door opened slowly as a woman, who looked to be about thirty, peered around the opened edge. "Yes?" she let out, obviously apprehensive at the sight of the pink-clad female who stood at her door with a covered basket and a tentative grin on her face. Hannah nodded, thinking the butler must have the day off. "Lady Hannah... *Gisborn* to see Miss Inglenook," she quickly corrected herself, not having much practice in using her new name. She wondered if the woman at the door was a maid or the housekeeper. The house didn't seem large enough to accommodate more than a few people. She held out her calling card, realizing too late she hadn't had new ones printed with her correct name and title. "I am Hannah... Forster," she offered, hoping her face wasn't displaying her nervousness.

Sarah Inglenook stared at the young woman who stood on her doorstep. *This is Henry's wife.* So, the rumors were true. That Henry had returned from his trip to London with a countess on his arm. Well, the woman was quite lovely. Fair in coloring, with blonde hair that fairy tales described as flaxen.

Young and glowing and quite the most ridiculous thing she had seen in the way of a woman in some time.

A rather large dog had seated itself just below the front step. Large brown eyes stared at her as if she might do harm to the young woman, but its overall expression was one of comical boredom. Sarah wondered for only a second if she should be fearful of the Alpenmastiff, but quickly decided the beastie meant no harm. "Sarah Inglenook," she finally replied, her oval face splitting into a grin as she curtsied. Laugh lines crinkled near the corners of her eyes, and her green eyes seem to be lit from within.

"Oh!" her visitor replied, stunned that the woman before her wasn't a servant. Sarah was dressed in a serviceable muslin day gown, her golden brown hair wound into a simple knot on the back of her head. Although she was of an age to wear a mobcap, she chose instead to leave her head uncovered when she was indoors.

Sarah stepped back to allow the countess into her home. The woman seemed friendly enough, but if she should find out about her and Henry—or had Henry told the woman about her? And about the son they shared? She would have to guard her every word until she learned how much the young lady knew.

"You have a beautiful home," Hannah said as she moved into the front room. Obviously set up as a parlor, the furnishings and draperies seemed new, as if the house had undergone a recent remodel. If she noticed Sarah's lack of a curtsy, she did not show it in her expression nor in her bearing. "Have you lived here long?"

Sarah regarded the countess for several seconds before taking a deep breath. "Almost two years," she finally got out. "Oh, where are my manners? Please, have a seat, won't you?" Again, she allowed a tentative smile, not sure if Henry or any of his servants might have told the new countess about her.

They must have, though, for why else would Henry's new wife pay me a call?

Hannah's eyes widened. "You mean, you've never lived at Gisborn Hall?" she asked, surprised that Henry wouldn't have insisted on having his son and his lover living with him.

Her eyes widening, Sarah swallowed. "No, of course not," she replied, stunned at the comment. As she wrung her hands together at her waist, Sarah regarded Hannah carefully. *She knows.* "I would not expect the earl to provide hospitality at his house," she explained, waving Hannah to a settee in the middle of the room. "Would you like tea?" she asked, nervous. She found herself hoping Hannah would decline the invitation and take her leave of the cottage. Then she could find Henry and determine what he had told his new countess.

"That would be lovely," Hannah said with a smile. "I hoped we might have the opportunity to get to know one another," she said brightly. "I realize most women would probably cringe at the thought of meeting their husband's mistress, but I have to admit, I have been looking forward to making your acquaintance ever since Henry told me about you."

Already on her way to the kitchen, Sarah spun around, her mouth open in surprise at Hannah's comment. *Mistress?* She expected to find the woman glaring at her, expected her eyes to be daggers, her manner to suggest Sarah would be cast out of the dowager house at first light. But her visitor appeared quite sedate as she lowered her covered basket to the floor and took a seat. "He is quite in love with you," Hannah added, wondering why her hostess would stare at her so. "Of course, you must already know that," she added with a knowing grin and a wave of her hand.

Sarah stared back, the words still making their way into her addled brain. Had the countess just claimed Henry *loved* her? And had she really said it as if it made her *happy?* "I wasn't aware he felt such affection for me, my lady," she countered, having decided long ago that his repeated requests for her hand in marriage were not claims of love but were instead desperate attempts to secure her as a wife so he wouldn't have to search for one during a Season in London.

She wondered at what kind of event he had found the chit that was taking a seat in her parlor. A ball, perhaps? Or a rout? *Not a rout,* she decided. Henry wouldn't even attend such an affair, and she rather doubted the delicate looking thing before her would, either. She pointed toward the kitchen. "I'll just be a moment," she added as she disappeared into the other room.

Sarah's heart beat in a staccato she was sure was visible through her plain gown. *Henry's wife was in her parlor!* Henry's beautiful embodiment of a fairy tale princess wife was sitting on her settee! *What is she doing here?* Sarah calmed herself with a slow inhalation of breath as she set up the tea service she used when Henry called on her. Thank goodness she kept it at the ready—she did not want the countess left alone in her parlor for longer than was necessary, or the woman might discover the hole in the upholstery of the wing back chair where Nathan had stabbed a small knife, or the place in the Aubusson carpet where his muddied shoe had left a stain the year before. "How do you take your tea, my lady?" she asked when she returned to the parlor with the tea service. She placed it on the low table in front of the settee and took the chair opposite from Hannah.

"Oh, you must call me Hannah," her visitor insisted as she leaned forward. "I do not want there to be any formality between us," Hannah added. She lifted the basket. "I had Cook make some scones and bread. I daresay she makes the very best scones," she added as she held out the basket toward her hostess.

Sarah took the proffered basket, the expression on her face one of surprise. "Thank you, my lady," she said in awe, realizing from the weight that the basket probably held enough baked goods to see her and Nathan through a week or more. Probably much more.

"Hannah," her visitor said by way of correcting her. "May

I call you Sarah?" she asked then, her head tilted in such a way as to suggest she really hoped they could be friends.

Sarah swallowed, surprised at Hannah's friendly nature but suspicious of the gift she bore.

Were the baked goods poisoned? Mrs. Chambers had never much cared for her. If the cook knew the items in the basket were for her, she might have made them with too much salt. Or poisoned them.

"I told Mrs. Chambers I was going to make some calls in the village," Hannah offered, once she realized Sarah wasn't going to answer her question. "Mrs. Batey made a list of several households that require a bit of charity, so I will visit those later—perhaps a couple of them today." She didn't add that there was another basket of bread out on the stoop, covered with a cloth, and under Harold's protection. She hoped Harold hadn't suddenly developed a taste for bread.

"Oh, of course," Sarah replied, realizing the bread and scones were probably just fine. She took a deep breath. "So, the earl told you about me?" she ventured, still expecting a fit of jealous rage to replace the rather calm façade the countess was displaying.

Hannah dipped her head. "He did, indeed. The very first day he called on me, in fact," she said as she remembered their ride in Hyde Park.

Sarah poured a cup of tea as she struggled to keep her face impassive. "Milk? Sugar?" she asked, glancing over the tea tray to be sure she had all the pieces in the proper place.

"Yes to both," Hannah replied with a smile. "I really wish you would consider moving into Gisborn Hall," she said with a sigh, noting there were no servants present. "There are plenty of bedchambers, and although there doesn't seem to be much in the way of a household staff, I'm sure we can find someone to see to your needs. And to Nathan," she added, wondering if Sarah would even consider the arrangement given she had probably lived in the dowager house since Henry inherited the earldom. "Is he here? I would so like to meet him."

Pouring a cup of tea for herself, Sarah shook her head. "I quite like having my own household," she replied gently, "Especially since Nathan will never inherit Gisborn's property." This last was said with a hint of regret, as if she had just then realized that by not marrying Henry Forster, she had relegated the boy to life as a bastard. "Nathan is with his tutor now. In the village," she explained, in answer to Hannah's other query. "Gisborn is quite adamant that he be ready for Abingdon School. He'll start there in the fall. It's close enough that Nathan can come home for Sundays, but he'll board during the school days. It's a good thing it's still another five months away. I know it will be harder on me than on him when he leaves," she said, stopping when she realized she was prattling. Dipping her head, she added a lump of sugar to her tea and stirred it quietly.

Hannah sipped her own tea. "I think it's so romantic that you and Gisborn have known one another since childhood and would remain a devoted couple even now," she commented, wondering why Sarah would seem so nervous in her own home. *Shouldn't I be the nervous one?*

Nearly spilling the cup of tea she held, Sarah stared at Hannah. "Romantic?" she repeated, not intending to sound surprised by the word. But never in the years Henry Forster had insisted on providing protection for her and her son could Sarah claim *romance* was involved. "I think perhaps I need to..." She stopped, not sure what to say. The countess had obviously jumped to conclusions about Sarah's relationship with Henry, but those conclusions must have been based on what Henry had told Hannah.

Just how had the earl described his relationship with her?

"Oh, dear." Sarah realized she had better set the countess straight on a few details while she had her alone.

Hannah waited for a moment while Sarah seemed to have a discussion with herself. She wondered then if her visit was a mistake. She was beginning to think she should have allowed Henry to make the introductions, to help smooth things over between the two women. But since she felt no jealousy, nor any animosity toward the mistress, Hannah thought it only proper *she* make the first move. "I have always believed that a man only ever loves his mistress, and that he only marries so that he might have a mother for his children," she stated, the mantra something she was quite sure was true. She had spoken the words often enough, sometimes to nods of agreement while other times to slightly shocked ladies who found the word 'mistress' to be an especially foul word.

Sarah stared at her as if she were one of those who found the word 'mistress' especially foul. *Oh, dear. She hasn't considered herself in that light*, Hannah realized as she regarded the mother of Henry's son.

"Well, I can tell you have spent a good deal of your life in London," Sarah said finally, a smile appearing along with a blush. She had heard the ladies of the *ton* could be quite glib about the men in their lives, but to hear one announce her total and complete acceptance of a mistress in her husband's life left her stunned in an amused sort of way. "I... I don't know what to say," she finally admitted. "Except that..." She leaned forward, her back quite rigid. "I have no intention of ever living under the same roof as Henry Forster. I have never considered myself his *mistress*. Nor do I expect to do so now that Henry has married," she announced with a firm shake of her head. She was still smiling, although it was more out of nervousness than of joy at having learned that Henry had finally married.

Hannah regarded her hostess, her face taking on the pink blush that showed her embarrassment. She struggled for a better word to use. "Paramour, perhaps?" she ventured carefully.

Sarah's eyes widened, but her shoulders sunk. Taking a sip of tea, she fought the tears that threatened in the corners of her eyes. "Perhaps," she agreed, holding onto her teacup as if her very life depended on it. "But I must inform you, Lady Gisborn—"

"Hannah, please," her guest insisted as she straightened.

Could a woman look any more lovely than the fairy princess who was sitting across from her? Her pale blonde hair had been braided and wound into an elaborate coronet on top of her head, and tendrils of hair curled into ringlets next to her ears and down the back of her neck. The pelisse she wore... *oh, good God, I should have asked her if she wanted to remove it*, Sarah realized. The parlor was warm enough. But she'd had no intention of welcoming the countess into her home. She expected whoever married Henry would despise her and require Henry keep hidden his bastard son. "But, you're a *countess*," Sarah spoke, saying the words as if the title prevented them from being friends.

Hannah arched an eyebrow. "And you could have been," she countered with a shrug of one shoulder. "So we're even."

Sarah blinked once, twice. And then she settled back into her chair, stunned at Hannah's simple rejoinder. Of course, Lady Gisborn was correct. If she had ever simply accepted Henry's suit, she could be Lady Gisborn. She allowed a tentative smile.

But then she would have to be *married* to Henry Forster. The smile disappeared.

If she were married to Henry Forster, she would have to tolerate his heavy-handed manner, his humorless demeanor, his controlling personality. The man was so good in so many ways, but she had no desire to *live* with him. And lately, she had no desire to share his bed, either. He was handsome. Too handsome. She'd had difficulty spurning his occasional desire to bed her, finally succumbing to his soft words and gentle touches. And that was the problem. Henry knew exactly where to touch her, exactly what to do to get her to agree to his wishes. But she had been quite insistent on just how he would take his pleasure, making sure he did so as quickly as possible so that he might be out of her bed and on his way back to Gisborn Hall. She never allowed him to spend the night in her bedchamber. And for those occasions when Henry insisted she and Nathan spend the night in Gisborn Hall, she spent them in his bed. She was quick to take her leave very early the following morning, not wishing to stay for a cup of chocolate, much less breakfast.

Now that Henry was finally married, and to a beautiful woman, Sarah had hope for her own future. Now, another man could ask for her hand, a man who would offer protection and a different home several miles away. He would give her the respectability she so craved. And perhaps children. She had always wanted more children.

She was nearly thirty. Being Henry Forster's woman, or *mistress*, as the countess had just described her, was no longer acceptable. She longed for a life as a wife and mother to legitimate children. "I have looked forward to Henry taking a wife for several years, Hannah. You cannot know how happy it makes me to know he has finally done so. Although you might accept his taking a mistress, it will no longer be me. If the earl comes expecting to bed me, I will turn him away and encourage him to honor his marriage vows," Sarah said quite firmly, her shoulders squaring as she sat up straighter.

Hannah stared at Sarah in surprise. "But, Henry *loves* you," she said again, her tone plaintive, the words so simple they sounded hollow. "Don't you love him?"

Sarah could not have predicted such a statement coming from Hannah. Nor could she have expected such a blunt question. She gave her head a little shake. "I am merely the mother of his son. He loves me for that. Nothing more," she tried to reason, her head shaking from side to side. "Please, Hannah." The name seemed hard for her to say. "Do not think of me as his mistress. Do not think of me as his paramour or his lover. If you must think of me at all, then do so only as the mother of Nathan," she pleaded. "And insist he bed you exclusively for as long as possible."

Hannah stared at Sarah for several moments, surprised by the woman's advice and left wondering how it was Henry could think this woman loved him.

Perhaps he didn't think it, though. He had never said anything about Sarah returning the affection he felt for her.

Could he possibly know she didn't share his feelings? That their relationship wasn't as mutual as he implied?

Hannah finally nodded. "He said he would visit me every night until I am with child," Hannah admitted in a voice barely above a whisper, finding the words easy to say to Sarah. "So, I suppose that will be at least two or three weeks, perhaps more," she reasoned, thinking of when her monthly courses were due in the event she did not conceive before then.

Sarah nodded slowly, her gaze dropping to her teacup. "That should be enough time," she murmured, not elaborating on what she meant by the comment. "Would you like more tea?" she asked then, realizing her own cup was empty.

Hannah gave her a wan smile. "No, thank you. I need to make some more calls," she spoke softly. "I have more bread to deliver."

"Mrs. Canker, perhaps?" Sarah suggested, her head angling to one side.

Hannah nodded. "Yes. And Mrs. Billingsly, too," she added, hoping she had the name right.

Sarah returned the nod. "They are both quite old and a bit infirm, but they are also very sharp," she said as she motioned to her forehead. "And Mrs. Canker will be quite pointed in her remarks, so do not take offense."

Smiling at Sarah's comments, Hannah leaned forward. "Thank you for speaking with me. I never thought it would be awkward for you to meet me, and of course it was. But I want us to be friends. Please accept my apologies," she said, taking Sarah's hand in hers.

The older woman glanced down at Hannah's hand covering hers, her face brightening with a smile. "Apology accepted, of course. Come for tea whenever you wish. And I wish you happy. I really do," she said, a faraway look crossing her face.

As Hannah retrieved her basket of bread from next to the front steps, she bid Sarah farewell. With Harold on her heels, she made her way to the other houses Mrs. Batey had described earlier that day.

Mrs. Canker was as Sarah described, causing Hannah to blush at least twice with her gentle ribbing and ribald comments. Mrs. Billingsly, a much quieter woman, made a few complaints about aching joints and voiced her surprise at receiving scones and bread from a countess. "'Bout time we had one here," the frail woman said, waving a crooked finger in Hannah's direction. "'Enry needs an heir."

Hannah felt her face redden for at least the third time that day. "And I desperately want a child," she countered with an embarrassed grin. "A boy first, I hope."

"Then it will be bottoms up for you, my lady," Mrs. Billingsly said with a nod. "On your elbows and knees if you want a boy and on your back if you want a girl." Her chin came up a fraction, as if to drive home her point. If she thought the instruction the least bit embarrassing, she did not show it in her expression or her demeanor.

Hannah blinked at the old woman. "Oh," she replied, not sure how else to respond to such a comment. *Was the old woman suggesting ..?* Of course, she was. Elizabeth had spoken of such positions. Many of them, in fact. "Well," Hannah said as she glanced around the sparse cottage and decided Mrs. Billingsly was doing fine on her own. "I really must be taking my leave. Do take care," she murmured as she made her way to the door and bade Mrs. Billingsly a good day.

While she walked, she spent the time thinking of Sarah's words and wondering at the odd impression she had of the mistress—or *not* mistress.

Hannah wondered if there was more to why Sarah didn't live at Gisborn Hall. As the mother of the earl's son, she and the boy should have been granted rooms, at least in the guest wing. Sarah had mentioned wanting to run her own household, but at what cost? She apparently had no servants, which meant she was spending a good deal of her days doing housework, laundry and cooking.

The woman seemed level-headed, seemed to run an efficient household, what little of it there was, and seemed to love her son over all else. So why wouldn't she consider Hannah's invitation? Sarah hadn't said Henry forbid it. In fact, she thought from some of the comments Henry had made that perhaps the mother of his child was a bit stubborn when it came to her independence, as if agreeing to live in Gisborn Hall would somehow rob her of that independence. And thinking about the way Henry spoke of Sarah and their son, it wouldn't make sense that he would begrudge them the comfort of the larger house and the staff of servants (although Hannah was beginning to think a few more might be in order if they ever hosted guests).

Sarah Inglenook did not wish to be Henry's lover. Or mistress. Nor did she love him—at least, not in the way Hannah would expect the mother of his child to feel toward a man who so obviously loved her.

Hannah thought of Mrs. Batey. The housekeeper had been at Gisborn Hall since before Henry took up residence there. Everyone knew servants were the best source of gossip and the history of a household. She would simply ask her. Mrs. Batey was sure to know why Sarah turned down her invitation.

The sound of running feet and Harold's gentle 'woof ' brought her out of her reverie. She turned to see a boy running in their direction, a huge grin on his face. Hannah stopped and called Harold to her side, not wanting the boy to be frightened of the large dog.

"Hullo!" the boy called out. He was nicely dressed considering his apparent age, with a scarlet coat, white linen shirt, cuffed breeches, clean stockings, and serviceable shoes. A hat was perched on his head, although it was too short to be considered a top hat. "Your dog is *huge*, miss," he said as he came to stand before her. Then he bowed, as if he suddenly remembered he was supposed to do it before he made a comment about the dog. Harold took the opportunity to wag his tail in greeting before obediently sitting next to Hannah.

Hannah curtsied, realizing from the boy's dark hair, deep blue eyes, and stern facial features that he had to be Henry's son. The resemblance was uncanny, as if she were seeing a younger version of her husband. "I am Hannah Forster, Lady Gisborn," she said as she held out her right hand, intending to the shake the lad's hand.

The deep blue eyes widened as the boy regarded her. He stepped forward, took her gloved hand, and quickly kissed the back of it, letting go his hold as if her hand was on fire. "Nathan Forster, milady," he managed to get out, his eyes still wide. "Pleased to make your acquaintance."

Allowing a wide smile, Hannah nodded. "And yours." She indicated Harold with a wave of her hand. "And this is Harold MacDuff. He's an Alpenmastiff," she said proudly.

As he had been trained to do, Harold dutifully held up a paw. Nathan glanced from the dog up to Hannah, as if he wasn't sure what to do. "You can shake his paw if you'd like," she said with a hint of encouragement. *Goodness, did the boy wonder if he was supposed to kiss the back of Harold's paw?*

A grin appearing on Nathan's face, he knelt down and shook Harold's paw. "Good boy!" he said before rising to his feet. Seeing the bit of dirt from the road on his knee, he leaned over and brushed it off with a few swipes. "He looks like Maggie, only a whole lot... huger," he commented. His eyebrow angled, not unlike his father's did when he was considering a problem, and amended his comment. "Larger. He is *larger* than Maggie," he said with firm nod.

Hannah wondered about Maggie, remembering the cook's mention of a Maggie, but at the moment, she was more interested in the boy. "Have you just come from your tutor's house?" she asked, turning to walk south. The dower house wasn't much farther up the road; the walk with Nathan would allow her to get to know him.

The boy sauntered along side, giving her a suspicious look. "How did you know?" he asked.

Shrugging, Hannah thought to say something flippant, but thought better of it. "I had tea with your mother earlier this afternoon," she explained. "I asked to meet you, but she said you were at your tutor's house. I hope you don't have to walk too far for your lessons."

Nathan continued to glance up at her, his facial expression giving away the turmoil that was going on in his brain. "Not too far," he replied in an off-hand manner. "Are you *married* to my father?" he finally managed to ask. His brow furrowed into a familiar shape. Henry's looked just like it when he puzzled over some problem.

"I am," Hannah replied with a nod, giving the lad a sideways glance, wondering if he would be pleased or not. Her comment was met with silence from the boy. He continued to trudge along at her side, his gaze directed straight ahead. Hannah couldn't help but notice his manner becoming more sullen, more sad, as if her simple acknowledgment had taken away any joy the boy had felt at having met her and Harold. "I do hope we can be friends," she offered in her lightest tone. "I would hate for you to think of me as a mean ol' stepmother."

The lad seemed to stumble at this last statement. "Stepmother?" he repeated. "You're my stepmother?" His voice was barely a whisper, but Hannah could tell from the question in his voice that he wasn't taking the news well.

Trying for lightness, she nodded. "Your father is quite proud of you. He told me all about you the very first time he took me for a ride in Hyde Park." She didn't add that it was the *only* time he had taken her for a ride in the park.

"He did?" Nathan repeated, his face still looking as if he had lost his best friend. "Isn't Hyde Park in London?" he asked. "Are you from London?"

Nodding, Hannah said, "Yes, it is, and yes, I am. Your father and I met and married when he came to London to acquire Ellsworth Park." She hoped it didn't sound as if they had only known each other a few days before they married.

The boy glanced up at her, still suspicious. "Did he

acquire Ellsworth Park?" he asked, trying to be sure he used the same word as Hannah even though he didn't seem to know quite what it meant.

"He did. He'll be adding it to his farmland just as soon as the irrigation ditches are ready." She paused in mid-step, realizing they had come up to the walkway leading to the front door of the dower house. "I must be making my way back to Gisborn Hall, Master Forster. It's been a pleasure," she said.

She leaned down and took his hand in hers, giving it a firm shake.

Startled, Nathan nodded. "Yes, ma'am," he answered. "I mean, my lady," he corrected himself. "Bye, Harold." And then he was running along the flagstones to his house, not looking back, even as he disappeared through the front door.

Hannah watched as her husband's son made his way to the dower house, wondering at the boy's strange reaction to her. Was he frightened of her? Was he worried for himself? Using the term 'stepmother' had certainly been the wrong word to use when describing herself. Perhaps Henry could help smooth things over with the lad. "Come, Harold. We're going to the kitchen," Hannah said with a sigh as she walked the lane to the estate grounds.

Hearing the word 'kitchen' had Harold's ears perking up. Hannah thought he picked up his laggard pace just a bit. *He's old*, she remembered, frowning as she watched him take the lead and head through the gate and up the cobbled path toward the house. Instead of heading to the front doors, Hannah instead walked around Gisborn Hall to the servants' entrance off the kitchen. Harold was waiting at the door, his tail wagging frantically.

Knocking a few times before she opened the door to peek in, Hannah allowed Harold to precede her and said, "Stay, Harold," before the beast had a chance to enter the main kitchen. After his initial meeting with the cook, Hannah didn't want Harold impaled by a meat cleaver.

"Hullo," she called out, ducking her head around the doorway from the hall into the kitchen.

"Lady Gisborn?" Mrs. Batey stood from the large trestle in the middle of the room, a quill in one hand as she gave a quick curtsy and regarded the countess with barely hidden surprise.

"How do, Mrs. Batey," she said with a nod. She glanced about until she caught sight of the cook's large arms lifting a stock pot onto the stove top. "How do, Mrs. Chambers."

The cook actually did a curtsy before saying, "Lady Gisborn." She went back to her stock pot, dumping a bowl of cut vegetables into what was apparently to be that evening's soup.

"I wondered if I might ask you something, Mrs. Batey," Hannah hedged. She turned to the cook. "Would it be permissible for Harold to join us?" she asked. "Perhaps you have some food scraps you need to get rid of. He'll eat anything," she added hopefully.

The cook exchanged a startled glance with the house-keeper, her reddened cheeks aflame, apparently embarrassed by the lady of the house being in her kitchen. "I just have some potato peelings at the moment, my lady," Mrs. Chambers offered, motioning to a prep table.

"That will be splendid. Harold," Hannah turned toward the door she had just come through. Harold, rather careful about entering a room he had been summarily shooed from only the day before, took two steps in and sat down, his attention on his mistress. "Mrs. Chambers says you may have the potato peelings." Hannah moved to the prep table, and pulling her glove from one hand, shoved the mess into a tin bowl, and took it over to where Harold sat. His tail wagged twice before he went to work devouring the mess. When Hannah turned around, Mrs. Chambers stood before her with a wet flannel.

"I didn't mean for her ladyship to do that," the cook stammered, holding the clean flannel in her direction.

"Oh, I have no problem touching potato peelings, Mrs. Chambers," Hannah said with a grin. "As the only girl in Devonville House, I spent a good deal of time in the kitchens with the servants," she said with a wave, hoping the older woman wouldn't find her as much of a bother as did the crotchety old cook her father had employed since before Hannah was born. She took the flannel from the cook and wiped her hands. "Thank you."

Mrs. Batey had returned to sitting at the trestle, her quill scratching a list on a long sheet of paper. She looked up when she realized Hannah was regarding her quietly. "You wished to ask me something, my lady?" she queried, her manner rather nervous.

Hannah nodded, noticing the cook had gone back to the stove. "I do not want to interrupt your work."

"Nonsense, my lady," Mrs. Batey replied. "I was just putting together the list for market for Mrs. Chambers. The best vendors will be selling tomorrow morning, you see, so we try to buy everything we need for the week."

Taking a seat opposite the housekeeper, Hannah smiled. "I'm sure I am supposed to be doing menus," she offered with an apologetic shrug. "Perhaps I could do them for next week in time for you to do your list?"

The housekeeper's eyes widened. "Of course, my lady." She could feel the cook's quick glance of surprise on her back. "His lordship is quite particular about some of his meals," she said carefully, wondering if she should turn down the countess' offer.

"Menu planning has been one of only two responsibili-ties I've held at my father's house since my mother died," Hannah countered calmly. "And the other one was acting as hostess to our visitors. I shall be sure to inquire as to the earl's likes and dislikes before I do any meal planning," she assured the housekeeper.

Mrs. Batey seemed so relieved, Hannah thought she might topple from the trestle seat. "Your help will be appreci-ated," the housekeeper said in a low tone, as if she were secretly confiding that Gisborn Hall lacked enough help. "Now, what was it you wished to ask?"

Hannah sighed. "It's about Miss Inglenook." A pan clattered over at the stove, the sound barely covering the gasp coming from the cook. Mrs. Batey's face, although trained to a level of impassiveness that suggested nothing could shock her, took on a look of shock. "Is there any reason that you know of," Hannah continued, wondering at their reactions, "Why it is she and Nathaniel don't live here in Gisborn Hall?" Even without looking toward the stove, Hannah knew Mrs. Chambers was regarding her with a look of surprise.

Mrs. Batey straightened and took a breath. "She lives in the dower house," she answered simply, as if Sarah could only live there.

"Yes. But, it seems to me that she and Nathaniel should live *here*." The housekeeper averted her eyes a moment, her face taking on a flush that Hannah realized was embarrassment. "Oh, Mrs. Batey, I am quite aware of Lord Gisborn's relationship with Sarah," Hannah assured the woman, causing the housekeeper's mouth to open, as if she had to breathe through it. "He loves her. He has since... I believe he said since they were in leading strings."

The cacophony that erupted from the stove forced Hannah to turn around. She found the cook staring at her in disbelief and several pot lids rolling about her work area.

"You must know, men only ever love their mistresses. Their only reason to marry is so that they have someone to give them children," Hannah stated, intending for both women to hear her comment. Her mantra, one she had repeated to all her friends and to her father on more than a few occasions, seemed to drop into a suddenly very quiet and tense room. Even Harold seemed to have stopped panting, although there was a hint of a whine. Hannah wondered if his eyes were rolling. He did that when he thought something was poppycock.

Mrs. Batey was shaking her head, as if she couldn't—or wouldn't—believe what the mistress of the house had just said. "My lady, I..." *don't know what to say*, was the housekeeper's first thought.

Had things gotten so bad in London that gentlemen no

longer married for love? Or at least affection? She had been in England long enough to know about some men and their propensity to employ whores and mistresses, but to have a lady of the *ton*, the daughter of a marquess, no less, announce that men only loved their mistresses and married merely to have legitimate children, well, this was quite unexpected. "I am quite sure Lord Gisborn did not merely marry you to have his children," she tried in a reasonable tone. Lady Gisborn was a beautiful girl. The man probably felt some affection for her. How could he not? She was as pleasant as could be, eternally happy and quite agreeable. There hadn't been a shrill demand, a thrown objet d'art, nor a raised voice since Lady Gisborn's arrival.

The same couldn't be said for Sarah Inglenook, however. It was as if Lord Gisborn's woman had decided to become as unreasonable as possible, almost as if Sarah no longer wanted Gisborn's protection nor his attentions.

And the poor girl wondered why Sarah Inglenook did not reside in Gisborn Hall?

"Oh, there was a dowry, of course," Hannah stated with a nod, as if that would be the only other reason Lord Gisborn would marry her. "Quite generous, if I'm to believe my father's comments on the topic." This last comment was made with a smirk, forcing the dimple to appear in Hannah's right cheek.

The comment did not illicit a response from the direction of the stove, and Mrs. Batey looked as if she could offer nothing more in response. Hannah straightened, realizing her forthright manner was unexpected. "I am a realist, Mrs. Batey. I know I sometimes look like I walked off the pages of a medieval fairy tale, but I am no milkmaid. Marrying Lord Gisborn was my best chance at finding happiness as a mother. He needs an heir. And a spare. And my other suitors only seemed to want my dowry to pay off gambling debts."

The air seemed to go out of Mrs. Batey as her shoulders slumped. Even the cook had turned her attention to the countess, one fisted hand planted firmly on her ample hip.

"So, I was wondering. Why is it Miss Inglenook and Nathaniel don't live here at Gisborn Hall?"

Before Mrs. Batey could even begin to respond, Mrs. Chambers stepped forward. "I'll tell you why," she announced, a rather grim look on her face.

"Mrs. Chambers!" the housekeeper tried to admonish her.

"She's too *independent*," the cook continued, as if she hadn't heard the housekeeper. "Always was. Why, she wouldn't even live in the dower house exceptin' as the old earl *required* her to as long as Nathan was living with her. The old earl adored that kid."

Hannah regarded the cook in surprise. "But, where would she live if she didn't have the dower house?"

The housekeeper leaned forward, keeping her voice very low. "His lordship would see to a house for her in the village, of course," she remarked. "They used to have one on the outskirts of Bampton after the boy was born."

"His lordship had to come back from Oxford every few days back then, to see to the girl," Mrs. Chambers added, wiping her hands on a towel. "But he still saw to his studies, even after the babe was born. Finished near the top of his class, he did."

Listening to the two women talk of Henry's earlier life brought a smile to Hannah's face. "He did right by her, at least," she offered, wondering why the cook would seem upset with Sarah's independent streak.

"And he would have married her, but the girl wouldn't have him. Thought he was too——"

"Mrs. Chambers!" The housekeeper gave the cook a quelling look. "I'm sure the countess is well aware of her husband's traits."

"Mark my words. Sarah Inglenook will be gone just as soon as the son is off to school," the cook added with a firm nod. "As I hear it, she's being courted by some cit in Bampton."

A loud gasp emanated from the housekeeper. "Mrs.

Chambers! That will be quite enough from you!" Mrs. Batey announced in a voice that actually sent the cook back to the stove.

Hannah remembered Sarah's odd comment implying two weeks would be *enough time*. Did she mean something other than what Hannah originally thought? That it would take her two weeks or more to get pregnant? Perhaps she meant that two weeks was enough time was something else. Enough time for her to make her own arrangements. Perhaps to become betrothed. *So Sarah must expect an offer for her hand from the cit in Bampton!* Sarah could be a married woman before Nathan left for Abingdon School.

That would leave Hannah with the earl to herself.

There was a moment when the thought brought a sense of calm to her, a feeling of satisfaction, as if having Henry Forster all to herself was what she truly wanted. Perhaps she did. Perhaps Henry would decide he preferred only one woman in his life. And if not, he could always take another as his mistress. Well, Hannah hadn't expected him to honor his marriage vows when she agreed to marry him. There was no reason to think that he would even if Sarah was married to another.

One thing was certain. Hannah would have to do every-thing in her power to see to it Henry spent his nights in her bed. It was the least she could do for Sarah until the woman was safely betrothed. Hannah thanked the servants for their insight and excused herself from the kitchen.

Making her way up the stairs to change for dinner, Harold following on her heels, Hannah thought of Eliza-beth's recommendations on how to keep a husband happy. She felt her face flush as she remembered some of Elizabeth's descriptions of things she had done in her marriage bed— even when round with child! Some of those acts she could not imagine herself doing, but some of them, well, she might have to employ a few if she wanted to keep Henry coming to her bed for another two or three weeks.

Once in her room, Hannah rang for Lily and made her

way to her dressing table. Lily would be able to fix her hair and help her into a suitable dinner gown. When the maid hadn't appeared after ten minutes, Hannah moved to ring the bell again. Her hand stopped, though, when, breathless, Lily hurried into the room. "I apologize, my lady," her maid managed to get out as she bobbed a curtsy. "I... I got lost," the girl said as her faced turned a bright red. "I still do not know my way around this house."

Hannah grinned and angled her head to one side. "It's quite all right, Lily. I just need to dress for dinner," she said as she stepped behind the screen. "I am thinking the gold velvet gown," she murmured, "And my hair is in dire need of a repair."

Lily dipped her head and hurried into the dressing room. *I should tell her*, she thought as she pulled the gown from a hook. *But if I do, I may never be able to leave Gisborn Hall.* She was all business when she emerged with the gown and a pair of slippers.

Holding her breath as if she thought someone might hear it, Lily crept down the hallway outside her room and made her way to the back door by the kitchen. She clutched her valise, the tapestry bag containing every stitch of clothing she owned along with a few mementos. If she could make it out the door and around Gisborn Hall without disturbing an animal, she would be able to reach the lane to the village and the road to Bampton just beyond it.

Thomas knew she was leaving her mistress to join him tonight. He would be waiting for her somewhere along the road past the village. He would have his gig and a horse. With luck, and the moonlight that shown down on the road, they would be well on their way to Gretna Green before the sky turned pink at dawn.

She was quite sure she had been silent as she closed the back door, putting down the valise so she could keep the door handle and bolt drawn back. Once she was sure the door was seated in its jamb, she reached down to pick up her valise. A shadow fell over her and she gasped.

"Where do you think you're going?" Billy whispered, his breaths showing up as white puffs in the air around them.

"Oh, good God, you scared me near to death!" Lily hissed back. Her heartbeats were already thundering in her ears. The shock of Billy O'Conlin being so close so suddenly had her breathless. "What are you *doing* out here?" she whispered, realizing the groom had to have already been outside.

Billy was about to admonish her for scaring *him*, but realized he would sound like a sissy if he did. "I was headin' to the kitchen for a bite," he replied, sounding every bit as indignant as he could. "Are you leaving?" he asked then, his voice softening. "Leaving the countess?"

He had been surprised when Lily Parker showed up in the earl's old carriage the day before yesterday. She was from a farm outside of Witney, her family in service to the landed gentry that lived in the main house there. When she had gone off to London to take a position in an aristocrat's home, Billy had thought she would never return to Oxfordshire. Others who had left for London, seeking employment or their fortune, never returned to Bampton-in-the-Bush.

Lily took a deep breath and let it out, her breath a white billow between them. "You cannot say anything to *anyone*," she whispered, resigned to having to admit her plan. "I have to meet Thomas near Bampton. We're going to marry in Scotland," she added, her bare hands pulled into fists against her coat. It was far colder than she expected; she had no winter gloves, and only a scarf to cover her head.

"You're gonna marry that prick?" he asked in disgust. "Lily, ya deserve better than him," he hissed. "*I* would be better for you than him," he said under his breath, his comment meant to challenge her assessment of Thomas Babcock. And, perhaps, make her believe he *would* be better than his former best friend.

"Billy O'Conlin!" Lily admonished him, trying to keep her voice to a hoarse whisper and nearly failing. "How dare you? Thomas has a good position in Bampton, and he's a year older than me."

"Which means he's, what? Eighteen?" he countered quickly. Had there been more than just moonlight to see by, Lily might have seen the hurt in Billy's eyes. He was seventeen. He had known her from their days helping with the harvest, always thought of Lily as someone he might court once they were of a certain age. And then Lily left for London and her position in Devonville House. Billy thought he would never see her again, and then, wonder of wonders, she had stepped out of the earl's ancient carriage looking ever so sophisticated, so confident in her crisp maid's uniform. And he had fallen head over ears in love with her.

"He's seventeen. He... he loves me." The words were spoken softly, as if she might be trying to convince herself as much as him of her suitor's conviction to her.

The groom shrugged, realizing he wouldn't be able to change her mind. What could he offer her? He might become the head of the stables or a footman someday, but he would always work in service to the earl.

He allowed his gaze to take her all in, from the top of her woolen scarf covering her golden brown hair down to her sturdy shoes. "You won't be getting far if you freeze ta death," Billy countered. "Come on," he said as he stuffed his hands into his pea coat pockets and headed for the stables.

Sighing, Lily followed him, not sure what he had in mind. She passed over the dimly-lit threshold and inhaled the scent of hay and horse manure. At least it was warmer in the stables. She watched as Billy scampered up a wooden ladder to a room above the stalls, surprised to realize it was his room. He disappeared and soon came out carrying a pair of work gloves. Constructed for labor as opposed to fashion, the well-worn gray gloves were at least warm. Lily pulled them on and wiggled her fingers. "I don't know that I'll be able to get these back to you," she spoke quietly.

"S'aright," Billy replied, his head leaning to one side. "The earl got me a new pair when he promoted me," he said with a hint of pride, hoping she understood that he was no longer the lowest of servants in the Gisborn household.

Lily regarded the groom. He couldn't be more than sixteen or seventeen, she thought. "Thank you. Please, Billy, don't say anything," she pleaded, a look of worry appearing on her face.

Billy shook his head. "You did leave a note for Lady Gisborn," he said more than asked. "Or Mrs. Batey?"

Dipping her head, Lily shook it. "I cannot write very well," she said, her eyes not meeting his. Her face reddened at the admission. "And I... I don't know anyone else on the staff I would tell—"

"Christ." The word came out in a whisper, Billy obviously not pleased with her decision to leave without so much as a fare thee well. "She'll think you were kidnapped or something gawd awful," he countered, incensed that she would just leave. "I'll keep your secret, Lily, but only until someone asks me directly, and then I'm telling."

Lily bit her lip but nodded. "Understood," she agreed. After all, who would ask the groom if he knew the whereabouts of a lady's maid? She gave Billy a knock on the arm and dipped her head again. "Thank you." Before she could change her mind, she took up her valise and turned to leave the stables.

Billy's hand reached out and ensnared her elbow, forcing her to spin around and face him. He moved one arm around her waist and another at her face. "Oh, Lily," he whispered, his face filled with pain. And then his lips were covering hers, his kiss as urgent as it was filled with passion.

Startled but unable to push Billy away, Lily allowed the assault, a series of sharp, bright stars stunning her vision. She closed her eyes and allowed him to do his worst, her own lips responding to his before she was even aware she was doing so. A moan escaped her throat as warmth surrounded her entire body, filling her from the inside.

The sound spurred him on as he readjusted how he held her against him. Suddenly, the fronts of their bodies were fitted together as if they belonged that way, her curves filling his voids, and his sharp angles and muscles nestling into the softness of her body.

A slight movement of his hand on her back, and she was pressing into him harder, not sure if she was doing the pushing or if he was simply pulling her closer. A shiver of pleasure passed through her entire body, followed by a tenseness that signaled danger. And then, just as quick as it had begun, Billy pulled his lips away from hers.

"Do not go, Lily," he whispered, his forehead pressed against hers.

Lily's eyes flew open. *What have I done?* This was Billy O'Conlin! This wasn't Thomas Babcock, the boy who she had fallen in love with so many years ago. Pressing her palms against Billy's chest, she pushed hard, grabbed her valise and hurried out of the stables, barely aware of her surroundings or of the sudden chill that infused her body as she made her way to the lane and the village beyond.

The walk proved invigorating; the chill deepened as she passed between the scattered farmhouses that made up the earl's village. She tried in vain not to think of Billy's kiss, not to think of how warm she had felt, of how their bodies had fitted together, of how truly bereft he had seemed on learning she was leaving the Gisborn household.

But she couldn't think of him now. She was on her way to meet her true love. Thomas. He would be waiting with a horse and carriage somewhere close to Bampton.

Only one animal, or rather, a whole lot of the same kind of animal, took exception to her midnight stroll when she passed in front of the Cavenaugh's house. The dogs whimpered and whined and one barked, its low 'woof' more of a warning than a threat. She increased her pace until the sound of the dogs no longer reached her ears.

She was almost to Bampton when she spotted a small conveyance parked alongside the road, an old bay in the yoke. At the sound of her approach, the huddled form atop the box turned and exhaled a cloud of white. "Lily?" she heard before she saw the form straighten. The movement startled the horse, but he had been hobbled and gave a snort.

"Thomas?" she countered, hurrying to reach the gig. And then Thomas was down from the box and wrapping his arms around her, his nose buried into the space between her shoulder and neck while her face pressed against his chest. "Oh, Thomas, I have missed you so much," she murmured, glad for the warmth of his body and the blanket he had draped across his back.

"Finally," he replied, a hint of annoyance in his voice. "Is that all you have?" the boy asked, motioning to her valise.

"Yes," she replied with a shrug. "Everything I own," she added, moving a gloved hand to his face. He was older than she remembered, the planes of his face straighter, his cheeks a bit more hollow, his eyebrows slashes on his forehead; she had to chide herself for thinking he would look exactly the same as he did when she had left Bampton over two years ago.

Thomas took the valise from her and lifted it into the gig. Then he turned and lifted her up, one arm behind her knees and one behind her shoulders. She let out a squeak of surprise, but gamely allowed him the impropriety. He saw to the horse before taking the reins, and once settled with the blanket wrapped around both their backs, they huddled close as they set off for the northern counties.

CHAPTER 13
HANNAH MEETS A FROG

*H*aving spent the late morning on a trek around the farmlands, Henry and Nathan picked their way back to the house. Nathan chattered about how he had managed to get almost to the river before hearing his mother's call for dinner the night before. Giving his son a sideways glance, Henry thought to correct him. The boy had been nowhere close to the river and had strict instructions not to go anywhere *near* the water unless Henry was with him. "What can be so fascinating about the river that you would wish to walk all the way there?" he asked, giving his son's hair a quick ruffle.

Nathan pulled away. "I just wanna see it," he countered, tilting his head up. "Last time I was there, it was frozen over." The sun made his dark hair glint with red highlights, very much like Henry's was displaying. It was at times like this he understood why so many in the village thought his son resembled him. At some point, he wondered if they wouldn't look even more alike. "Would it be okay for me to go to the river if someone else was with me?" he asked then, pausing for a second to pick up a multi-colored rock. He held it up for Henry to look at, the earl turning it in his hand several times to determine if it might be worth anything.

He tossed the rock back to Nathan. "As long as someone

is with you, then I suppose you can go to the river," Henry agreed, a hint of reluctance in his voice. Had he not been so busy with work on the irrigation system, he would have taken his son earlier that afternoon.

They mounted the steps to the house. The front door opened even before they reached the landing at the top. "Luncheon is served in the dining room, my lord," Parkerhouse stated as he shut the door behind Nathan. "Will Miss Inglenook be joining us?"

Henry shook his head. "Not today." He gave Nathan a slight nudge in the shoulder. "Come. Let's wash our hands."

A positively blood curdling scream came from somewhere near the top of the stairs following by an "Oh!" that gave absolutely no indication as to the state of the person who had just screamed.

"Hannah!" Henry was already on the stairs, taking them two at a time as Nathan scrambled behind him. Wondering only for a second if he should first knock on the countess' bedchamber door, he instead simply opened it, thinking Hannah was in some kind of mortal danger. He pulled up short, though, Nathan barreling into him from behind and then repositioning himself at his father's side as the earl stared at his wife.

Hannah stood quite tall, and quite beautiful, Henry thought as he took in the sight of her with one arm bent at the waist and holding what appeared to be a moss green lump in her outstretched hand. "My lady," he managed to get out before Hannah's attention turned to him and to Nathan, her eyes hinting at amusement. "Are you well?" he asked, staring at her hand.

"Ribbit!"

The sound came from the green lump, which seemed to pulse as Hannah held it in her hand. "I am quite fine, my lord," she answered with a nod, still holding the frog in front of her. Then her other hand reached out so a finger could stroke the frog down its back. Nathan's eyes boggled at the sight of Hannah holding his prized frog. "However, this poor frog was in my sewing basket," Hannah continued, pulling the creature closer to her body so that it was nearly nestled between her breasts.

For a moment, Henry found himself quite jealous of the little amphibian. *I could be a frog. Kiss me, Hannah, and I'll turn into a prince.* He shook his head at the odd thought.

"I cannot fathom how he would have gotten in there," her expression quite innocent as she glanced in Nathan's direction. "I would never allow any of *my* frogs to get into my sewing basket. I would be quite bereft should one impale themselves on a pin or a needle!" she reasoned with a shake of her head.

Nathan's eyes widened. "You have frogs?" he questioned, the awe in his voice unmistakable.

Hannah gave him a look that suggested his question could hardly warrant a response. "Well, of course. Doesn't everyone?" she asked with a shake of her head. "Well, I should amend that claim, of course," she said as she moved forward, still carrying the frog at her bosom. "I didn't bring mine with me from London," she explained as she looked up at Henry and gave him a wink. She handed the frog out to a still-awestruck Nathan. "It's not really *proper* for a countess to keep frogs as pets," she whispered.

Nathan reached out to take back his prized frog. "His name is Mr. Snotball, on account as he looks like—"

"Nathan!" Henry interrupted, his eyes rolling heavenward as he realized what had happened. Of all the underhanded, cruel and unusual pranks the boy could pull on his new stepmother...

"A snotball!" Hannah finished for him, her enthusiasm far too accommodating. "So, then he must be yours then," she said with some humor, handing out the frog so that Nathan could retrieve it.

"Yes, my lady." And, then, as if he realized his mistake in having admitted ownership of the errant frog, Nathan added, "He must have escaped and thought your sewing basket was the basket I keep him in at home."

Hannah had to suppress a knowing smile, her eyes occasionally glancing in Henry's direction. "Well, let's hope he doesn't make that mistake again. I should hate for him to become a pin cushion," she said with a arched eyebrow.

"Oh, no, my lady," Nathan said with a quick shake of his head. "He knows better now."

Henry regarded Hannah with a roll of his eyes and a newfound respect for her way with children. "Luncheon is served in the dining room," he said by way of invitation. "We were... we were just on our way to wash our hands, weren't we?" he asked as he looked down at his rather happy son. "And Mr. Snotball is *not* invited to join us for luncheon," he stated in a rather firm voice.

Nathan looked suitably chastised, but then his brows furrowed, an expression that perfectly matched his father's. "Wait. If you have frogs, my lady, then why did you scream just then?" he asked, his brows furrowing even deeper.

Henry nearly swatted Nathan for his impertinence, but Hannah gave him a quick shake of her head.

"He asked me to *kiss* him!" she answered with an expression that suggested she was quite insulted. "Claimed he would turn into a prince if I did!" This last bit was delivered with enough disbelief that Nathan turned his expression of awe onto his frog.

Henry merely rolled his own eyes, not quite sure if he should admonish his wife for her fib or take her into his arms and kiss her senseless for showing such perfect grace in the face of an assault by a frog. Deciding he could kiss her senseless sometime before dinner that night, he placed his hands on his hips. "You both need to wash your hands before we can go down to eat," he announced, his voice very businesslike.

Hannah's bearing, quickly returned to that of a lady. She motioned to Nathan, and they hurried off to her bathing chamber. "You can leave the frog in my bathtub," Henry heard Hannah suggesting as his wife and son disappeared behind the door. "Just be sure to come get him after luncheon. Harold quite likes frogs, and I shouldn't want Mr. Snotball to become his next meal," she was explaining quite calmly.

"Ewww!" he heard Nathan respond. Henry put his hands to either side of his head, shaking it in disbelief.

Nathan's visit and the clear skies prompted Hannah to take a walk. Harold lumbered along beside her as she made her way down the lane toward the village. Deep in thought over Nathan's episode with the frog and wondering about Lily— she hadn't come to her room to help her dress that morning— Hannah was quite surprised when Sarah was suddenly beside her.

"May I join, you?" the older woman asked, a shawl pulled around her shoulders.

Hannah beamed at her husband's former lover. "Of course. I thought to walk a ways."

"No particular destination?" Sarah asked, reaching a hand up to brush some stray hairs from her face. Her tightly wound hair was covered by a serviceable bonnet.

Shaking her head, Hannah regarded the woman who walked alongside her. "None. I am feeling a bit sorry for myself." At Sarah's arched eyebrow, she continued, "My maid has gone missing without so much as a word or a note."

Sarah seemed startled by the comment. "Did she come with you from London?" she asked, her brows furrowing. Why would a maid make the trip from London to Oxfordshire and then disappear?

"She did, but she was originally from Witney. I think she may have relatives there, and I have reason to believe there is a boy—someone named Thomas Babcock, perhaps?" Hannah heard Sarah's inhalation of breath and turned to regard her. "Do you know him?"

Placing a hand over her mouth, Sarah sighed. "Your maid must be Lily Parker." At Hannah's surprised nod, she sighed again. "Those two have wanted to wed for years. Mr. Babcock is employed by Mr. McDonald at his posting inn near Bampton. The boy was just promoted to oversee the taproom.

I imagine his promotion makes it possible for him to afford to take a wife."

Hannah sighed, realizing her almost worst fear had come to pass. Her worst had been that something dastardly had happened to Lily, that she was spirited away in the night by a highwayman or someone determined to do her harm. "I will miss her. She was always able to manage my hair," she said with a wave toward her head. "And she was a good laundress."

Sarah made a comment about good help being hard to find. "But, surely, there is someone at Gisborn Hall who can become your abigail," she said, her arms folded across her chest, as if the shawl wasn't quite enough to ward off the spring chill.

Shaking her head, Hannah replied, "I am not so sure. I rarely see servants about. I am beginning to think there are only a few on staff. Either that, or they are all hiding from me!" The two shared a giggle before Hannah remembered the frog and told Sarah about what had happened in her bedchamber. The more she related of the story, her face quite alight with humor, the more distressed and horrified Sarah's expression became.

"You should have had the earl beat him senseless," Sarah claimed, outrage clear on her features.

"It was just a *frog*," Hannah replied with a shrug, surprised at Sarah's sudden anger. "I have an older brother who used to pull such pranks on me. Your son doesn't have a sister he can torment—"

"Thank goodness," Sarah breathed, yanking the shawl tighter around her shoulders. "I am so *sorry*. I cannot believe—"

"I think he feels a bit threatened by my presence," Hannah interrupted, hoping she could make Sarah understand Nathan's behavior and go easy on the boy. "I have tried to be sure Lord Gisborn spends as much time with the two of you as he did before my arrival, but I cannot help but think he is at Gisborn Hall more than usual. Is that... is that the case?"

Her hands tying the ends of the shawl into a knot, Sarah gave Hannah a sideways glance. "Nothing has changed in that regard," Sarah said, almost as if she wanted it to. She sighed and paused in mid-step. "May I... I wish to speak freely, milady, but I would like some assurance my words will not reach his lordship's ears," she said, as if she was about to impart news the earl would find offensive.

Hannah frowned as she regarded Nathan's mother. "Oh. Of... of course. Rest assured I shall not share your comments with anyone." After all, who would she share them with? It wasn't as if any of her friends were available for afternoon tea and the latest gossip. A pang of guilt interrupted her thought. Just because Lady Bostwick wasn't available to spend every morning with her in the parlor, why couldn't she invite Sarah to do so? Or other ladies of the village? There were apparently several members of the landed gentry some-where near Bampton. She could invite them to Gisborn Hall for tea.

"You seemed rather surprised that I was not especially upset at Gisborn having taken a wife."

Hannah angled her head to one side. "I was," Hannah acknowledged. She thought a moment, deciding she could be frank with Sarah. "I knew he left for London expecting to buy land, and instead, he came back with another woman's dowry and me as his wife. I would expect you to be angry. Hurt. To feel betrayed."

There.

She had spoken the words out loud—for herself and for Sarah to hear. It was a rather harsh way of looking at the situ-ation, but when it came down to it, that's exactly what she thought would happen.

Her brows furrowing as she considered Hannah's odd comment, Sarah shook her head. "I felt none of those things. In fact, *relief* would be a better word to describe my reaction at hearing Gisborn had finally taken a wife," she stated quite firmly. "It meant I was free to make my own life." After a pause, her brow furrowed. "Another woman's dowry?"

Nodding, Hannah shrugged. "I suppose I feel as if I am his third." She paused, thinking of something from long ago. "No, his *fourth* choice," she murmured, a heaviness settling over her.

Sarah brows furrowed as she considered the comment. "How could you have been his fourth choice?" she asked, befuddled. "Who else would Gisborn have married?"

Hannah turned to face Sarah directly. "You, first. He loves you. He has since you were children. You bore him a son—"

"I was *never* an available choice for him, and he has known it for all of our adult lives," Sarah said with such conviction it caused Hannah to step back. "Gisborn might be an earl, but he is a farmer first and foremost. I have lived in this area for my entire life, my lady. I promised myself I would *never* become a farmer's wife," she stated firmly. "I do not want that life for myself nor for my children," she added her head shaking from side to side.

Astonished at Sarah's confession, Hannah had to blink several times. *That is what I am. A farmer's wife.* Henry had made that clear in the library her first day at Gisborn Hall. *I am a countess, too.* She hadn't been at Gisborn Hall very long, but she couldn't find fault with the life there. Yes, her husband spent long hours out of doors, seeing to the irrigation trenches, and to a greenhouse that was being built, and to the laborers in the fields. But she hardly thought of him as a farmer. But Sarah obviously knew of the hard work required to keep a farm, the work required during every hour of daylight to make sure crops were planted, watered, harvested and sold. She knew of the disasters that could render a farm a failure—drought, insects, disease. "You were a farmer's daughter," Hannah spoke softly when she realized why Sarah would not want the life for herself.

Sarah's head jerked as if she had been slapped across the

face. "I was," she acknowledged. "I promised myself I would marry a man who owned a business. I want my children to live in a town, with other children to play with. I don't want their entire existence to be doing chores and seeing animals slaughtered and praying for better weather because one bad season can send a farmer to debtors' prison."

It was Hannah's turn to look as if she had been slapped. "You are about to marry someone, aren't you?" she whispered, her breaths coming faster. Mrs. Chambers had been correct with her bit of gossip in the kitchen.

Sarah inhaled and held her breath for several steps, as if she was trying to decide if she could admit her secret to the countess. "You can say *nothing* to Gisborn, but yes, I am being courted. Mr. McDonald—the man who owns the posting inn in Bampton where Mr. Babcock works—he... he is a good man. A widower. I have known him almost as long as I've known Gisborn, and he feels *affection* for me. And I for him, truth be told," she murmured, a wan smile appearing. "With luck, we shall marry about the time Nathan goes off to school. At some point, once Mr. McDonald is ready, I shall tell Gisborn of my plans. " She took a deep breath, as if putting a voice to her thoughts had emboldened her. She returned to Hannah's earlier worry. "Now, since I could never be a choice for Gisborn's wife, that leaves you as third. Which is ludicrous. Whoever would have preceded you?" she asked, her manner quite stern.

Hannah considered Sarah's comment. Wouldn't she know about Lady Jennifer? Gisborn's betrothal to the late Wainwright girl was known in London parlors, mostly because he was nearly fifteen years her senior. Some claimed he had only met the girl once, when she was quite young and he wasn't yet aware he would be an earl someday. His uncle had to have been behind the arrangement. "He was betrothed to Lady Jennifer Wainwright," Hannah offered finally. "Although he has said nothing about her death in the fire last year."

Sarah nodded at the mention of the Duke of Chichester's

daughter. "Although he was fond of her, I do not believe Gisborn ever intended to *marry* her. He had nothing to do with the arrangement, although he was present when the late earl and Wainwright signed the papers," Sarah said with a hint of sadness in her voice. "She would have been like a younger sister to him. Nothing more." She regarded Hannah again, as if she had put that choice out of the running. "Who else?"

Taking a deep breath, Hannah let it out slowly. "Lady Charlotte Bingham. The Earl of Ellsworth's daughter." Hannah could tell from Sarah's reaction that she was unaware of the betrothal Ellsworth had arranged on behalf of his daughter, Hannah's other best friend. "Part of her dowry was Ellsworth Park—"

"He didn't *buy* it?" Sarah interrupted, her face taking on a look of astonishment as she paused in mid-step, remembering Hannah's earlier comment about Gisborn coming home with another woman's dowry.

"No," she answered as she shook her head. "Ellsworth had already signed over the land to Gisborn before he even reached London. Gisborn agreed to the arrangement—he knows Lady Charlotte—"

"We used to play with her, when the Binghams came from London for the summers," Sarah said, her eyes glazing over. "She was a very beautiful girl," she whispered quietly. "I was always a bit jealous of her," she added, her face reddening with the admission. "She held a good deal of sway over Gisborn. He would do whatever she told him to do. I spent an entire week thinking Gisborn had kissed her and..." She broke off, her eyes darting about as she realized her mistake in admitting she had, at one time, had feelings for the man.

"You do love him, don't you?" Hannah spoke quietly, trying hard to ignore the other comment about Gisborn doing whatever Charlotte told him to do. "It's perfectly understandable. I expected you—"

"I did. Back then. I was very young. Very naïve. He was already quite handsome. But I've grown up. I've grown *old*,"

Sarah stated firmly. She sniffled, as if she was fighting back tears. Quiet for a few moments, her thoughts obviously on the past, Sarah straightened. "What happened with the betrothal to Lady Charlotte?" she asked, her brows furrowing. The news of Gisborn having taken property as Lady Charlotte's dowry was still a surprise to her. She wondered if she would have felt more jealous had Gisborn married Charlotte instead of the woman who walked by her side.

Hannah shrugged. "Charlotte loves Joshua Wainwright, the new Duke of Chichester. She had been betrothed to his late brother since she was a child. But, according to Gisborn, Chichester intended to marry her. And he did. They were married shortly after Gisborn left Sussex." She didn't add that their wedding date was the same as her own.

Sarah shook her head, surprised at learning there were others who were supposed to be Henry Forster's wife. "So, how was it he came to marry you?"

Smiling finally, Hannah sighed. "Lady Charlotte told him to ask me for my hand," she said, tears welling up. "And, as you said, he does whatever Charlotte tells him to." She pulled a handkerchief from a pocket in her gown, embarrassed. Waving a hand in front of her face, as if she could fan away the tears, Hannah felt so conflicted, she knew not what to think or do. *Charlotte was responsible for Henry coming to her. Charlotte was the reason he had asked for her hand. Charlotte was the reason they were married.*

For a moment, she didn't know whether to thank her best friend, or to despise her for her involvement. Certainly her friend had meant well. Certainly she had told Gisborn why he should consider Hannah. "A man only ever loves his mistress and marries another so that there is a mother for his children." *Damnation!* How could she have ever believed that mantra? How could she believe she would never love a man? Never want him to love her? *I've been a fool!*

Sarah watched Hannah's conflicted emotions cross her face, saw the tears. "Although he holds Lady Charlotte in high regard, I doubt he married you because she *told* him to,"

Sarah countered, her head shaking. A movement in the distance caught her attention, but for only a moment. Nathan was heading in their direction, his afternoon with the earl obviously at an end. She needed to get back to the dower house and see to dinner. Taking Hannah's arm, she turned them around and headed south toward the dower house and Gisborn Hall.

Harold, having decided the women would be standing in the middle of the road for the rest of the afternoon, had settled onto a nearby patch of grass and was napping rather loudly. At the sudden movement of his mistress, he lifted himself up and sauntered after her. When he noticed Nathan, his pace picked up and he rushed to meet the boy.

"Why, then? Why did he choose me?" Hannah asked, her tears under control. *Good grief!* She had made a fool of herself just then. But Sarah's words had been so true. He had even admitted Charlotte had told him to seek out Hannah. How could she have been so blind when he came courting?

Blind.

Love is blind, she thought absently. And deaf and dumb.

I love him.

"I think he loves you," Sarah said with a shrug before she lifted a hand to wave at Nathan.

Dumbstruck, Hannah stared back at Sarah. She blinked, hoping the tears had subsided as quickly as they had appeared. She heard Sarah's words again in her mind, stunned the woman would think such a thing. *How could she know how Gisborn felt?*

Hannah finally let her gaze drift to the boy whose frog had startled her earlier that afternoon. The boy who had his father's eyes. The boy who could look as stern and as serious as his father. The boy who had his father's wicked sense of humor. He would be upon them at any moment, Harold barking and jumping around him as he skipped his way along the road. "Is it wrong for me to want him to? I want him to love me," she finally admitted. "Very much so."

Sarah gave her arm a reassuring tug. "He needs you,

milady. He may not know it yet, because he can be stubborn and high-handed and proud, but he needs you. So, just love him, and eventually he'll sort it. It always takes the men longer to realize these things," she added with a wink as she pulled her arm from Hannah's so that she could wrap it around her son's shoulders and greet him.

And Hannah watched as mother and son embraced, her heart clenching as she considered Sarah's words.

"*Y*ou were brilliant this afternoon," Henry said in a whisper, his arm pulling Hannah's body atop his as he rolled off of her and into the mattress. He had entered her suite from the dressing room door, his robe not even tied at the waist, to find her in front of the fireplace reading a book. He had taken great pleasure in undoing the laces of her gown, although he wondered why she would still be dressed when it was after ten o'clock. He half-expected to find her asleep.

There was a feminine giggle from somewhere near his armpit. He felt her lips on one of his nipples, and he inhaled sharply. She was getting quite good at pleasuring him, even when he claimed he could take no more in that regard.

"I just adored the look on his face when I convinced him I had frogs of my own," Hannah whispered, her lips returning to his nipple and then the soft skin along the side of his chest. She thought briefly of her talk with Sarah that afternoon. At this very moment, she could believe what the older woman had claimed.

He loves you.

"Which, of course, you did not," he countered, his smile more because of her lip's ministrations than his comment. When there was no reply, he lifted his head. "Now would be the time to agree with my brilliant deduction," he ventured, his post-coital brain finally clearing to allow reasonable thought.

Hannah paused in her exploration of Henry's ribs.

"Remember, I had an older brother," she countered before her lips took purchase on another rib and suckled playfully.

"Oh, God," Henry exhaled, his chest heaving with the words.

"He was worse than his frogs," she added before taking the opportunity to grasp his semi-hard cock in one hand and stroke it from base to tip and back down the other side.

"You minx!" he admonished her before her giggle erupted from beneath his arm.

When they awoke the next morning, the room bathed in a golden-pink light, Hannah found herself encased by Henry's body, her back tucked against his front, his knees behind hers and his arms wrapped around her in a protective cocoon.

"How long before your maid arrives?" he asked, his lips kissing her hair.

Hannah sighed. "I'm not sure she's ever coming," she whispered back.

There was silence for a moment as Henry seemed to digest the information. "What are you saying?" he asked, his body tensing.

Hannah turned in his arms, her shoulder against his chest. "She attended me the night before last, but I did not see her at all yesterday, nor did Mrs. Batey. I believe she has left the household, perhaps to marry."

Henry lifted himself onto an elbow, his brow furrowing. No servants just left his employ! They usually said something, resigned, or at least left a note. "Marry whom?" he asked, his manner quite stern.

Hannah recalled the name on the note Lily had left to be mailed and from her discussion with Sarah. *Thomas Babcock.* According to Sarah, she thought Babcock and Lily had planned to marry for some time. "Do you know Thomas Babcock?"

Staring down at her, Henry's face hardened. "Oh,

Christ," he swore. He was suddenly up and out of the bed, grabbing his dressing gown. "Did she talk to anyone?" he asked, his ire apparent.

Startled by his sudden anger, Hannah pushed herself up until she was seated on the edge of the bed. "Not that I know of. I only asked Mrs. Batey. And then Sarah told me..."

But her last words were spoken to thin air as Henry was out of her bedchamber, through the dressing room and into his.

"What is it?" Hannah asked, coming to her feet and hurrying to her husband's room. Unlike him, she didn't reach for a gown and entered his room entirely naked.

"Thomas Babcock is a *rake*," Henry said in an angry tone. He was standing before his tallboy, pulling out a pair of drawers. He turned to find Hannah staring at him, her unclothed body a distraction he couldn't deal with at that moment. With her long hair only partially covering her breasts, their tips puckered in the cool air in the room, she looked like a woodland nymph.

He picked up his dressing gown and moved to wrap her in it. "As much as I *adore* seeing you this way, and believe me, my lady, you, *naked*, is probably my favorite thing to see, especially first thing in the morning, you really must cover yourself, or you will become *Murphy's* favorite thing to see. He's on his way up as we speak," Henry explained as he ushered his wife through the dressing room and into her bedchamber.

Ignoring his comment, Hannah turned and reached for his arm. "Is she in danger with this Babcock boy?" she asked, her face displaying her concern.

Henry dared not share his initial impression. Her maid would certainly be ruined; beyond that, he wasn't sure what Babcock would do. "I don't know. I'm going to find out, though," he vowed. And then he left her when he heard Murphy enter his bedchamber.

Henry considered what he should have done to the rake after what Babcock had done with the Coley girl the year before. Babcock had taken the village girl in the dead of night. He had promised her a wedding in Gretna Green. But the couple never got that far. The second night on the long ride, he had convinced her to spend a night in a Stratford inn, but without enough money to take two rooms, he had talked the girl into sharing a bedchamber. Once he had taken her virtue, he had quit the room and returned to Oxford-shire, claiming the girl had taken employment at the inn. When her father found her days later, she was indeed working at the inn, but only because Babcock had left her with no money. She was stranded, trying to earn enough funds to return home.

Wrapping her arms around the front of her body, Hannah struggled to remain calm. The scent of Henry's cologne reached her nostrils as she gathered the fabric of his dressing gown around her. Inhaling deeply, she took comfort in the now-familiar scent. Lily knew Babcock. Certainly she wouldn't leave with him if she thought she would be in danger. Lily would be fine.

Hannah glanced around her room, realizing she would be dressing herself again this morning. With Lily gone, she had no one to assist her with dressing for dinner, either, but if Henry intended to go after the young couple, he probably wouldn't be home for dinner. Perhaps Mrs. Batey could send up a servant girl to assist her, even if the household staff already seemed rather meager. She could manage, she decided, until arrangements could be made for a replace-ment. She had done her own hair yesterday; she could do it again today.

And in the meantime, her husband seemed quite adept at removing the pins from her hair and undressing her before bed. She hoped he would return by that time.

Henry spoke in terse sentences with Murphy. "What do you know of Thomas Babcock these days?"

Murphy stiffened as he held a waistcoat for his master to slip into. "I... I have heard he has been promoted at the The Romany Inn. I believe he is to be in charge of the taproom," his valet informed him. There was a formality to his words, but a definite impression of disgust under the comment.

Henry regarded his valet as the man held out his topcoat. "What do you know about Lily Parker?"

Murphy stared at Henry for several seconds, not sure of his meaning. "I rode with her from London, of course. We spoke very little, although she mentioned she was looking forward to returning to Oxfordshire. I have not seen her since... since the night before last at dinner, in the kitchen," he said as his brows furrowed. "There was some talk at dinner last evening as to her whereabouts, but Mrs. Batey thought she was in Witney to visit her family. Has something happened?" he asked, smoothing the fabric of the topcoat over his lordship's shoulders.

Henry snorted. "Doubtless. She may have left with Babcock, but I don't know that for certain."

Murphy stared at his master. "If she left, she had to do so in the middle of the night," he remarked.

"Who would have seen her leave?"

The valet considered possibilities. Most servants were in their rooms before midnight; the household seemed to keep early hours, farm hours, not at all like the households in London. "None of the household staff, if she didn't want to be seen," he said as he considered the possibilities.

Nodding, Henry did a quick check in the cheval mirror before departing the room. "Someone had to have seen her," he countered as he headed to the hall and down the steps.

"What do you know about Lily Parker's departure from the household?" Henry had made his way straight to the stables, figuring if anyone on the Gisborn estate knew anything about the comings and goings of personnel, it would be his newly promoted groom. For all intents and purposes, Billy O'Conlin was still a stable boy, but Henry had plans for him.

Billy stared at the earl with an arched brow. He was carrying a bucket of water intended for Thunder. He had promised Lily he would tell no one of her clandestine trip two nights before—as long as no one asked him a direct question. He sighed. Henry Forster was asking him directly. "She left about midnight the night before last, my lord," he answered, setting the water into the stall with Thunder.

Henry stared at the groom. "Why didn't you stop her?" he asked, his eyebrows furrowing.

Billy's head dipped before he raised it and considered how to answer. "I tried. Believe me," he said with a kind of exasperation that Henry took as the younger man's inability to deal with a member of the opposite sex.

"Christ! Where was she headed?" Henry asked, his ire apparent. "My wife is worried sick," he said, although, come to think of it, Hannah hadn't seemed particularly concerned. Just resigned to having lost her maid. But Billy didn't need to know that. "She thinks she might have run away to get married."

The groom's eyebrows lifted at the comment. "I asked her if she left a note for her ladyship, and she said she hadn't because she couldn't write well," he said, his disgust at the situation evident in the tone of his voice. "She was to meet Thomas Babcock somewhere on the road to Bampton. And she said they were going to Scotland to get married."

His shoulders slumping, Henry regarded Billy and sighed audibly. The last thing he had time for was a trip north in pursuit of a young couple intent on marriage in Gretna Green. Although Babcock probably didn't intend to get that far. "Christ!" he swore, his nostrils flaring at the news. "Did you think that maybe *someone* should know what she told you?" he asked, his anger increasing.

But Billy didn't back down from the earl's confrontation. "Aye, my lord. Aye, I did. She made me promise not to tell anyone unless... unless someone asked me directly. And it took over a day, dammit, for someone to come out here and ask me directly," he cursed, his own anger increasing. It was apparent he had forgotten he was addressing an earl. "Do you honestly think I would have let her go if I thought I could stop her?" he asked rhetorically. He wasn't angry with the earl. He was angry at himself. Angry that he hadn't prevented Lily from leaving that night.

His brows furrowing at Billy's outburst, Henry stared at the young man for several seconds. "You feel affection for her, don't you?" he countered, his voice softening with the realization.

Billy's eyes closed and he held himself very still. "Ever since... yes, for a long time," he acknowledged, his head lowering.

Henry thought he heard a sob coming from the boy, wondered what had happened between Lily and him when she had left. He licked his lips. "Saddle up your choice of a horse," he ordered. "Load your saddle bags with grain and apples. I'm going to see what I can get from the kitchen."

Billy lifted his head, his face showing his confusion. "Pardon, my lord?" he asked, his civility toward the earl restored.

"We're going after them," Henry replied, turning to leave the stables. "I'll see to some food for the road. Get your horse and Thunder saddled, and we'll be on our way. With luck, we should be able to catch up to them before they get to Stratford on Avon." He turned to go, but Billy's shout had him turning around before he reached the back door to Gisborn Hall.

"Why?" Billy had called out, his mouth open in astonishment.

Henry shrugged. "Because Thomas Babcock is a prick, and Lily Parker deserves better," he answered with a shrug.

For the first time in two days, Billy smiled. "Aye, my lord," he murmured in reply. And then he was off to saddle two horses and fetch his bedroll.

CHAPTER 14
ALL IN A DAY'S WORK

"*I*'ll be back in two... three days at most," Henry said as he held Hannah against his chest. His news of the trip he and Billy were taking to retrieve Lily was such a surprise to Hannah, she could only stare, open-mouthed, at her husband. "I doubt I'll be back in time to... to share your bed tonight," he stammered, feeling a pang in his gut that surprised him. "But, with luck, we might be back late tomorrow or the following day. They can't have gone far in a gig," he reasoned. "And they probably don't have much money—"

"She has a ten-pound note," Hannah stated, her face displaying the guilt she felt. *I should have said something about Lily's absence,* she realized. But she thought the girl had merely left to visit relatives in Witney, which wasn't so very far away. It wasn't until Sarah had said something about Babcock being a beau that she thought Lily might be gone for good. "My father gave it to her after our wedding—as compensation and a sort of 'thank you' gift, I think," she explained, her face taut with worry.

Henry lowered his head so that his forehead touched hers. "Damn," he whispered. That kind of money meant they would be able to change out the horse, stay at an inn, eat well. *Move faster.* "Pray for her. I'll hurry back," he whispered, capturing her lips with his own in a kiss that was urgent and heartfelt. He pulled a note from his waistcoat pocket. "As quickly as you can this morning—these instructions must reach Frank Coley, my man in the field. Murphy knows to go with you. Will you see to it they're delivered?" he asked, his forehead still pressed against hers.

Hannah took the note, her eyes lifting to meet his in question. "Of course, but, wouldn't your foreman expect your valet to deliver them in your stead?"

Henry closed his eyes, his lips thinning. "Frank Coley has no regard for Murphy. He's a servant. Act as my countess and Coley will regard you, respect you," he explained quickly. "He... he values class and holds dear to traditions. Can you do this for me?"

Nodding, Hannah fingered the note. "Of course, my lord," she answered, a quirk on her lips. "Perhaps I will even stay and watch the men work," she added with a lifted eyebrow.

"You minx!' Henry countered, thinking she was teasing. His face took on a serious expression again, though, and he sighed.

"I miss you already," Hannah whispered, lifting herself on her toes so that she could kiss him again on his lips and cheek. "Be well."

Henry sighed and nodded. Then he was gone.

Armed with Henry's instructions for that day's laborers, Hannah was glad to have something to do besides menus and needlework.

Having managed to dress herself in a riding habit, she hurried out to the stables. A footman helped her saddle a small horse before he prepared a horse for Murphy, claiming the earl would have his head if he allowed her to ride to the western edge of the estate without benefit of a chaperone. Soon, Murphy was seated on a stallion and Hannah was perched on a gray gelding, the note tucked into a pocket.

The instructions seemed simple enough, although there was also a drawing and scratches along the side of it that were probably a legend of some kind. Hannah thought to ask Murphy about them, but decided time was more important than understanding her husband's diagram. They took off for the western border of the earldom just before nine o'clock. It took only fifteen minutes to reach the work crew. Shovels and picks were wielded with a good deal of enthusiasm as the men dug up the loamy soil, the trench already several feet wide where it would connect with the river once that last bit of land was hewn away.

Riding as tall in the sidesaddle as she could, Hannah motioned for Murphy to stay back. He rolled his eyes but pulled up, allowing her to move again at a trot as she surveyed the workers. A few looked her way, their gazes suggesting they appreciated what they saw, but most continued to fill their shovels and hoist the dirt onto a series of growing mounds behind them. Hannah made sure to stay out of their way as she pulled the instructions from her pocket and reread them. Now that she was seeing the work being done firsthand, she could better understand Henry's instructions and the diagram. She also understood the enormity of Henry's plan. The ditches were wide, and their length was the entire distance from the river to the front edge of the farmlands—the crew doing the digging numbered at least fifty. No wonder they had been able to do the east side trench in a week.

"Ma'am?" a man called out from atop a horse. Dressed in a wool topcoat and doeskin breeches, he looked nothing like the laborers. He spurred his horse and made his way to her side.

"Mr. Coley?" Hannah spoke, keeping her voice steady. She had to admit to feeling out of her element. At the man's tentative nod, she held out her hand. "Hannah Forster, Countess of Gisborn," she spoke firmly.

Frank Coley's eyes widened. "My lady," he responded,

awkwardly taking her hand. Hannah gave his hand two firm shakes, hoping they felt as firm to the foreman as she meant to convey with her handshake.

"The earl asked that I act in his stead today," Hannah said as she held out the written instructions. "Do you have news or any messages I need to relay to Gisborn?"

The foreman took the note and opened it, studying the cryptic message and drawings. His expression took on a look of appreciation, his brows rising as he considered the note. "May I inquire—have you read this, my lady?" he asked, his eyes squinting as he faced east, the sun nearly blinding him.

"Of course, Mr. Coley," Hannah replied with a nod, keeping her expression as impassive as possible. "Did you have a concern? Or a message you wished me to relay to the earl?" she repeated, hoping he wouldn't ask any questions she couldn't answer.

"No, my lady," he answered finally. "The earl is quite clear with his instructions," he said, indicating the note.

Hannah thought to ask if she could stay and watch the progress, but then realized by asking permission she would be putting herself at the mercy of the foreman's opinion. She was a countess; she could simply stay and watch if it suited her.

It suited her.

She took the reins and guided her horse so it cantered far behind a line of workers on the west side of the trench, her ride taking her almost to the river's edge. The water line was high here, no doubt due to the spring run-off; the winter had brought more snow than usual, but the river's movement was slow.

Hannah imagined what would happen when the gates were lifted for the first time. Water would rush into the trench, bouncing in waves as it first hit the west bank, rebounding to splash against the east bank before settling into a smoother flow as it filled the ditch. That meant the sides of the trench closest to the river would be in danger of caving. The middle part of the trench walls would be carved out by the blasts of the water when the gates were raised and the water rushed to fill the ditch, eroding the supports for the edges of the trench. She made a mental note to ask Henry how the trench walls would be reinforced.

"Is there a problem?"

Hannah nearly started at the sound of Murphy's voice. He had ridden up to join her at the edge of the river.

"Not yet," Hannah answered with a shake of her head. "I'll speak with Gisborn about my concerns," she said, keeping her chin as high as she could.

"Mr. Coley may wish to hear them first, my lady, so he can make corrections," Murphy countered, realizing he was being impertinent in his suggestion. "I beg forgiveness," he added then, his lips thinning.

Hannah regarded her husband's valet, wondering how much he knew of the plans for the irrigation ditches. "I did not take offense." She glanced back at where the ditch would intersect with the edge of the river. "I have seen Gisborn's plan for how the gates will be built, but the drawings did not show this area just beyond the gates. It's possible he has already specified some kind of reinforcements in the wall of the trenches."

Murphy's brow furrowed. "Reinforcements?" he repeated, not understanding why she would think there would need to be any in soil that was mostly clay this close to the river's edge.

Determined not to show any hesitancy in her reply, Hannah shrugged. "The rush of the water from the river will no doubt be quite strong against that edge," she pointed to the west side of the trench, "When the gate is opened. Then the water will wave up," she motioned with her hand, "And strike down hard on the east bank," her hand curving and arcing to show the motion of the water, "Until the flow evens out. The west bank will suffer erosion and might cause the top edge to eventually collapse inward and create a dam, preventing the water from entering the ditch."

Murphy stared at her. He blinked. "How is it you know

this, my lady?" he asked, his brows furrowing. *Her ladyship talked just like his lordship!*

Hannah lifted an eyebrow and regarded her husband's valet. "Have you never played in the water, Mr. Murphy?" she asked with a hint of amusement. "With your frogs and tadpoles?"

The valet stared at Lady Gisborn, so stunned at her question he blinked again. *Frogs?* Before he could regain his normally impassive expression, Hannah flicked her reins and directed her horse back along the length of the trench, slowing as she reached the laborers. In the short amount of time she had been by the river, they had extended the ditch another five feet to the north. The mountain of soil on the west side of the trench continued to grow longer, creating an earthen dam for one side of the trench. Water would then be forced to flood the fields to the east.

"Gisborn will be pleased with your men's progress," Hannah said as she pulled alongside the foreman.

Frank Coley regarded her with a hint of wariness. "Thank you, my lady," he said in acknowledgment.

Raising her voice so it could be heard by several of the workers nearest to them, she said, "Do be sure the men are given a chance to drink water and have a suitable break for elevenses and luncheon," she said, more as a suggestion than an order. "I'll leave you to your work. Good day, Mr. Coley."

Coley's eyebrows shot up. There was a fraction of a second where he thought to counter her suggestion and instead held his tongue. "Yes, my lady," he murmured, watching in surprise as the earl's wife nodded and took her leave of the work crew. Coley had no doubt she would be back, probably at least one more time that day.

Hannah kept her smile reined in until she was past the edge of the field and almost to the stables. She had never behaved in such a manner before, acting every bit the earl's wife with her comments to the foreman. Without having actually looked at the men who overheard her suggestion about breaking for lunch, she knew they were surprised, pleasantly surprised. And they would no doubt put in more effort if their thirst was slaked and their hunger staved off. She wondered what kind of treats Mrs. Chambers could bake up in time for an afternoon repast.

CHAPTER 15
A RESCUE OF SORTS

For at least the fourth time that day, Billy O'Conlin was sure he saw the back of Lily Parker on a slow-moving gig. And for the fourth time, he felt despair when he discovered it wasn't her. He and Henry were already past Stow, but it seemed as if the miles were going by too slowly as they made their way north.

"Patience," Henry spoke from his left. He had allowed Thunder to catch up to Billy's mount, knowing the horse liked to be in the lead. Had Henry any interest in raising race horses, Thunder would likely make a good stud. "They have a whole day on us."

The groom glanced over at his master. "But if Babcock is driving that dog cart he uses to haul wood, and if he's using the nag he calls a horse, we might have caught up to them by now."

Henry was wont to agree; it was possible the couple had taken an entirely different route on their way to Scotland, but it wouldn't make sense to take the lesser traveled roads. The threat of highwaymen or damage to the dog cart wheels dictated they follow the main roads. Discreet inquiries along the way suggested the couple had pulled over near Widford and napped in the cart as the horse drank from a stream. That had been the morning before.

Another account had a couple asking about rooms at an inn just south of Stow late last evening. Henry remembered Billy's tense reaction. The Coley girl had been ruined at an inn much farther up the road. He could only hope for Billy's sake—and for Lily's—that Thomas Babcock was holding out until they were too far from Bampton for someone to follow and expect to catch them.

They had just passed through Moreton when Henry spied a lone figure on the side of the road. His brows furrowed as he strained his eyes, not sure if the person was old or young. Billy caught his gaze and followed it. His breath caught as he realized it had to be Lily.

His horse was up for the race with Thunder. Any girl would be frightened to death on seeing two horses speeding in her direction, clearly intent on an intersecting course with where she was trudging along the side of the road. But as they slowed their mounts, Billy barely stopping his own before dismounting, Lily gave no indication she even noticed them.

"Lily!" he called out, running up to her. At first, she gave no indication she recognized him, her steps barely large enough to move her forward. He stared at her, finally reaching out to stop her. "Lily," he said more softly. Lifting her chin with a finger, he gasped as he saw her chapped lips, the smear of dirt across one cheek interrupted by tear stains. Her eyes were hollow, distant. And then, as if she had been awakened, her eyes cleared.

"Billy?" she whispered, her voice cracking.

Still on his mount, Henry came up alongside the couple and glanced back north, wondering how long Lily had been on foot. Where was the dog cart? Where was Babcock? The girl was still wearing her livery, but the white apron was no longer very white and the black gown was stained with mud. If she had been wearing a bonnet, it was long gone. Her honey brown hair hung loose. "Christ!" Henry murmured. He dismounted and pulled a canteen from a saddlebag. "Lily, drink this," he ordered, pushing the canteen toward the girl.

Billy took it and held it as Lily took a long gulp and sputtered. "Easy," he said, pulling it away so she couldn't drink too much at once. When she finally indicated she'd had enough, she turned to regard the earl. All at once, her eyes filled with tears.

"I... I think I killed him," she murmured, a sob interrupting her claim.

Billy stared at her, realizing at once she meant Babcock. "Where?" he asked, stunned by her words. For the past twenty miles, he had wanted to do just that to Thomas Babcock. He had been so worried for Lily, so angry at Babcock for having arranged her middle-of-the-night disappearance from Gisborn Hall. He heard Gisborn's hiss and another curse, was aware that the earl had mounted his horse. Seeing her tears, he fished in his pocket for a handkerchief and held it out to her. She seemed surprised by the gesture, and although she took the square of linen from him, she merely stared blankly.

"Stay with her. If you can, get her on your horse and head toward home," Henry ordered. "I'll catch up. We'll get rooms at the White Hart inn in Stow," he said added before spurring Thunder to head north.

Billy nodded, putting his arm around Lily's shoulders while he spoke in a soft voice. "It's all right, Lily. I'm here. I'm not letting you leave ever again," he murmured quietly. He helped her onto the saddle, leaving her legs hanging off to one side as he mounted and held her against the front of his body. "Hang on," he urged her, taking one of her limp arms and wrapping it around his waist and back. He placed her head into the small of one shoulder and wrapped an arm around her. Once he was sure she would stay on the horse, he took a quick look north. He wasn't surprised that the earl and his horse were no longer visible. He was tempted to follow, tempted to learn the fate of the rake who had taken the girl he loved. Gisborn had said to head south, though, so Billy flicked the reins and did so, cradling Lily as he set a pace that would keep them both seated.

When Henry hadn't returned by midnight that night, Hannah finally took to her bed. She clung to the pillow Henry usually ended up on after their nights of lovemaking, his musky scent lingering in the fabric of the covering. She inhaled deeply, taking comfort in the smell. She was bone tired. Worry—about Lily and for Henry out there somewhere on a quest to find the maid—on top of her first active day as a countess, had taken its toll.

The irrigation project was coming along faster than she would have thought possible. At Hannah's request, Mrs. Chambers had baked dozens of biscuits, filling a basket for Hannah to take to the work site late in the afternoon. The men had been shocked to see her return, and even more stunned when she dismounted and carried the basket to each and every man, holding it out so they could help themselves. Their eyes wary, occasionally glancing toward the foreman, they all gave her deep nods and murmurs of thanks. Once all the laborers had the opportunity to take a biscuit, she offered the basket up to Frank Coley. The foreman nodded to her and helped himself to the last biscuit. "Thank you, my lady," he said cautiously, his manner quite serious. "If I may speak freely," he said in a low voice. Without waiting for Hannah to agree, he went on, "If the men are to stop for tea and biscuits, they get less work done."

Arching an eyebrow at the foreman, Hannah turned her gaze to where the men were lined up along the west edge of the ditch. Most were digging with renewed vigor, several breaking out into song as they filled their shovels and hoisted the dirt behind them. "It looks to me as if they're getting *more* done, Mr. Coley," she countered. "I can only wonder how much more they would get done if there really was tea." With that she strode back to her horse, remembering only then she didn't have a mounting block on which to stand. She was about to step into the stirrup and raise herself into the sidesaddle when a burly man was suddenly there, holding out his hands. He had laced his fingers together into a step.

"Why, thank you," she said as she placed her boot into his hand and allowed him to lift her until she was seated.

"My pleasure, Lady Gisborn," the man said. He tipped his hat and bowed before taking up his shovel and returning to work.

That last act by an overworked man had her nearly in tears as she made her way back to the stables. And now, she found her nerves were raw. She had spent far too much time wondering about Lily, worrying about Henry, chastising herself over not having mentioned the maid's disappearance. Had she done so when she first realized Lily was gone, Henry might have sent a footman or Billy after her and not gone himself.

Because Henry had gone after Lily, Hannah realized he wasn't doing it because she had asked him to—he obviously thought Lily was in some kind of danger from the Babcock boy. Hannah wondered what he knew.

What had Thomas Babcock done in the past to make Henry go after the couple?

Would Mrs. Batey know? If not, Mrs. Chambers would certainly know. The cook seemed to know the village gossip, and she seemed willing to share it when it was asked of her. Too late to seek her out tonight, Hannah decided she would pay a visit to the kitchen first thing in the morning. She planned to, anyway, to be sure the cook had enough stock on hand to bake another round of biscuits for the laborers. It was the last coherent thought she had before collapsing into the bed linens. "Harold, up," she murmured.

The dog lumbered to the side of the bed and pushed himself onto it, settling himself into a curled mass on the side of the bed where Henry usually slept. With Harold's weight in the bed, Hannah was quick to fall asleep.

Henry rode at least another mile before coming up to an abandoned dog cart, one wheel broken and the horse gone. Dismounting, he led Thunder around the cart as he surveyed the damage. Lily's valise was still in the back. Glancing around, he dared a peek inside. Once he confirmed it was merely filled with ladies things—clothing, mostly,—he hoisted it from the cart and attached it to the saddlebags on Thunder. Then he was off again, heading north.

Had he allowed Thunder full rein as the horse seemed to want, having been fed some grain and an apple, Henry would have missed the body sprawled in the grass along the side of the road. Instead, he was almost past it before steering Thunder to stand next to it. Henry knew even before he dismounted that the boy was still alive; there was a steady rise and fall of his upper body as he breathed. In the field beyond, an old horse with a pronounced swayback stood regarding him. As if he were being summoned, the horse began making its way to the road, finally stopping as Henry bent to turn over Babcock's body.

There was a mournful moan as the boy's face appeared in the growing twilight. His nose bloodied and a purpling bruise shown around one eye, it looked as if Thomas Babcock had taken several punches to the face, and the way a hand went to his chest made Henry think he might have been kicked as well. "Can you stand?" Henry asked as he regarded the boy.

Frowning and finally making the effort to raise himself on one arm, Babcock sat up.

"Forster?" the boy managed to get out, a drop of blood forming where his lip was split. He reached up with the back of his hand to wipe it away.

Henry stiffened. "That would be *Lord Gisborn* to you," he countered, allowing some annoyance to color his voice. "Where's Lily Parker?" he demanded, wondering if the rake would admit what had happened. If Billy had followed his orders, the groom and maid might be in Stow by now. He had said they would spend the night at the White Hart; with any luck, Billy would be able to secure rooms before Henry arrived. The horses needed to rest, and he knew Lily needed a bath and a comfortable bed.

Babcock stared up at him, a look of astonishment on his battered face. "I... I don't know. She... she left," he stammered, his eyes darting about as if he was surprised she wasn't nearby.

"She left?" Henry repeated, his manner becoming more impatient. "Did you... did you *ruin* her?" he asked, his ire increasing as he stared down at the boy.

"No!" Babcock answered, his brows furrowing. "No," he said again, his voice quieter. "She wouldn't let me near her," he added, his eyes lowering. He had pulled one knee up and had an arm resting on it. There were scratches across his forearm.

Henry regarded Babcock for several seconds, wondering if the rake would admit anything. "And why was that?" he prodded, wondering if Babcock would tell him what happened.

"I didn't have enough blunt for the trip," Babcock hissed. "I thought she had some, but she claimed she didn't, and when I told her we'd have to stop and earn some, she... she got angry."

Biting his lip in an attempt to stifle his growing impatience, Henry inhaled. "And just how did you expect to earn money, Babcock?" he countered. A moment before, he had felt pity for the boy, thinking to aid him in mounting the old nag that stood grazing nearby. Now, he felt such contempt for Babcock, he wasn't about to see to his welfare.

The anger in Henry's voice had been impossible to ignore. Babcock braced himself. "When we got to Moreton, I suggested she offer herself to a gentleman in the pub where we ate dinner," he explained, his voice becoming stronger as he relayed the details. "Seeing as how she was going to be giving up her virtue to me in a few days anyhow, I thought she could make a pretty penny—men like virgins. She could earn enough to get us to Scotland."

The back of Henry's hand struck Babcock so hard across the jaw, it sent the boy reeling backwards. The boy's howl pierced the growing gloom of night. When the sound faded, Henry took another deep breath. "If you ever so much as *touch* another girl from my earldom or from even Witney, I will have you drawn and quartered in the public square," he vowed, having a hard time keeping his voice even, "And I'll allow Lily Parker to do the honors," he added, wiping the blood from the back of hand with his handkerchief. He took satisfaction at the look of fright that filled Babcock's eyes, the nod the boy gave from his position on the ground.

With that, Henry mounted Thunder and sent the horse flying south toward Stow.

CHAPTER 16

BILLY DECLARES HIS INTENTIONS

As Lily slept against the front of his body, Billy couldn't help but wonder what she had done to make her believe she had killed Thomas Babcock. The lifeless look of her eyes when he had first found her haunted him. It was as if her soul had left her body.

On the way to Stow, she had regained consciousness a few times, one of those times asking if she could turn around in the saddle and ride the opposite direction. Billy had quickly reined in his mount, helping her to turn around and get as comfortable as she could. She clung to him as he increased their pace, her head resting against his shoulder. Not wanting to be caught traveling after dark, Billy was relieved when lights appeared ahead. Once he was in front of the White Hart, he managed to dismount as a stable hand rushed out to greet them. Billy helped the maid down, holding her up when her legs refused to do so at first.

"The Earl of Gisborn will be along shortly," Billy said to the stable boy. "Are there two rooms available?" he asked. He fished a coin from his pocket, one Henry had given him the day before when he had brought his horse back from the fields. "Until then, here's all I've got."

The stable boy pocketed the coin and gave him a nod. "Go on in and see Mr. Fisher."

"Thanks," Billy replied. He led Lily up to the entrance, hoping the innkeeper wouldn't ask too many questions. The man was quick to meet them at the door, his face showing displeasure when he took in the sight of a weary traveler and a girl who looked as if she had been spirited away from a gentleman's household. "The Earl of Gisborn is on his way. This here is one of the maids from Gisborn Hall. She was kidnapped," he claimed before the man had a chance to ask. "We need two rooms please, and a bath for the lady."

"Oh, my," Mr. Fisher replied as he turned to call out to another employee. "And just who are you?" he asked as he returned his attention to Billy.

"Billy O'Conlin. I'm a groom at Gisborn Hall. This is Lily Parker. She's the new countess' maid. Wasn't even in residence two days before she was taken," he said with a shake of his head. Although Lily seemed wide awake, she didn't offer additional information nor refute what he was telling Mr. Fisher. Tiredness overwhelmed Billy. "I'm sure she could use some tea and something to eat," he added, his own stomach growling at the thought of a decent meal.

The innkeeper must have noticed. He finally took action, leading them to a room on the second floor. A servant carrying a can of steaming water entered the room ahead of them, pouring the water into a beat-up copper tub in front of the hearth. A fire was already set and warming the room. Another servant followed, pouring more water into the tub while the innkeeper's wife appeared with flannels, linens, and a ball of soap. "Is it true we're to have an earl stay with us this evening?" she asked, her eyes alight with excitement.

Billy gave her a slight grin and a nod. "Henry Forster, Earl of Gisborn," he acknowledged. "He should be here any moment. He had business just north of Moreton. He said he would meet us here at the White Hart."

Mrs. Fisher beamed. "I'll get my best room ready right away," she offered, taking her leave of the room. "And dinner will be ready in an hour." The servants exited and the innkeeper gave him one last suspicious look before he, too, left the room.

Lily seemed to lose any strength she had, slumping against him. "Bath," she sighed.

Taking her meaning, Billy realized she wasn't going to be able to undress herself if she was half asleep. Glancing around, he moved her to the edge of the bed and got to work undoing the fastenings of her apron and gown. He knelt before her and removed her shoes, noting the holes in the bottom of both soles, wondering how long they had been there. Sliding his hands up her calves, careful not to lift her skirts too high, he set to undoing the garter ties. Then he began rolling her stockings down her legs, trying to ignore the feel of her skin as he did so. Standing her up so her back was to his front, he pulled off her apron and peeled the bodice of her dress down her body, trying to seem nonchalant about removing her clothing. She wore no corset, just a chemise. He stifled a gasp at the sight of her body in the translucent garment. Through the fabric, he struggled with the fastening of her drawers while trying to avert his eyes. If his gaze lingered too long, Lily would think he was ogling her, and he didn't want her thinking he was trying to take advantage, especially after her ordeal. Her fingers soon replaced his, and the drawers slid to the floor.

"Should I leave your gown on?" he asked, his voice barely above a whisper.

Weary, Lily leaned against him. "It will get wet," she answered in a weak voice. "Just take it off," she said. Tears welled in her eyes, as if she had lost all her strength and any sense of modesty.

"Shh," Billy whispered, holding her up as he undid the ties and pulled the chemise from her body. "I'm not looking," he said as he reached down to capture the back of her knees with one arm before lifting her to the tub. Then he carefully lowered her, trying to avert his eyes and finding he simply could not. She was beautiful in the lamplight, her skin milky white, her honey gold and brown hair glinting. With most of her body submersed in the water, he concentrated on her face. "Is it permissible for me to...?" He glanced around and found the ball of soap on top of the flannels. Lifting it in front of her, he continued, "Wash you?"

Tears still streamed down Lily's face as she glanced away and nodded. Billy reached over and kissed her forehead, recognizing her blush for what it was. "It will all be fine, Lily. We'll be back at Gisborn Hall tomorrow," he promised, dipping a flannel into the water before smoothing it and the soap over one of her arms. He gently followed it with a flannel full of water, rinsing her arm as he lifted it from the water. He did the shoulder closest to him before moving to the end of the tub to do her back. "Lean forward," he whispered. She did so, wrapping her arms around her legs, resting her cheek on her knees. An occasional sob wracked her body as he smoothed the soap over her smooth skin, gently rubbing the slick suds with his palms before rinsing away the bubbles.

He had moved to the other arm when a small knock sounded at the door. Before either he or Lily could react, the earl peeked in. Aware he was all alone in a room with Lily Parker, with Lily Parker naked, Billy swallowed.

At least Lily's back was to the earl.

Henry regarded his groom with a arched eyebrow, wondering for just a split second if the boy had witnessed the bath he had taken with the countess only a few nights ago. "Is she well?" he asked in a whisper. He wanted to ask far more, like how the hell Billy had managed to get the girl completely undressed and into a tub without her being comatose, but he bit his tongue.

Billy glanced at Lily's face, realized she was dozing. "She will be, once she has something to eat, my lord," he whispered.

The earl nodded. He felt bereft at not being able to share a bed with Hannah that night. He had thought of her far more than he expected to on this trip. Christ, he had only known her a week and she was already consuming his thoughts! Which, he supposed, was why he understood perfectly well what Billy was going through, thinking the girl he loved was lost to him.

"Did you intend to stay with her tonight?" Henry asked, his voice a hoarse whisper. "I can arrange for another room for you." He was confident Lily was still left with her virtue intact, no thanks to Thomas Babcock, but he would require the boy to marry his wife's maid if they shared a room. He thought perhaps Billy knew damned well he would be expected to offer for Lily.

"That won't be necessary," Billy replied. "I'll sleep in a chair. I... I don't want to let her out of my sight, my lord. And I have every intention of making her my wife when I can afford to do so."

His eyes widening at this proclamation, Henry gave Billy a look of admiration. "I don't suppose Lily has any say in the matter," he teased as he slid Lily's valise through the opening. His arms crossed as he continued to peer through the crack in the door.

Billy didn't reply, but gave the earl a shake of his head.

"Ask Lily if she still has her ten-pound note," Henry demanded, his manner again serious. He was worried that Babcock might have stolen it, or gambled it away their first night on the road.

Cocking his head to one side, astounded to hear the maid would have that kind of blunt, Billy regarded his future bride.

Lily lifted her head from her knees and whispered, "It's safe."

Billy turned his attention back to the earl, nodding.

"That's a relief," Henry breathed. Pushing himself away from the door jamb, he added, "Don't dawdle. Mrs. Fisher is bringing dinner up to the parlor in a few minutes." Then he pulled the door shut.

Smiling at the earl's comment, Billy continued washing Lily, his strokes gentle, especially when he moved to lay her back against the tub so he could wash her hair. With her eyes closed and her breathing slow, Billy realized she had fallen asleep. When he had finished rinsing her hair, he moved to her front. Awakening slowly, Lily stilled herself, stunned to find the groom's soapy hands smoothing over and around her breasts, down her front, around her ribs, and to the fronts of her thighs. And just as carefully, he used the flannel to rinse the areas that peaked above the water. Then he moved to her legs, his ministrations slow and deliberate, so careful and reverent, she wept. He ended with her feet, rubbing the soles where her shoes had worn through. Standing up, he reached for a linen and unfurled it. "Give me your hand," he whispered, holding two corners of the linen so that it hung down in a curtain in front of him.

Lily looked up and glanced back down at the water. She reached up and felt his hand grasp hers. She held the other across her breasts, realizing almost at once that it was far too late to be modest. Not only had Billy seen her entire body unclothed, he had touched almost every inch of her with his soapy hands!

Once she was standing, Billy wrapped the linen around her body and then lifted her from the tub the same way he had put her in there, eliciting a squeak of surprise from Lily. He put her down on the bed and hurried to get her another flannel from the pile. Wrapping it about her hair, he found her gazing at him with tear-filled eyes. "It's all right, Lily," he said. He kissed her on the forehead before retrieving her valise from where the earl had left it. "I can help you dress if you'd like," he offered.

"I can do it, Billy," she murmured, nodding as she made the claim. Spurred into action, she opened her valise and began removing several items. When Billy didn't make a move to at least turn around, she arched an eyebrow at him. "I dress myself every day," she hinted, holding her finger out and spinning it around to indicate he should turn around and give her some privacy.

"Oh!" he acknowledged as he turned away from her. "You know, though, that when we're married, I'll be more than happy to help you with your buttons and laces and... fastenings," he offered lamely. When Lily didn't reply right away, he went on, "I think the earl would allow us larger quarters in the main house, now that I'm a groom," he added, a hint of pride coloring his voice when he mentioned his promotion. When she still hadn't said anything after another long pause, he sighed. "Of course, I realize you haven't yet agreed to marry me."

Lily's arms were suddenly around his waist, her front pressed against his back as she laid a cheek against his shoulder. "Nor will I, until you ask me properly, you bounder," she whispered.

Billy stiffened, wondering if she was still wrapped in flannel or if she was naked. He turned around in her arms, relieved and perhaps a bit disappointed to find her fully clothed. "I will, Lily, just as soon as I have a right proper ring and your father's permission," he promised, holding her body hard against his own.

"Billy," Lily murmured after a moment.

"Aye?" he responded, pulling away from her so he could look at her face.

"*You* need a bath. Now," she said, pointing at the tub. And before he could protest, she was undoing his buttons and pulling his clothes from his body.

*I*t was midday, under gray leaden skies, when Henry rode up to Gisborn Hall. Somewhere farther back on the road, Billy and Lily were riding in a gig pulled by a single draft horse. Hannah caught sight of Henry from the second-story window of a guest room overlooking the road that led from the village. She had been watching from the window since ten that morning, knowing it might be another day or more before she would witness the arrival of her husband from his rescue mission. And seeing Lily riding, arm in arm with the young groom, she realized it had been more than just a successful rescue. After what she had learned from Mrs. Chambers regarding Thomas Babcock and what he had done to the Coley girl last year, Hannah was beside herself with worry. Seeing the young groom and her maid looking happy to be in one another's company, she could only hope they might have a future together. A future at Gisborn Hall.

Hurrying down the stairs and out the front doors, she ran until Thunder cleared the main gates and was taking his rider toward the stables. On seeing Hannah, though, Henry reined in his mount and halted before her. Jumping down, he captured her in his arms and spun her around until she giggled in delight. Harold was at his feet, his tail wagging so hard it created a slight breeze against their legs.

"I've been so worried," Hannah breathed, not releasing her grip on her husband.

Henry stared down at her, his smile faltering. "Lily is fine," he assured her.

"I know. I saw from the upstairs window. But I was still worried about you," she managed to get out, her face taking on the pink blush. "Did you take a room at least?" she asked. "Have dinner at a decent inn?"

Closing his eyes for a moment, Henry nodded. "Yes, of course," he replied, giving her a reassuring hug. "Even had a bath, although you wouldn't know it now," he said with a grin.

"I don't care," Hannah replied with as shake of her head. "Just so you're *back*." They walked in silence up to the house, Henry leading Thunder until a stable hand came out to retrieve the horse. Before they could go inside, the curricle came through the gates. Hannah smiled as she watched Lily tentatively wave in her direction. She waved back. "Mrs. Chambers is baking biscuits for the laborers. I'll take them out at four o'clock. Would you like to join me when I go to check on their progress?" she asked. "It's a wonderful ride. I was out there just after nine this morning, and they had completed nearly twenty feet of the trench just this morning." She paused a moment and added, "When I asked if Mr.

Coley had any concerns or questions to bring to your attention, he said he did not."

Henry stared down at her. "What did you say about biscuits?" he asked, his brow furrowing.

Taken aback by the question, Hannah sobered. "I'm having Mrs. Chambers bake biscuits for this afternoon's four o'clock break," she repeated as she entered the house. "Well, it's not really a *break*, since all they do is grab a biscuit from the basket and eat it whilst they continue to shovel dirt, but it really seems to lift their spirits, and they seem to work just a bit harder afterwards."

Parkerhouse was removing Henry's coat from his shoulders as Henry considered his wife's words. "And you know this... *how* do you know this?" he asked, his manner far too serious. He had been gone for just over a day and a half and his wife was feeding his work crew *biscuits*? He thought of some of the men who had been hired for the job, thought of them ogling his wife as she brought them biscuits.

When he first rode through the gates and saw Hannah running to him, he thought he might take her to his bedchamber and have his way with her, but he thought he should get back on his horse and find Mr. Coley.

Hadn't the man said anything to stop her? *Biscuits?*

"Well, because I did it yesterday," Hannah replied, her manner tentative. "Mr. Coley doesn't give the men very much time to eat luncheon, and they don't stop for tea, since there is no tea, and, well, it just seemed the right thing to do—"

"My lady, they're a *work* crew," Henry countered, annoyance in his voice. He was tired, he was sore, and the last thing he wanted to deal with was a problem on the west irrigation project. "They don't stop for tea and biscuits!" he nearly yelled, his voice sounding far too harsh. Taking a breath, Henry held it for a moment, raked his fingers through his hair and eyed the ceiling above them. He hadn't meant to chastise her quite so harshly, but the tears limning

Hannah's eyes made it apparent he had. Dipping his head, he shook it. "I'm sorry. I—"

"It's all right. I thought... I just thought that when you asked me to take the instructions to your foreman, that you also wanted me to check on their progress and I *did*," she said, one slippered foot stomping as tears poured down her cheeks.

Tears! Damn! Not knowing what else to do, Henry lifted her chin with a finger and kissed her lips. It wasn't a long kiss, not even a passionate kiss. Just a simple kiss in an attempt to make things better. "Thank you," he said in a whisper. He kissed her again.

"You're welcome." She sniffled, and he pulled out a handkerchief. "Thank you," she murmured as she took it and wiped her tears.

"Do you know how much they—?"

"Two-hundred and ninety feet yesterday," she managed to get out between sniffles. She sobbed again, realizing she had no idea if that was good progress or not.

Henry stared down at her. "The entire width?"

She nodded. "And a bit more at the river."

"And today?"

"They had another twenty done when I was there at nine this morning." She dared a glance up at him, wondering if he was pleased or displeased. The stunned look on his face didn't indicate one way or the other, but she could have sworn he said something about the east side taking a week to complete. The west side would be done much sooner than that.

Henry blinked. Blinked again. And then he kissed her, hard, and cupped her face with both his hands. "Damn!" he got out as he pulled away from her.

Hannah shook her head, still not certain if he was pleased or not. "Is that bad?" she asked in a weak voice.

His arms were suddenly around her shoulders, pulling her body hard against his. She let out a squeak of surprise before she felt a burble of laughter erupt from him. Then he was lifting her into his arms and taking her up the steps, his face a study in delight. "My lady, we're going to need more biscuits," he announced as he flung open her bedchamber door and tossed her onto the bed.

After bouncing a couple of times, her skirts flying up so her stocking-clad legs were on display, Hannah stared back at her husband. She gave him a tentative smile. "So, you're not angry with me?" she whispered.

Henry settled himself on the bed next to her, his head shaking from side to side. "No, my lady," he murmured. "Just mad for you." And then his lips captured hers in a series of kisses that did not end until almost four o'clock.

*A*s he did the fastenings of Hannah's riding habit, Henry allowed his mind to wander. *I should go see Sarah. I should pay a visit to Nathan. I need to check on the status of the greenhouses.* But, at that moment, exhausted by his travels and yet somehow invigorated by the afternoon tryst, he decided it could all wait until after he checked on the work crew.

Henry had allowed Murphy to dress him but thought Hannah should wait until later in the evening before asking for Lily to see to her, perhaps to dress her and do her hair for dinner. He had given leave to Billy to see to Lily's resettling; he knew she was quite embarrassed over the entire ordeal with Thomas Babcock. They hadn't discussed anything over dinner at the inn. Despite having had a bath, Lily still looked lost and out of sorts. It wasn't until that morning, when he had mentioned Babcock wasn't welcome on his lands that Lily realized the rake was still alive.

"He's not dead?" she asked as she held a piece of dry toast, regarding it as if it might make her sick if she ate it. "I was sure—"

"Were you the one who gave him the shiner?" Henry asked then, remembering how the boy had looked when he had turned him over.

The flush of red that colored Lily's face gave him the

answer he expected. He turned to Billy. "Don't ever anger this girl," he ordered with just a hint of humor. "She can break your nose, split your lip and leave you with a black eye."

Smiling now as he remembered Billy's open-mouthed look of admiration and respect, Henry explained he would be riding back to Gisborn Hall, but that they would riding in a rented conveyance. Once they were there, a groom could return it to the inn and retrieve Billy's horse. Although Billy had volunteered for the duty, Henry told him he couldn't go — he was to see to Lily's comfort and begin setting up their room in the main house. Now that 'Bill O'Conlin' was a groom, he would have to give up his room in the stables.

Billy had been so surprised by the earl's proclamation, by the earl's calling him 'Bill' instead of 'Billy', he could only thank the man and give Lily a shrug when he saw her look of surprise.

"Your maid will be getting married soon," Henry spoke in a quiet voice as he nudged Hannah to turn around.

His wife's eyes widened in surprise, a flash of worry touching her brow. "Are you requiring Mr. Babcock to...?"

"God, no," Henry interrupted her. "She will marry Billy O'Conlin. They'll have a room together here in the servants hall in the main house," he explained, taking her hand and leading her down the stairs.

"But, he's... he's so young!"

"He and Lily are the same age. And given what happened on this trip, well, I figure it best the two are settled together." They took the hall to the kitchen, Hannah leading, so she could retrieve the basket of biscuits, and Harold following at Henry's feet.

She was looking back at him, her surprise still evident. "Did he ruin her?" she whispered. Her eyes grew wider. "Or did the Babcock boy?" She stopped in her tracks, forcing Henry to stop short and Harold's head to careen into the back of his knees. Henry nearly toppled backwards onto Harold, but Hannah reached out and grabbed onto his arm, helped him to regain his footing. She saw the flash of anger in Henry's eyes even before his curse filled the tiny hallway.

"Damned dog!" he shouted. He had turned, Hannah thought perhaps to kick Harold, but the dog had made a hasty retreat to the end of the hall and sat with his head hung low.

"Henry!" Hannah admonished him, her eyes wide with shock at what she considered a minor offense on the part of Harold.

"Damn it, Hannah! That dog will be the death of me," Henry cursed again, his ire quite apparent.

Reeling back at the shout as if she had been slapped across the face, Hannah stared back at her husband. He rarely called her 'Hannah'—almost always said 'my lady' when he addressed her—and yet he cursed quite easily using her given name. She had to force herself not to breathe, not to allow the tears that pricked at the corners of her eyes to form into drops and stream down her face. "I'll be certain he is *never* in your way again, *my lord*," she hissed, before turning and making her way through the kitchen, grabbing the basket as she sailed through the back door. Despite her sudden anger, she felt a wave of relief when she realized Mrs. Chambers wasn't in the kitchen but perched on a stool just outside the back door plucking feathers from a chicken.

"Hannah!" Henry called after her, stunned at her rebuke. He dared a glance back at Harold and could swear the dog was shaking his head at him, as if to say he had made a big mistake and he's better do whatever he could to set things right.

Leaning up against the hall wall, he took two deep breaths before calmly making his way out the back door and to the stables. Hannah's horse was already saddled; she was on the mounting block and placing her feet in the stirrups when he motioned for the stable boy to get his horse.

"My lady," he said as he rounded the mounting block and stood to one side of her horse's head. "I wish to apologize and ask that you please forgive me for my outburst back there," he said in a very quiet voice.

Sitting as high as she could in the saddle, her attention on the basket she was positioning for the ride to the west irrigation ditch, Hannah struggled to keep the tears at bay. She finally looked over at him, stunned to find that, even though she was mounted on a horse, he was nearly on level with her. Then she realized he had climbed one of the steps of the mounting block.

"Oh, Henry," she whispered, still struggling to keep the tears from forming. "You *cursed* me," she whispered hoarsely.

"I did not curse *you*, Hannah," Henry replied too quickly. "I cursed the *dog*." Even as he made the clarification, he remembered the dog shaking his head from side to side and wished he hadn't just made the comment. *Christ, was the dog becoming his conscience now?* Hannah's expression had not changed one iota. In fact, he was quite sure she was going to burst into tears.

"That dog *loves* me, Henry. Until I bear a child, he is the only *being* on this planet besides my father who does!"

Hannah's words were like a slap across Henry's face. He stared at her, his brows furrowing in a combination of shock and shame. "I beg your forgiveness, Hannah," he said in a very quiet, very controlled voice, his mouth mere inches from her ear. "I may love another, but..." He shook his head, his lips pressed together as if he feared what he might say. "I do feel *affection* for you, my lady," he whispered. Reaching over as far as he dared given his precarious perch on the mounting block, he kissed her on the cheek. "I thought of you to distraction whilst on this trip. I missed you terribly."

Hannah's breath caught. She dared not look at him at that moment for fear she would become a watering pot and slide off the sidesaddle and into his arms. Given his precarious perch on the mounting block, she was sure they would go tumbling down onto the ground right in front of Mrs. Chambers.

Then he would no doubt curse again.

She would be in his arms, but she decided the display of affection wasn't worth the aftermath.

"I promise I will never again curse Harold. Nor you," he whispered urgently. "Tell me... tell me what I can do to make it up to you," he offered, the memory of Harold shaking his head at him suddenly in his mind's eye. He watched as Hannah seemed to give a great deal of thought to his offer, and he began to worry. *Should I offer a diamond pendant? Or a necklace and matching earbobs set with sapphires?* Perhaps he should have put a limit to what he was willing to do, what he was willing to spend.

"Bed me, and only me, every night for another three weeks," she whispered, aware that the stable boy had just brought Thunder out of the barn.

Henry blinked. He blinked again, not quite sure he had heard his wife correctly. "You do realize that I don't consider bedding you to be a form of *punishment?*" he countered, his head shaking.

Hannah's gaze met his just then, and she bit her lower lip. If he was in her bed, then he wasn't in Sarah's. That's all she could think of—that's what she had thought of every day for the past week and would probably think for the next week, for she had only extracted a promise of two weeks from him that afternoon in the coach on the way to Gisborn Hall. And the longer she kept him out of Sarah's bed, the more likely it was Sarah would have time to accept an offer of marriage and Henry would never be welcomed in her bed again. "Then, you agree?" she asked, her lower lip trembling.

Blinking again, Henry leaned over and kissed her cheek. He had hurt her with the curse, he knew that. And he knew Harold was important to her. So he thought she was letting him off too easily. What was he to do but agree? "God, yes," he whispered. "I promise." With that, he bounded down from the mounting block and quickly climbed onto Thunder, knowing she watched him as he did so. When he caught her gaze again, she was giving him a brilliant smile.

"You minx!" he called out as he watched her take off

toward the west, her bearing on the small horse making it very apparent she was a countess—*my countess.*

Thunder closed the gap between them long before they reached the western border and the group of men who were shoveling to the rhythm of a work song. He drew his horse up next to Frank Coley's mount as Hannah continued her ride to the group of men farthest away. He watched in awe as she dismounted and carried her basket to the rows of men, holding it out so each man could help himself to a biscuit. They bowed and smiled as if she was the single brightest spot of their day, returning to work with renewed vigor.

"I have to admit, she knows what she's doing," Mr. Coley offered when Henry didn't say anything by way of a greeting.

Henry shook his head. "I assure you I was not happy about the situation when she first explained it to me," he countered, hearing a new song break out amongst the workers that had taken biscuits. One man called out the words while the others repeated them back. He could make out something about 'four o'clock' and 'biscuits' and 'the Countess of Gisborn' and 'the fairest in the land', but not much else. Once each man had helped himself, Henry watched as Hannah made her way back to her horse. Two men had hurried up to her horse, one of them with his hands laced together to form a step while the other held onto the reins. When she was seated, the men bowed and hurried back to their shovels.

"Christ! They love her," Henry murmured, not quite sure how he felt about his wife garnering such attention from the group of laborers. He watched in silence as she made her way toward him, her basket again perched atop the pommel in front of her.

"The way to a man's heart," Mr. Coley said with a shake of head. And then Hannah was there offering him one of the last biscuits before her mount cantered back around to Henry's side. She held out the basket for him. One biscuit remained at the bottom.

"Thank you, my lady," he said as he dipped his head and

helped himself to the biscuit. The thought of something to eat reminded him it had been far too long since his last meal at the inn in Stow. "May I inquire as to what's for dinner this evening?" he asked then, keeping his voice low enough so only Hannah could hear.

A hint of panic flashed through Hannah. She didn't know if dinner had been planned since the earl wasn't sure he would be back from his trip. But she remembered Mrs. Chambers plucking a chicken outside the back door as they had made their way to the stables. "We're having chicken, my lord," she answered, giving him a look that suggested all was well between the two of them.

Henry's eyes widened. "My favorite!" he replied happily.

Hannah smile faltered. Didn't he say that about every dinner? She gave him a nod and then she was off again, surveying the east side of the trench for the entire distance back to the river before turning and cantering back toward the work crew. Henry watched as she stayed well away from the opening, her eyes taking in all that had been accomplished since she was last out there this morning. When she reached the end of the trench, she waved to the work crew and headed back over the fields to the stables.

Henry watched her go, a hint of pride rising in his chest. Hannah was turning out to be the perfect countess, a good wife, and a very willing bed mate.

He would have to send a note to Charlotte Bingham Wainwright, the Duchess of Chichester, letting her know how happy he was with her recommendation.

CHAPTER 17
NATHAN PLAYS PIRATE

"**C**ome with me!" Nathan's plaintive wail sounded again. "We can pretend our ship is moored at the dock and we're loading new treasure!"

Andrew rolled his eyes and glanced around his yard, his impatience with his best friend growing. Nathan had shown up more than ten minutes before, Harold at his heels, claiming it was time to go to the river. "I tell you, I can't! My father wants me to help with stacking firewood. If I'm not here when he gets back, I'll be feeling it on my backside for the next week!"

The sky was almost cloudless, it had actually warmed up to be a comfortable spring day, his tutor had excused him early because he had to be in Bampton for a meeting, and Nathan had decided This Was The Day. His father had said he could go to the river as long as *someone* was with him. Andrew certainly counted as someone.

"Well, how long will that take?" Nathan asked, one hand going to his hip. He had seen his father strike a similar pose to great effect, although he had to admit, it was more effective on a body that wasn't wearing short pants.

Andrew waved to the wagon parked in the drive in front of the barn. It was loaded with cut wood that lay every which way. From the looks of it, Andrew and his father would be stacking wood until the dinner bell chimed.

"Oh," Nathan said dejectedly. "All right. Well, I'm going to my father's then," he said, making his way back to the road. Harold followed. The dog had taken to spending his days with Nathan, a constant companion as the boy attended his lessons with his tutor and played with Andrew until his mother's call reminded him it was time for dinner.

The two had made it to the edge of the Gisborn estate, just past the dowager house, when an idea began to form. *Harold was someone.* He was, in fact, larger than most some-ones. And he was certainly willing and able to join Nathan on his quest to see the river. Taking a quick detour, Nathan headed for the path the workers had created while digging the east irrigation ditch. All he had to do was follow the path. It was a straight shot to the river. "Come on, Harold," he urged the dog, who seemed to hesitate before finally relenting and following Nathan. "We're going to the river!"

Harold gave a quick 'woof ' and followed his master's son.

Nathan hadn't expected the distance to the river to be so great. He could see the stand of trees that lined the fast-moving River Isis from where the path began. In what seemed like forever (but was probably only thirty minutes), Nathan and Harold loped along until they were finally step-ping up and over a hillock. At the top, Nathan yelped happily. Just below him, the river rushed over rocks and downed trees, the sound so loud he could barely hear himself shout. Harold let out a 'woof ' and made his way down to the river's edge, his front paws sinking into the muddy banks as he dipped his head to the water. He was soon lapping up water as if he hadn't had a drink all day. Which, Nathan real-ized belatedly, was probably the case.

The boy followed the dog to the edge of the water, not paying attention to the way his boots sank into the mud. He knelt next to the dog, dangling his hand into the freezing water. Shards of ice still clung to some of the downed trees, but water could be seen rushing beneath the translucent layers.

Nathan was soon busy exploring the hollowed log that extended over part of the water, its branches keeping it suspended over the water where it ended in the middle of the river. Scrambling onto one of the roots, he climbed up and onto it until he was standing several feet above Harold. "I'm a pirate and this is my ship!" Nathan yelled out happily, his arms outstretched.

Harold lifted his head from the water, his attention on the boy. He barked and jumped forward, his paws landing in squishy mud.

"I am the captain of this ship and you are my..." He struggled to think of what Harold could be on his ship. The dog was certainly too big to be his parrot. And he couldn't talk. "My first mate! Aye, matey!" he called out in triumph. He turned and ran out onto the log, barely aware that his impulsive behavior had Harold in fits. The dog bounded to the end of the log, his front paws lifting his body so he stood against the side of the log as he continued to bark at the boy. "Take the wheel while I check out the gangplank !" Nathan cried, his face full of joy as he turned and spread his arms again.

Harold stilled himself, watching the boy intently. Nathan stared back at him, his face turning serious. "Bad dog," he said. "You're supposed to take the wheel and keep my ship from the enemy." And then Nathan turned and, holding his arms out on either side of his body, began to walk farther out onto the log. Water rushed below the rotting trunk, its force causing the log to waver and shift beneath him. Nathan continued to hoot and holler in delight as he made his way to where a branch stuck straight up out of the log. "The mast is in danger of breaking," he called out, his hand grasping the branch as he attempted to step around its base.

The sudden change in his weight on the log caused the

entire tree to twist, and within seconds, it had shifted so Nathan was suspended over the frigid water, one hand still gripping the branch while the other flailed in the air. Neither of his feet could reach the log. "The mast has broken, matey!" he yelled, his voice still indicating joy.

But the emotion was quickly replaced with horror as he realized what was beneath him.

"Harold!" he called out. "Help!" He managed to get his other hand up and around the branch so that he hung suspended over the fast-moving water. "Help! Father!" he called out, the sound of his voice swallowed up by the roar of the rushing water.

Harold pushed off of the log and bounded into the water, his massive body well above the surface of the water for several steps. He stood staring at Nathan for a few seconds, as if he were wondering if he should head into the water. Nathan let out a cry of pure panic as one hand lost its grip on the branch. Harold surged into the current, swimming with giant, lurching motions until he was under the boy.

"Help!" Nathan cried out one more time before he lost his hold completely and fell into the bracing water. The air rushed out of his lungs at the impact with the cold water. The last thing he heard before he was covered by the icy blanket was Harold barking.

Harold's mouth clamped onto Nathan's coat and held tight as he tried to negotiate the swift current. Paddling with all his might, he found solid ground, but not before they had traveled some distance from the downed tree, and only because the current had slowed due to another series of fallen trees. It was in the eddy created by that dam that Harold was able to swim to the edge of the water and pull Nathan's body to the edge. Panting as he grasped the boy's coat sleeve with his teeth, Harold tugged until the boy was entirely out of the water. When Nathan didn't respond to his inquisitive nose nor his tongue, Harold stood over him and barked. He pulled at the boy's soaked clothing, pulling him farther onto the muddy bank, barking between pants. Still, Nathan lay prone and unresponsive.

Harold hurried up the bank, through the trees and over the hillock that fronted the river, racing through the newly plowed field toward Gisborn Hall. In the late afternoon light, his body might have appeared as a large rabbit as he hopped the furrows, his barks unheard by anyone near the house. Too old to keep up the pace, he lessened his run, panting hard as he finally made it to the stables.

His mistress was greeting the earl. Billy had just taken the reins of his horse and was leading it to the stables when Harold increased his pace and lunged toward the couple.

"What brings you out here at this time of the day?" Henry asked as he joined Hannah where she stood near the stables.

"You, of course," she answered with an embarrassed grin. A pink flush was blooming on her face. "I was hoping you might join me for tea."

"Woof!"

The earl turned in the direction of the sound he had just heard. "An invitation I am most willing to accept, my lady," he answered, his brows furrowing.

Noticing his concern, Hannah turned in the direction of the sound to see her dog limping toward them. "Harold?" she spoke, her voice registering alarm.

Harold hurried to Henry. He barked and then jumped in the direction from whence he came. "What is it?" Henry asked Hannah.

Hannah crossed her arms. "It's not time to play, Harold," she admonished the dog, recognizing the familiar advance and dodge technique he used when he wanted to play. After what had happened the last time Harold annoyed Henry, Hannah wanted to ensure her dog never again bothered the earl.

Harold stood and barked several times. He ran up to Henry and nipped at his boot. Then he ran off in the opposite direction.

"Harold MacDuff!" Hannah cried out, startled at her dog's behavior.

"Damned dog!" Henry said under his breath as he held out his boot, careful to be sure Hannah couldn't hear him curse the dog. There was no sign of damage, but the dog had clearly gotten his teeth around most of it. Harold turned around and ran in circles, barking incessantly.

"Something's wrong," Hannah said in a voice that commanded attention. She realized her dog's fur was wet, which could only mean he had been in the river.

"I agree. I do believe it's time for your dog to take his place in the stables," Henry said with a good deal of anger. Hannah was shaking her head, though, slowly making her way toward the dog.

"No, Henry. Something's *wrong*," she repeated. She began moving as quickly as her skirts would allow, following Harold as he turned and headed out into the field.

"Hannah!" Henry called out, alarmed at his wife's behavior. *What the hell?* But he had heard the alarm in her voice, heard the tinge of panic, and now she was running over the furrows in the field, following her damned dog as it bounded over the newly plowed field. "O'Conlin!" Henry called out, turning to hurry toward the stables.

Billy emerged from just inside the door, his hands still holding onto the reins of Thunder. "Yes, my lord?" he asked in surprise.

"I guess I'm not done with him yet," Henry said in a heavy sigh as he yanked the reins from the stable boy. He was mounted on Thunder and racing after his wife and Harold before he was even properly settled in the saddle. Despite the speed of Thunder, he was amazed at how much ground Hannah had already covered as she hurried after her dog.

"Hannah!" he called out, slowing his mount until he was abreast of her. He reached down and motioned for her to grab his arm. Her eyes wide, Hannah reached out, and in a quick and frightening motion, she was airborne and then seated quite firmly in front of her husband.

"Where the hell is he going?" Henry shouted above the sound of Thunder's hooves as he pounded over the furrows.

Hannah struggled to catch her breath, her head pressing into Henry's chest. "The river, I think. He's wet!" she managed to get out, realizing Harold's path followed one he had already made through the freshly turned soil. She could see up ahead where it had broken the top edge of furrows all the way to the edge of the field. Beyond that, there was a stand of trees that fronted the river. "Oh, Jesus," she heard Henry say.

Thunder had caught up to Harold, but Henry spurred his horse to move beyond the dog, following the tracks clearly marked ahead. Once they were past the fields, they could hear Harold barking behind them as they picked their way through the trees and to the river bank. In the growing gloom of twilight, Hannah looked in vain for a sign of something, someone.

Harold broke through the trees several yards west of their location, barking as he did so.

"There!" she called out, pointing to where a body lay on the river bank. In only a moment, she was gripped around the middle and was being lowered to the muddy bank. Her slippers sank into the soft mud as she tried to make her way to the boy who lay lifeless next to the water. "Nathan!" she heard from somewhere to the side.

Henry had knelt next to his son, moving his hand beneath the boy's head to cradle it. His clothes and hair were soaked. "Nathan!" he shouted again.

Panting hard, slobber dripping from his mouth, Harold nudged her arm. "Oh, Harold," she murmured, wrapping one arm around the dog's neck. "Good dog," she said as she allowed the dog to lick her cheek. She considered how long it had been since Harold had found the boy. But Harold was damp. He had obviously been in the river, too. "He couldn't have been here long. Harold would have run the whole way," she said in desperation.

She watched as Henry lifted Nathan from the muddy

ground. "He's alive," he said, a whoosh of relief sounding as he took a deep breath.

"Take him on the horse," Hannah ordered, her other arm wrapping around Harold's neck. Henry gave her a questioning look. "I can walk back with Harold," she added, her breaths still coming in short gasps, as were Harold's. "Go!" she said, a bit too harshly.

Adjusting his hold on his son, Henry nodded to his wife.

He lifted his son to the saddle and then mounted Thunder. He rode off, cradling the boy's body to his front. He turned around several times as his horse raced back toward the house, looking in vain for Hannah and Harold. Before he could confirm they were following him, he was back at the house, Billy running out to help, and Mrs. Batey calling out to Parkerhouse to send for a doctor, and Mrs. Chambers bringing hot towels to wrap around Nathan.

*H*enry had no idea how much time had passed from when he had left Hannah and Harold at the riverbank to when the doctor arrived and was seeing after his son.

Cold, wet, and disoriented, Nathan woke to find a cadre of people staring down at him. He grinned. "I walked the gangplank," he said proudly, his blue eyes all mischief.

His father stared down at him with a look somewhere between concern and anger. "You mean, you walked *off* the gangplank," he retorted.

The memory of what he had been doing just before the log twisted sideways was replaced with the nightmare of hanging over the icy river. "I tried holding on," Nathan said, his voice suddenly feeble. "But I lost my grip." He lifted his head to look around the room, between the people that made up the crowd that hovered over him. "Where's Harold?" he squeaked. "He was my first mate," he said, trying to make it sound like everything was fine. Surely, everything was fine.

"Oh, damnation," Henry said, his hand coming away

from his son's head. He looked around the room, expecting to find Hannah amongst those in the parlor. When he realized she wasn't there, he left his son's side and hurried out into the hall. "Hannah!" he called out, making his way to the stairs. Certainly she had arrived home safely. Harold was with her.

He'd had every intention of going back after her, every intention of taking a mantle with him to wrap around her. The evening had already turned chilly even before he had returned with his son. If she was still out there.

"Here," he heard her quiet voice. Henry turned to see her sitting on the floor of the vestibule, Harold's huge panting body spread out over the tiled marble floor. Hannah had her arms wrapped around his neck, much the way she had when he had left her at the riverbank. The dog's fur was still damp from his swim in the river.

"Hannah!" he said as he rushed to her side, lowering himself to his knees. "Good God, I'm so sorry. I—"

"How is he?" she interrupted him, her face streaked with tears. Mud lined the hem of her skirts and was smeared over most of the rest of her gown from when she had lowered herself to the river bank. Her slippers, ruined from mud and water and the walk back to Gisborn Hall, had been abandoned near the front door. "Is he alive?"

"He'll be fine," Henry replied. "He's a Forster. Too dumb to die of exposure," he said in the most self-deprecating manner he could manage. "He was walking the gangplank and apparently fell in," he said by way of explanation. "Says he doesn't remember anything after hitting the water."

Harold lifted his head and whined.

"Harold must have fished him out," Henry said quietly.

Nodding, Hannah lowered her face to Harold's head. "Good dog," she whispered as she allowed a wan smile.

"Cook said she would make him a special dinner," Henry said with a matching smile. "Come on," he said as he stood up and held out his hand.

Just then, the front door flew open. Sarah rushed in, out

of breath and quite agitated. Her eyes flew to Henry. "Is he here?" she practically shouted. "Oh, Henry, I swear you had better take the switch to him…" Her voice trailed off as she took in the sight of the Countess of Gisborn sitting on the tiled floor with the top half of her muddied dog cradled on her lap. "Oh," she managed to get out, offering an awkward curtsy.

Hannah had to suppress a grin. *I must look a sight in my ruined gown, my tear-stained face.* "How do, Sarah. Nathan is here and apparently on the mend," she said quietly, thinking someone had been sent to fetch the boy's mother.

Sarah's eyes widened again as she looked between Hannah and Henry. "What happened?" she asked, her gaze finally resting on Henry. "He was supposed to be home before dark," she claimed in a voice that couldn't seem to decide if it was panicked or angry. Hannah thought perhaps it was a little of both.

From her vantage point on the floor, Hannah watched as Henry held out an arm to Sarah. Her shoulder was suddenly under his as he wrapped an arm around her back and led her to the parlor, all the while explaining what had happened in a calm, quiet voice, his head tilted down so his cheek almost rested on the top of her head.

Stunned at how easily Sarah had curried his sympathy, how quickly Henry had taken her under his wing—literally! —Hannah felt a stab of… *anger?*

No.

How could she feel anger? Sarah was Nathan's mother. Henry loved her. Of course, he would do everything he could to calm her, to reassure her that everything was going to be fine.

Sniffling, Hannah acknowledged the emotion she felt as jealousy. Henry had been about to offer his assistance in helping her to her feet, and then suddenly, he was seeing to Sarah.

Gulping back a sob, Hannah hugged Harold so hard he let out a whine of complaint. Which only made Hannah cry harder. "Oh, Harold," she whispered, burying her face into his neck.

When she had finally cried her last tear, Hannah managed to get herself to her feet and make her way to her bedchamber, leaving Harold to sleep in the vestibule.

CHAPTER 18
HAROLD DISAPPEARS

Mrs. Batey hummed while she dusted the round table near the entry, her white mobcap askew and her cheeks the reddest Hannah had ever seen. Despite the calendar's insistence that it was April, Hannah wore a winter gown and her thickest silk stockings. She had even donned another petticoat as protection against the chill in the air. That morning's sunrise had been a glorious pink and ruby and promised a clear, warm day. It had been anything but.

"Have you been outside, Mrs. Batey?" Hannah asked as she wandered past the housekeeper, her eyes on the front entry windows. She could swear she saw something just then fall from the sky. Too slow to be a raindrop, she thought it might be snow.

"Goodness, no, milady. It's far too cold to be out if I don't have ta be," the older woman answered, a faint northern county accent tinging her voice.

Hannah stood before the windows staring out at a rather gray scene. It was snowing. This was the kind of weather Harold had been born for, she considered, remembering her father's tale of having acquired the dog from some monks in the Italian Alps. Harold had been a puppy then, old enough to leave the den but not yet trained in how to search for travelers in trouble. He had done a magnificent job in rescuing and warning them about Nathan, though, and she felt a great deal of pride that he had been the one to lead them to the poor boy.

She recalled the look on her husband's face when Harold had come to him, barking frantically and pulling at Gisborn until she'd had to explain that something was wrong. Harold would never behave that way unless someone was in trouble or needed help. And once Nathan was safely home with his mother and Gisborn had finally, very late, taken his leave of his mistress and their son, he had come straight to her and thanked her for insisting Harold join them at Gisborn Hall.

Vindication, she remembered thinking on her dog's behalf. But she still felt that pang of jealousy. She had wondered if more had happened at the dowager house than just the two of them tucking Nathan into his bed. Had he bedded Sarah? Had he told the mother of his son that he still loved her? She had almost gathered enough courage to ask him.

But Henry kissed her. Gently, at first, and then with more force, his mouth taking possession of hers, his tongue opening her lips to plunder her mouth and render her entirely helpless. She had clung to him, returned the kiss as best she could, and made the quiet mewling sounds he seemed to understand as permission to take her. A simple kiss would have done the trick, she thought, for the touch of his lips to hers made her insides seem to take a tumble and liquid heat to build between her thighs. Within moments, she had been ripe and ready for him to impale her. And yet, he had taken his time in undoing the buttons down the back of her ruined gown, spent an unbearably long time removing it and her corset, and it seemed forever before he had her chemise off her body. He had continued to kiss her as he stretched her out on her bed, covering her body with his own, even though he still wore his linen shirt and breeches. His lips had traveled from her mouth to her neck and ears and the long column of her throat before taking purchase on each nipple. By then, her fingers had wound themselves into his thick, dark hair, their gentle guidance pulling his face down so that her breasts were covered with his nips and licks and kisses.

When her cries of delight and pleasure finally escaped, she was sure he would undress and take her then. She felt her frantic pulse deep inside, her core throbbing in anticipation for him. But he simply moved farther down the bed, farther down her body to move his lips onto the soft white flesh of her thighs and then into the dark curls. She hadn't been conscious of spreading her legs for him, of tilting her hips so that his tongue could circle into her swollen folds and tease her womanhood. *But I must have!* For when the ecstasy had taken her, she remembered crying out his name, remembered how her entire body had finally succumbed to the pent up waves of pleasure that simply washed over her again and again until she had sighed.

Her hands were still in his hair, she realized then. Stroking his head with the ends of her fingernails, she felt a shiver pass through him as he pulled himself away from her womanhood. She wasn't aware of his shirt coming off his body, of his breeches being removed or of anything else until he was covering her with his body again. Knowing what to do, she had her thighs wrapped around his back even before she felt the moist tip of his engorged manhood enter her wet sheath.

The sudden sensation of fullness caused her to inhale sharply, and he paused, holding himself very still, waiting for her to make the next move. Tilting her hips up more, her motion forced him deeper into her. She was aware of his gasp then, of his groan, as he held himself still for a very long moment. And then he was pulling out, slowly, until she was sure he was leaving her body.

Not quite sure of what she should do to stop his retreat, she clenched on him, wrapped her arms around his torso and pulled. There was a strangled groan, and he was back inside, deep and hard and filling her, the sensation rather pleasant.

The rhythm of his quickening movements was easy to match, her hips lifting to meet his as he buried himself inside her again and again. And then the tension she had come to realize was arousal and cresting pleasure overwhelmed her. She clenched hard on him as the climax took her entire body in undulating pleasure.

The growl that emanated from him began low in his body and erupted as his body spasmed hard against her and in her and over her. And then he was pressed against her, his head buried into the space between her neck and shoulder, his body surrounding her, enveloping her in warmth, his heartbeats pounding against her breast much like she knew hers had to be pounding against his chest.

They lay like that for a very long time.

When he finally attempted to leave her body, she had clung to him, her "No!" the only sound besides his ragged breath near her ear. So he had wrapped his arms around her body and turned onto his back, taking her atop him while he reached for the bed linens and covered them both. Before sleep took her, she was aware of his lips on her forehead, of his heartbeat beneath her palm slowing with each breath, of his satisfied sigh as sleep took him.

Hannah wondered if she had pleased him. She would have asked him had they woken up together. But when she had opened her eyes to the red hues of that morning's sunrise, Henry was no longer in her bed. On the pillow where his head had been was a small velvet pouch. Hannah stared at it for a long time before she lifted it between two fingers and studied it.

The satin rope drawstring, drawn tight at the opening, loosened when she pulled at the gathers. A golden chain with a ruby pendant slid out like liquid onto the bed linens. Startled, Hannah touched the warm metal with one finger and studied the round-cut stone in its gold setting. The ruby glimmered in the odd morning light, casting its red hues this way and that.

Glancing back where she had found the pouch, she saw a parchment folded into a tiny square.

For my wife, For my countess, A ruby I give thee, For all that you have done, Henry.

Hannah reread the masculine scrawl several times, touched that Henry Forster would bestow her with such a jewel before she had even borne him a child.

Her hand reached to her belly, caressing it protectively. Had his seed taken root? Could she already be with child? A smile appeared on her face as she thought of a baby playing with Harold, how patient he would be with a toddler grabbing handfuls of his hair and begging to ride him like a horse. Harold would be good with their baby, she thought.

Where was he?

She hadn't seen the beast that morning. "Have you seen Harold?" she asked, turning from the glass of the vestibule window where her breath had created intricate patterns of frost on the pane. Her thumb and forefinger absently caressed the ruby pendant at the hollow of her neck.

Mrs. Batey paused in her dusting of the potted palm in the hall, as if she had to give the question a good deal of thought before she answered. "No, milady. I haven't seen him today. If he's got any sense, he had been in the kitchen where it's warm, though."

Hannah regarded the housekeeper for a moment. "I rather doubt Mrs. Chambers would allow him to spend too long in there," she countered, remembering how the cook reacted upon meeting the Alpenmastiff the first day she had been in residence. At least the cook was more accepting of him now that she knew he ate scraps. It saved her from having to dispose of them.

Her alarm increasing, Hannah moved past the housekeeper and down the hall to the back servants' stairs, her slippers tapping on the stone. She was nearly running when she reached the kitchen, its comforting warmth at odds with the rest of the house.

Mrs. Chambers looked up in surprise at her arrival from the servants' entrance.

"Have you seen Harold?" Hannah asked, breathless from her rush from the front of the house.

The cook wiped her forehead with an arm while she gave Hannah's question consideration. "No. Well, not since early this morning. I tossed him a hock from the mornin's bacon right out that door there," she amended as she waved toward the back door. "I rather think the beastie would be awfully hungry, seeing as how he didn't eat last night," she added.

Furrowing her brows, Hannah remembered the dog's exhaustion. When they had returned from the river, Harold had barely made it into the house before collapsing onto the floor of the vestibule. Once Sarah and Henry had gone into the parlor, she had finally pulled herself up from the floor and encouraged Harold to follow her to her room. He had done so, but it seemed to take a great deal of effort for him to climb the stairs. Once he was on his rug at the foot of the bed, he had settled down and immediately gone to sleep.

Meanwhile, since she couldn't undo the fastenings of her ruined gown, Hannah spent time in the bath, washing off the remnants of mud from her body and the gown as she considered what might have happened to Nathan. She unrolled her dirt-caked stockings and slippers, wondering if Lily would be able to put them to rights. Removing the pins from her hair, she brushed it out, wondering if Henry even liked the scent of honeysuckle that wafted around her.

Hannah thought to spend the rest of the night in the library reading a book. But then Henry had returned to the house and made love to her in that slow, exquisite... she shook the carnal thoughts from her mind.

Hurrying to the back door, Hannah opened it and gave the side yard a look, finally calling out Harold's name. When he didn't appear, she pulled herself back inside.

Damnation! It was getting cold and there were more

snowflakes swirling about. Where could he have gone? He wouldn't be with Henry—the earl was visiting tenants to explain more about the irrigation and flood control channels and the greenhouses that were already fully framed on the fallow land near the stables. There weren't even any laborers working on the irrigation ditch that day; the cold had kept everyone indoors.

Nathan! Perhaps he had gone back to Sarah's house. Hurrying to her room, she donned another pair of socks and half-boots before pulling on her warmest pelisse. Back in the vestibule, she grabbed her gloves and mantle and a muff she found amongst the outer clothing hanging on hooks, silently cursing Harold for having disappeared on such a cold day. Then she was out the door and walking as quickly as she could to Sarah's.

The dowager house appeared deserted; a knock at the front door wasn't answered. She called out Harold's name, but the dog was nowhere to be found.

"Lady Gisborn?"

Hannah whirled to find Sarah on the arm of a man she didn't recognize. Tall and just a bit on the portly side, he had a friendly face and wore clothing that suggested he was a well-to-do cit. *This must be the man who Sarah spoke of—the man who was to ask for her hand in marriage!*

Hannah wasn't able to give the man more than a slight nod to his generous bow. "Oh, Sarah, I was about to call on you," she said, her breathless state causing Sarah's eyebrows to furrow.

"What's wrong, milady?" Sarah asked, aware of Hannah's growing distress. She intended to introduce her escort to Hannah, but realized the countess was in no mood for pleasantries. Sarah gave the key to her house to the gentleman. He moved around Hannah to unlock the door.

Hannah shook her head. "I... Harold is missing," she finally got out, realizing at the last second that her concern sounded overwrought even to her own ears. He was a dog.

He was covered in thick fur and bred for weather like this. *Why am I so worried?*

Sarah's mouth opened, as if she intended to reply with a platitude. But she was aware of what Harold had done the day before, aware that her son could have been lost to her had the dog not come to his aid and then led rescuers to the poor boy.

And she saw Hannah's distress.

"I have not seen him since last night, milady," she replied carefully. "And he didn't come to the house this morning. Nathan is with his tutor," she added, waving a gloved hand down the lane toward the village. "Surely he'll come home when he gets hungry?" she half-asked, hoping to assuage the noblewoman's concern.

Even bundled up against the growing chill, Gisborn's lady was beautiful, Sarah considered. Beautiful in appearance and in spirit. She had been more generous and tolerant than Sarah could ever imagine of a lady of the *ton* to be. She behaved as if Sarah, as Henry's first love, had first rights to the man. Did the woman not realize how much Gisborn had grown to care for his wife? He might have required a push in the right direction, but certainly Lady Gisborn was perceptive enough to realize Gisborn felt affection for her.

Hannah shook her head. "I suppose," she finally replied, feeling ridiculous for overreacting to a missing dog. "I apologize. I am keeping you from warmth and tea. Please excuse me," she begged as she curtsied and hurried off down the lane.

Sarah watched the countess take her leave as the innkeeper moved to take her arm and lead her into the dower house. "Do you suppose she loves the dog more than she loves her husband?" Tad McDonald asked in a whisper, a tinge of teasing in his voice.

His future bride shook her head. "Equally, I should think," Sarah replied with an arched eyebrow. Realizing Tad was standing aside to allow her to enter the house before him, she stole a glance back at the retreating figure of Lady

Gisborn one more time before hurrying into the warm house.

A young boy, loading bricks into a wooden cart, paused as he saw Lady Gisborn approach him. He bowed rather properly considering his dirty face and muddy breeches. Hannah afforded him a quick curtsy before asking about Harold. "Yeah, I seen him." The boy pointed in the direction of Gisborn Hall. "Just after luncheon. He was walking out that way. Into that field along the new ir'gation ditch," he said before returning his attention to the bricks.

Hannah turned to follow the direction his finger had indicated. "Thank you," she replied with a nod, feeling relief in knowing the dog wasn't headed toward Bampton. That village was nearly two miles away! Trudging back toward Gisborn Hall, Hannah followed the footpath that bordered the eastern irrigation ditch. Dead plants crunched beneath her half-boots as she made her way. Her gaze occasionally scanned the horizon in search of the brown and white hairy beast.

Her alarm had long since turned to growing annoyance at the missing dog. *How could he?* He had proven his worth only the afternoon before, and now he had gone and run off and made her worry to the point of nearly being sick. Snow was falling in large, wet flakes. Unaware of the cold until the moment she noticed the larger snowflakes, Hannah realized the sun would soon set and twilight would cause all the colors to turn gray. If she didn't find Harold before nightfall, she would... what would she do? Cry, certainly. *I seem to be doing far too much of that lately*, she admonished herself.

Harold was her best friend, her *only* friend here at Gisborn Hall. Her girlfriends were married now. *In love with their husbands*, she thought, her mind going back to last night when Henry had been so loving. Her heart clenched just then.

Would he ever feel for her what he felt for Sarah? Would he ever only think of her when they made love? Only think of her in the morning when they were in the breakfast room?

Only think of her when they were having tea, when he would reach out and give her a quick kiss on the cheek while she poured? He had done that just the day before yesterday. And then Harold had to lift his big, hairy head and regard her poor husband with that look that suggested he had best leave his mistress alone.

Harold!

Was that him? She hurried toward a brown and white mass nestled against a small hillock at the far end of the field. Sounds of flowing water came from beyond the hill. *The river?* she realized, surprised she had come so far. The river marked the back border of the earl's lands! This was very close to the place they had found Nathan. Nearly running, she called out Harold's name. A puff of white cleared from in front of her face when she finally knelt next to the hairy beast. "Oh, Harold, is *this* where you've been all day?" she asked in exasperation, her gloved hand stroking the long hair. "Nathan knows better than to come back here alone," she chided him.

When Harold didn't move, she crawled to where his head rested on the ground. There was no evidence of trauma, no sign he had been hurt. But his body didn't move. No white puffs appeared near his head. "Oh, Harold, no," she whispered, tears welling up even before she fully realized what had happened. Why didn't he move? Why did he come here? He was *old*, of course. Far older than any dog his size had a right to be. But here? *Now?* She could not bear to believe Harold was gone.

Hannah pulled a glove off her hand, burying her fingers into the downy fur at his neck. He couldn't have been dead long, she thought. He was still warm. Collapsing onto his body, one hand stroking his ear, she burst into tears. "No," she cried, a hiccup interrupting her plea. She continued to weep as sobs shook her entire body.

How could her only friend in the entire world die? Never had she felt so alone. Never had she felt so bereft. She couldn't remember feeling this much despair when her mother died, but she must have, she thought. Even when a modicum of sense told her she was a countess and shouldn't be prone on the body of her deceased dog, Hannah continued to cry until exhaustion and cold took their toll. Before long, she fell into a fitful sleep.

"Pray it doesn't rain tomorrow, Mrs. Batey," Henry said with a grin as he allowed his valet to help him remove his greatcoat. "With any luck, we'll get a better start on the center irrigation ditch." His nose was red from the chilly air, but he was obviously happy at the progress the team of laborers had made that day on the greenhouses.

The earl seemed in such good spirits, the housekeeper considered keeping her concern for the countess to herself. But Henry Forster knew something was wrong even before she answered his greeting. "What is it? What's happened?" he asked, a hint of urgency in his voice.

Mrs. Batey rung her hands together. "May be nuthin', milord," she replied with a shake of her head. "But... Lady Gisborn hasn't returned. And from the looks of your coat, it's gotten even colder out there." A flurry of snowflakes had sailed off Henry's coat as Murphy removed it from his shoulders.

Henry eyed the housekeeper with an arched eyebrow. "Hasn't returned from... from where?" he asked. Hannah hadn't said anything about making calls. She didn't yet know many people in the area. And it was far too cold to be out delivering food to the two infirm women she had made deliveries to just a few days ago.

"I don't know," Mrs. Batey replied, her hands now held out on either side of her plump body. "She was looking for the dog, you see, and when she couldn't find him in the house, she got dressed for the weather and left. And no one has seen her come back." The old woman looked as if she was about to cry.

Panic gripped Henry. If she was *with* Harold, he wouldn't be overly concerned about Hannah, but if she was out looking *for* the dog, where would Harold have gone?

Sarah's.

Henry took his greatcoat from a surprised Murphy and tossed it over his shoulders, the capes swirling as they settled onto his frame. "I think I may know where they've gone. Tell Billy to keep my horse saddled, though," he ordered before hurrying through the vestibule and out the front doors. It would be twilight shortly. Surely Hannah would know enough to come home before darkness settled over the estate, before the cold and snowfall worsened.

Forcing himself to remain calm, Henry merely walked to Sarah's house, his strides longer than normal. The windows were lit with lamplight, and the chimney emitted a curl of smoke laced with the scent of herbs. Although it was his right to simply enter the dower house, he knocked, calling out Sarah's name. When she opened the door, a hint of surprise showing on her face, she curtsied. "You haven't found the dog yet?" she asked, saying the words before waving him to enter.

Henry shook his head, realizing just then that Hannah's search for the dog probably started at the dower house. "Actually, I was looking for Lady Gisborn. Is she here?" he asked, thinking he sounded like a jealous husband who didn't want his wife and his lover to socialize.

Sarah's eyes widened in alarm. "Oh, Gisborn," she breathed, one hand going to her chest. Nathan appeared next to her, his face lighting up when he realized his father had come to call.

"Hello, son," Henry said as he held out his right hand. The boy took it and shook it firmly.

"Did Lady Gisborn find Harold?" the boy asked. "Andrew said she was real worried when she asked where he went off to." There was a hint of excitement in his voice. "I thought he might be here when I got home from my tutor's, but mum says he didn't pay us a visit today."

"Shush, Nathan," Sarah said, her hand reaching out to hold onto her son's shoulder.

"Where did Harold go off to?" Henry queried, the sensation of panic gripping him again. It would be dark soon. It was getting colder, and more snow was falling.

"Andrew said he was heading through the field. Like he was going to where I was playing yesterday," he added with a guilty grin. "Can I come with you?"

Sarah held onto her son's shoulder more tightly, her knuckles whitening with the pressure. "You're staying here, Nathan. I'll not have you out there in this weather," she said more to Henry than to her son.

Before Sarah even finished her statement, Henry took his leave of the dower house and was off at a run, heading back toward the stables. How long had Hannah been gone? If she had found Harold, why wasn't he back at the house? Or had she stumbled? Hurt her ankle in a rabbit hole? Was she lying in the field somewhere, covered with snow and freezing to death?

Billy stood holding the reins of his horse, his slight body shivering in the growing gloom. "Good evenin', guv'nor," the groom said as Henry acknowledged him with a nod, grabbed the reins and mounted Thunder all in one smooth move. And then he was off, spurring his horse into the field. Despite the grayness of twilight and the slight covering of snow, he could make out the path they had followed through the newly plowed field the day before.

Occasionally pausing to call out Hannah's name and scan the horizon for signs of her or Harold, Henry felt his panic turn to fear. What could have happened? He was almost to the river. Certainly she wouldn't have gone to the river.

Unless she was running away.

No, she couldn't. She wouldn't leave him. He was sure of that. Not after last night. Not after the night they had spent together. Not after the way she had responded to his kisses, to the way he had made love to her, to the way he had held her afterwards as if she were the most important thing in his world.

Which she was.

Barely aware of his last thought, Henry caught sight of an

arc of jet black against the stark white of snow that covered the side of the hillock separating the field from the trees at the river's edge. He slowed his mount, allowing the horse to pick his way carefully to the mound.

Good, God! He was off his horse and kneeling next to Hannah even before he was quite sure it was her. One of her hands seemed embedded in something; in the growing darkness, it took him a moment to realize Harold was under her. He pulled her body up and against his, relieved to feel warmth on the front side of her body but aware that her back had been exposed to the cold for some time. "Hannah, my love," he whispered, his lips seeking her throat. He felt the pulse there and breathed in relief.

"Harold," he heard in a faint whisper. Hannah's eyelids were wet, as if she had been crying. Henry regarded the mass of fur for a moment. Too still to be asleep, Harold lay on his side with his eyes closed. Henry was aware of what must have happened even before he felt the dog for any signs of life. Harold had come back to the mound to die. Back to the place very near to where he had rescued Nathan. *Where Nathan had nearly died.*

Realizing he could do nothing for the dog, Henry cradled Hannah in his arms. Her eyes were still closed, her body too chilled and her breathing so slight she seemed lifeless. Holding her tightly against the front of his body, he carefully mounted his horse. He wrapped his coat around her as best he could before digging his heels into the horse. The stallion set off at a run, following the path through the field and back to the stables. Without waiting for Billy to claim his horse's reins, Henry dismounted, clutching Hannah against the front of his body as he did so. And then he was running, running into the house and through the vestibule. He didn't hear Mrs. Batey gasp or Parkerhouse's "Dear God" as he passed them.

"Where's the largest fire?" Henry demanded, barely slowing down as he made his way to the stairs.

"Lady Gisborn's room, milord," Parkerhouse replied as he watched his master take the steps two at a time.

"I'll speak with you later," Henry called down, disappearing into Hannah's room with his wife still bundled in his coat, the hem of her mantle floating beneath. He settled himself into the largest chair in front of the crackling fire, positioning Hannah so her back was to the flames and her front was nestled against his body. Her arms were encased in his greatcoat, the garment still wrapped tightly around her body. Henry cupped one of her cheeks with his hand, placing it so it rested against his shoulder.

"Is she ill, my lord?"

Henry knew he should have expected the housekeeper, but he was still startled at the sound of her voice. "She's alive," he answered, surprised at the relief he heard in his voice. "Harold is not, though. Can you have cook make some tea and chocolate, please? And have Murphy bring the brandy from the library." A list of tasks was forming in his mind, but at that moment, he wanted to get Hannah warm and awake. He could find out what had happened later.

Mrs. Batey hurried from the room, barely getting out a "Yes, milord," as she did so.

Taking a deep breath, Henry realized it was probably the first in a long time. The fear he had felt at thinking he had lost Hannah had been palpable. How could a woman he had only known a couple of weeks have such an effect on him? Yes, she was beautiful, but her physical beauty had nothing to do with how her simple presence in a room seemed to make it so much brighter. Or how her simple kiss on his cheek made him feel so glad to be home when he returned from a day working in the fields. He had been looking forward to that kiss tonight, he realized, the thought buoying him after the setbacks his laborers had encountered while working on the new ditch. They hadn't even worked that day due to the chilly conditions.

Unconsciously, his grip on Hannah tightened, and he absently kissed the top of her head as he considered what life would be like without her. Sarah was becoming distant, almost as if she no longer wanted him as her lover and protector. His son would be going to Abingdon soon. *Empty*, he thought, his lips returning to Hannah's head. Only she had angled her head up, and his kiss fell on her forehead, the heat of her skin searing his lips. He pulled her away from his body, startled to see her cheeks bright red. *Fever!*

"My lord?" Murphy stood near the doorway, unsure if he should enter the lady's bedchamber. A crystal decanter hung from one hand while two glasses were in another.

"Come," Henry called out, repositioning Hannah so he could remove his coat from around her body. "Help me get this off of her. I think she has a fever," he spoke in a voice that sounded like one that had commanded soldiers.

Murphy was there in an instant, having deposited the brandy and glasses on a nearby table. The valet expertly removed the coat and mantle, placing them both over one arm. Then he knelt and undid the laces of her half-boots, pulling them off as he turned his gaze up to meet Henry's. "Should I have Parkerhouse send for the doctor, my lord?" Murphy asked, his brows furrowing. Lady Gisborn's boots were stiff from the cold, although he noted she wore more than silk stockings beneath them.

Henry gave the question some consideration. With the snow and growing chill in the air, it would be cruel to require the physician to make the two mile trip from Bampton. Not to mention the poor footman that would have to make the trip to Bampton in the first place. "No. I'm rather hoping brandy will be medicinal enough. Would you pour some? And where is Lady Gisborn's maid?" he asked as he noticed the valet still held his wife's boots and mantle.

"Miss Parker is not in residence, my lord," the valet paused as he considered how to tell his master that it was the maid's day off. "She is visiting her parents at the Coley house," he finally got out. At Gisborn's look of disbelief, he added, "Miss Parker is due back first thing in the morning."

Boggled, Henry bit back an angry retort. Lily was barely

back from her trip with Babcock and now she was off to Bampton. The sooner she and Billy were married, the better.

Murphy took a deep breath. "At the risk of sounding impertinent, my lord, has Lady Gisborn… has she mentioned anything about the lack of staff here?" he asked, keeping his voice low. "I realize this is not the best time to be bringing up the matter," he said by way of an apology.

Henry shook his head. Not only had Hannah not mentioned any concerns she might have had about the lack of maids and kitchen help, she hadn't spoken one word of complaint when Lily had gone missing. She had even dressed herself and arranged own hair. What other daughter of an aristocrat would have been so accepting of such conditions? And not voice a word of complaint? His uncle's years of miserly behavior might have left the earldom flush with funds, but the cost to correct the years of—how had Lord Bostwick put it?—*deferred maintenance*—would drain the coffers if Henry wasn't careful. Well, there was certainly enough to hire more staff, more maids, at least. "I hear the Stewards have a daughter who is seeking employment in service," Henry stated by way of a suggestion.

Murphy's eyebrow cocked up. "Do you wish me to inform Parkerhouse?"

"Yes," Henry spoke firmly. "We need another maid or two in this house."

"Very well, my lord," Murphy said, handing a glass of brandy to Henry as he did so. He left the other on the table next to his master and took his leave of the room.

Henry brought the glass next to Hannah's lips, thinking the smoky scent would be enough to awaken her. Although she didn't stir, Henry heard her faint whisper of "Harold".

Oh, how he wished she would say his name like she did that damned dog's name!

He was about to chide himself for his uncharitable thought—Harold had saved his son, after all—when he heard his name whispered.

And it did sound like a prayer. As if she had overheard

his thoughts. "Hannah?" he whispered. He put down the glass and shook her gently, stroked the back of a finger down one of her cheeks. Her lashes fluttered and then opened. "Thank God," he breathed, holding her tighter against his body.

Hannah stared up at Henry, her mind a jumble, as if she couldn't tell where a dream stopped and reality began. "Henry?" she whispered in reply. She attempted to push herself away from his body, to look around at their surroundings. "Where? What?" she murmured.

His tense body relaxing, Henry repositioned her on his lap and kissed her temple and forehead. "Do you think you can take some brandy?" he offered, holding the glass to her lips. Hannah gave him a look that suggested he should not be offering her spirits, but she sipped a bit, not the least bothered by the strong flavor or the burn she felt as it reached the back of her throat. "You've had an awful shock," he whispered.

The words seemed to bring her back to reality. He felt her body tense, saw her cornflower blue eyes widen before tears welled up in them. "Harold died," she whispered, one gloved hand covering her mouth.

"I know, I... I found you with him. He went back to the same place where he and Nathan were yesterday." He didn't know what else to say so he merely held her for a few more minutes, coaxing her to drink more of the brandy. When she had drained the glass, Henry set it aside and then used two fingers to begin pulling the gloves, one finger at a time, from Hannah's hand.

"He was old, you know," Hannah whispered before a sob wracked her body. "It's been at least ten years since Father brought him back from Italy," she explained, her tears subsiding nearly as quickly as they had started. "He was still a puppy then. Father was allowed to take him from the den because he was generous with his support of the monks that lived in the Alps. They rescued his friend, you see. Mr. Aldenwood was injured in a mountain pass..."

The name startled Henry. He had just removed one glove and was about to start on the other. "Aldenwood? The adventurer?" Henry interrupted, remembering how her father had described the man who was known to have traveled the world. The man who was now claiming the effects of a volcano would make this growing season especially difficult in Northern Europe. Henry still hadn't decided what to plant, or even if he should give credence to Aldenwood's prediction that the summer would be too cold and rainy to support a decent crop at all. If they could get the final drainage ditch dug, they could at least channel the excess water to the river. But even wheat required sunlight to grow. One large greenhouse was under construction. There was plenty of timber to erect the frame of the second greenhouse. He had already talked to the glazier in Bampton about glass panes. If the man wasn't able to make enough for a greenhouse or two, then oilcloth could be used in its stead.

Henry's mind was racing when he realized Hannah was still speaking.

"Yes," Hannah nodded. "He had a badly sprained ankle, so my father continued without him until he spotted an Alpenmastiff on the trail. The dog had supplies—he had been sent by the monks to help them, you see," she explained in a whisper, "And one of the bitches had given birth to a litter a couple of months earlier. The monks couldn't afford to keep all the dogs, of course, so Father was allowed to take Harold." She took a deep breath and sighed, burrowing herself against Henry, fighting the sobs she could feel coming from the very center of her body.

Mrs. Batey hurried into the room with a tray of cups and two pots. "Tea and chocolate, my lord," she said as she set the tray on the table nearest the fireplace. "How is she?"

Henry gave the housekeeper a cursory glance. "I think she has a fever, but she seems in one piece, at least." His wife had fallen asleep, her occasional jerks and trembles suggesting her sleep was filled with nightmares. "Could you help me get her into bed?" he whispered, slowly rising to stand with Hannah's limp body held in his arms.

"Of course, my lord," Mrs. Batey replied with a nod, hurrying to turn down the bed linens. "I'll see if I can't find a nightrail—"

"Behind the pillow," Henry said as he motioned with his head toward the front of the bed. He had to fight the sudden flush he felt coloring his face. How many husbands knew where their wives kept their bed clothes? Of course, it was there because that's where he had stuffed it after removing it from her body the two nights before, hiding it from her so she couldn't insist on pulling it back on after they had made love.

He thought of this morning, of how hard it had been to take his leave of her and the warm bed, of how hard his erection had been even as he made his way through the cold room to his own. It had been that strange tug on his heart that made him leave the ruby pendant and chain on her pillow when he had returned to her room to say his farewell for the day.

Sitting her on the bed, Henry noticed the ruby pendant as it caught the faint lamplight, red streaks flashing out from where it rested in the hollow of her throat. *She's wearing it!* He placed the front of her body against his as he leaned over to undo the series of buttons down her back. He was aware of Mrs. Batey's barely contained gasp as he lifted her to a standing position and lowered her bodice and sleeves. "Can you ..?" he hinted, keeping Hannah up as the housekeeper stepped forward and stripped his wife of her gown and petticoats.

"At least she put on more petticoats," Mrs. Batey commented as she removed the third one. "Should I leave her stockings on, my lord?" she asked then, not sure if the earl expected her to remove his wife's corset and chemise while he was still in the room.

"Are they dry?" he asked, reluctantly pulling his attention away from Hannah's bare shoulders and the curve of her neck. A quick memory of Lady Charlotte's back, with its series of black stitches marching between her shoulder blades, came unbidden. Where Charlotte would have scars from those stitches—from the wound put there by a horsewhip— for the rest of her life, Hannah would have smooth, creamy skin that molded beautifully over sensuous shoulder blades and the delicate bumps of her spine. It took every fiber of his being not to stroke that smooth skin right now, not to place the palm of his hand against that space between the triangular bones and simply revel in touching her, in allowing the warmth of his hand to seep into her.

"A bit damp, I think," Mrs. Batey replied with a shake of her head. "And cold," she added under her breath, her head shaking as if she couldn't fathom the countess' strange foray. She pulled the stockings and socks off Hannah's feet before loosening the ties of the corset. Giving the earl a questioning look, she waited until Henry nodded.

"She is my wife. I have seen all of her, Mrs. Batey. You needn't worry about propriety."

The housekeeper had to close her mouth quickly or risk looking like a fool to her employer. A few tugs and a swish of the fine silk of her chemise, and Hannah was left bare. With the warmth of the fabric removed from her, Hannah's skin turned to gooseflesh. Mrs. Batey quickly pulled the nightgown over Hannah's head while Henry helped to smooth it down around her body. Satisfied she was ready for bed, Henry lifted her into it. "Parkerhouse brought up brandy. Could you refill her glass? And I could use a cup of tea," he murmured, thinking this had to be the most he had asked of the housekeeper since he had moved into Gisborn Hall upon his uncle's death. "And could you bring up dinner when it's ready? Along with a hot brick? My lady's feet are freezing," he added then, pulling off his boots and stockings.

Mrs. Batey nodded nervously, not accustomed to the earl undressing in front of her. She hurried over to the tea service, pouring a cup while she tried not to watch as Henry climbed into the bed, positioning himself so he sat against the upholstered headboard before pulling Hannah into his arms and the bed linens up and over the both of them. And then, her face a bright red, Mrs. Batey gave him the tea, left the glass of brandy on the night stand, and performed a quick curtsy before leaving the room.

Henry placed a feather pillow behind his back and pulled another to prop up the arm that held Hannah. Downing the tea, he leaned over Hannah to place the cup on the night stand. She murmured something unintelligible, a tinge of sadness in her voice.

He sensed quite suddenly the growing spot of wetness in the linen of his shirt under where her head rested. *She's weeping.* His heart clenched, a sudden need to comfort her overwhelming him.

Sighing, Henry rather wished he had completed undressing, even if it would have scandalized poor Mrs. Batey. Deciding he could at least get out of his breeches, he moved Hannah to his side and pushed them off under the covers, tossing them over the side of the bed.

Even before he could reposition Hannah in his arms, she had turned onto her side, her body clinging to his bare thigh, one arm bent so her hand rested next to his manhood and her head rested on his hip. He had to stifle a chuckle. At the moment, that area was the warmest part of his body. But if she opened her eyes, she might not appreciate the sight of his manhood only inches in front of her.

Lifting her back onto his body, he held her close, whispered into her hair and sprinkled feather kisses along the top of her face, telling himself he was checking for fever. She was warm, and the weight of her curled body made Henry succumb to the drowsiness that suddenly enveloped his entire body. Within moments, he was sound asleep.

CHAPTER 19

HANNAH FALLS IN LOVE
WITH HER HUSBAND

Hannah stared out the window, her elbows resting on the sill as her chin lay atop her hands. She had awakened to find the household quiet and Henry gone from the bed. She was sure he had been there, holding her, stroking her arm and kissing her temple as she wept and shivered.

Or had she dreamed that?

Had he spent the entire night in her bed? She remembered feeling protected. The thought reminded her of why she had felt such sorrow.

Harold. *Poor Harold.*

The excitement of the day before yesterday, when he had rescued Nathan from the river, had obviously been too much for his aged heart and his old body. To have chosen to die so near to where Nathan had nearly lost his life, though—perhaps he had done so because he knew she would look for him there.

She wondered if she could ask Gisborn to have his body buried where he lay. Would he think her request foolish? She couldn't stand the thought of Harold laying out on the hillock like that. A tear escaped the corner of her eye. Thinking she should wipe it away, she instead ignored it and continued to stare out over Gisborn's lands to the south. If she squinted, she might make out the tops of the tress that lined the riverbank.

The farmland went all the way to the river and extended to the east and west beyond her line of sight. Instead of the typical one-acre strips of farmland that surrounded Bampton, Gisborn had managed to combine his tracts into several large farm fields for his tenants.

The fact that he worked with his tenants to improve their situation seemed out of the ordinary for an earl. Instead of the seven pence a day a typical farmer in Bampton might earn, Henry was determined that those who farmed his lands would earn eight pence a day or more. He was so unlike the other men of the *ton!* She knew of no other earl that labored in his fields—most had estate managers to oversee such details, and even those men wouldn't dirty their hands with the actual working of the land. But Gisborn was up early every day, riding out on his horse to wherever the next project lay unfinished. He was a responsible land owner, she realized. A good man.

He is my husband.

She sighed as she continued to stare out the window.

Henry strode into the entry hall, glancing into the various rooms as he passed them, hoping to find Hannah awake and dressed and doing whatever it was countesses were expected to do every day.

But the house was strangely quiet.

Perhaps she had gone calling on the villagers, he hoped. He found Mrs. Batey dusting the statuary in the parlor. "Good morning, Mrs. Batey," he greeted her, not wanting to startle her with his sudden presence for fear the bust of his uncle's father would tumble from its perch on a wooden pedestal.

"Oh! My lord, I did not hear you come in!" she answered, flustered. From the way she couldn't quite meet his gaze, Henry thought she was no doubt remembering the sight of him undressing his wife the night before. Or perhaps she had seen him sleeping whilst he held Hannah when she delivered the dinner tray later that night.

Before she could say more and in an effort to stave off further embarrassment, Henry asked after Hannah. "Is Lady Gisborn making calls?" He could immediately tell from the way the housekeeper's eyes darted about that Lady Gisborn was most certainly *not* making calls. "What is it, Mrs. Batey? Is she here?" *Good God, would she have gone running off again?* If so, Henry hoped she wouldn't have gone back to where Harold had died. He had arranged for two of the laborers to retrieve the corpse, although he wasn't yet sure where he would have them bury it.

"She's still in her bedchamber, my lord," the housekeeper answered, her hands nervously wringing together in her apron. "I took chocolate up to her at ten, but when I checked on her again at eleven, she hadn't touched it. She just stares out the window, my lord. She's still in her night clothes, but she must be freezing."

Henry was out of the parlor and taking the steps two at a time before Mrs. Batey could finish her sentence. When there was no response to his knock on Hannah's bedchamber door, he opened it slightly and peered around the opening. "My lady?" His first glance was to the bed, but it had been made up and looked as if it hadn't been slept in. Then his attention turned to the only source of light in the room. As he feared, Hannah was still staring out the window, her forearms resting on the sill and her chin resting on one arm. She wore no dressing gown or even a blanket against the cold—she would certainly be chilled to the bone.

Quite unaware she was no longer alone, Hannah sighed. What would she do without Harold? He had been her constant companion for nearly ten years. At some point, she would have a baby to care for, a baby to play with and to feed and put to bed and to love. But that would be at least nine months away! What would she do in the meantime?

"My lady?"

Oh, so now I am hearing things, she thought with derision.

I should get dressed. I should get something to eat. I should...

"Hannah!"

Startled, she sat up straight and turned to find Henry staring down at her, the worry so evident in his eyes that she thought something horrible had happened. But what could be more horrible than Harold dying? Another tear fell from the corner of her eye. "My lord?" she finally replied, realizing the earl was indeed real and perhaps a bit impatient and standing rather close. She could feel heat radiate from his body.

"Good God, Hannah, you'll *freeze* sitting there like that!" His arms were suddenly around her, lifting her from the chair and pulling her stiff body against the front of his. Warmth seeped into her, wakening her other senses. She was shivering, although she had been unaware of it until the heat from her husband's body became apparent. Her mind seemed slow, unable to form a coherent thought. Where was she? And where was Lily? Shouldn't her lady's maid be here to dress her?

"Hannah."

Her name was said in a sigh as she was vaguely aware of being lifted and taken to her bed. A mound of bed linens were suddenly covering her body, although she clung to the source of heat that still held her. "You're frozen!"

The words were apparently said to admonish her, but Hannah couldn't figure out why.

"How long have you been sitting there like that?" Henry asked in a whisper, his lips coming down onto her forehead.

She rather liked those lips, she remembered. They were soft and firm and forceful and forgiving and...

"Hannah, my love," the voice said again, only this time there was no admonishment. *My love.* What a very nice thing to hear in that voice she found so comforting. Coming from the body that was so warm and so hard and so very male. He smelled of musk and eau de cologne with just a hint of spice.

So why at this moment would she think of Harold? Harold was warm. But he was also hairy. He slobbered. He sometimes smelled like a dog. But he was so... *had been* so devoted. Another tear spilt from an eye and ran down her cheek. It didn't make it far, though. For the tip of Henry's tongue reached out and captured it before his lips pressed against her cheek.

"Hannah. Please. Say something," he urged her, one hand cupping her other cheek to force her head to turn toward him.

Hannah's eyes widened. "Oh, Henry. Poor Harold. He died and..."

Henry's lips covered hers, cutting off whatever else she was about to say about the dog. Hannah tried to return the kiss as best she could, but she was shivering so badly she didn't seem to have control over any of her limbs. Or her lips.

When Henry pulled away, she made a sound of disappointment. A small smile appeared on his lips before his kissed her again. "I've seen to Harold," he finally said, hoping she wasn't so addled she would misunderstand his words.

Hannah was suddenly very aware of where she was and who was speaking to her. "Will we bury him?" she asked, hoping that's what he meant. She sniffled.

"Mmm," Henry responded with a nod, his lips coming back down onto her forehead. "Do you suppose you might be able to drink some chocolate now?" he asked, brushing a lock of hair from her forehead.

Hannah smiled. "Chocolate sounds wonderful. I'm so hungry," she added, her hand moving to her belly. She glanced in the direction of the mantel clock and her eyes focused on the time. She returned her attention to Henry. "Noon?"

"Afraid so," he answered, kissing her forehead again.

She rather liked it when he did that. It made her feel loved. Her heart clenched. Henry couldn't love her. He loved another. He loved Sarah. *I need to guard my heart*, she remembered. If her husband continued as he was doing these past few days, she would find herself quite in love with the man. But his heart was clearly owned by the woman who bore him his son. Hannah could have him in her bed, but she would never have his heart.

Hannah wondered when he was finding any time to spend with Sarah. He always seemed to be working or here at Gisborn Hall. Perhaps with his promise to bed her for another few weeks, he had decided to forego visits to Sarah. *He is supposed to be bedding me every night, so when would he have the opportunity to spend a night with Sarah?*

Certainly not last night.

Last night, she had been quite bereft, making a watering pot of herself over the loss of Harold. But Henry had been by her side the entire night, holding her close in bed and comforting her whenever she wept. The thought of his warm body atop hers came unbidden. She needed to give him an heir. They should be making love. The sooner she bore him a child, the sooner she would have something to love.

Something to replace Harold.

"Harold." The name came out in a whisper. The tears started anew.

A frustrated sigh escaped Henry. He was up and out of the bed and out the bedchamber door. Hannah listened to his heavy footfalls as they made their way down the stairs. The front door slammed.

Harold!

Henry berated himself even before he was out the front door. Harold had been Hannah's constant companion for ten years. Lady Charlotte had warned him, had told him that if he wanted Lady Hannah, he would have to accept Harold, too. Well, he had.

He *thought* he had, at least.

How was he supposed to compete with a dog for Hannah's affection? *A dead dog, no less.*

Affection?

The thought brought him up short. What the hell was he thinking? Why should he expect Hannah to feel any affection toward him? Sarah was his love. Hannah was his wife. Hannah would merely be the mother to his legitimate children.

She married him knowing that. She married him knowing that men only ever loved their mistresses and only had wives to bear them their heirs.

So, why did he suddenly yearn for Hannah's affection?

Perhaps because he was feeling affection for her? *Am I?* Because, if he was, he had to wonder about Sarah. He certainly loved her. He had for over ten years. *Could I love two women?*

Hannah and Sarah were so different from one another. Sarah was practical and strong and independent. She could never be a milk water maid like so many of the debutantes in the *ton*. It was part of what appealed to him. Part of what he found so endearing about her. And yet, lately, she had shown very little interest in him or his life. She carried on as if they had never been a loving couple, almost as if they hadn't been parents to a boy nearly old enough to attend school. What would happen when Nathan went off to Abingdon in the fall? Would Sarah withdraw more? Or would she return to her loving self, a willing partner in his bed? A confidante and a friend?

Feeling at a loss, Henry pondered his future with Sarah. He then thought of Hannah, of how she would look when she was carrying his child—a nymph with a rounded belly, her braided hair wrapped in a silver blonde coronet atop her head, ringlets dancing at her temples, one hand resting protectively at her midriff while the other held a flower to her nose. He could hear her laughter, the melodic sound coming in response to Harold as he barked and bounded about at her feet. He smiled at the thought of her delicate face alight with the glow of impending motherhood. He thought of her holding their babe in her arms, of how she would look holding it to her swollen breast as it feasted on her, her feet tucked under Harold as he napped in front of the rocker. He could almost feel jealousy at that thought, that his son would be held so close and Harold would always be by her side. Jealousy and... he nearly stumbled as he thought about the image he had created of her and their child and *Harold*.

Harold was in his mind's eye, but he would not be there with Hannah and their baby. He couldn't be.

Henry tried again to imagine Hannah with just the babe and found he could not. Harold had been a part of her since he had met her. He had been her constant companion for a very long time.

Shaking his head, Henry was finally aware of where he was headed. Tom Cavenaugh's cottage, he realized. Tom had what he needed to give Hannah. She would need something to get her through the next year, until she would give birth to their first child and have something of her own—of theirs— to love.

He wondered if she would ever love him. *God, what am I thinking?* He married her because she would tolerate Sarah. And, apparently she had found Sarah so agreeable, she had asked the woman to move into Gisborn Hall!

What was she thinking?

Did she not realize he couldn't host his lover under the same roof as his wife? *Such an unselfish act, though*, he considered. What other woman of the *ton* would not only marry him knowing he had a woman he loved, but a bastard son, too? Most would be too scandalized to even consider his suit. And yet Hannah had done so knowing she might be ostracized by the *ton* should more of them discover his secret.

They would, of course. Probably in the fall, after Nathan was enrolled at Abingdon. Word would get out that the bastard son of the Earl of Gisborn was attending school. And the boy's stepmother was the Countess of Gisborn, the daughter of the Marquess of Devonville. Having a father for a marquess could only go so far to assuage the *ton*.

Mistress.

Henry winced at the label. He had never once thought of Sarah in those terms until the past two weeks. She had borne him a son. He loved her. But did she still love him? His heart clenched again as a strange feeling passed through him, one he was sure he hadn't experienced before. Perhaps he would stop at Sarah's cottage. Just to look in on her and Nathan. It would only take a few moments. He would be able to tell from Sarah's reaction if his fears were unfounded or not.

A curl of smoke was wafting out of one of the chimneys of Sarah Inglenook's residence. At least she was home, he considered. He strode up to the front door and rapped on the painted wood. "Sarah?" he called out. A quick glance about the property made him realize Nathan must be inside or at his tutor's house—the yard was deserted but for two chickens who pecked at the ground.

The sound of a bolt being thrown made him turn around. Another moment, and Sarah appeared in the barely opened doorway. Her eyes were wide with surprise. "My lord?" she said with a hint of question, her legs bending into a curtsy. She opened the door wider but didn't step aside to allow him entrance.

Henry regarded her for a moment, stunned at how different she looked. Her hair, normally wound into a tight bun at the back of her head and sometimes covered partially with a mob cap, was rolled into an elegant chignon. Ringlets surrounded her face. Her usual muslin day gown, brown or gray and topped with an apron, was replaced with a deep blue round gown, and she wore white gloves. Henry bobbed his head in a bow. "Good afternoon, my lady," he said, the appreciation in his voice evident. "Are you about to make calls?" he asked, never having seen her dress quite so nicely unless she was headed to church.

Sarah blushed. "No, my lord—"

"Henry," he insisted, his eyebrows furrowing at her formal address. She never called him by his honorific. He had expressly forbid her to do so.

"Henry," she hissed, stepping aside and using one hand to invite him in. "It's not proper for you to call on me here. You're a married man now," she whispered hoarsely.

Annoyance replaced the sense of satisfaction he felt upon

seeing Sarah looking so smart. He wondered if the gown was new. Had she purchased it with the pin money he gave her every week? Or had she made it from fabric purchased in Bampton? "You're the mother of my child. I'll call on you when I wish," he responded more harshly than he intended. He dipped his head as if apologizing. "Where is Nathan?" he asked, expecting his son would have come out of his room when he heard his father's voice.

Tensing at the severe way in which he spoke, Sarah lowered her gaze. "He's with his tutor, of course," she replied with a heavy sigh. She was none too pleased at the earl's appearance. If he didn't leave soon, the man who was scheduled to take her for a ride to Bampton would show up to claim her, and then she would have to tell Henry who he was and why she was going for a ride with him. "I'm sure Mr. Thomas would not mind you paying a visit. And I'm quite certain Nathan will not object." She said the last with a forced smirk, hoping to lighten the mood.

Henry seemed distracted and short-tempered. Were things between him and his new wife already strained? Had Hannah decided she did not care for Henry's high-handed manner?

Or was it something else?

Had he come expecting to bed her? *Not now, Henry*, she thought as she pinched her lips together. "How is Lady Gisborn fairing? I take it she found the dog?" she half-questioned, hoping the change of subject would remind him he was married. *Honor your marriage vows*, she pleaded in silence.

"I fear Lady Hannah is quite distressed," Henry replied, remembering the quest he had been on before he detoured to the dower house. "The dog died yesterday. Out near where Nathan was found."

Both of Sarah's gloved hands covered her mouth, and her eyes were wide. Moving into the parlor, she stood very still for a moment. "What... whatever happened?" she whispered as her face contorted with grief.

Surprised by her reaction, Henry wondered if perhaps the loss of Harold was more serious than he had figured. "He was *old*. All the excitement from the day before." He moved into the room and watched as a tear collected in the corner of Sarah's eye. *Oh, not her, too,* he thought, wondering if all the women in the village would shed tears for the deceased beast. "He was just a *dog*, Sarah," he said, his teeth clenching.

Sarah's eyes widened, a flash of anger unmistakable in their smoky green depths. "How can you *say* that?" she demanded, her fists turning to balls at her sides. One held her gloves— they would be terribly wrinkled if she held onto them like that for much longer.

Henry leaned against the settee on his outstretched arms, his head turned slightly to one side. "What? That he is a *dog?*" he countered. "A good for nothing beast who..."

Not having his attention on Sarah, Henry was at a complete loss to understand why his cheek suddenly stung with a sharp pain and his vision was impaired by a series of stars that danced across his eyes. For, until it impacted the side of his face, he was quite unaware of the flat of Sarah's hand as it arced through the air.

"You *ass!*" Sarah cried out.

She didn't bother trying to shake out her hand. The shock of the impact had to have caused her as much pain as she inflicted. Henry knew it had to have hurt. She might have even broken a bone or two. But the rage on her face made it quite apparent it would be some time before she was aware of anything but her anger toward him.

Recoiling from both the pain of her slap and from her ire, Henry stared at her in disbelief. "Sarah," was all he could manage to say as he stared at her.

"You're an *ass*, Gisborn!" she spat out, her head shaking back and forth. "I cannot believe that sweet, beautiful woman would agree to be your wife when you are such an unfeeling, uncaring *beast!*" Her hands back to clenched fists, she stalked to the fireplace and turned around, anger still evident on her face. "That dog saved our son's life—"

"I am quite aware—"

"That dog is the reason your *son* was able to wake up this morning—"

"And I do appreciate—"

"That dog is the reason we still *have* a son!"

"I understand the—"

"That dog was Lady Gisborn's only *friend!*"

Henry stared at Sarah, his face contorted into a look of startled disbelief. Never had she raised her voice like this. Never had she challenged him. Although she had punched him that one time, when he had left her alone at her request (she *demanded* he do so, as he remembered it). And a few other times in their youth, but usually because he had started a fight.

"That dog was like a *child* to Lady Gisborn. He was all she *had* in this world!" she whispered hoarsely, a wave of her hand indicating her definition of the 'world' was Gisborn's earldom. "And now he is *dead*, probably because he saved your son's *life*. And you have the *gall* to claim he is just a *dog?* How *dare* you?" At some point, tears had sprung to her eyes, and now several escaped to stain her cheeks. "How dare you?" This last came out as a whisper.

Not sure how to respond and even more discomfited by Sarah's tears, Henry took a deep breath. And then he did whatever he did when tears were involved. He moved closer and wrapped his arms around her shoulders, drawing Sarah against his body, wanting to provide comfort and soothe her anger away—especially to soothe away anger that was directed entirely at him. Her shoulders were tense, unforgiving, though. Her head didn't bury itself into his shoulder to take comfort there. After a moment, Sarah let out a very long sigh, her shoulders finally giving in and her entire body relaxing under his hold. She wept quietly into his shoulder.

Her words still echoed in his mind.

That dog was like a child to Hannah.

Well, he supposed he should have treated Harold like a... like a stepson, then. The dog *had* saved his son's life.

Henry pondered what to do. What to do to appease Sarah as well as to honor the hairy beast. *Give him a proper burial.* Bury him in the family plot on the east side of the property. Order a headstone from the local mason. Allow Hannah her bereavement. Having recently been in mourning for her mother and sister, the woman must certainly knew how to grieve.

"I am on my way to the Cavenaugh's," Henry finally spoke, his voice soft against her hair. "I mean to ask about the litter of puppies their bitch gave birth to before I left on my trip to London."

At the mention of the puppies, Sarah sniffled. Angling her head up, she regarded her protector. "They are adorable, Henry. If I could afford to feed a dog as large as they will be in a year, I would have you select one for me, too," she claimed, her face lighting up with the statement. She was furiously wiping away tears with a handkerchief she must have pulled from a pocket in her gown. Henry realized belatedly that he hadn't offered his.

If I could afford to feed...

What did she mean by that? He supported her. He could certainly afford food for a dog! "I will see to it," he stated with a quick nod. When he saw her surprised expression, he wondered again at her nice clothes and hair. "Were you about to go on a call?" he asked then, an uncomfortable sensation creeping into his awareness. "Or is someone about to call on you?"

Her eyes closing for a moment, Sarah swallowed. She lowered her head. "The latter. Mr. McDonald offered to take me to Bampton. To shop," she added, hoping the arrangement didn't sound as scandalous as she was thinking it would. "He has a very fast curricle, so I shouldn't be gone long, and Nathan knows to go to Andrew's house when he is done with his studies."

Henry had thought her slap quite painful, but now Sarah's words were like a blow to his stomach. A *man* was calling on her. Another man. A man for whom she was dressed rather nicely. She looked pretty, he thought. Certainly not like Hannah, for Hannah was far younger and more beautiful in her nymph-like, fairy tale princess way.

But even though Sarah would turn heads today, she was still *his*. She would still require his permission to make the trip. It wasn't as if McDonald was considering anything beyond being a driver for her. The man certainly knew Sarah was his. She was of an age that she no longer required a chaperone. And she wouldn't think about taking a lover. She couldn't. She was the mother of his child.

"I take it Mr. McDonald is due at any moment," Henry said, his ears detecting the sounds of horses coming up the lane. Sarah deserved an afternoon shopping, he realized. He could not begrudge her that simple delight. "Give him my regards, and enjoy your trip," he added as he leaned over and kissed Sarah on the cheek. Surprised at his comment, Sarah kissed him, a quick peck meant as an acknowledgment of his blessing and perhaps as an apology for her having slapped him. She rarely kissed him.

"Thank you, Henry, truly," she spoke in a whisper, her eyes opening to meet his. He was sure he saw surprise there, perhaps even relief. He nodded and gave her a quick kiss on the forehead.

Before he could change his mind, Henry departed the dower house. He nearly ran the length of the path to the lane, avoiding Tad McDonald's curricle as it had taken the circular drive along the side of the house. The man owned a nearby posting inn and tavern, the profits of which made McDonald one of the wealthiest men in the Bampton area.

Henry supposed if Sarah were seen in McDonald's company, there would be talk. But everyone within two miles of Gisborn Hall knew Sarah was his... his *mistress*. He grimaced. The word seemed so wrong for what they had shared. Sarah was more than a woman he bedded when he felt the need for release. He had loved her for almost his entire life. She would have been his wife—his countess—had she not been so damned stubborn!

He shook his head and remembered why he had set out on this trek to begin with. Why hadn't he thought to ride Thunder? The horse was probably still saddled next to the stable. He could have been at the Cavenaugh's and back home by now.

Reaching into his pocket, he felt for coins and pulled out several. How much would Cavenaugh want for a puppy, he wondered? The man was so proud of his brown and white long-haired beast, claiming it had been a gift of a friend who had returned from a Grand Tour of Europe. Apparently, the dog was pregnant when it arrived in Great Britain, although there was nothing said about the breed of the dog or if the puppies were fathered by a dog of the same breed or not.

He wasn't sure what to expect, exactly. He had only heard tales from his valet and Mrs. Batey that the pups were brown and white like their mother and made "adorable mewling sounds," this last a comment made by Mrs. Batey, not Mr. Murphy.

Had Mr. Murphy made such a claim, Henry thought he might have to dismiss him.

At least six weeks had passed since the pups were born; perhaps he would be able to take one home to Hannah now.

Approaching Cavenaugh's small farm cottage, he heard the dogs well before he saw them. And when he did, he had to admit to feeling shocked, for at least three of the beasts looked like miniature versions of Harold. Well, not so miniature, he realized when he got closer to the pen. Several were bounding about, grabbing at one another's tails and jumping on each other's backs. The 'adorable mewling sounds' had been replaced with yips and yowls. The 'woof ' he heard had come from the bitch, who had pressed herself against one of the pen's wooden posts and was watching the chaos with a distinct look of annoyance. On closer inspection, Henry thought she looked enough like Harold to be of the same breed. If Cavenaugh's friend had taken the Grand Tour of Europe, he had no doubt included the Alps in his trek and come across the same monks that Henry's father-in-law had during his tour there ten years ago.

"My lord!" Tom Cavenaugh called out from the edge of his field. He trotted up to the front of his property and gave the earl a bow before extending his right hand.

"Mr. Cavenaugh. I see you are the proprietor of a rather large nursery," Henry said with a grin as he nodded toward the pen filled with puppies. Were there four? Or five? They didn't stand still long enough to be counted, and they were certainly larger than Henry expected for dogs that couldn't be much more than six weeks old.

The farmer rolled his eyes. "When ol' MacLeod dropped off Maggie, here," he pointed to the mother of the brood, "I thought she seemed larger than she was supposed to be. He thought it quite the thing to bring a pregnant bitch from the Alps, the bounder. But the man has no place to keep such a beastie. And I've grown rather fond of her. She's a good mouser," he claimed with a proud nod.

A mouser? Well, given how large the dogs were, he supposed they had to be able to eat anything. Perhaps one of the dogs would be good for something more than a companion for Hannah, Henry thought. "Are these... Alpenmastiffs?" he asked as he waved to the pups.

"Heard of 'em, have you?" Tom commented in surprise. "They're rare, apparently. Some men in a mountain cave—"

"St. Bernard monks," Henry interrupted him.

Tom's eyebrows shot up. "You know the story then?" he questioned, impressed by the earl's apparent worldliness.

"Until he died yesterday, Lady Gisborn had one," Henry explained quickly. "Harold MacDuff was ten years old. She is quite *bereft* at his loss. I was hoping I could buy one or two of these off of you." He knew just the one for Hannah, too—a male whose patches of light brown and white most closely matched Harold's. Although he was fairly rambunctious, Henry thought perhaps the little monster would settle down as it aged.

He could only hope.

Tom Cavenaugh gave the earl a look of surprise. "Buy one?" he repeated, a look of wonder on his face. "Begging your pardon, my lord, but you can *have* your pick. Maggie is done feeding 'em, and I certainly can't afford to keep 'em all," he countered, his expression very serious. "Could you give Lady Gisborn my sympathies? If she had him ten years, he was probably like a child to her. My wife, may she rest in peace, probably would have allowed Maggie to sleep in our bed—under the bed linens no less," he added, his expression dour.

Henry wondered if perhaps Maggie was already sleeping in Cavenaugh's bed, if for no other reason than to get some peace and quiet from her noisy pups. He tossed Tom a coin. "I want that one," he said as he pointed to the small version of Harold MacDuff. "And if Miss Inglenook wants one as she claims she does, I'll have her come down and pick another."

Tom caught the coin, a look of surprise crossing his face when he took in the denomination. *A sovereign! For a dog?* He followed the direction of Henry's finger. "Good choice. Wasn't the first out, but he's not the runt, either." The farmer stepped into the pen and scooped up the fur ball. When Tom came to where Henry stood at the pen wall, he held the squirming mass out to the earl.

Henry froze.

He had never held a dog before.

He owned dogs. Two of them. Spaniels for hunting. But he had never held them in his arms nor treated them as pets. Suddenly, he was holding a rather heavy, wiggling, warm bundle of brown and white fluff. Huge brown eyes stared at him before a yawn revealed a rather large mouth, a very long tongue, and rows of sharp, white teeth. Floppy ears, huge paws and a tail that swished from side to side... despite knowing what it would look like when full grown, Henry couldn't help but find the little bugger *cute*. And before Henry had a chance to readjust how he held the pup, it fell asleep.

"They do that," Tom commented as he watched the earl

try to position the dog for easy travel. "They're busy as can be, and then they just flop down and sleep for a few minutes."

Placing the sleeping beast so its head rested on his shoulder, Henry held one hand under the dog's bottom. He hoped he didn't look too ridiculous. It was a long walk back to Gisborn Hall. "Thank you, Cavenaugh," he said as he waved at the farmer.

"I'll save a good one for Miss Inglenook," the farmer promised as he waved.

The little dog didn't stay asleep long, and when sharp claws had done their worst on his top coat, either in an attempt to climb onto his shoulder or get down from it, Henry finally let the dog down. The pup stared up at him and looked back from whence they came. "Come, Harold," Henry commanded as he continued on his way to Gisborn Hall. Although the pup seemed unsure at first, he was soon running and walking along side Henry, occasionally giving his new master a questioning look as they made their way down the dirt lane. Just before they reached the front doors to Gisborn Hall, Henry turned to regard the pup.

He was pissing on one of Mrs. Batey's rosebushes.

Well, the bush was a long way from blooming, and if Aldenwood's prediction about this year's growing season turned out to be true, then there probably wouldn't be any roses. Henry reached down and scooped up the pup from his perusal of a boxwood. "Come, Harold," he stated, placing the dog back onto his shoulder. Harold squirmed a bit but seemed to realize the only way down was a long way down. Apparently deciding he liked being on the earl's shoulder, Harold licked Henry's ear.

Stunned and not too pleased to have the pup licking him, Henry was about to put him back down. But he caught the look the little beast was giving him. A damned familiar look. It was as if they had already made each other's acquaintance, and Harold was reminding him he had better not make a cake of what he was about to do.

"I am making it right with my wife," Henry said quite firmly, almost chastising himself when he realized he had spoken out loud to the dog. "You just better do your part. And no piddling on her."

Harold behaved as if he was listening to Henry, his eyes quite wide and attentive, so the earl continued. "You have to be a foot warmer, and a bed warmer, and a mouser, and you must guard Hannah and keep her safe when I cannot be there."

A pink tongue intersected his cheek, the abrasiveness against his afternoon beard a surprise. Closing his eyes, Henry couldn't help but grin at the pup's antics. Still, he glanced about to be sure no one had seen his reaction.

Henry rather hoped the front hall would be empty. He wanted to get Harold up and into Hannah's room before any servants saw him carrying the little beastie in such a manner. He couldn't begin to imagine the talk below stairs should that happen.

Thank goodness Parkerhouse was not at his post. Henry took the stairs as quickly as possible and hurried to his wife's door. He knocked once. When he didn't hear a response, he peeked in. The bed was empty. Scanning the room, he saw Hannah where he had found her that morning, her arms resting on the window sill as she looked out over his lands. *At least she has a blanket around her shoulders*, Henry thought sadly. And the fireplace was lit and warming that part of the room.

Harold squirmed to the point that Henry lowered him to the floor. Even before the pup could get his traction on the wooden planks where there wasn't Aubusson carpet, he was off and running awkwardly toward Hannah, his tail wagging so hard Henry thought he might knock over a piece of furniture. He hurried in the puppy's wake, wanting to see Hannah's reaction when she noticed him.

He wasn't disappointed. He was suddenly *in love*.

"Oh!" Hannah cried out, a sound so joyful he wanted to hear it again and again. Her face had changed instantly from one of infinite sadness to pure joy. The puppy had its front paws on Hannah's knees, its tongue reaching out to lick whatever of Hannah he could reach. Hannah turned to find Henry gazing down at her, a hesitant smile on his face. "Where... how?" she asked as she reached down to capture the puppy and bring it onto her lap. Now that he had full access to his mistress, Harold was licking her neck and chin as Hannah giggled in delight. Her hands were smoothing the fur on the sides of the dog as he continued to show his excitement and affection.

"He piddles," Henry warned her.

"Oh, they do that," Hannah replied with a shrug, apparently unconcerned that Harold might soil her beautiful night rail.

"His mother lives about a mile from here. She has at least three others and appeared quite happy to give him up," he said in answer to her earlier question. He really couldn't be sure the expression on the dog's face was that of happiness. Relief, perhaps. It was really hard to tell with dogs.

"What is his name?" she asked, cradling him so his tummy was turned up. She was rubbing it with a couple of fingers while the pup's tail swished over her night rail.

Surprised by the question, Henry bit his lower lip. "I called him Harold on the way home. He followed me when I wasn't carrying him," he said with a shrug.

"Harold," she repeated, her face turning up to give her husband a brilliant smile. "He does look an awfully lot like him," she murmured, scooping the puppy into her arms and placing it against her shoulder. "He's perfect, Henry.'

She stood up from the chair, the blanket falling from her shoulders. A pensive smile on her face, she reached up and kissed his cheek.

Henry was briefly reminded of Sarah's earlier kiss, but found he valued this one more.

"Thank you, Henry," she whispered. And then her free arm wrapped around his neck while she reached up to kiss him on the lips.

Henry wrapped his arms about her waist, pulling her up and against the hard planes of his body. Despite the pup preventing him from hugging her as hard as he wanted to at that moment, the puppy's squirming ceased when he returned the kiss. His tongue gently parted her lips until he was tasting her teeth and tongue.

Her soft moan spurred him on so that he deepened the kiss. Through the thin fabric of her nightgown, he could feel the curves of her soft body as his hands pressed into the small of her back before moving down to cup her bottom and up to grasp one shoulder. The heat of his hands seared her back as he did so.

Another soft moan escaped her when Henry tried to pull away. She had slipped her free hand between their bodies to press her palm against the growing bulge in his breeches. A growl emanated from Henry, but he recaptured her lips and kissed her hard before pulling away with a gasp. Hannah was already undoing the buttons of his waistcoat, her deft fingers working their way down the garment before moving to the fastening of his breeches.

"Hannah." He barely got the word out as he noticed Harold sleeping soundly on her shoulder. The sight seemed somehow right, as if the pup was supposed to be sleeping on his wife's shoulder at three o'clock in the afternoon. But not right given what she was doing to him at the moment.

Hannah had slipped her hand down the loosened fall of his breeches and through his drawers. His engorged cock was in her hand, her thumb caressing the top of the wet bulb while her fingers gripped him. Cursing softly, he struggled to maintain his balance.

Whatever was she doing? It was daylight, for God's sake. Had he locked the door? She was lowering herself before him, and her hand left his cock for a moment only to return to grip and stroke it harder than before. Her other hand had slipped behind his buttocks to pull down his breeches and drawers.

When he glanced down, he saw Harold sleeping on the

carpet below, well away from where he stood. A shiver of pleasure shot up his body, forcing his attention back to what Hannah was doing. Her tongue was sliding along the length of his manhood!

How did she know to even try such a thing?

A mix of horror and admiration clouded his thoughts as he realized what was about to happen. "Hannah." He spoke her name again in the hope she would pause or stop. When she did not, Henry stepped back. Her grip on him gone, he labored to regain his breath as he watched Hannah struggle to regain her balance.

Her face turned up to him, her body perched on her haunches, bare feet peeking out behind her night rail. "Did I... did I do it wrong?" she whispered. She looked as if she might cry.

"No," Henry breathed, reaching down to hook his hands beneath her arms and pull her up. "Quite the contrary, actually," he managed to get out before stripping his waistcoat from his body. His shirt quickly followed, making him wonder when she'd had time to undo his cravat. Or had he even been wearing one?

His boots made a *thunking* sound on the carpet before his arms wrapped around Hannah and moved her to the bed. She was pulling up on the fine lawn of the night rail when he simply stripped it from her body. Her nipples were already hard pebbles, her skin flushed with desire, the pupils of her eyes so dilated her blue eyes were nearly black. Kissing one nipple, he kneaded the other with an impatient thumb until he felt her body trembling.

God, she is beautiful in daylight, he thought as his gaze swept over her slender frame.

He lifted her onto the bed and followed to hover over her as she moved to the middle and left one leg bent. With her hair spread out over the pillows and her body beneath him like a banquet, Henry slowly trailed his tongue down the front of her, caressing her nipples, her belly, her hips and finally the insides of her creamy white thighs before cupping her bottom in his hands and tilting her hips up so that his tongue could lick and tease her engorged womanhood.

Her quiet mewling increased as her chest arched up. One of her hands clutched the bed linens, as if to anchor her body to the bed. One of his hands moved to cup her breast, her nipple firmly planted in the palm of his hand as he started the slow rotations that matched those he was doing with his tongue. Her ecstasy came hard and quick, her cry of his name muted by her other hand covering her mouth.

Hannah had never thought anything could feel as pleasurable as what he'd just done to her. She reached down to hook her hands beneath his arms and pull him up and over her body. Henry didn't need the invitation—he plunged his hardened cock into her wet sheath in one swift motion, burying himself to the hilt. His growl filled the room before he stilled himself. And then he began moving, pulling himself out and pushing back into her in a slow, methodical rhythm.

Hannah would have none of it. She clenched down hard on him when he was buried in her. When he pulled out, she clenched again. His next thrust proved his undoing, for she closed herself onto him with such force, he could no nothing but allow his release. Even while his seed spilt into her, he rocked his body one more time before settling his head next to hers on the pillow. His body collapsed onto hers, and he let out a very loud sigh. "You minx," he whispered in her ear. He kissed the earlobe as he listened to her giggle of delight.

"I could not wait," she whispered back, her voice sounding seductive against his ear.

"For what?" His words were filled with surprise.

"To hold you like this." Her arms had wrapped around his lower back, one hand resting on his bottom while another took purchase on his lower ribs. "Thank you, Henry," she whispered, kissing his ear and the space below it.

Thank you? She was thanking him for bedding her? He allowed a chuckle to burble up. "You're welcome, my lady. Anytime, actually. I have to admit I have never been seduced in the middle of the day. You took me quite by surprise." He lifted his head, which seemed to weigh a hundred stone. "Whatever possessed you to do that?" he asked, his gaze traveling over her naked body. *And who told her how to do it?* Had she held a man's organ before? Or had she seen illustrations? Or lithographs of sexual activities?

He was imagining Hannah in a large bed with her tongue lathing across some overweight duke's... He shook his head to clear it of the offending image. Until he had taken her virtue two weeks before, she was a virgin. Her reaction to his nakedness, to the way he held and stroked her... just the blood of her broken maidenhead on the bath linens had been a testament to that.

The sun dipped low behind clouds made red and angry from the dust in the air; the late afternoon light left Hannah looking golden. Her firm breasts were still topped with engorged nipples. He reached over with his tongue and teeth and nipped at one. "However did you know to do that to me?" he asked in as neutral voice as he could manage. Although his cock was still firmly inside her, he could feel himself slipping out little by little.

Catching her lower lip with a tooth, she turned to gaze at him. Her face had begun to flush with the question. "Lady Bostwick. She recommended I try it with whomever I married."

One eyebrow cocking into a sharp arch, Henry stared down at her. *Lady Bostwick?* He remembered Lord Bostwick at the Attenborough's ball. No wonder the man had seemed so happy. He was married to a wanton woman! "And what else has Lady Bostwick recommended you do to me?" he asked. His voice took on a teasing tone now that his fears of her having spent time in bed with some other man were clearly unfounded.

Hannah's face turned that bright pink he found so fetching. "She... She says I should use my imagination," she hedged, not wanting to get too specific. "And she says I should demand my husband bed me every day, even when I am with child."

Henry considered her words. "Does she now? I suppose George must be a very exhausted man," he said, not exactly teasing. *And very happy.* "Does he really accommodate his wife's demands?"

She nodded, her head still on the pillow. "George Bennett-Jones dotes on Elizabeth," Hannah answered with a hint of mischief. "He will do *anything* for her. He loved her from the moment he first saw her," she said in a voice that had quieted to a whisper.

Henry stared at Hannah for a very long time. "That *dog!*" he finally said, a grin belying his comment. "How did a man with such an ugly puss manage to land a beauty like Lady Elizabeth?" he asked under his breath. He slipped completely out of Hannah. He couldn't help but grin at her moan of disappointment. "You are more beautiful than she is, by the way," he added, hoping Hannah wouldn't take umbrage at his comment about Lady Elizabeth.

Moving her arms over her head and stretching her body in what looked like a writhing wanton to Henry, Hannah suppressed a grin. "George is rather handsome when he smiles. Or so Elizabeth says, at least. When they returned to town for the Season, Elizabeth and I called on one another every day, and she told me all about her life with him."

An eyebrow arched up on Henry's forehead. "It sounds as if she told you far too much if she was describing how she pleasured her husband," he countered with a snort. "I do hope she didn't go into *too* much detail." When he glanced back at Hannah's guilt-ridden face, he noted the pink blush was back. It seemed to cover her entire body, in fact. "I see."

Any hint of humor in Hannah's face was gone, replaced by an expression that suggested she might cry at any moment. "If she hadn't told me, I wouldn't know what... what to *do*, my lord," she reasoned, "Would *you* have told me?"

Henry stared at her in surprise. "Henry," he corrected

her, as he tried to decide how best to answer her question. "I don't know that it's *appropriate* for a wife to do something like *that*," he finally got out. He remembered that Sarah had tried once, a long time ago, but he had pulled himself away, thinking that only lightskirts and courtesans would engage in such practices. But how did he know? He had never employed any ladies of the night. He hadn't wanted to since the time he and Sarah had experienced their first coupling.

Thinking of Hannah using her tongue on him was so out of context from what he expected of a virginal fairy princess — even her just sharing a bed with him seemed odd, as if the woman he married was suitable only for display in the pages of a fairy tale. And yet, he did feel *lust* for her. Every day since that first time he had seen her playing with Harold, in fact. He had wanted to bed her even then.

"Did it please you?"

His head snapping up to regard Hannah, Henry furrowed his brows. "What?" he asked, his mind still on his thoughts of her as a virginal princess. "Oh, um. Yes," he admitted with a nod. "Very much, actually."

Damnation! Now that he knew what it was like, he would likely beg her to do it the next time they were together.

Hannah sighed happily before allowing the smile to fade from her face. "I know you weren't pleased with me. Were you angry, though?"

Henry lifted his head, wondering why she would ask such a thing.

"Over what happened to Harold," she added in a whisper. "My reaction, I mean."

Furrowing his brows, Henry rolled off the top of her body and lifted himself onto one elbow. "You were mourning," he stated simply. "I could not find fault with that," he reasoned, trying to keep his voice from betraying how he had felt earlier that day.

She was right in that her mourning had caused him a great deal of concern. He wondered if, when he died, would she mourn him like she had mourned Harold? She had been sitting in a rather cold window for hours on end, weeping, putting her own life at risk. She could have caught a terrible cold. Or influenza. Or a fever. Perhaps she was already carrying his child, in which case she was endangering it. "Are you with child?"

The question startled her. "I... I don't know," she replied with a shrug. She hadn't felt any different during the two weeks she had been at Gisborn Hall, but how did one know if you were pregnant when it wasn't yet time for your monthly courses? Seeing his genuine concern, she lifted a hand to his face. "I'll know soon, though."

A thumping and mewling sounded from somewhere along the bottom of the bed. Peering over the side of the mattress, Henry found himself face to face with the puppy, who had stretched himself as tall as he could with his front paws at the top of the bedskirt. His hind legs tried to push his body up and onto the bed, but he was still far too small to make the leap. Chuckling, Henry reached over and captured the ball of fur, pulling it onto the bed. The excited puppy stepped onto and over Henry's body, inciting a series of 'oofs' and 'ows' out of Henry as he made his way to Hannah, who giggled as the little beast snuggled into a space between her body and her arm, his tongue hanging out and his body panting with the exertion.

Henry sat up on the edge of the bed. "He's probably thirsty and starving," he said as he reached for his shirt. "And he needs a bath."

The floor was littered with their hastily removed clothing. He was rather glad Murphy wouldn't come into Hannah's bedchamber. His valet would have a fit if he saw the way Henry's clothes had been scattered about.

As Henry pulled on his shirt, he nearly chided himself for the missed time working on the estate. But the sight of his naked wife lying satiated and prone on her bed, her skin all golden in the late afternoon sunlight and the panting puppy against her body, quickly put that thought out of his head. "If you wish it, I will come to you later tonight," he suggested. Did expecting to bed her twice in one day seem selfish? Even now, his manhood was hardening at the thought. He pulled on his drawers and breeches as quickly as he could, hoping she wouldn't notice.

She noticed.

"I would like that," she purred, a suggestive grin lighting her face. "And, if you are so inclined, you are welcome to stay with me when we are finished," she added, hoping she didn't sound as wanton as her words made her out to be.

What was happening to her? It was as if she wanted nothing more than to stay in bed with her husband and make love all the time!

If he was in her bed, it meant he wasn't in Sarah's bed.

She swallowed hard at that thought. *Guard your heart,* she warned herself. The last thing she could allow to happen was to fall in love with her husband. And yet, truth be told she was quite sure she already had.

"I'm thinking I will be so inclined," Henry responded with a wink. "I don't suppose you know what's for dinner?" he asked then, buttoning up his waistcoat.

Hannah's eyes glazed over as she remembered the menu for that night's dinner. "Onion soup, roast chicken, carrots, beans, rolls, lemon tarts," she counted off, her voice trailing off. She glanced up at Henry, whose face was split by a huge grin. Leaning over her, he gave one nipple a quick kiss. "My favorite!" he claimed, and then he took his leave of his rather startled wife.

CHAPTER 20
SARAH MAKES AN ANNOUNCEMENT

A week later

The hour was long past ten. Where could Henry be? He had said he was going out after dinner for a quick visit with Nathan. But he did that nearly every night. And he always returned before nine. Sarah was quite insistent that her son be in bed by nine. So where could Henry be?

Two weeks, Hannah thought. A fortnight. He had promised her two weeks before he would return to Sarah's bed. But then she had made him promise to bed her every night for another three weeks as punishment for his cursing Harold. Her stomach did a somersault, threatening to toss up the wonderful dinner they had shared only a few hours ago. Why should she feel so bereft? He loved Sarah. He had for a very long time. So why did the thought of him sharing her bed bring such a feeling of emptiness?

Hannah's hand went to her belly for at least the tenth time that night. Her courses were three days late. *I must be with child!* The thought warmed her, although there was still an ache in her heart. Perhaps she was merely late. Perhaps she would wake up in the morning to find... No, she would not even think it. She couldn't think anything but the best news right now. It was all that buoyed her as she listened for the front door.

Voices. She sat up straight in bed, startling Harold enough that the puppy lifted his head and regarded her in surprise. Had she fallen asleep? No, the mantel clock above the fireplace showed eleven. But familiar footsteps sounded on the stairs. She had never felt such relief. And, although they paused for only a second outside her door, they continued farther down the hall. Then she heard his door close, perhaps too hard, and the latch clicked into place.

Holding her breath a moment, Hannah thought perhaps he only meant to undress and put on a dressing gown. Then he would come to her through the dressing room door. But after another ten minutes, when the house was still eerily quiet, she crept out of bed, pulling on her own dressing gown. He had locked his hall door, she was sure, but perhaps the connecting door through their dressing room would still be unlocked.

She motioned for Harold to stay on the bed and went into the dressing room. A sliver of light shown beneath his door, but there were no sounds of movement, nor were there changing shadows in the light. Placing her ear against the door, she listened for a moment. The sound of her own heartbeat nearly drowned out the odd sounds she heard from his room.

Sobbing? That couldn't be right. Testing the door handle, she found it unlocked. When she peeked around the edge of the door, she was stunned to find her husband sitting on the edge of the bed, his elbows on his knees, one hand covering his face as he wept. Wondering if she should let him know of her presence, she immediately chided herself for even pausing to consider what to do.

Something was *wrong*. Her husband was upset.

Even if there wasn't anything she could do for him, she should at least show that she was concerned. Hurrying to his side, she placed a hand on one side of his face and kissed his temple. "Henry, what's wrong?" She felt alarm when she realized his tears could be for his son. "Is Nathan ill?" Whatever could be so awful that Henry Forster would be reduced to tears?

Barely aware that Hannah was somehow next to him, her dressing gown unfastened and her nightgown undone at the top, Henry allowed his head to drop against her bosom. The scent of honeysuckle wafted from her body, enveloping him in familiar comfort as her arms wrapped around his shoulders. *Where had she come from?* It was late. She should be asleep.

He felt her kiss on the side of his face and turned his head in that direction. His lips found hers for a quick kiss, but a sob interrupted what needed to be a much more thorough kiss.

"Please, tell me, Henry," she whispered. She had undone the knot of his cravat and was working to loosen the linen before her fingers moved to his waistcoat. He had divested himself of his topcoat, but there was no sign of it in the room.

Henry allowed his head to roll back to her bosom. He could feel her heartbeat thundering under his ear, the pulse too fast. *Hannah!*

"What's wrong, Henry?" she asked with a bit more urgency.

Henry's eyes cleared. He glanced about, realizing they were in his room. The connecting door to the dressing room was open, and Harold sat on the threshold, his head cocking to one side as if he, too, wondered what was wrong. "Sarah has accepted an offer of marriage."

The words came out leaden, his voice so hoarse he didn't recognize it as his own. Hannah's strokes down his arms and back ceased as she stilled her entire body. But her heartbeat thrummed on, increased in speed perhaps, as he left his head where it lay.

A cacophony of emotions swept through Hannah at that moment. Relief, that nothing was wrong with Nathan. Sorrow on Henry's behalf, for she knew he loved Sarah. Happiness for Sarah, for she secretly knew the woman was no longer satisfied with being whatever she was to Henry. Hope for herself, for she knew at that moment she carried his child. She had to. That news alone would help Henry recover from his shock and agony.

Wouldn't it?

"You gave her permission to do so?" Hannah whispered the query, her hands starting their gentle strokes across his back and down his arms as she held him. His tears had penetrated the fine lawn of her gown, plastering the translucent fabric against her breast.

"Mmm," he responded, his head nodding. "Although she did not ask as much as tell me." His voice was clearer now.

"Did she tell you *whom* she is to marry?" Hannah kept her words quiet and soft, aware that the tension in his body was sprung tight and could unravel at any moment.

Henry stayed very still for several minutes. "Tad McDonald."

Although the name should have been a surprise to Hannah, she felt guilty. She had known even before he said the name. Sarah was quite besotted the last time Hannah had paid a call on her, the day Sarah described her upcoming trip to Bampton to shop as if it was the most important day of her life. Perhaps it had been. Perhaps it was that day that Mr. McDonald had asked for her hand. Perhaps she had known that day she spoke with Hannah—she had seemed about to burst with happiness knowing Henry was married. She had welcomed Hannah so warmly, seemed so intent on telling her everything, although the woman couldn't exactly admit to having fallen in love with another man. Not when the earl was her protector and the father of her child. But there had been that light in her face, that glow that spoke volumes about how a woman felt.

"I lied to you," Henry's voice broke into her reverie, the words so unexpected she nearly gasped. "I didn't just go to Sarah's to spend time with Nathan. I went there..."

Hannah could sense the tension in his body increase, as if anger and betrayal had suddenly replaced his sorrow.

"I went there to... to bed Sarah. It has been more than a month since I .., and I meant only to renew my relations with her." His breathing had quickened, and his head no longer lay pressed against her. "She is mine, after all. It is my right!"

Hannah let go her hold on him, not sure how to respond to his revelation nor to his rising anger. Or her own flash of... was that jealousy she felt just then? She took a deep breath and reminded herself that Sarah was marrying another. "I figured as much when you did not return earlier," Hannah offered, hoping her conciliatory tone would calm him. The words seemed to have the opposite effect, though. He stood up from the bed, his fists clenched at his sides.

Hannah dared a glance at them before returning her gaze to his face, trying hard not to allow fear to show in her eyes. Henry caught the look, though, and followed Hannah's quick glance. He unclenched his fists. Biting his lip, he looked around as if he wanted to punch something. "*Damn* her!" he whispered hoarsely.

Starting at his curse, Hannah's eyes widened. Should she tell him now? *No, not when he was so angry.* Perhaps another approach. He had gone to Sarah's expecting to bed her. *So bed me instead,* she thought quickly. Despite his anger and sorrow, the thought of him atop her this very moment sent a thrill through her body. The space between her thighs began throbbing with need, her nipples hardened, and somewhere in her core, desire bloomed. "Take me instead," she ordered, her chin thrust out. "Pretend I am Sarah. Bed me the way you do her."

The challenge seemed to catch him by surprise. His brows furrowed. He looked at her with a sideways glance and shook his head quickly.

"Do you undress her, or does she take off her own clothes?" Hannah asked then, rising to her knees on the bed. She slid the dressing gown from her body and tossed it to the side. "Does she remove your clothes?" She reached out to capture the ends of his cravat. She yanked the linen from around his neck and moved to pull his shirt from his breeches. He stepped away, pulling his shirt off his body in a quick motion, his breaths quickening. His hands were undoing the fastenings of his breeches, his eyes boring into hers the entire time. He wore no boots or stockings; he had to have removed them when he first got into the room. With one swift yank, his breeches were off his body. Standing before her, naked, his cock hard and upright, his chest heaving from breathing too fast, Henry looked every inch a predator.

His prey still stood on her knees on the bed, her lips parted and her eyes smoldering, daring him to do his worst. The outline of her erect nipples shown through her night-gown, the dark space above her thighs apparent through the translucent fabric.

Hannah held her breath as he advanced, an arm like steel wrapping around her waist to force her knees from beneath her. As she fell to the bed, he had the front of her gown between his fists, the cloth rending as he pulled it apart from the top. She stifled the cry of alarm that was about to erupt from her as she felt the shredded fabric flutter to the sides, her arms still encased in its billowy sleeves. His body descended onto hers. She knew instantly there would be no foreplay, no gentle kissing or stroking or licking. Henry was hell-bent for intercourse, hard and fast.

And, at that moment, Hannah's need matched his.

Opening her legs as his body dropped, she moved to wrap her arms around his neck. He captured them both and forced them above her head, pinning her wrists with an iron grip as his hardened manhood drove home in one hard, unforgiving thrust, filling her instantly. Her upper body rose up in reaction, her heavy-lidded eyes opening wide before returning to their smoldering glare. "Yes," she hissed, not knowing what else to say to such a frantic assault. The cant of her chin dared him to do it again, and he took the challenge, pulling himself all the way out of her body before plunging back into her as her legs wrapped around his back, her ankles anchoring one another to his back. Her hips lifted to meet his thrust, forcing a growl to escape as he met the unexpected counter thrust and felt the cage of her legs around his body.

"Hannah," he hissed back, his mouth coming down onto one of her breasts, his lips and teeth suckling and biting so hard she was sure she would be left with bruises.

Her chest lifting in response, Hannah gasped, her hips again meeting his in the hard, fast rhythm he had quickly established. Although she thought she should feel fear at his animalistic behavior, she instead felt excitement. Arousal. Primal lust. In only one more thrust, she would peak, she would crest and the waves of pleasure would cascade down around her and she would be lost. But what of him? "Now!" she groaned, her chest lifting again, her back arcing as he filled her.

Henry's mouth came off her breast. "I will *not* spill my seed on this bed," he growled in response. "Never again!" His cock left Hannah's body and plowed into her one more time, this time her sheath clenching on him so hard he was forced to allow his climax, forced to allow his seed to spill into her, forced to allow a wave of sharp and sudden pleasure to grab him and violently toss him and leave him gasping for air and seeking respite in the soft body that lay beneath him, the body that was caught in its own spasms of pleasure so violent he had to let go of her wrists so he could hold himself up for just a moment more.

Released from his hold, Hannah's arms spread out on either side of her body, the white, billowy sleeves of her ruined nightgown making her look as if she bore angel's wings. Her hair, spread out on either side of her head, formed a halo on the pillows. But her eyes were still black, black with desire, black with *fury?*

Didn't Sarah allow him to take his pleasure whilst he was inside her? Did Henry always have to withdraw and spill his seed in her bed?

He must have, when Sarah said, "Now." Hannah had meant it only as a warning of her impending orgasm, not a demand that he withdraw from her. And then Hannah remembered Sarah's words. *I have known I will never have another child with Henry. I make sure of it.* All those years Henry spent with Sarah, and yet he could never have her the way he he'd had Hannah these past few weeks. He could never share in the pleasure of a mutual orgasm, of the sensation of being torn apart in splendid release and put back together piece by piece with the gentle undulations of a woman's secret place.

Henry's gaze slowly cleared as his body put itself back together. He still hovered over her, his upper body held up on elbows that threatened to give way at any moment. And he swept his eye over the body beneath him. Hannah looked every bit the angel, her breasts still lifting and lowering with her every labored breath, her smoldering eyes clearing to finally meet his in mutual recognition.

"Oh, good God, what have I done?" he got out as he tried to lift himself from her body. Her legs were still wrapped around his buttocks, though, preventing his spent body from lifting away from her. He collapsed down, burying his head in the pillow next to her head, her spread arm beneath his collarbone. "Oh, Hannah," he whispered, his voice sounding as if he might cry.

"Shh," she answered, turning her head so her lips could capture his ear and kiss it gently. They lay like that for several minutes, until Hannah's legs were too tired to hold up any longer. She slowly lowered them along the back of his thighs before allowing her ankles to unlock and her feet to take purchase on the coverlet.

"Why, Hannah?"

The simple question caught her off-guard, forcing her to stare at the ceiling, a ceiling she realized she had never seen before. They had only ever shared her bed.

She thought for a moment, trying to decide how to answer his simple question. "I am your wife. I could not stand by and do nothing when you needed *this*," she replied quietly, wincing with her explanation. She could have stood by and watched his agony. She could have returned to her room and left him to his mourning. He would recover one day, realize he had a wife he needed to bed every night if he truly wanted an heir. She would never deny him her body.

He knew that, too.

At least, he certainly knew it now.

"We rarely kissed."

Surprised at the odd comment, Hannah had to suppress a gasp. She brought her free hand to rest on the back of his shoulder. "Why ever not?" she asked in a gentle whisper.

Henry turned his head on the pillow so that his face was very close to the side of hers. "She thought it too intimate. Too... telling, I suppose."

Sighing, Hannah swallowed. "How sad," she replied, her voice quiet, its tone matching the word. Perhaps Sarah would find kissing more appropriate with Tad McDonald. When they were husband and wife, society would accept her as something other than the earl's paramour. "I rather like it when you kiss me," Hannah added, sighing when she heard his 'mmm' in reply.

"I had no idea I would *enjoy* it as much as I do," he countered, his voice sounding sleepy. His body seemed to start just then. He raised himself up to hover over Hannah before his lips came down onto hers. The kiss was soft and warm, unlike anything they had shared that night. When he pulled away, he said, "I do not want our child to have been conceived this night," he said, pulling himself out of her. He winced when he saw what his teeth had done to one of her breasts. "Oh, Hannah, I am so sorry," he murmured, his glance passing between her face and her bruised breast. "I... Sarah requires... she can only..." He stopped and gave a helpless shrug. "It's almost impossible to bring her to ecstasy unless there is some... some pain," he finally got out, his frustration with his ex-lover quite evident.

Hannah felt empty as he left her body, but with his explanation, she was glad she was probably already with child. No wonder his lovemaking had been so violent. She had thought him merely angry at Sarah's decision to marry. A decision Sarah had obviously made without first seeking his blessing.

At the reminder that Henry would no longer be sharing Sarah's bed, Hannah placed a hand on the side of his face. "Will you seek another to be your mistress?" she asked, hoping her question wouldn't anger him. "I know you will always love her. She is the mother of your son."

"No," he whispered, turning his body so that he lay on his back. "I believe it is time to concentrate on more important things."

Hannah turned on her side, nestling her head into the small of his shoulder. "What might those be?" she asked sleepily, thinking he referred to the improvements to the property or the farm equipment or the restoration of Ellsworth Park.

Henry kissed her head. "You, of course. And getting you with child," he said with a wan grin. How much simpler everything would be from now on, he realized. How could he think he could keep Sarah satisfied when he could offer her nothing but a life as a mistress? She had long ago made the decision not to be his wife despite his every overture. It was time he let her go to make her own life.

He felt Hannah's hand pulling on his wrist, moving his hand so that it settled on her belly. She had placed her small hand over the top of it, her fingers settling between his before she gave him an incandescent smile. At his look of shock and the sudden movement that left her flat on her back and him on his side with his hand still resting on her belly, Hannah giggled.

"I am not yet positive." she tried to get out before his lips took purchase on one of her nipples. "Oh!"

"But?" Henry managed to get out as he moved his lips to her other nipple, kissing it more gently. He had bitten it far too hard earlier.

"I am three days late with my..."

His lips were on hers even before she could finish her

sentence. When he finally pulled away to nip her earlobe, he whispered, "You have made me the happiest man in England. Even if you are not yet with child."

Hannah smiled, her heart filled with more gladness than she could ever imagine feeling. "Let's make sure I am, then."

Henry regarded her for a moment and then finally nodded. "As you wish, my lady."

CHAPTER 21
LITTLE HAROLD MAKES A
DISCOVERY

"The main trench along the western line is complete, my lord," the foreman announced as Henry rode up on Thunder to review the progress of the laborers. Despite the cooler temperatures, several men were perspiring as they leaned on their shovels and drank from canteens.

Henry dismounted and surveyed the ditch that now stretched from the river to the north edge of the field. He stepped down into the trench and looked toward the river. The final earthen dam was still in place, although once the gates were built, that would be dug out to allow river water to flood the trench. He could only hope the trench wouldn't have too many low spots that might trap water, or high spots that would prevent water from filling the trench along its entire length. "Excellent work, Mr. Coley. If this weather holds, Mr. Perkins and his crew should be able to start the gate tomorrow. And your crew can move to the central trench."

Frank Coley nodded. "Very good, my lord," he replied, wiping his forehead with the back of his arm. "The stakes marking the channel are in place, of course, and Mr. Filbert will see to staking the gate openings just as soon as he is back from Bampton."

Filbert was the surveyor responsible for making sure the

guide markers for the trenches were installed in straight lines perpendicular to the river. He had also seen to it a section of the eastern field had been plowed so that there would be end guides for the trenching to follow as the laborers dug the central ditch. Henry could only hope the lay of the land was level enough for everything to work once the trenches were flooded.

"I'll have Cavenaugh bring his oxen and plow the day after tomorrow. With the plows here and in the village, the rest of the furrows can be done in three or four days," he figured, hoping he wasn't waiting too long to get seed in. He wanted the infrastructure for irrigating in place before he had the valuable seed planted. If the weather remained too chilly, though, it wouldn't do any good to plant too soon anyway.

The construction on the greenhouses was progressing. If what Aldenwood predicted came true and there was no summer, Henry wanted the greenhouses in place and producing whatever could be planted under their protection, preferably fruits and vegetables. A building crew had completed the framing for the second greenhouse the day before. A glazier from Bampton would begin the installation of glass panes as soon as the frame was complete. There wasn't enough glass in all of this part of Bampton to cover both greenhouses, but with glass on the south-facing roofs and walls, oilcloth could be used on the other surfaces to keep the structures warm.

Henry heaved a sigh of relief when he realized the first greenhouse might be ready in just a few weeks.

He remounted his horse and tipped his hat to his foreman. "Send these men to their homes, Mr. Coley, but pay them for a full day." When the men nearest to him heard his announcement to the foremen, they broke out in cheers. He gave Thunder free rein and headed toward the stables behind Gisborn Hall.

That day's post had brought word of Hannah's dowry from her father. The Marquess of Devonville had arranged for it to be deposited into Henry's bank account. With more than enough to pay for the buildings and for the gates to be built, Henry was feeling generous. *The Gates of Hannah*, he thought with a grin.

Henry was nearly to the stables when Harold bounded toward him from the north. The puppy was barking, the sound deeper than it had been his first day at Gisborn Hall. Thinking the dog was merely greeting him, Henry gave him a nod and continued on his way toward the stables. But Harold was soon racing ahead of the cantering horse, turning in circles and then running back toward the southeast. When the dog looked back and saw that Henry wasn't following him, Harold barked again.

Henry watched the dog turn in a circle and run back toward him. When the dog reached the area in front of where Thunder was about to step, Harold turned and barked again. Thunder was forced to step sideways and finally come to a halt as Henry pulled on the reins.

Angry at the little dog's odd behavior, Henry cursed. He stared down at Harold, intending to scold him. But the dog raced off toward the southeast again, stopping and turning as if he expected Henry to follow him.

Curious as to the dog's behavior, and remembering the late Harold's similar behavior when he was trying to get Henry to the river, Henry spurred Thunder to follow the dog. Harold was soon bounding over the furrows that had been dug earlier that day, his white and brown fur appearing and disappearing as he leaped over each furrow edge and landed in the depression in between.

At one point, Henry realized Thunder had gone too far. Harold's bark was coming from behind them. Turning the horse around, Henry spotted the pup, the front of his body and head peeking over the top edge of a furrow as he resumed his barking.

Wondering if the dog was involved in some form of play, Henry allowed Thunder to pick his way back toward the little beast. He slightly cursed at the thought of some of the furrows being trampled not only by his horse but by Harold.

He dismounted once he realized Harold wasn't moving from the spot from where he stood guard.

Hands on his hips, Henry stared down at Harold. "What has gotten into…?" His words faded as he realized Harold stood over a spot in a furrow where he had obviously done some digging beyond what the plow had accomplished earlier that day.

Scattered on the freshly turned earth were several coins. Leaning down, Henry picked up one and brushed the dirt from it. The sovereign gleamed in the afternoon sunlight. He knelt down and retrieved several more coins, all sovereigns.

Tail wagging furiously, Harold bounded to the other edge of the furrow and let out a small *woof*.

Henry turned to regard the pup. "Indeed," he replied, wondering if Harold had seen the coins as they were dropped by whomever guided the plow horse. But then he noticed the rotting remains of pasteboard. As he pulled several pieces of pasteboard out of the ground, more coins appeared.

Harold was suddenly in the middle of the mess, his paws digging quickly to further separate the remains. With another low *woof*, he buried his snout into the ground.

"Harold," Henry said with a shake of his head. "Your mistress is not going to be happy when she sees how dirty you've managed to get."

Harold's head appeared from the hole, his bared teeth displaying his latest find. Henry stared at the dog before glancing down at the collection of coins.

The memory of his son telling him of the lost pirate treasure came to him in a flash as Harold dropped a dirt encrusted object into Henry's outstretched hand. Then the dog pulled his back legs under him and sat up, his head cocking to one side as Henry fingered the object until the small clods of dirt gave way to reveal the gold and ruby of his signet ring.

"I'll be damned," he breathed, holding the ring up before Harold. "My ring. You found my ring, Harold."

Standing up briefly and turning in a tight circle, Harold

wagged his tail before he returned to his sitting position. Henry gave him a pat on the head before gathering up the coins. "You found the buried treasure! These are Nathan's," he said as he rubbed the dirt off several of the sovereigns, showing each one to the dog as if he would understand. There were nine in all; Henry couldn't be sure if his son had buried any more than that in the pasteboard box that made up the treasure chest he and Andrew had created that day just over a year ago.

Shaking his head, Henry pushed the treasure into a golden pile. "Good dog," he said with a nod. "Let's get these home." With that, Henry cradled the coins and ring in one hand against the front of his body while he mounted Thunder. He directed the horse back toward the stables while Harold ran along side, his tail waving behind him.

Henry wondered how he should tell his son of the find. Perhaps he would just package them into a pasteboard box and give them to Nathan later that night when he paid him a visit. His son would be thrilled to discover his birthday presents had been found, and probably even more thrilled to find out they had been found by little Harold.

Or perhaps he would keep them until Nathan's eleventh birthday and give them to him then.

The excitement he felt at having found the treasure was too much to bear, though. When he dismounted, he handed the reins of Thunder to a stable boy and hurried into the house by way of the back door into the kitchen.

He wondered what Hannah might think. She would certainly be distressed to see Harold's front paws covered in dirt as they were right now. He could imagine his wife admonishing the poor pup even as the two of them approached the door to the kitchen.

"My lord?" The voice of the cook sounded as surprised as Henry had been only moments before.

"Yes, Mrs. Chambers, it's just me. And what has Lady Gisborn decided we're having for dinner this evening?" he asked, hoping the cook wouldn't notice Harold following him into the house. He was aware there had been an issue with the late Harold and his first visit to the kitchen.

"Beggin' your pardon, my lord, but Lady Gisborn says if you was to ask, I was to tell you 'tis a surprise and not be telling you. But you'll like it just fine, if you catch my meaning," she said, one eye winking as she wiped her hands on her dirty apron.

Henry gave the cook his best grin and motioned for Harold to follow him.

Harold paused and gave the cook an imploring glance. "Oh, would you look at the wee one. Got into some trouble now, did he?" she spoke in a good natured voice, not sounding angry in the least.

"Actually, he got my son *out* of a good deal of trouble today," Henry countered. "If you can keep your tongue, I'd be much obliged," he said as he held out his ungloved hand. The signet ring, still caked in dirt, shown from his fourth finger.

The cook took a closer look. "Well, I'll be!" she breathed, her hands coming up to cover her mouth. "Harold found that, did he?" she whispered, obviously impressed with the pup.

"He did, indeed. But he's gone and gotten himself dirty in the process."

"Oh, don't you be worrying none about that, my lord," Mrs. Chambers replied with a wave of her hand. "I can see to it Billy gets him cleaned up right quick." She turned and yelled in her more annoying imitation of a Welsh milkmaid. "Billy! Git your sorry bottom in here right quick!"

Henry had to keep himself from rolling his eyes as Harold gave him a tentative glance and the cook moved toward the door from which he and Harold had entered from the stables. The young groom hurried into the kitchen, breathless. "Yes, ma'am?" he offered, his cap coming off his head and his body bending in the middle as he bowed to the earl. "My lord," he murmured, his face turning a scarlet red.

"Bill," Henry replied, giving the young man a nod. "Are

you leg-shackled yet?" he asked, keeping his voice as serious as possible.

The groom shook his head. "The second reading of the banns is this Sunday, my lord. Lily's father gave me permission to ask for her hand the Sunday after we got her back, and she agreed to marry me," he said, his chest puffing out just with the news.

Henry gave the groom a nod. "And are you settled into your new quarters yet?"

Billy dared a glance at the cook before he shrugged. "I'm moved in, but seeing as how we're not married yet, Lily is still in her room, my lord," he answered, his face reddening as if Lily might already be sharing his bed.

The earl remembered the night he had seen Billy bathing Lily and wondered if he should have seen to a special license for the couple. But since they were going about their wedding the more traditional route, Henry found he couldn't argue with how things were progressing. And then the thought struck him—if he and Hannah had waited for banns to be read for three weeks prior to their wedding, they still wouldn't be married!

"Where will the ceremony be held?" the earl asked then, wondering if he and Hannah would be invited to attend.

Exchanging glances with Mrs. Chambers, Billy took a breath and said, "The chapel in Bampton, my lord. Lily and I were hoping you and your countess could be in attendance. That is, if you don't have any place else you have to be that day," he added, making Henry wonder if the groom really wanted him to attend.

"We'll be there," Henry said with a nod. He glanced down at Harold. "I'm sure you must be wondering why you were called in," he said, nodding in the cook's direction.

Mrs. Chambers took her cue. "Get some water heated up and give the pup a bath. Use the tub you used for big Harold when last you done it. And see to it he gets a treat." She turned to the earl. "I saved the trimmin's from last night's ham for him," she said, giving Henry another wink.

"That was very considerate of you," he offered, wanting her to know she could continue doing such things with the dog in mind.

The large woman beamed, her rosy cheeks reddening with embarrassment. "Thank ye, my lord." She returned her attention to the groom, and, as if she hadn't just been the sweetest thing to the earl, she said, "Now git going!"

Billy hurried off, calling Harold to follow him. Harold looked up at Henry, as if he was asking for permission to follow the groom. Henry nodded and waved him off. The puppy gave a short 'woof ' and hurried off after the young man.

"Thank you, Mrs. Chambers," he said with another nod before making his way out of the kitchen and up the servants' stairs. He hadn't gone far before Parkerhouse stepped out of his quarters.

"My lord?" he said, obviously surprised to find the earl on the servants' stairs.

"Yes, Parkerhouse. Would there be a pasteboard box about so big," he held out one hand to indicate a small size, "That a gift of coins might fit into?"

The butler puffed out his chest as he considered the earl's question. "I believe there is one in your study, my lord. Your latest book arrived in it last week. And there's a letter for the countess on your desk."

Henry considered what book that might have been. One on farming, no doubt. "That should do, Parkerhouse. See to its placement on the desk in my study. I'll need it directly following dinner."

He thought to give the coins to Parkerhouse for him to clean and put in the box, but some things were too important to have a servant do. He took his leave of the butler and continued up the stairs, wondering if he might catch a glimpse of Hannah before she changed for dinner. Opening the door that led to the main hall, he caught sight of her conversing with the housekeeper. She held a long sheet of parchment, and Hannah and Mrs. Batey were both studying it. His heart clenched as he watched her face light up in delight at something the housekeeper had just said.

He continued to watch, leaning his tall body against the door frame.

In only a moment, the countess seemed to sense that someone was watching her. She slowly turned to find the earl, his arms crossed over his chest and one foot crossed over the other, doing just that. "My lord!" she spoke with a hint of surprise. She excused herself and moved to stand before him as the housekeeper hurried off with the parchment. About to curtsy, Hannah was suddenly pulled hard against the front of his body. "Oh!" she managed to get out before Henry's lips came down onto hers.

Although he had frequently kissed her without preamble in their bedchambers, he had never blatantly done so where anyone could witness their indiscretion. Hannah finally reached her hands to his neck and returned the kiss, a slight moan escaping before Henry eventually released her.

"Good afternoon, my lady," he whispered, his nose grazing her temple and forehead before his lips touched her forehead.

"And to you, my lord," Hannah whispered back. She quickly glanced around, thinking a footman or maid might be witnessing their tryst.

"There's a letter for you in my study. And no one saw us," Henry whispered, his arms wrapping around her waist and holding her hard against his front. "I have it on good authority that no one is here but us," he murmured. The sound of a throat clearing had him grasping Hannah closer to his body as he moved to protect her from their interloper.

"Pardon me, my lord," Parkerhouse said in his most bored sounding tone. The butler moved by the couple and headed toward the study, disappearing into the room without a backward glance at the earl and countess.

Clearly mortified, Hannah had to move a hand to cover her mouth. "Henry!" she managed to get out before her husband let her go.

Not the least bit embarrassed at having been found in error, Henry grinned. "Come, my lady. I have something to show you," he said with a hint of mischief.

Hannah's face turned bright pink.

"Not *that*, my lady," he said as he realized his manhood had created a bulge in his doeskin breeches. "These," he said as he held out his handful of sovereigns.

Her eyes widening at the sight of the dirt encrusted coins, Hannah gave him a curious glance. "Where did you find them?" she asked, one long finger pushing the top one aside to reveal another below. She thought there had to be at least a half-dozen in the stack.

"I didn't. Harold did," he said as he turned and offered her his arm. Hannah placed her hand on it and walked alongside him as he explained what had happened in the newly plowed field the year before. "Parkerhouse is getting a box for me now. Once I have these cleaned up, I'll see to it they're returned to Nathan."

Hannah's mouth formed an 'o'. "He'll be so relieved to learn of their discovery," she breathed. "But what of your signet ring? Wasn't that in the same treasure box he buried?"

Henry grinned as he held up his other hand. The ruby caught the candlelight of a nearby torch. "Safe and sound, although it needs a good cleaning," he announced proudly. "As does Harold. Billy is seeing to that right now."

Hannah stopped, a look of horror on her face. "What is it?" Henry asked, his brows furrowing.

Hannah shrugged but did not return the earl's gaze. "Are you angry with him?" she asked, her voice very quiet as they entered his study. The pasteboard box was already on his desk, its lid sitting off to one side.

Henry's brows continued to show concern. "Of course not. He found the treasure, Hannah," he said with a shrug, as if Harold's behavior could be excused because something good had come of it. "He's actually a very good dog. Just as loyal as his predecessor and a bit better looking, I must say."

He found the letter Parkerhouse mentioned and was about to hand it to her.

At that, a brilliant smile appeared on Hannah's face. Henry's heart seemed to clench at the sight of it, but he reminded himself they were talking of her pet just then. He imagined her making that brilliant smile when told that one of their children had done something good. "Now, I just want to get these coins cleaned up before I package them in this box," he said, giving her a peck on the cheek. "And then I'll get dressed for dinner." He glanced at her again, his gaze locked on her when he noticed a look of mischief on her face. "What is it?" he asked. Dumping the coins onto his desk, he moved to wrap his arms around her waist.

"I think you should leave them just as they are, with their bits of dried mud," she murmured in a quiet voice. "The way real pirates might find them." She gazed at him through her lowered lashes.

Henry chuckled. "And what, pray tell, do you know of real pirates, my lady?" he teased, giving her a peck on the forehead.

"Only what I read in stories, of course," she replied with an arched eyebrow. "Just because I look like I stepped out of the pages of a fairy tale doesn't mean I've only read those kinds of books."

Intrigued by her comment, Henry moved a bit closer, one arm moving up to her shoulder. "And what story might you be thinking about this very moment?" he whispered, his lips taking purchase on her temple.

Hannah inhaled sharply, thinking fast to come up with the most titillating tale she could think of. She was now certain she was with child, but once she told Henry, she feared he would no longer come to her bedchamber every night. He had only promised to bed her every night for another two weeks. The thought of spending her nights alone made her feel quite bereft, empty even. "Lady Godiva," she whispered, her lips moving to leave their mark along his jaw.

She felt Henry's body stiffen and then wondered if she should have come up with a different tale.

"I do not tax my tenants beyond their ability to pay," Henry whispered back, his teeth capturing her earlobe. "In fact, I do not tax them at all," he added, sounding as if he had taken umbrage at her suggestion that he was an autocratic leader.

Hannah let out a slight squeak. "I was thinking of you more as the noble steed," she clarified, her eyebrow arching when Henry caught her naughty look. "You know. The horse she rode so fast and so hard as she was making her protest."

Henry stared at her for a very long five seconds. Then he glanced about the room as if in a panic. "Well, I... I can't very well take you on the desk," he murmured, his attention moving to various chairs, tables and even the fireplace.

Moving to the door, Hannah drove home the bolt lock, turned, and leaned her back against the panel. With her hands behind her back and her head resting against the door panel, she regarded her discomfited husband with that arched brow. "Lady Godiva *mounted* her horse, Henry. Not the other way 'round," she said in a voice so silky she didn't recognize it as her own.

She stepped forward, removed a slipper using the toe of her other slipper, and lifted her foot to the edge of the desk. With one hand, she raised her skirt to just past the knee, revealing a shapely calf encased in a sheer silk stocking. "You'll have to play my lady's maid first, of course. And then the horse."

Henry gulped. "I can do that," he said, his voice not sounding the least bit in control. He moved to the other side of the desk, his hands reaching out to rest on her leg. That's when he noticed the clear outlines of hardened nipples beneath her bodice. She was aroused, there was no doubt of that. The fact that her nipples were evident meant the minx wasn't wearing a corset!

And then he had to remind himself that he had left that morning before helping her dress. But Lily was back to being her abigail. Which meant... *had she planned this assignation?* Had she chosen not to wear a corset in anticipation of seducing him? The thought excited him, addled him so thoroughly he found himself quite willing to do whatever she asked.

Slipping a finger under the edge of the silk, he managed to get the stocking to roll down her leg. When it popped off the end of her toes, she lifted her other leg and gave him an expression of feigned boredom. He quickly removed the stocking on that leg, rather proud he was able to do so without snagging the silk.

Lowering her leg from his desk so that she stood on bare feet, Hannah waited patiently while Henry regarded her with barely controlled lust.

"Lady Godiva was *naked*, Henry," she whispered, wondering why he was staring at her with such a besotted look on his face. She could hardly believe what she was doing, but Elizabeth had been quite insistent that play acting was good for a relationship. *Keep him guessing, Hannah. Keep him interested. Keep him entertained.*

Blinking, Henry moved to stand behind Hannah. His hands were at her shoulders in an instant, his fingers fumbling to undo the buttons down the back of her gown. "I can do this," he said again, his voice sounding husky. "I've become very good at it these past few days," he said, referring to her frequent requests of assistance when undressing for bed. As a testament to his words, the gown, along with her chemise, were pulled up and off of her body.

Inhaling sharply, Hannah realized she was completely nude. Turning only her head, she could feel Henry's eyes raking over her backside before she saw him step up to press the front of his body against her back. His hands had moved up to cup her breasts, his lips to press against her temple.

Hannah resisted the urge to simply allow him whatever he thought he was about to do. Reaching behind her, she undid the fastenings of his breeches, knowing she had successfully freed them when his turgid cock sprang forth to press against her spine. Her hands moved to grab handfuls of his shirt and lift them from his breeches. A shiver arced through her when she heard his growl, although it was probably from his fingers wreaking havoc on her nipples and breasts. She turned her body around to face his, her hands pushing down on his breeches.

Realizing her breasts were no longer in his hands, Henry blinked and saw to removing his shirt. In a moment, he, too, was standing naked in the study.

Hannah gave him a brilliant smile, her face pinking up as she did so. "Time for my ride," she said, placing the flat of her hand against his chest and maneuvering him backwards toward an armless chair. Breathless, Henry sat down, hard, and leaned back, watching through heavy-lidded eyes as Hannah placed her hands on his shoulders and swung one shapely leg over his lap, straddling him. Her swollen breasts were suddenly across from his mouth, her wet sheath coming down onto his erection. In an instant, he had her impaled and trembling as his hands gripped her bottom and his mouth took purchase on a nipple.

"I am afraid this may be a very short ride," Hannah whispered between gasps for air as his manhood filled her. She was so aroused, it would take but a moment for ecstasy to send her into oblivion. Her arms wrapped around his neck. She held on as she lifted and lowered herself on her toes. Then she realized Henry's hands, branding her bottom and hips with their heat, were lifting and lowering her as well.

Henry was suddenly as deep inside her as he would ever be. She clenched hard on him, desperately wanting his ecstasy to match hers. "Henry!" she cried, gripping his back with all her might. The matching groan from Henry sent vibrations through both their bodies. His mouth let go of her breast to say her name in a breathless prayer as his entire body spasmed into pure pleasure that had him almost rocking out of the chair. He stilled himself and once again buried his face into the soft white skin of her bosom.

Boneless and breathless and quite shocked at what she

had done, Hannah slumped against Henry's chest, the side of her face coming down to rest on his shoulder.

"I find myself very jealous of horses," Henry murmured, the words muffled against her skin.

A giggle burbled up from Hannah. "You needn't be," she countered playfully.

Henry lifted his head to regard her, a smile still on his lips. It faded slightly as he took in the sight of her blushed body, so wanton and lush and lovely. He realized he should have removed the pins from her hair, so that the silken mass might form a curtain around them. "What... what was that all about?" he asked, his brows furrowing. He made a move as if to lift her off of him, but Hannah clenched hard on his manhood while her hands clung to his neck.

"No, please," she begged. "Don't leave me just yet."

Frowning at her response, Henry tightened the hold of one arm around her back while he lifted a hand to cup the side of her face, wondering at her sudden look of fear. "Hannah, what is it?"

Shivering, Hannah shook her head. A tear had formed in the corner of one eye. She blinked several times in an effort to prevent it from escaping, but it did so anyway, leaving a wet trail along her cheek.

Alarmed, Henry straightened in the chair, his hold on her tighter. "Hannah!" He wiped the tear away with his thumb. "Are you hurt? Did I hurt you?"

Hannah was shaking her head, though, and sprinkling the top of his head with urgent kisses. "No, no, nothing like that," she whispered, dipping her head so that she might see his eyes. "I received a letter from Her Grace, the Duchess of Chichester," she finally said, her voice so small Henry barely made out her words.

"Lady Charlotte?" he said, his face brightening. Then, when he considered Hannah's hesitant manner, he grew concerned. "Is she well?"

Nodding, Hannah loosened her grip from around his neck but left her hands firmly on his shoulders. "Very. She and His Grace plan to make a spring trip to London so that she can make amends with her father. And then she and the duke would like very much to pay a visit here before the Little Season starts in the fall. That is if my lord is agreeable with the arrangement."

Henry frowned at her sudden formality. "A moment ago, you were Lady Godiva and I was your *horse*, as I recall. You're to call me 'Henry'. Especially when we're alone. Even when I'm a horse," he added with feigned amusement. But he saw the unsure look on his wife's face turn to something approaching fright. "Of course, she and the duke are welcome to visit. I, in fact, *invited* them to do so. Any time they wish. Ellsworth Park..."

He paused, wondering if Hannah knew of the details of his brief betrothal to Charlotte Bingham. He had spoken of her when he first courted Hannah, but he avoided telling her he might have married Lady Charlotte. Had he forced the issue, Henry was quite sure Charlotte would have agreed to the union. But even then, Charlotte had known there would always be a rift between them over the circumstances of the betrothal. The woman would have a scar for the rest of her life because of that damned betrothal. Now that Charlotte was married to a man who had his own scarred visage, Henry wondered if the duke knew how her scar got there. If he did know, had he been forced to accept his less than perfect duchess out of a sense of guilt? Or had he simply fallen in love with the lady and married her in spite of it?

The latter, he decided, realizing he needed to tell his wife why he held the title to Ellsworth Park. She was Charlotte's friend. She would understand what had happened.

He was about to continue his comment when Hannah placed a hand along the side of his face. "Ellsworth Park was part of her dowry," Hannah spoke softly. "She wrote to me about what happened."

Embarrassed when he realized Hannah knew more than he thought she would, Henry nodded. Charlotte was her best friend. Of course, the duchess would have written to

Hannah. She would have explained what happened that day when Henry showed up at the Wainwright estate intending to ask for Charlotte's hand in marriage. "The deed had already been signed over to me. When we agreed we shouldn't marry, she insisted I keep Ellsworth Park. To keep it from her cousin."

Hannah nodded. "I know. And I... I am in her debt," she stammered, her eyes searching Henry's. At his quizzical expression, she added, "If it hadn't been for Charlotte, do you think... would you have ever... sought me out? To be your wife, I mean?" The last words came out in a mere whisper, Hannah's lips trembling.

Henry stared at her for several seconds. Would he have pursued Lady Hannah, the daughter of a marquess, if Lady Charlotte hadn't directed him to do so? Would he have been so bold as to show up at Devonville House and request an audience with the marquess in order to ask for the man's permission to court his daughter when he hadn't even met the chit? And, if not, would he have eventually met Hannah? He would have been forced to attend a Season in London in search of her. Someone certainly would have introduced them at a *ton* ball or a musicale or a soirée. But the possibility of *never* meeting Hannah—he found he couldn't imagine such a scenario.

"I would have *had* to," he replied quietly. "I cannot imagine my life without you," he added in a hoarse whisper, his face displaying an expression of shock.

Hannah's heart clenched at his simple words. "Nor mine without you," she whispered back.

Henry's arms were like steel bands around her body, pulling her against him so hard she couldn't breathe. "You send word back to the duke and duchess. Tell them they *must* visit. I insist they do so. Perhaps late August, when the pheasants invade the wheat fields. Joshua and I can hunt while you and Charlotte..." Hannah's lips were suddenly covering his, cutting off his words with an urgent kiss.

Stifling the urge to laugh at her enthusiasm, Henry

returned the kiss in equal measure. At some point, he felt her hand reach around to grasp one of his hands to pull it between them. She placed it against her abdomen, covering it with her own as she did so.

Henry pulled his face away from hers, a look of surprise on his face.

"While Charlotte and I share stories of impending motherhood," Hannah finished for him.

Staring at her for several seconds, his expression of surprise not changing, Henry slowly smiled. "You're sure? She is sure?" he asked, his face brightening even more at her answering nods. "Oh, Hannah," he breathed, wrapping his arms around her and holding her far more gently than he had the moment before.

He pressed his face into her bosom, inhaled the scent of honeysuckle and musk and felt a profound happiness he hadn't felt since the birth of his son. So he was startled when a sob racked the soft body he held. His head jerked up to find Hannah crying quietly. "Oh, Hannah," he repeated in an entirely different tone of voice. "What is it now?" he asked as he reached up to stroke her face. *Why do women who are with child have to cry so much?*

Struggling to breathe, Hannah, hiccuped and whimpered before saying, "We... had an agreement... that you would b-bbed me... every night until I was... w-w-with child," she barely managed to get out.

"Yes," Henry replied hesitantly, wondering at the sadness in what little of her voice he could make out.

"Does that mean... y-y-you won't be... sharing my b-bbed anymore?" Hannah inhaled deeply, as if steeling herself for his response.

Henry stared at her in disbelief. He remembered the day in the coach when they had made the agreement. He thought they had made it with Sarah in mind. And then, a week later, he promised Hannah he would bed her every night for three weeks to make up for having cursed her dog. He hadn't made that promise with Sarah in mind.

Perhaps Hannah had *her* in mind, though.

Perhaps Hannah had decided she didn't want Henry and Sarah to continue their relationship as lovers. The mother of his child had made it perfectly clear his conjugal visits were no longer welcome the night she told him about her impending marriage to Tad McDonald. And Henry had begun to wonder if they ever had been.

With Sarah out of his life, at least as a lover, did Hannah really think he was going to quit spending his nights with her? Now that she had him so besotted he could barely think straight? So bewitched he actually came in from the fields every day for luncheon just so he could see her? So addled he would play horse to her Lady Godiva in his study? In the late afternoon, no less?

"Actually," Henry finally spoke, "It means I won't be *bedding* you anymore, my love," he said quite sternly. The sound of Hannah's sob could probably be heard through the entire house, and his heart clenched hard at how cruel his words must have sounded just then. "However, I intend to make *love* to you as often as possible. Your bed, my bed, this chair," he said wearily, realizing he was still buried deep inside her. "I would suggest the large table in the kitchen, but Mrs. Chambers can be rather prickly, and I shouldn't like to be naked anywhere near her meat cleaver."

Hannah's body stilled so suddenly, Henry had to pull his face away from the soft breast was cradling his cheek. He had been listening to her heartbeats, the tattoo a gentle rhythm under his ear until this latest round of tears. The tempo had turned to one more closely matching her heartbeat after he had pleasured her, after she had been brought to ecstasy and was clinging to him as if her very life depended on it.

"Are you... teasing?" she whispered, sniffling.

Henry angled his head over the chair back, taking in the sight of Hannah's tear stained face, her tentative smile, her soft white shoulders, the crest of her collarbones and the round, pink-tipped breasts he so adored. "I assure you, my lady, I will be at your beck and call whenever you ever wish to make love."

Hiccuping, Hannah lowered her head to his shoulder. "Oh, Henry," she whispered, her lips nipping at his earlobe and kissing the space between his neck and shoulder. Within a moment, she felt his hands slide to her hips and his manhood harden inside her, his breaths quicken and his pulse beneath her breasts increase two-fold. Even before his hands could lift and lower her, her toes began pushing her up and lowering her around his straining cock. "I do not think Lady Godiva had quite the right idea," she managed to get out just before Henry placed his thumb onto the swollen space where their bodies met and merged.

"Right idea, wrong horse," Henry countered, just before the growl of his tightening body erupted from his throat. Had they been anywhere but the study, he might have allowed the entire sound of his pleasure to escape. Instead, he simply groaned and covered Hannah's mouth with his own as ecstasy took them.

Henry wore only his breeches as he helped Hannah to redress. Given her few garments, it didn't take long to make her presentable enough to get up the stairs and into her bedchamber to change for dinner. He reminded her of the letter that still lay on the desk.

Hannah regarded the wax seal on the back. "It's from my father," she said as she opened it. Reading in silence for a few minutes, she lifted her head to find Henry's gaze on her.

"Is everything good at Devonville House?" he asked carefully.

Hannah finally nodded. "Lady Winslow is now the Marchioness of Devonville," she said as a brilliant smile appeared. "They married by special license the day before yesterday."

Grinning, Henry took her into his arms. "So, now *you* have a stepmother," he said before kissing her on the nose.

"But she's not wicked, not in the least," Hannah said, surprised at his comment.

"Neither are you," he countered. He handed the paste-board box with the coins to her. "And just to prove it to my son, I'm thinking *you* should be the one to give him back his treasure."

Hannah gave him a curious glance. "As long as I can give credit where credit is due," she stated, imagining how she and Harold would go in search of Nathan to present him with his pirate booty.

"If you mean Harold, then, of course," he agreed. "Come on, Lady Godiva. We need to get dressed for dinner," he reminded her, lightly slapping her bottom with the palm of his hand.

"Oh!" she got out in response, her gaze sweeping over his bare torso. "Do you honestly think you'll make it all the way upstairs without being seen half-naked?" she teased, grabbing her stockings from the desk and sliding her feet into her slippers.

A burble of laughter erupted from Henry. "You see what you've done to me, you minx?" he accused, grabbing his shirt and pulling it over his head.

The afternoon tryst had been as exciting as it was enlightening and satisfying. Perhaps it was right that Lady Bostwick had been so free with her recommendations on how a married couple could enjoy one another. He wondered at how loyal, or *deaf*, perhaps, the servants must be in the Bostwick household, to have their master and mistress behave so, yet he heard not a hint of scandal about their lives whilst he was in London.

Henry considered how his own servants had been behaving lately. He remembered the cook's words, implying tonight's dinner would be special. "Hannah. Who have you told?" he asked. "About the babe, I mean."

Hannah blinked. "Only you. When I first suspected, that night when..." She allowed the sentence to trail off, not wanting him to remember how bereft he felt the night Sarah had told him of her intention to marry Tad McDonald.

Furrowing his brow, Henry thought back to the cook's

comment. "Mrs. Chambers doesn't know?" he asked, one eye cocking.

Hannah shook her head. "I don't see how she would."

"Nor Mrs. Batey?"

Hannah shook her head again. "I wouldn't speak of such a thing with either of them," she insisted. "At least not yet. Why?"

Henry held her close for a moment. "I think they must suspect, is all," he managed to get out. "Come, let's dress for dinner. I am especially curious as to tonight's meal," he said as he led her out of the study and up the stairs.

Surprised by his comment, Hannah shook her head. "Beef steak, potatoes, carrots and Yorkshire pudding," she said with a shrug, as if there wasn't anything particularly special about the menu.

Henry laughed, his hand tightening on hers as he lifted her hand to his lips. "My favorite meal, of course," he said, continuing to chuckle.

Hannah's eyebrow arched in confusion. "You say that about every dinner menu," she countered, wondering at his comment.

Henry wagged an eyebrow. "I do. Keeps them guessing," he said with all the mischief he could manage.

CHAPTER 22
PIRATE BOOTY NO MORE

Hannah donned a cloak and made her way down the cobbles and through the front gate of Gisborn Hall, the pasteboard box filled with sovereigns under one arm and Harold at her heels. She timed her departure to match when she expected Nathan Forster to be making his way home from his tutor's house. She was just past the dower house when she spotted the boy making his way home from the other direction. Harold's ears perked up and he was suddenly racing toward Nathan, an occasional bark coming from his ever expanding body.

"Here boy," she heard Nathan say as he lowered himself to the road and waited for the dog to jump onto him. The impact knocked him over backwards. A series of shouts and giggles erupted from the earl's son as Harold proceeded to lick the boy to submission. "Stop! Someone save me," Nathan was shouting in between his giggles.

"Harold!" Hannah called out, suppressing a giggle of her own. The puppy ceased his tail wagging and pulled his head up from Nathan's face. "Sit!"

Harold immediately complied, tucking his bottom under him and acting as if he were guarding his own recently acquired pirate booty.

"Good afternoon, Nathan," Hannah said in greeting as

she stepped up to the boy. He quickly got up from the ground and bowed quite formally. Although he was dusty and quite disheveled from Harold's attentions, Nathan was obviously a happy child.

"And to you, Lady Gisborn," he said in reply. Despite their having frogs in common, the boy still seemed ill at ease with his stepmother.

"Harold was out playing pirates in the eastern fields yesterday," she said by way of introducing the topic of her visit. "And he made quite a discovery." At Nathan's quizzical expression, one that reminded Hannah so much of her husband when he was working to solve some problem, she pressed her lips together.

"Oh?" Nathan prompted. He seemed to swallow, as if he thought he might be in some kind of trouble.

Hannah nodded. "He uncovered pirate treasure!" She pulled the pasteboard box from under her arm and held it out to Nathan. "I believe you may have been the pirate that buried it?"

Nathan's eyes widened in disbelief. He took a step back and glanced up at Hannah and then back down at the box she held out to him. "My sovereigns?" he whispered.

Hannah shrugged. "I don't know. You'll have to open it, I suppose," she said, still holding the box out to him.

Wagging his tail, Harold stood up and walked around in a tight circle before sniffing the box and sitting back down again. Nathan finally took the box from Hannah and removed the lid. His eyes boggled at the sight of the dirt-encrusted coins. A finger dipped into the box and moved the coins around. He looked back up at her. "There was a ring," he said, his eyes filled with disappointment.

"Oh, Harold found that, too. He already gave it to your father," Hannah hurried to assure him.

A grin finally appeared. He turned to the dog and scratched Harold behind an ear with his free hand. "Good dog," he said. Looking up again, his brow furrowed much the way Henry's did when he was worried about something. "Did he *really* find the treasure?" he whispered.

Hannah nodded. "He really did. Took a while for him to convince your father he had found the treasure, though," she added with a roll of her eyes.

Nathan stood up, holding the box in both his hands. "Thank you, my lady," he said with a nod.

Smiling, Hannah nodded. "You can call me 'mother' if you wish. Especially since your little brother or sister will be calling me that," she said with careful encouragement.

Nathan's eyes widened again. "I'm going to be a big brother?" he asked, his face taking on an expression somewhere between delight and fright.

Laughing, Hannah nodded. "Perhaps when you're home from school at Christmastime," she acknowledged. "Oh!" she managed to get out as Nathan dropped the box of coins, and his arms wrapped around her waist, and his head pressed against her midriff.

Not sure what to do, Hannah wrapped her arms around Nathan's shoulders and held him close for a moment. Harold jumped up, apparently deciding that he, too, needed some attention. And in a moment, Nathan was laughing and picking up his treasure and waving farewell and heading for the dower house as if nothing unusual had occurred.

After he disappeared behind the door, Hannah glanced down at Harold. "Come on you little beastie, it's time for your dinner," she said, tears collecting in her eyes. She turned, Harold at her heels, and saw Henry watching her from where he leaned against the gate to Gisborn Hall. With his arms crossed and one booted foot crossed over the other, he looked every bit the nobleman.

Keeping her steps measured, she moved to meet him. She raised her eyes and gave him a smile. "Hello, my lord," she said, a tear streaking down her cheek. Henry had her in his arms before she knew what was happening. *Like father, like son,* she thought just then, reveling in the feel of the father's hold on her as he buried his head in the space between her neck and shoulder. Wrapping her arms around his neck, splaying her fingers into his hair, she rested the side of her face against his chest. "I hope all our other children are just like him," she murmured into his shirt.

Henry kissed her head. "Just the boys, I should think," he murmured, removing one arm and turning so he had one arm around her shoulders. She slid one of hers around the back of his waist. "I rather hope the girls are more like you, or we're doomed," he said as they made their way up the cobbles to Gisborn Hall, Harold hurrying on ahead and around the house to where his dinner would be outside the back door.

Hannah's melodic laughter filled the air around them. "They'll be farmer's daughters," she said in voice that suggested she was warning him they might be hoydens.

Snorting at the comment, Henry kissed her temple. "Do you mind so much being married to a farmer?" he asked then, leading her up the front steps.

"Not at all," she replied happily. "If you were a man of leisure, I'd be inclined to believe you would drink and gamble and spend your nights whor... not in my bed," she countered with a raised eyebrow. "I would mind that."

A slow smile spread over Henry's face. "Does that mean I can spend every night in your bed for the rest of our lives?" he teased, a grin slowly spreading across his face. The front door opened, Parkerhouse stepping aside as they made their way over the threshold.

"Every night," Hannah replied with a heavy sigh.

"Oh, good," Henry said with feigned relief. "So, what's for dinner?"

Hannah gave him a glance out of the corner of her eye. "I have absolutely no idea," she replied in a teasing voice.

"My favorite!"

THE WAINWRIGHTS PAY A VISIT

The first greenhouse, with its panes of glass installed on the south facing roof and oilcloth around the remaining surfaces, was a beehive of activity the days following its completion. Rows of corn seed were planted to take up half of the building while a variety of other vegetables were planted in the remaining space. Small orange and lemon trees were planted along the southern side in the hopes the warmer, sunnier location would help them thrive. The planting in that building hadn't even been completed when the second greenhouse was ready for its rows of cucumbers, melons, strawberries and other assorted vegetables. Meanwhile, the seeds for wheat, beans and barley were planted with seed drills in the furrowed fields.

Over the course of the next few weeks, reinforcements were installed along the walls of the trenches to prevent erosion, a concern Murphy voiced with his master a few days before the irrigation gates were installed. He gave credit to Hannah for having mentioned it during one of her biscuit deliveries, and Henry made sure to thank her for her experience of having played in the water as a child. He was still concerned about the fact that she had done so, especially with frogs.

The first gate to be installed, on the central irrigation

ditch, proved difficult to maneuver into place and to anchor into the ground. Once it was, though, the remaining earthen dam was dug out and the gate was left to settle into place for another day before the door was raised. The crew of laborers broke into hearty cheers as Henry tugged the rope that was threaded over a pulley and watched as the gate raised. Water gushed into the trench and slowly began filling the furrows in the fields.

Longer support legs were welded onto the other two gate frames as anchors in the hope they would prove sturdier with their installation. With the help of a team of draft horses and a framework and pulley, the gates for the east and west ditches were installed the following week. Although everything worked as Henry had hoped, rain fell every day during the last week of May. The gates were closed and the caps to the large clay pipes at the ends of the trenches were opened up to allow the excess water to drain from the fields and irrigation ditches.

As Aldenwood had predicted, the rest of the summer proved to be cooler and rainier than usual. The ditches on the Gisborn farm ended up being used for drainage rather than for irrigation. From May to September, the gray skies and prolonged rain made for slower growing crops. Despite a late snowfall in June, none of the Gisborn crops failed completely. The earl and the tenants that farmed his fields struggled to keep the fields drained, directing some of the water into the greenhouses and the rest into the ditches. Meanwhile, despite the lack of regular sunlight, the plants in the greenhouses seemed to thrive.

With the harvest still seven weeks away, the rain stopped for several days and the land began to dry out. It was during this respite from the colder weather when the Wainwrights came calling on the Forsters.

"Carrying a child becomes you," the Countess of Gisborn said in a hushed voice, linking her arm into the Duchess of Chichester's as the two made their way along the riverbank. The River Isis, or Upper Thames as some referred to it, gently flowed under the late summer sky. The afternoon, not nearly as warm as usual, was the perfect time to walk the grounds of Ellsworth Park and Gisborn Hall while their husbands hunted pheasants in a field nearby.

"And you, too," Charlotte replied with a mischievous smile, not absolutely sure Hannah carried a child, but certain enough to make the comment.

Hannah paused in mid-step. "How... how did you know?" she asked in surprise, her own smile lighting an already glowing face.

Charlotte squeezed Hannah's arm, moving to face her friend. "You glow like you have a dozen candles inside you. I have never seen you look more stunning," she said as she angled her head.

From the moment she and Joshua Wainwright, the Duke of Chichester, had arrived at Gisborn Hall, Charlotte was sure her best friend was with child. "Even at your coming-out ball, you did not look this glorious." Charlotte regarded her friend for a moment more, happy for her in that Hannah had married a man who needed an heir while she needed nothing more than a child to love.

"Early January, I think," Hannah stated before Charlotte could ask when she might deliver.

"So soon?" Charlotte retorted, an eyebrow arched in a teasing manner. "Oh, Henry must be thrilled." Despite his having inherited an earldom from his uncle, the Earl of Gisborn would always be simply Henry Forster to her. Just a week after he had left her in the garden at Wisborough Oaks, she had received his letter thanking her for the suggestion that he consider Lady Hannah Slater as a wife and hoping that, despite what had happened that day in the duke's garden, they could remain friends. The following day, she received Hannah's short note saying she had accepted the earl's proposal of marriage.

"Henry is beside himself, although, after reading George's letter last week, he may be feeling a bit frightened," Hannah said with a shake of her head.

George Bennett-Jones, Viscount Bostwick, had sent the note to Henry following his 'recovery' from having personally delivered his baby boy. His wife was quite shocked when her water broke shortly after they had been intimate. The poor man had been caught unawares—Elizabeth's labor had been so quick, there had been no time to summon the midwife, and the only servant in the household at the time had been the cook, who at least knew enough to boil water and supply a suitable knife for cutting the umbilical cord.

In the end, David Morgan Bennett-Jones was born into his father's nervous but capable hands. George's one additional comment in his letter had been that, although he continued to share the marriage bed with Elizabeth and their newborn, he was quite relieved to have a few weeks off from sexual intercourse since, he wrote, *I am exhausted. Who knew a woman with child could be so ripe and ready for intimacy any time of the day or night?*

Hannah could only wonder how Elizabeth had fared during the childbirth.

Charlotte giggled. "Wait until you hear from Elizabeth," she countered, her hand coming up to her mouth. Her face was flushed. "I don't know how they'll tell David when he's old enough to hear the tale, but I'm sure George will think of something."

Inhaling sharply, Hannah turned to regard her friend. "And what *did* she write about it?" Hannah demanded to know. She could only imagine how Elizabeth would behave during childbirth. *Probably with a good deal of complaining, screaming, making threats...*

"She was... humbled, I think," Charlotte replied, her head dipping slightly. "George had just given her some diamond and emerald baubles and she insisted they..." She lowered her voice to a whisper, as if someone might overhear them. "Have sexual intercourse, which apparently, they'd already done a couple of times earlier that day because her back was hurting, and George didn't know what else to do for her to help alleviate the pain. The next thing they knew, he was stuffing pillows behind her and telling her she had to hold onto something other than his hand because he needed it to deliver their son!" Charlotte ignored Hannah's wide-open eyes and added, "She said George was so calm and firm with her—told her what to do—then their son was suddenly in his arms and he was weeping uncontrollably. Elizabeth said she cried worse than the baby." This last was delivered with an elegantly arched eyebrow. "She's nursing the babe herself, since they'll be in the country until after Christmastime."

Hannah held both hands to her mouth, wondering how she could convince Henry to bed her only hours before their baby was born. And how would she even know when that was? "Do you suppose intercourse was the key to having an easier delivery?" she asked, her dimple appearing.

Shrugging, Charlotte allowed a grin. "I have reason to believe Joshua will think so," she hinted, her face turning a bright pink despite her bonnet. They walked along for awhile, sharing a companionable silence as Harold ran up to join them, tagging alongside Hannah. Aware that Charlotte wanted to say something, Hannah regarded her with a sideways glance.

"What is it?" she asked, looping her right arm into Charlotte's left.

"I was wondering how Henry reacted when you told him you were with child," Charlotte murmured, her eyes bright. "I would have loved to have seen his reaction."

Hannah grinned, dipping her head. "Oh, Lottie, you should have seen his face. I told him at one point I thought I might be, but I didn't tell him I was absolutely sure until the day after I got your news that you and His Grace were coming to visit," she explained, a hand moving to rest against her abdomen. When she heard Charlotte's sudden inhalation of breath, she turned to regard her friend.

"Did you think he would object to our visit?" Charlotte asked, her brows furrowing in concern, thinking the countess had used the good news of her pregnancy to counter the bad news of the Wainwrights' impending arrival.

"Oh, heavens, no!" Hannah managed to say, knowing it wasn't quite the truth. She had been worried that day before their afternoon tryst in the study, but Henry had made it very clear he hoped the Wainwrights would accept his offer of hospitality. "He feels quite beholden to you, Lottie, and not just for the gift of Ellsworth Park. As do I, actually," Hannah said happily, her brilliant smile displaying white teeth between berry-colored lips.

Charlotte grinned as she watched her friend, remembering the welcome Henry had given her when she and Joshua arrived the day before. He had kissed the back of her hand and then apologized to Joshua before leaning over to kiss the corner of her mouth and to whisper, "My sweet Charlotte," in her ear. The exchange was not the least bit awkward, nor did Joshua seem to mind the liberty their host had taken.

"So, you two suit one another then?"

The former Lady Hannah Slater blushed and continued to stroll along the river bank. "We do, indeed. I am finding married life quite pleasant, actually. Not at all how I expected. But I know it's all because of Henry. He is nothing like the insipid gentlemen I met at balls during last Season," she explained as they continued their walk. "From the time he came to Devonville House to meet with my father about courting me, he has been everything I could want in a husband." At Charlotte's quick inhalation of breath, Hannah glanced at her friend. "Do not fret, for I truly do not expect him to ever say he *loves* me," she added quickly, thinking Charlotte might be concerned for her heart. "But he dotes on me as if he does, Lottie. He brings me bouquets of flowers. Gives me the most exquisite jewelry. He's quite careful about our time together. He actually asks me during dinner if it might be acceptable for him to visit me later." She said this last part in a hushed voice, as if she thought someone might overhear. "As if I must grant him permission to bed me!" She didn't add that Henry spent every night sleeping next to her.

"As he should!" Charlotte countered, secretly pleased to hear the man she might have married was treating her best friend with such courtesy.

Hannah grinned at that, and then blushed bright red before saying, "I have never denied him, of course. And one time, I went to *his* bedchamber, very late at night!" That had been the time when Henry had come home from Sarah's, just having learned she had accepted Tad McDonald's marriage proposal.

"Hannah!" Charlotte exclaimed, covering her mouth in mock horror at her friend's admission. She wasn't about to admit that she woke up next to Joshua every morning, sometimes so aroused she simply used her new-found skills to seduce him from his slumber. He never seemed to mind waking to her kisses and gentle touches, although he accused her of being wanton on several occasions.

She was never left with the impression that he found that trait *objectionable,* however.

"Henry is an amazing man," Hannah continued proudly. "He spends at least an hour each day at the dower house with Sarah and their son. I tried to insist that those two move into the main house, but Sarah refused. She was quite determined to keep to her station in life, and she wanted her son to grow up understanding that, although he will be an educated gentleman, he will never be a member of the *ton.*"

Charlotte considered the news about Sarah and the bastard son Henry could never declare an heir. "It is most unfortunate our odd laws do not allow for his first son to inherit," she murmured, hoping Hannah wouldn't take offense. Hannah's firstborn son would inherit the Gisborn earldom upon his death, after all.

Sighing loudly, Hannah nodded. "As I said, Henry is not like the others in London. I find I rather like that he is a very hard worker, and he sees to the welfare of all his tenants and his employees. A life of leisure does not suit him, so I rather think the *ton* would not think kindly of him if we lived in Town," she explained with a shrug, alluding to the members of the peerage who shunned those that performed any kind of work, even if they had to do so to make a living. "And he informed me very early on that he has no plans to take a mistress," she added, her brows furrowing, as if the news had somehow bothered her.

Finding the comment odd, Charlotte gave Hannah a sideways glance. "He told me he loves Sarah," she said quietly. "I expect he wishes to remain loyal to her."

Hannah shook her head. "At one time, yes. But Sarah has decided to move on with her life," she said with a sigh. "Just after they made arrangements for their son to attend Abingdon School next month, Sarah told Henry she had accepted a proposal of marriage from an innkeeper in Bampton. I think the earl was very *hurt*, but he gave her his blessing. He could have refused to allow the marriage, of course, since he provided protection for her."

Hannah recalled how Henry had seemed so broken after Sarah had told him about the innkeeper's proposal, as if his entire world had come crumbling down around him. He had been sobbing when she went to his room and offered herself to him. The sex they had shared that night had been frantic and a bit rough and somehow exciting, but Henry had said he never wanted it to be like that again. "I am the only woman he beds."

Charlotte stopped on the path and stared at her friend in disbelief. "Indeed?" she responded, her mouth remaining open in a most unbecoming manner. "Oh, this is... this is most unexpected," she murmured before her attention returned to Hannah, remembering Henry's declaration of love for his childhood sweetheart and the mother of his son.

Her friend nodded. "It was for me, as well, for that very evening, when he didn't come to me in my room, I went to him and spent that night in his bedchamber. He clung to me as if his very life depended on it, Lottie. I felt pity for him," she said quietly, her gloved hand clutching her skirts. "And that's when I told him I thought I might be carrying his child. I wasn't yet... well, I wasn't yet *certain* that I was, but I was sure enough, and he needed... he needed a lifeline, I think," she said with a sigh. "I do not mind telling you that I found myself quite in love with him just then." A tear appeared in the corner of her eye and escaped to run down her cheek. She quickly wiped it away and held her head higher.

"Oh, Hannah," Charlotte gasped, wrapping her arms around her friend, feeling such a mix of emotions. "I think he must love you," she whispered, hoping that was truly the case, especially if Sarah's affections lay elsewhere.

Hannah nodded again, but she seemed uncertain. "Ever since that night, he's been bringing me flowers and gifts and he's been *kissing* me in the most inappropriate places!" She said the final words in a hoarse whisper, as if being kissed by her husband was somehow scandalous.

Despite Hannah's obvious confusion about her feelings for the Earl of Gisborn, Charlotte giggled, biting her lip when Hannah gave her a look of mortification. "He's courting you, silly goose," Charlotte said with a huge smile.

Hannah gasped, her hand once again going to her belly. "But, we're already married!" They had come to the hillock that separated the field from the river, the hillock on which Hannah had found Harold just after he had died. The dog now rested in the graveyard on the east end of the Gisborn lands, his plot marked with a simple headstone that read, "Harold MacDuff. Lifelong friend." The smaller Harold stood at the base of the hillock and sniffed, occasionally lifting his head to glance at Hannah as he did so. Hannah gave him a wan smile and shook her head.

Shrugging, Charlotte took Hannah's arm and started them along the path back towards Gisborn Hall. "And so you'll be married and in love with one another. It's really a rather pleasant way to spend life, I'm finding," she said brightly.

Hesitating a moment, Hannah lowered her voice again.

"So then, you and Wainwright are finding marriage pleasant?" she asked, her question rather hesitant. "I know you claimed you *wanted* him for your husband, but Elizabeth was quite worried about you marrying the duke."

"Because of his scars?" Charlotte guessed, remembering the reaction of her friend when she insisted she still planned to become the Duchess of Chichester despite her betrothed's ruined face.

"I suppose," Hannah agreed carefully, not wanting to admit that she shared their mutual friend's concerns. "You do not seem to mind his disfigurement, but *do* you?"

Charlotte took a deep breath, realizing that she would be answering such a question for the rest of her life, although no one but Hannah or Elizabeth would dare ask it of her directly. "We all have scars, Hannah. Some just aren't so visible," she responded quietly. "At least with 'His Grace with half a face', I know where they all are. And some are ticklish," she said in a teasing voice.

Hannah gasped at the familiar phrase. "Lottie!" she admonished her. "I cannot believe you actually said that!"

Allowing a broad smile, Charlotte regarded her dearest friend. "I love him, Hannah. I cannot imagine my life without him," she stated happily. "Marriage has changed my life." She paused a moment as she considered how to say what she was thinking. "There is something about men when they are about to be," she paused, not quite sure how to put it. "There is something about..." She struggled to find the right word.

"Impending fatherhood?" a male voice interrupted in a teasing voice.

The women whirled around to find the Duke of Chichester and the Earl of Gisborn, hunting muskets in hand, on the path directly behind them. The two wore long tailcoats in deep russet and browns, buckskin breeches and top hats with small brims. Their hunting boots were scuffed from having been dragged through tall grasses. A footman, similarly dressed, followed them carrying a string of several pheasants attached to a pole while a white and black spaniel serpentined his way along the path. The three men bowed to the ladies, tipping their hats as they did so.

Charlotte gasped, wondering how much of their conversation the two men had overheard. *Not much*, she realized when she noticed that they would have had to come out of the trees along the river just after she and Hannah had turned to head back toward the house. She curtsied, as did Hannah. "Your Grace, my lord," they spoke quietly, their cheeks blushing at being caught gossiping.

"You were saying, Your Grace?" Henry hinted as he held out his arm for Hannah, leaning over to kiss her temple as he did so. Hannah arched an eyebrow in Charlotte's direction, hoping the duchess noticed her husband kissing her as she had claimed he had been doing so much of lately.

"Yes, do tell," Joshua encouraged Charlotte as he held out his arm for her.

Charlotte shook her head as she placed her hand on his arm. "Perhaps *you* can explain it, Your Grace," she countered. "What is it about impending fatherhood that makes men so loving?" she asked in a teasing voice. She could hear Hannah's delighted gasp and wondered what the earl thought of her query.

"Don't you mean lovable?" Joshua replied, taking joy in teasing her.

"I rather like that I could be considered lovable," Henry stated, daring to glance down at Hannah as he made the comment. She kept her eyes steady and forced herself not to look up at her husband, afraid if she did, she would have to agree that he was lovable and then say so in front of their guests. "Wainwright, does this mean that you are experiencing impending fatherhood?" Gisborn asked lightly.

"Indeed," Joshua replied proudly. "In December, if I am to believe the math involved. So I am more lovable. And apparently more *loving*," he added, stealing a glance at Charlotte and enjoying her discomfort at the change in the conversation.

"Perhaps *attentive* is a better term," Charlotte offered, thinking that the word 'loving' might be too much to admit to for the earl.

Henry shook his head. "Not a strong enough word to describe a man when he knows his wife is about to bear him an heir," he stated firmly, lifting his arm so Hannah's hand was close enough that he could lean down and kiss the back of it. Surprised, she looked up then, catching his gaze as he gave her a wink and a grin.

"I do hope I am being attentive," Joshua put in, his brows furrowed. "I do try," he said in his own defense.

"And you're doing a rather splendid job of it," Charlotte agreed, leaning toward him as they walked so their bodies bumped against one another. Joshua countered by leaning toward Charlotte so that they bumped again with the next step, making her smile at his antics.

"So, then, Gisborn, am I to understand that you are also experiencing impending fatherhood?" Joshua asked, his tone conversational.

"Indeed, although 'impending' implies very soon, and I will not be a father until next January," he stated proudly.

Joshua nodded. "Congratulations are in order then! And if 'attentive' is not a strong enough word to describe you, then what word would you use to describe yourself, Gisborn?" he ventured, causing Charlotte to inhale slightly and lift her head to shake it so that only Joshua could see her alarm.

The earl slowed his steps, his attention once more on his wife. "I would need more than one word, Your Grace," he replied softly. "For I find myself loved and in love."

Charlotte held her breath as she watched Hannah look up at the earl, a look of astonishment on her friend's face.

"Which is a surprise to me," Henry continued, "For I thought a man could only love one woman during his lifetime. But I find I love three."

A chorus of "Three?" responded in unison to this stunning bit of news.

"Now, you really must explain yourself, Gisborn," Joshua admonished the earl, wondering if the man realized to what he had admitted.

"Gladly," Gisborn stated, a slight grin on his face. "First, there is Sarah, the first woman I loved, who I grew up with and who bore me a son, despite knowing—insisting, rather, that she would never be my wife," he explained patiently. "And then there is your wife."

Joshua stopped in his tracks, a stab of jealousy roused in him so suddenly he had no words while Charlotte's eyebrows arched in surprise, her shocked expression meeting Joshua's look of astonishment before moving onto the equally stunned expression on Hannah's face.

"Who loved me enough as a *friend* to see fit to recommend her best friend as my wife. I shall love her for that until my dying day, I'll have you know," he said with a good deal of emphasis.

Charlotte and Joshua exchanged awkward glances, both finally smiling as the earl continued his explanation.

"And then there is my wife, whom I have fallen deeply in love with over the course of the past few months, although if I were pressed, I would have to admit I was probably in love with her the first time we rode together in Hyde Park, when she told me she wanted nothing more in life than to be a mother."

Hannah stared up at Henry, her mouth forming an 'o' and her breath held as she gazed at him. "Oh, Henry," she breathed, placing the side of her head against his coat and the palm of her hand against his cheek. Henry moved his free arm around her shoulders and held her for a moment before leaning down to kiss her on the top of her bonnet.

"I can only claim the one love," Joshua stated emphatically, tapping one boot as he pulled Charlotte against his body and kissed her bonnet.

"And one is quite enough for you," Charlotte responded firmly. "I am not sharing you with anyone," she added for good measure, surprised she could make such a claim in the company of others.

Joshua inhaled slowly and let it out, suppressing the smile he felt when he noticed Henry's raised eyebrow in his direction. "Of course, Your Grace," he agreed with a nod. "My, but you are a willful woman," he said under his breath, intending for all of them to hear his comment.

Charlotte angled her head to one side and gave her duke a prim smile. "You wouldn't have it any other way."

Joshua smiled in return. *No, I wouldn't.*

"So, my loving and very lovable wife, what are we to have for dinner this evening?" Henry asked as they made their way to Gisborn Hall.

Hannah grinned and gave Charlotte a sideways glance. "I am thinking pheasants under glass, mashed potatoes, beans and bread," she said aloud. And then, under her breath, she whispered, "And I'm having you for dessert."

Henry's eyes widened as he nearly stumbled in his tracks. "Oh, now, that really *is* my favorite meal!" he announced happily.

Thank you for taking the time to read The Seduction of an Earl. *If you enjoyed it, please consider telling your friends or posting a short review. Word of mouth is an author's best friend.*

Thank you,
Linda Rae Sande

EXCERPT

Read on for an excerpt from Book I in "The Sons of the Aristocracy" Series

Tuesday Nights

Michael Cunningham, the second son of a viscount, was minding his own business as he strode toward the Ship. He intended to take a room at Shipley's only inn, the establishment promising a clean room and hot meals for the few days he would be in the Horsham District of Sussex. Although his family's small estate, Cunningham Park, was just south of Horsham, he thought the daily trip to Shipley would take too much time away from his opportunity to meet with Harold Waterford. Sir Richard Waggoner had taken a risk in arranging for him to meet with the businessman, and Michael didn't want to disappoint either of the gentlemen by not being available on an hour's notice.

So it was a surprise and a bit of an annoyance when his attention was suddenly diverted. A young lady's scream, followed by a drawn out cry of "No!" had him stopped in his tracks. Michael glanced around, realizing almost at once that the sound had come from behind the inn. Hurrying around the whitewashed stucco building, he spied the source of the scream. A young woman, her back pressed against the inn's carriage house, was pinned in place by a taller young man, his bent arm pressed across her throat. Dressed in trousers and a wool shirt, he looked like he belonged at the edge of the flock of sheep that were grazing just east of town. But this wolf had his lamb at a distinct disadvantage, and Michael was quick to act on the lamb's behalf.

"Now, see here," he shouted, reaching out to grab the attacker's shoulder. He instead ended up with a handful of shirt, lifting it so the man was suddenly off his feet and turned facing him.

"Wh ..?"

Before the predator had completely turned to see who it was that had him pulled away from his prey, Michael's skills as a pugilist took over. His right fist struck the man's jaw, and then Michael let go of the shirt. Dazed from the blow, the young man stumbled backwards and landed on his bum, his nose dripping blood while one hand reached up to his cheek.

"The young lady said, 'no'!" Michael yelled, uncurling his fist and stretching his fingers to determine that, thank the gods, none were broken. He needed that hand to take notes whilst in his meetings these next few days. "You go near her again, and I'll see to it every bone in your body is broken," he vowed.

His eyes wide as saucers, the young man nodded. "Yes sir," he mumbled, his hand still rubbing his cheek.

Michael's attention turned to the young lady whose back was still against the wall, her arms straight while her palms were flat against the stucco. Although her bodice was a bit askew, and her face had a look of astonishment, she seemed in one piece.

At least she hadn't had a fit of the vapours and fainted on him.

"Are you hurt?" he asked, careful to keep the tone of his voice as neutral as possible. He didn't want the girl as frightened of him as she was of the man who was scampering backwards like a crab toward his escape.

For the first time in several seconds, Olivia Waterford let out the breath she'd been holding. She was sure Eli Blaylock was about to kiss her. Perhaps about to have his way with her, although she still wasn't quite sure what that would have entailed. Ruination, certainly!

Her green eyes, still quite wide, took in her rescuer. Tall — at least six feet, she surmised—dark haired and broad of shoulder, he had a rectangular face defined by a rather square jaw and straight eyebrows. Under those brows were blue eyes, eyes that had seemed full of mischief when he confronted her attacker but were now regarding her with a great deal of concern. His broad nose was a bit crooked, but not so much that it looked out of place. And his lips made it rather difficult for her to remember what it was that had just come out of them only a moment ago. *Kissable lips*, she thought, just as she remembered how they were described in a novel she had finished reading only the week before.

Olivia blinked in an attempt to remember what it was he had asked.

"My lady, are you unhurt?" Michael asked then, moving closer so he might determine if she really was about to faint. *Don't faint, whatever you do, don't faint.* He glanced down to her hands, noticed how one was flat against the carriage house wall while the other clutched a reticule and what looked like a terribly wrinkled hanky. One knuckle on her fourth finger was red; he reached out and carefully pried her hand away from the wall, lifting the finger so he could examine it. The knuckle was bleeding from a deep scratch. He wondered if she had attempted to defend herself or had merely scraped it on the stucco. "You're bleeding," he murmured before placing his lips over her finger. Sucking on the wound for a moment, an action that seemed to bring the young lady back to awareness, Michael tasted the iron tang of blood before he pulled away to examine the wound again. He noticed how long and slender her fingers were, how pale and beautiful her hand was, despite there being no gloves in sight. Her fingernails were perfect ovals, trimmed short but not bitten off. He imagined a ring at the base of that finger. A sapphire would look most becoming, he thought, with a diamond or two on either side. And then he chided himself. *Why am I thinking about jewelry?* he wondered, the thought nearly bringing a grimace to his face.

Once he determined that the injured knuckle had stopped bleeding, he dared a glance at his patient's face. She was younger than he first thought, but quite pretty, with mahogany hair caught up in a bun at the back of her head. Her smoky green eyes were tilted up at the outer corners, giving her a slightly exotic look despite her youthful cheeks and pert nose. But those lips—reddened from her attacker's attempt at a kiss—were full and sensual. *Kissable lips*, he thought, and was about to find out for himself when he remembered he had just rescued her from such an assault. He took a step back.

Staring at her rescuer, Olivia forced her mouth closed. She dared a glance beyond the man. At least the yard was still abandoned; no one had witnessed Eli's attempt on her virtue nor this man's unusual ministrations with regard to her finger. She turned her attention to where his lips had just been and arched an eyebrow. Her knuckle, where it had intersected one of Eli's teeth when she attempted the same move this man had accomplished with a good deal more ease, was no longer bleeding. A shiver passed through her as she relived the sensation of his lips against her skin, of how his warm hand had held hers with so much care. *Was the man a doctor?* Well, whoever he was, he was giving her that look again, as if he expected her to say something.

"It appears I am now," Olivia answered finally, her eyes lifting to meet his. "And to whom shall I address my gratitude?"

Michael let out the breath he had been holding for that moment. "Forgive me." He removed his hat and bowed. "Michael Cunningham, at your service," he spoke formally.

Giving him a smile, Olivia pushed herself away from the carriage house wall and curtsied. *So this is Mr. Cunningham!*

Her father had made mention they would be hosting the man for a few days – something having to do with a business venture he was considering. Mr. Cunningham was certainly younger than she expected given her father's typical business associates. "Olivia," she replied finally, reaching out with her hand to shake his. The man intercepted it with his own gloved hand and raised it to his lips. He kissed the back of her knuckles before she quite realized what was happening and had to still the sound of a gasp when the renewed dart of pleasure shot up her arm.

Either he was a gentleman or a bounder. She wasn't sure which just yet.

"Pleased to make your acquaintance," he said with a nod as he let go of her hand.

Olivia found that her hand suddenly felt leaden without his support. "And yours. Thank you, truly, for what you did." She looked toward where Eli had crawled off, disappointed that the boy had escaped.

In fairness to the would-be rake, Eli had been dared by his friends to kiss her. His first attempt the week before had ended when she'd managed to get a knee shoved up into his groin before he could get her against any wall. His second attempt had been interrupted by his mother's shout—the woman had no doubt been a Welsh milkmaid in her younger years. This attempt, though, had been carefully calculated and timed for when she exited the mercantile with a package in one arm and her reticule and gloves in the other. She'd been unable to use her fists until she dropped her parcel, and by then, Eli had her in the inn's yard and halfway to the wall.

"You're welcome, of course," Michael replied before tearing his eyes away from the young lady. He glanced about the yard, rather surprised that no one else had joined them to determine the fate of the young lady. Certainly someone else had heard her cries.

"Mr. MacFadyen is at the mercantile. To pick up his weekly order," Olivia said, realizing her rescuer was probably wondering why no one had come out of the inn at the sound of her scream. The comment reminded her about her package. She glanced about, trying to remember just where she had dropped her book. Somehow her reticule and gloves were still clutched in her uninjured hand. *My poor gloves*, she thought as she realized how tightly she'd been clutching them.

Furrowing his brows, Michael regarded the young lady for a moment. "I take it Mr. MacFadyen is the proprietor?" he half-asked, trying to remember the name of the family that was supposed to be in residence.

Olivia shrugged as she regarded her gloves. "He runs the pub portion of the inn on behalf of the owners," she explained as she moved away from the carriage house wall and walked toward the front of the inn. "Which is why Eli chose this particular place to try to kiss me," she explained, affording Michael a sideways nod. She spotted her bonnet and hurried towards it, surprised when Michael beat her to it and had it in hand before she could even reach the spot in the small lawn where it had landed. "Thank you," she added as she regarded the hopelessly crushed hat.

"Allow me," Michael countered, using the fist from one hand and fingers of his other to pop the straw back into shape. He regarded the bonnet inside and out before holding it out for her inspection. "It's not perfect, but—"

"It'll do!" Olivia interrupted, amazed that the man was able to restore the bonnet to a wearable state. She allowed him to place the bonnet on her head, adjust it and tie the ribbons while she pulled her wrinkled gloves onto her hands. "Thank you again, Mr. Cunningham," she added, resisting the urge to add that he would make a good lady's maid. No need to embarrass the man.

Especially since her mother was expecting him for dinner that evening.

ABOUT THE AUTHOR

A self-described nerd and lover of science, Linda Rae spent many years as a published technical writer specializing in 3D graphics workstations, software and 3D animation (her movie credits include SHREK and SHREK 2). An interest in genealogy led to years of research on the Regency era and a desire to write fiction based in that time.

A fan of action-adventure movies, she can frequently be found at the local cinema. Although she no longer has any tropical fish, she does follow the San Jose Sharks. She makes her home in Cody, Wyoming.

For more information:
www.lindaraesande.com

www.ingramcontent.com/pod-product-compliance
Lightning Source LLC
Chambersburg PA
CBHW020919110726
47900CB00001B/210